SILVER & SMOKE

SILVER & SMOKE

THE ASHES OF THEZMARR
BOOK THREE

HELEN SCHEUERER

To all the women who've been told to smile.
Let the world see what happens when you do.

REGARDING REFERENCES
TO PLANTS AND POISONS

Some are true, some are not.
It's safest not to guess which is which.
Don't try this at home.

Dorinth

Delmira

Thezmarr

The Bloodwoods

Hailford

The Chained Islands

Harenth

The Broken Isles

Ciraun

Naarva

The Scarlet
Tower

The Veil

THE MIDREALMS

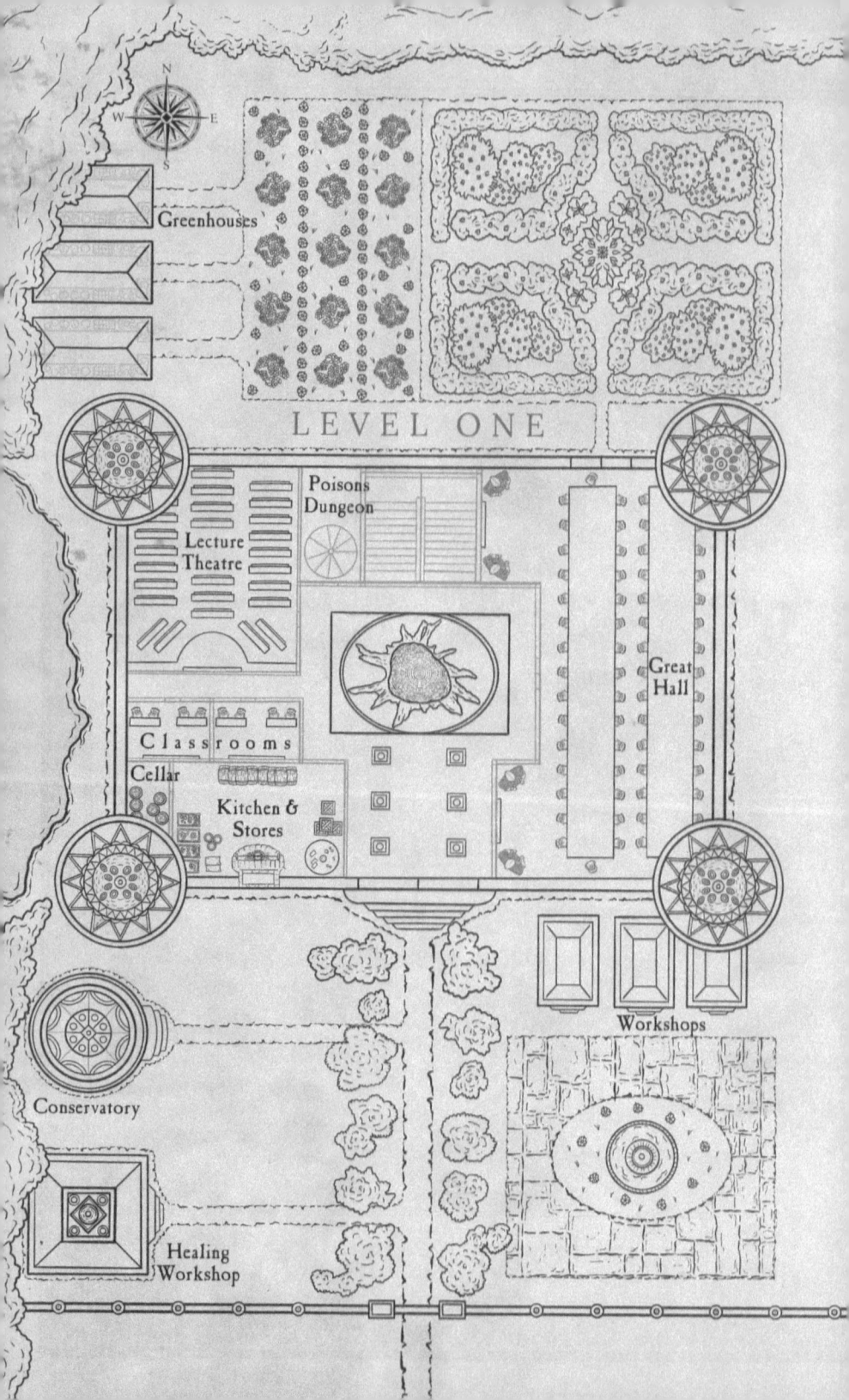

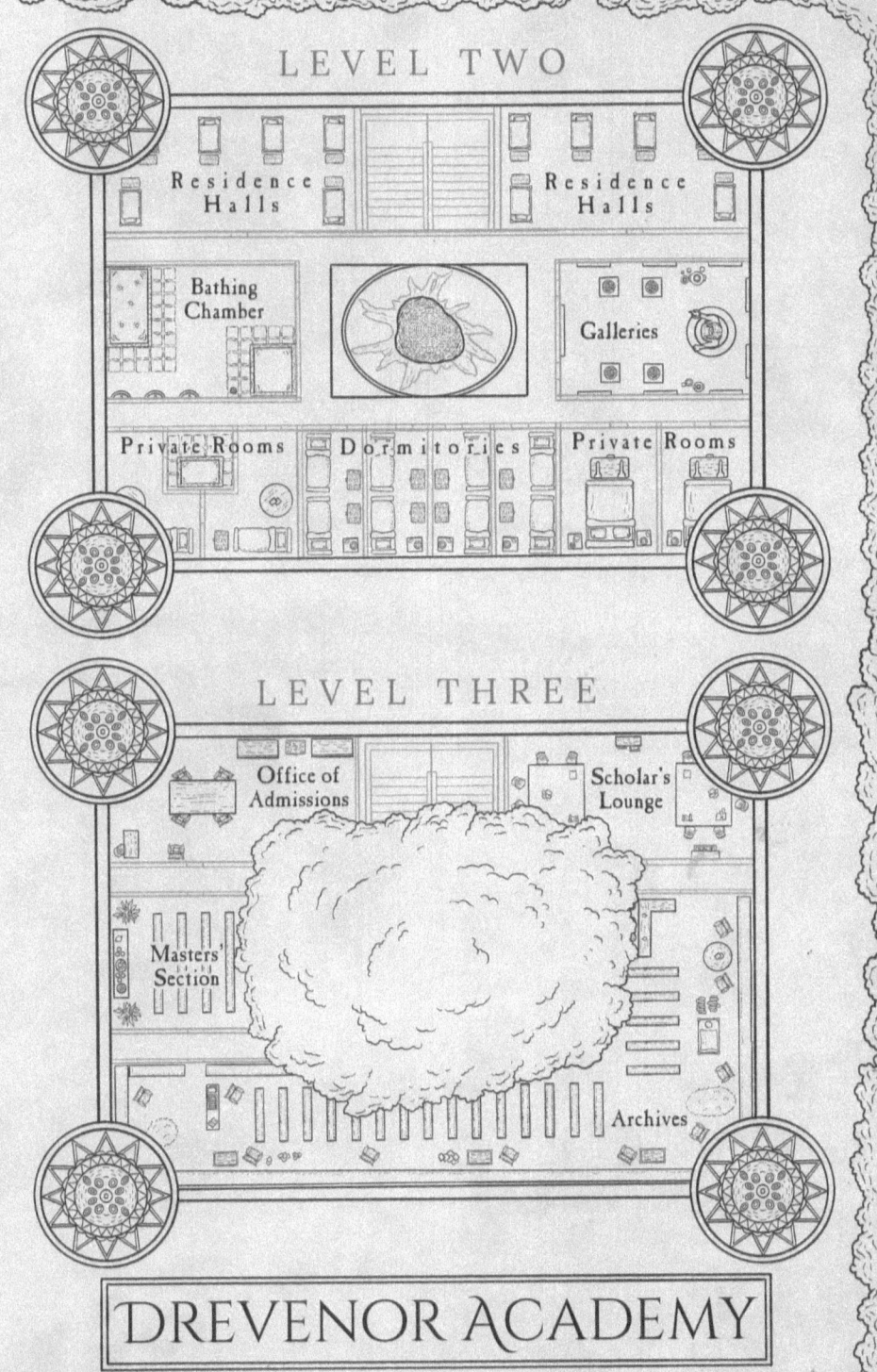

LEVEL TWO

Residence Halls

Residence Halls

Bathing Chamber

Galleries

Private Rooms

Dormitories

Private Rooms

LEVEL THREE

Office of Admissions

Scholar's Lounge

Masters' Section

Archives

DREVENOR ACADEMY

"Gold will turn to silver in a blaze of iron and embers, giving rise to ancient power long forgotten."
—Prophecy from the Seer Queen of Aveum

CHAPTER 1
WREN

"A good alchemist understands patience. A better alchemist masters it."
—Alchemy Unbound

"Your Bear Slayer is dying."

Lord Lucian Devereux's words still echoed in Wren's mind. The private study room in the archives had suddenly felt too small, as though the walls were closing in around her as the nobleman continued.

"It's a slow-releasing poison... How's that for irony?"

Fear had spiked through her, but she refused to let it show to the bastard before her. "When did this happen?"

"When Elderbrock rescued Queen Reyna. My spies within the People's Vanguard tell me Silas the Kingsbane targeted your Warsword specifically. A toxin made just for him as he was fighting to save the winter queen..."

1

Heart pounding, Wren had lifted her chin in defiance. "Poisons are my specialty," she replied coolly. "I can analyze any toxin; I can make any antidote. I thought I'd proven as much to the masters of this academy."

"Perhaps, Your Highness," Darian's father drawled. "But with what *time*? How do you hope to save him when you have the dark alchemy cure to produce for the midrealms? An army to raise? And a kingdom to defend?"

Wren's eyes narrowed. "Say whatever you came here to say, Lord Lucian."

"Marry my son."

"What?" Wren blurted, almost laughing. It had to be a joke, some sort of sick prank. Her? With Darian—the Lord of Larkwood Valley? A sour taste spread across her tongue.

"Marry Darian and the poison's ingredients and methods are yours," Lord Lucian continued, undeterred. "I have alchemists in my employ too, Elwren. They are quite certain of its composition, but you'll never break it down in time yourself. The Warsword will die before you find an antidote."

Wren scoffed. "You're lying."

"If you want to take that risk, it's the Bear Slayer's life you gamble. But if you want proof, ask your former mentor. Farissa Tremaine can vouch for my findings."

Wren's blood ran cold. "Farissa...?"

Lord Lucian dipped his head in confirmation. "Marry my son, and when you do, I will provide you with what you need to save Torj Elderbrock. A marriage to an influential man is a small price to pay for that, surely? Not to mention all the resources that the Devereux name will afford you. You have an hour to decide."

Wren's throat constricted. "I..."

"Your affair with the Bear Slayer is over, Elwren," he told her. "Make my son look the fool, and Torj Elderbrock's life will be forfeit."

Now, the sight of the Warsword on his knees was almost enough to bring Wren to hers. She still wore the gold dress she'd been forced into for the public announcement of her engagement to Darian, and it was stealing the breath from her lungs, as was the warrior before her.

"Then tell me how to serve you, my queen." Torj said the words with reverence. On his lips, the title didn't make her want to shrink away—it made her want to rise from the ashes. It made her want to *fight*. With Lord Lucian's threats still ringing in her ears, she was all the more determined.

"You stand at my side," she told him, her fingers closing over Torj's, a tether of gold and lightning linking them. "And we destroy them all. Together."

The Bear Slayer dipped his head, his silver hair gleaming in the last rays of the sun. "This is yours now." He pressed the dagger he was holding into her hands.

It was familiar, and it was not. Wren recognized Naarvian steel, but it was lighter, daintier than the weapon she often borrowed from him. And there was an inscription down the blade: *Iron & Embers*.

"I had it altered," he explained. "It's the right weight and balance for you now. A queen needs a blade as much as any warrior."

A lump formed in Wren's throat. She knew they had

3

only minutes to spare as she traced the hilt, noting the silvertide roses that had been engraved there. "It's..."

Torj looked pained. "Too much?"

"Perfect," she finished, her eyes burning. "Thank you. I love it."

He nodded, satisfied. "Good."

Wren wished she could savor the moment. She wished there was more *time*. But she was taking a risk simply by being here after the deal she'd made with Lord Lucian. She had agreed to his terms, a fact that still made her insides churn. But Torj had been *poisoned* by the enemy. Even as they spoke, a toxin coursed through his blood, threatening to take him from her, piece by piece.

To Wren, it stood to reason that if she had mastered one cure, she could master another. She had discovered the might of the silvertide rose, amplified by her own storm magic, and she suspected that the plant could be the key not only to saving the midrealms, but to saving Torj as well. She just needed time.

The difference between poison and cure is simply a matter of dose, she told herself.

Wren sheathed the blade in her belt of potions and tugged on his hands. "I'm going to save you," she vowed.

"If anyone can, it's you." Torj reached for her, cupping her face, his fingers trailing down to her throat, tracing the scar there.

Wren's heart seized as she pulled back sharply, scanning the grounds in a panic. "Don't—"

Torj flinched, his gaze dropping to her hand, where his touch lingered on the diamond adorning her fourth finger. *Darian's* ring.

"Are you going to tell me how this happened?" the Warsword said quietly, his eyes fixed on the glimmering stone.

Wren pulled her hand away completely, hating herself. His pain was so raw, she could feel it pulsing in her own breast.

"There was no time," she told him. "And you were too close to it, too emotionally connected. I had to make calculated decisions, and I had to make them fast."

The Bear Slayer made a noise of disbelief, his eyes dipping back down to the ring on her finger. "It wasn't all that long ago you were pretending to be *my* wife..."

Despite the rising panic in her chest that they'd be seen —that the ruse would be over before it had truly begun— Wren turned to Torj, full of anguish. "Perhaps a day will come when I'm not pretending."

Gods, she wanted to believe it, with every desperate fiber of her being, but first... they had to survive. *Torj* had to survive.

His silence told her he heard the doubt in her voice.

"Kipp or Dessa will explain everything," she said. "But for now, I have to keep my distance. I *must* act the part. Your life depends on it—"

Torj shook his head. "That *can't* be the only way, Embers."

"Trust me," she pleaded, turning back to the academy, her anxiety peaking in waves of nausea. "*Please.*"

Kipp was waiting for her at the foot of the academy stairs, practically bouncing on the balls of his feet. "Hurry up," he hissed. "For this to work, you need to enter *with* your betrothed."

Wren suppressed a wince at the term, and she didn't dare look back to see the expression on Torj's face. She knew he had followed. She could feel his presence behind her, his gaze boring holes in her back. He deserved answers, but right now, she could not be the one to give them to him, especially as they rounded a corner and saw who was waiting.

Lord Darian Devereux looked as stately as ever. The fine clothes, the regal posture, the well-practiced smile on his lips... All a stark contrast to the rugged warrior at her heels.

"Thanks for keeping her company for me," Darian said to Torj with a smirk, reaching for her hand.

"Furies save us," Kipp muttered, pinching the bridge of his nose.

Wren tensed, on edge. Everything she'd precariously built was poised to come crashing down around her. Darian's touch, his kiss on the back of her hand, felt *wrong*. And all she could think of was the Warsword now beside her, who was practically vibrating with rage, magic rolling off him in waves—*her* magic.

"Torj, please," she implored at a whisper, but Darian pulled her toward the door to the hall—

"You gave my father your word that you were done with the brute," Darian said, loud enough for anyone to hear. "Now *smile*, my love." He gave a dazzling grin of his own. "You're about to gain access to everything you need to be a queen of the midrealms."

CHAPTER 2
WREN

"What an alchemist measures in their flask determines what follows in the crucible, and, like the scales of fate, can tip on a single grain of intention."
—Arcane Alchemy: Unveiling the Mysteries of Matter

The doors swung open, and they were greeted with a near-deafening cheer. Wren hardly recognized the hall, which, not so long ago, had still been in repair. Now, the space was extravagant, everything dripping with luxury and opulence. Bouquets of flowers were pressed into Wren's hands. Well-wishers invaded her space, kissing her on both cheeks, declaring, "You're a perfect match!"

It spoke of Lucian's power and resources that he'd managed to bring an event like this together so quickly. There was no doubt in Wren's mind that the cogs of the nobleman's plans had been whirring for quite some time, and now could not be stopped.

Wren and Darian were swallowed by the crowd, and when she looked back, she couldn't see the silver-haired Bear Slayer in their midst any longer. That was for the best. She should never have asked this of him.

"Congratulations," someone cried, embracing Wren and showering her with more kisses. She didn't know who any of them were, or where they had come from, but it was a carefully staged production orchestrated by Lord Lucian—an effective means of spreading the news of the pending Devereux and Embervale union to the people who mattered most, at least in his eyes. She hated that she was here instead of her workroom. She needed to study Torj's blood. She needed to consult the Master Alchemists about his poisoning. She needed to harvest more silvertide rose. Instead, she was here, caught up in Lucian's charade while the toxin sunk its claws deeper into her soul-bonded.

"Thank you," Darian called out beside her, pinching her arm to snatch back her attention. "We couldn't be happier. Isn't it wonderful to have a burst of joy amid all the warmongering? It's just what the midrealms need—*hope*."

"Indeed, Lord Devereux, indeed."

The voices all sounded the same to Wren, all with that silken quality she'd come to recognize as masking hidden agendas.

Servants rushed forward to unburden her of the flowers and offer food and drink. Numb, she shook her head and waved them on, mumbling her thanks. It felt jarring to be here amid the sparkling wine and silver trays of tiny delicacies, while beyond Drevenor's walls, conflict festered.

Darian led her through the throng of people, and she caught glimpses of familiar faces on the outskirts: Thea, Wilder, Dessa, Audra, Farissa... Cal and Kipp were with a group of soldiers, Kipp gesturing enthusiastically with his empty glass. But Wren had known him long enough to see that it wasn't his usual carefree demeanor—that beneath the grin and mirthful gaze, he was calculating.

Kipp met her eyes and offered a subtle dip of his head, a reminder to Wren that she had her own role to play. After Lord Lucian had visited the archives and delivered his threat —or *proposal*, as he called it—she had strategized with Kipp for as long as she could. She would do whatever she had to do to save the Bear Slayer's life, and to stop what was now the most valuable kingdom in the midrealms from falling into the wrong hands. It was their plan that unfolded around them now, and Wren had to make it convincing.

She steeled herself as she looped her arm through Darian's and walked about the lavish hall, making idle small talk with nobles from all around the kingdoms. She smiled when expected, blushed at compliments, and deferred to her "betrothed" for all *serious* matters, as any good woman would do. She hadn't grown up in a noble house of lords and ladies, but the Thezmarr of her youth had always been a place where women were barely meant to be seen, let alone heard. When she'd become the Poisoner and found herself among the trappings of wealth, things had been much the same, only with prettier decorations.

As she moved through the flock of people, Wren felt a pair of eyes burning a hole through her: those belonging to Lord Lucian Devereux. Her chest seized. Had he seen her go to Torj in the gardens? It certainly wasn't beneath the bastard to have her followed, but she'd thought that single risk was necessary, to tell Torj she loved him, to assure him—

Beside her, Darian tapped a silver fork to his glass, calling for silence.

The room fell quiet at once.

"My future bride and I thank you for your congratulations and support for our union," he said smoothly. "We are thrilled that in a time of conflict, we have managed to find love."

Despite wanting to recoil from his words, and from his touch as his arm slid around her waist, Wren leaned in, her body soft and pliant, her eyes wide with adoration, ever the besotted fiancée. She had been many women in her time. Alchemist. Poisoner. Lover. And now, the future wife of Darian Devereux. She hoped this lie was the last mask she wore before she shed all pretenses and became her true self. The one who would battle tyrants and rule a kingdom with her soul-bonded Warsword at her side.

Make my son look the fool, and Torj Elderbrock's life will be forfeit. Lord Lucian's words were never far from her mind, but they came back to her now, loud and clear, as he scrutinized her from across the room. It was Torj she thought of as she rested a hand on Darian's chest, ensuring her engagement ring sparkled in the candlelight for all to see.

He beamed down at her as he spoke. "But even amid the celebrations, we cannot forget—we are indeed in a time of impending war." His voice rang out across the room, full of command. "And now that the houses of Devereux and Embervale are to be joined, we must ensure that my wife-to-be doesn't lose her beloved kingdom. So, we thank you for your compliments and assure you that your names will be the first on the invitation list for what is bound to be a spectacular wedding, but we must retire with our trusted council for the evening."

There was an array of final toasts and salutes, but soon, the hall was emptying, leaving only the essential players behind—the players Lucian had chosen for his agenda, and those Wren and Kipp had ensured would be with them every step of the way.

Darian motioned for her to sit at the head of a large oak table on the far side of the hall, pulling her chair out for her. Kipp, who she'd named her royal advisor, took the seat to her left. Audra, the High Chancellor, and all the alchemy masters took their places, while Thea, Wilder, and Cal stood on the outskirts, and Lord Lucian took the seat opposite her.

In addition, Wren gaped at the presence of King Leiko, Queen Reyna, and Regent Liora, their guards now lining the walls... Lord Lucian must have set this plan in motion long before he cornered her in the archives if he'd managed to call the rulers of the midrealms back into council so soon.

She saw a blur of silver from the corner of her eye, but she didn't dare seek the Bear Slayer's gaze. Not here. Not with Darian seated to her right, his hand covering hers for all to see on the table's surface. Not with Lucian watching her like a hawk.

All at once she seemed to be staring down at yet another war assembly. Wren finished her study of the group and found there was one notable absence.

"Where's Zavier?" she asked.

Lord Lucian cleared his throat. "If I may... Given that the

prince's actions sought to protect an enemy of the midrealms from our justice, might I suggest that he be forced to abdicate his throne?"

Shock rippled down the table in the form of whispers and gasps.

"Abdicate?" Wren frowned. "He has only just been crowned. Naarva has only just been reunited with its ruler."

"And that ruler put the realm at risk," Lord Lucian countered.

Wren turned to the High Chancellor and Audra, the latter meeting her gaze.

"The Prince of Naarva has been confined to his rooms and is under guard," the Guild Master said.

"Given the threat of war in the midrealms, I think we can table the discussion of the prince for now," Lord Lucian offered smoothly. "We must address the matter of the usurper. He targets Delmira for its fertile lands, yes?"

"Not just its lands," Wren said slowly. "But the silvertide roses upon it. They are the key ingredient to the cure for his dark alchemy—a means to defeat Silas. But... recently, I was fortunate enough to obtain a vial of shadow magic from Warsword Hawthorne. I experimented with that vial and the silvertide, which led me to discover that the roses are double-edged. Broken down and properly distilled, they cure, but utilized whole, they feed dark magic, potentially amplifying his existing power beyond measure."

"The difference between poison and cure is simply a matter of dose," Master Norlander murmured from where he stood on the outskirts of the room.

Wren nodded. "Exactly. Whoever rules Delmira controls the silvertide roses, which are the key to defeating the usurper. The roses have the power to banish his corrupted alchemy from the midrealms... or invite it in. If Silas gets a foothold in my kingdom, he will have the ability to strip the rulers and Warswords of their magic, and he won't stop there. He will take the kingdoms one by one."

"And how exactly is he going to do that?" Lucian asked sharply.

To Wren's surprise, the masters of Drevenor looked to her. Then again, she supposed, between her opus and her time on the battlefield, she had the most experience with the foe they now faced.

She cleared her throat. "Silas was—*is*—a keen alchemist himself. He has been using a dark form of the art since he made himself known to us, but furthermore, he has sought shadow war relics and has been extracting the same magic that was used against us then—gathering the bones of monsters and drawing out any lingering power. Warsword Hawthorne proved that when he brought back a vessel of shadow magic from one of Silas' laboratories." Wren suppressed a shudder.

"Where is he finding such things?" Queen Reyna said quietly.

"Old battlefields, former wraith lairs," Wilder chimed in. "I'm guessing that's where he held you captive, Your Majesty. He had such items when the Bear Slayer and I rescued you."

The moniker was like a blade to Wren's heart, but she still refused to seek him out. She had to keep her mask in place. It was only when she met the gaze of the High Chancellor across the table that a bolt of realization shot through her.

She addressed him directly. "Do we have such artifacts here? Artifacts from the war? You have chroniclers writing up the history..." Wren recalled the biased questioning of Magnus Crane easily enough.

"We do," the High Chancellor said slowly. "Purely for scholarly purposes, of course."

"Of course," Wren replied evenly. "But Drevenor has them in its possession?"

He nodded. "Some."

"Some? What does that mean?" Audra asked sharply.

"Well, a portion of that wing was destroyed in the initial attack during the novice graduation ceremony."

Wren's stomach bottomed out, and across the table, Audra and Farissa's expressions mirrored her own.

Thea let out a low whistle. "So, you're saying that during that battle, Silas stole historical artifacts containing old shadow magic and is now using them against us?"

Silence hung across the table like a heavy fog.

Audra pushed her spectacles up the bridge of her nose. "High Chancellor, you'll need to direct my warriors to the remaining artifacts. We'll need to set up additional guards at once. Or better still, remove them from the academy entirely."

The academy's leader dipped his head again, pale-faced.

"So, what does this mean for our enemy's power?" Lord Lucian pressed on.

Wren fought the urge to let her head fall into her hands. Instead, she answered calmly. "When applied, shadow magic distorts any natural alchemy at play. For those who fought in the last war, it's how we suspect the howlers were made."

"Howlers?" Darian prompted, turning to her. "Are those monsters?"

"By the time the shadow magic is done with them, yes," Wren told him, ignoring how her fingers were growing clammy beneath his. "They were men once, cursed by shadow, whose voices were replaced by blood-curdling howls. They were lost to cravings of violence and destruction."

Lord Lucian's eyes narrowed. "Have there been any sightings of such things?"

Audra spoke up. "Not according to our scouts. But I will send word to Talemir Starling. It's my understanding that the shadow-touched folk still have a crop of sun orchids, which we used against them last time... The thing about this usurper is that, beyond the fact that he's digging up old wraith bones and extracting shadow magic, we don't know how he was able to match the strength of a Warsword."

"In the battle at the novice graduation, he drank a potion, didn't he?" Thea interjected, her brow furrowed.

"He did," Wren confirmed. "But I suspect that's only one part of this... He has to *get* the strength from somewhere first."

Thea dipped her head in acknowledgment. "Do we have information as to his movements?"

"According to my spies, he was poised to march on Delmira a matter of days ago," Lucian replied. "My sources say he will aim for the capital, Dorinth, and establish a stronghold there in the ruins of the old castle, for it's the only place Princess Elwren can be legally crowned queen."

"A challenge, no doubt," Darian declared. "A dare to the rightful heir to come and claim her throne."

"One you expect all the kingdoms of the midrealms to answer to, no doubt," King Leiko said, a clear note of bitterness in his tone.

"I have no expectations," Wren told him coldly. "Though the midrealms should understand the threat... If the usurper holds Delmira in his grasp, he has the might of the silvertide roses to further his dark agenda, and they are out of our own hands to create any countermeasures. That means the rest of the kingdoms and their freedoms will be next."

King Leiko's narrowed gaze fell to Wren and the gold dress she still wore. "And how does the heir of Delmira plan to respond?"

Before she could answer, Darian swept in. "We shall visit the noble houses of the Devereux bannermen, gathering allies to Princess Elwren's cause, calling in old oaths. We shall build an army in her name with every resource of the Devereux name at her disposal." Darian brought her hand to his mouth, his lips brushing her knuckles. "The world is at your feet when you are by my side, my love."

Wren's breath hitched as she caught Torj's stare across the hall. His sea-blue eyes were full of fire, watching them from the shadows as Darian referred to her as *his*.

I belong to you, she called down their soul bond.

But there was only silence.

"Well?" King Leiko demanded abruptly, staring at her expectantly. "Is what Lord Darian saying true? Are these your intentions?"

If someone had told Wren at the end of the shadow war that this was where she would end up, she would have scoffed in disbelief. She wasn't made to be a queen. She loathed the games of the rulers and nobility, but here she was, playing the biggest game of her life, with the highest stakes on the table. And so, Wren refused to falter, refused to let a tremor into her voice. She didn't look away, didn't shrink back from the challenge. Instead, she stood and braced her palms against the table.

"We *cannot* let Silas take Delmira. It houses the most potent silvertide roses in all the kingdoms, which could be our cure, or our poison. The usurper already has shadow magic in his possession, and in the hands of an alchemist and a tyrant, the consequences would be catastrophic. As such, my education as an alchemist at Drevenor is at an end. My duty is now to Delmira, to the midrealms... and I intend to take back what is mine."

CHAPTER 3
TORJ

*"Denial is about as useful a cure as opium—deadly comfort that
only hastens the inevitable."*
—Wisewoman Vara

Torj was going to *kill* Darian Devereux. He was going
to squeeze the life out of him with his bare fucking
hands. Devereux's father, too. The whole damn family was
poison and the midrealms would be a better place in their
absence. Rage was consuming him like a fire from within,
burning and burning, the flames almost out of control—
until Wren's soft voice sounded in his mind, her words
echoing through their bond.

I belong to you...

But the ring on her finger said otherwise.

Perhaps a day will come when I'm not pretending.

Before them all stood a queen announcing her

intentions to the world, which both soothed and tore at his heart. The midrealms deserved a ruler like her: perfectly flawed, duty-bound and strong, smart and cunning. Only she could unite the kingdoms against Silas and protect the silvertide roses that might be their only salvation against his spreading shadow magic.

Torj watched the council disperse, his shoulders bunching with tension. Whether it was because of Darian or not, Wren could never marry him. Not now.

As though the prick could sense his turmoil, Darian tucked a strand of hair behind Wren's ear and laughed at something she said.

"Easy, brother," Wilder murmured beside Torj.

It was rich, coming from Wilder. He knew if anyone so much as looked in Thea's direction wrong, Wilder would punch through their chest and rip their heart out. Now, his fellow Warsword was poised in readiness, as though he expected he'd need to hold Torj back at any moment. Which was a fair assessment, especially as Wren and Darian made their way around the table, talking to the stragglers, including Darian's father. Torj could see the ruthlessness in the older nobleman's eyes as he surveyed Wren, no doubt weighing up how much she was worth in his schemes.

"You have been poisoned, *my Bear Slayer."* Wren had said she'd done this to save him, but Torj knew the Devereuxs, and he didn't want either viper near her—

"Torj?" Dessa obstructed his view of the betrothed couple.

"What is it?" he said, trying to peer around her.

"Wren asked me to run some tests," she replied. "We

need working samples of your blood to show the masters. They might be able to help."

That caught his attention. "What?"

"Can you come with me?"

"I need to speak with Wren." He was already pushing his way toward her. In that moment, he didn't care what she'd agreed to with Lucian. He wasn't going to let this happen. He'd burn the Devereux name to the ground before he did.

"Now's not the time," Wilder cut in, giving him a shove toward the door. "Thea's got her."

Sure enough, Thea, the Shadow of Death, was standing shoulder-to-shoulder with the future Queen of Delmira. Neither sister so much as glanced in his direction, and to Torj's frustration, Dessa was pulling him away from them. He didn't want to let Wren out of his sight. The last time he'd done that, she'd wound up engaged to the fucking Lord of Larkwood Valley.

Trust me, she had begged.

At last, Torj gave in. It would do no good to make a scene —well, more of one than he'd already made. He didn't speak as Dessa took him to one of the workshops on the level below, with Wilder following quietly on their heels.

Night had well and truly fallen outside, but there was no end in sight to this awful day being over. Torj felt wrung out. As though he had experienced every emotion on the spectrum in a short space of time and was now in some sort of daze. So much so that he paid no attention to his surroundings, until Dessa pricked his finger with a sharp pin.

Snatching his hand back, he shot her a glare. "What was that for?"

Dessa didn't seem fazed by his tone. Instead, she grabbed his hand again, squeezing the tip of his finger until a bead of blood formed. "I told you, we need to determine what poison was used so we can counter it. We need samples to work with—"

"I feel fine," Torj ground out.

"Well, you will," Dessa told him, pressing his finger into a shallow dish, smearing his blood on the fine glass and repeating the motion in another. "For a while, anyway. From what I know and from what Wren told me, it's something slow-releasing, something you won't feel until it's too late."

Just like Silas' strategy, Torj thought. *Infiltrating slowly, corrupting from within, until the shadow magic has spread too far to stop.* He exchanged a grim look with Wilder. "Great."

"Look on the bright side: you're in the best possible place to be poisoned," his fellow Warsword offered unhelpfully.

"He's right," Dessa added. "Wren believes the roses might be the key to your cure too. I just need to get a few samples for us to study. Then you can be on your way out of Drevenor—"

"What are you talking about?" he interrupted.

Wilder replied this time. "Our orders from Audra are to investigate the villages outside of the city. To gather information on the numbers of the People's Vanguard, to determine what sort of foothold they have with the common people."

"You mean I won't get to see Wren tonight?" Torj blinked, not even feeling the pin prick his finger this time.

"'Fraid not," Wilder said with a note of apology.

Torj was ready to throw the workbench through a window. "She said she would explain, or that Kipp would."

"And she will," Dessa reassured him. "Just—"

Torj shook his head, turning for the door. "I can't just leave without talking to her. I can't—"

"You *have to*," Wilder told him. "You being near her like this puts the whole plan in jeopardy. Lives hang in the balance. But you'll get her back, brother, I swear it."

Torj stared at his brother-in-arms for a moment, the only other man who knew what it was like to love and lose an Embervale sister. "You swear it?"

Wilder bowed his head. "Yes."

"Then get me the fuck out of here before I rip the smirk right off that highborn prick's face."

As they rode away from the academy in silence, Torj's thoughts were of Wren, as they always were. He wondered what she was doing at that very moment—if she was with Darian, or if she'd managed to extricate herself from him by now. Was she standing at her workbench in her room, pondering over her crucible? He would have liked to think she was in the conservatory, digging up supplies for her potions... or in the gardens, where she looked the most free. The reality was that she was likely being dragged into another meeting with the vipers. He knew Thea would guard her with her life, that there was no one better for the

task than the midrealms' most revered Warsword, and yet...
He was *soul bonded* to Wren. She was *his* to protect, and he
wasn't there.

"Has there been news of Vernich?" he asked Wilder,
inquiring after their senior Warsword, who'd gone missing
not long ago. Anything to stop his mind churning over
thoughts of Wren and who she was with.

His friend sighed. "None. He's still missing. There have
been no reports, no sightings pertaining to his
whereabouts. Audra is pushing hard for his safe return."

"I'll bet," Torj muttered. "If Silas can take down one of
the three original Warswords from the shadow war, that
might be enough to turn the people against us entirely. And
without unified kingdoms standing behind Wren, Delmira
won't stand a chance. The silvertide roses will be in his
hands, turning our potential cure into his ultimate
weapon."

The hour was growing late, and their venture was only
just starting, which only made Torj want to turn his horse
around even more. What if Wren was wrong? What if he
hadn't been poisoned, and it was all just a ruse designed to
force her into an alliance with the Devereuxs? He certainly
wouldn't put it past the bastards. They were more than
capable.

It felt like an age had passed, but as they finally
approached the first village on the outskirts of Highguard
city, something shining on a stone wall caught Torj's eye.

"Hawthorne," he said, signaling to halt. "You see that?"

Wilder followed his gaze, frowning. "What is that?
Blood?"

Torj urged his stallion closer to the wall, the moonlight

illuminating something wet. Removing his riding glove, he dragged his fingers through the moisture. It didn't have the same coppery tang he associated with blood.

"Paint," he declared, guiding Tucker back so he could survey the wall from afar.

Is this a better world? the vandalism read.

"That's not the People's Vanguard motto..." Wilder said slowly.

As Torj turned to Wilder, he heard a shout from within the village. He moved on instinct, charging on horseback toward the commotion, Wilder close behind him.

A crash echoed from the village square, followed by angry shouts. The details unfolded in fragments as they rounded the corner: a ring of villagers, the torchlight illuminating faces twisted with rage. Two men were grappling in the center, one with a bloody nose, the other nursing a swollen wrist. Behind them, an overturned cart spilled apples across the packed earth.

"This is your fault!" one man spat, lunging forward. "My brother's *dead* because you couldn't keep your mouth shut!"

"And *my* brother has lost his mind because of you!" the second screamed back.

"Stand down!" Torj's voice cut through the chaos, carrying the full weight of his authority. Most of the villagers startled at the sight of him—his warrior garb and the war hammer strapped across his back. But the two men remained locked together, deaf to everything but their own fury.

Torj saw no trace of enemy alchemy. This was just a poor village on the outskirts of the city, and yet... there was the same animosity here, the same anger. The shadow of

Silas' influence was spreading like a disease through the midrealms, village by village, just as Wren had warned. If he discovered the silvertide roses, his corruption and strength would be amplified a thousandfold. And if he sought to destroy them... there would be no stopping him.

Wilder was already moving. He jumped down from his horse and slipped between the fighters with the same efficient grace as always, his hands finding pressure points that made fingers spring open, weapons clattering to the ground.

Torj stepped in from the other side, creating a physical barrier between the men as they struggled in Wilder's vise-like grip. "Enough," he snapped.

The sudden stillness that fell over the crowd told him they'd stumbled into something far more significant than a simple village dispute.

"What is going on here?" Torj demanded.

Both men blanched, but the one with the broken nose had the gall to meet his gaze.

"You have no business here, Warsword," he said. "Look around. You're too late."

Torj surveyed the group. Their faces were gaunt, their clothes tattered, and there was a hungry gleam in many of the eyes staring back at him.

"Am I to understand that you are *not* affiliated with the traitor group known as the People's Vanguard?" he asked.

Someone made a show of spitting on the ground.

"Tell us what happened," Wilder prompted.

A woman broke through the crowd, pushing to the front to address them. "A commander did come through here, weeks ago. He told us of their so-called better world, and all that Silas the Kingsbane was offering folk like us. Our mayor said we'd think about it, and he left... but not long after, a lot of our people started acting strange. Angry and violent... That's what these two here are having words about."

Torj exchanged a glance with Wilder. "This commander... Did he give you anything? Potions? Weapons?"

The woman shook her head. "We offered our hospitality. He shared a meal and then went on his way."

"Who shared the meal with him?" Torj asked.

The woman looked around, brows knitting together. "They're all gone now... or dead."

A cold dread settled in Torj's gut. This wasn't just about claiming a throne—Silas was systematically corrupting the common folk, building an army from within. And with each village that fell, he grew closer to Delmira and the power of the silvertide roses—however he would choose to use them. But if there was one thing Torj knew about tyrants, it was that they never stopped at one kingdom. The Kingsbane would not stop until the entire midrealms was under his heel.

The race against time had already begun.

CHAPTER 4

WREN

*"The slow boil heats a crucible just as surely as the rapid one.
Both waters reach the same deadly temperature; one simply
allows an alchemist to mistake gradual inevitability for safety."*
—Toxic Tales: Chronicles of Lethal Elixirs

W ren and the Devereux company left the academy by carriage in the night, well after Wilder and Torj had departed under Audra's orders. It was for the best. It had taken over a decade, but Wren now understood that she couldn't help herself when it came to the Bear Slayer— and so, with Lord Lucian watching her like a hawk, removing herself from the situation was the only option. One slip-up and she'd condemn Torj to death. One mistake and there would be no army at her back to defend Delmira. Wren would maintain the ruse for as long as she could, to buy them all time.

She glanced at the travel case by her feet. Dessa had equipped her with ample supplies of Torj's blood, the cure she'd used on Queen Reyna, and a generous store of silvertide roses wrapped in silkspore. Her notebook was open in her lap, a mess of scribbled calculations and variables, along with a list of agricultural experts to write to.

As the carriage rattled over the uneven road, she could feel Lucian's disdain from where he sat opposite her, wrinkling his nose at the ink smudges on her fingers. She would have to keep her experiments hidden from her noble company, but no one was going to keep her from her work, not even a fucking Devereux.

Their carriages drew to an abrupt halt the following nightfall at the first bannerman's manor. It was an imposing building, with several groundskeepers still at work in the sprawling gardens and a dozen servants lined up at the sweeping staircase to receive them. Wren knew little about their hosts, only that they had been loyal to House Devereux for over a century and had contributed men on several occasions where local confrontations called for it.

"Welcome to the Briar estate," Darian told her, exiting the carriage and offering her his hand.

"Briar?" she echoed with a frown, accepting his help. The prickling of her nape told her people were watching, so she quickly schooled her face into a more neutral expression. She didn't have the energy to bat her lashes at her supposed fiancé, though.

Darian didn't seem to notice. "They're a noble house from Harenth, though they have estates all over the midrealms."

Harenth. A bitter taste spread across Wren's tongue as she recalled the ring bearing the Briar family sigil in her box of keepsakes back at Drevenor, souvenirs from a job well done.

Wren once again took in the sight of the stately manor. Climbing roses sprawled across intricate latticework while frescoes and mosaic tiles adorned the outer walls, leading to beautiful arches embellished with filigree detailing. "And they're your bannermen?" she asked. "Who is the head of the house? I need to be able to formally greet our gracious hosts, don't I?"

"Hamond Briar and his wife, Agnes," Darian told her. "He took over the estates and the relationship with the Devereux name after his brother passed away a few years ago."

Briar. One of the many names on her ledger. One of the many she had struck from its pages.

"I look forward to meeting them," Wren replied, allowing Darian to usher her toward the entrance.

"Agnes loves to host," he said. "And loves to plan a wedding even more. I expect she'll want to give her input before the night is over."

Wren was shown to lavish guest quarters to freshen up before a formal engagement dinner to be hosted in their honor. Thankfully, the nobility could be counted on for their numerous rooms and their preference to separate unmarried men and women. Thea went in first and did the usual security sweep, the action causing Wren's heart to ache, her hand drifting to the dagger at her belt as memories of Torj surged forth.

"You're invading my privacy," she hissed. "You have no right to go through my things, to—"

"No right?" He rounded on her, halting his sweep of the bathing room. "I have every damn right. I vowed to protect you, and that's exactly what I'm doing..."

"Ridiculous doesn't even cover it! You're rifling through my things! You're attacking random men in the corridor—"

Torj crossed the room in seconds. "He wasn't a man."

Wren glared up at him. "No? You're suddenly an expert?"

Torj laughed darkly. "If you need a comparison between a boy and a man, I can definitely help with that..."

"Looks like your future husband thinks of everything," Thea said stiffly, snatching Wren from her train of thought.

She blinked, the word *husband* echoing in her mind. "What?"

Thea pointed to a garment bag hanging on the wardrobe door. Shimmering blue fabric spilled out from where it had been opened.

"Furies save me," Wren cursed quietly. "No wonder the common folk are angry. Once more we're on the brink of war and all the nobility can think to do is throw a fucking party?"

Thea sighed. "It was always this way."

"Then you'd think we would have learned something by now," Wren quipped, reaching for the buckle of her potion belt. While she got dressed, Thea went to the elaborate drinks cart by the window overlooking the grounds below and poured them both a glass of something clear.

She tapped her drink against Wren's. "Perhaps you'll be the one to break the cycle."

Wren said nothing. Instead, she tipped the liquor back, nearly choking at the searing burn down her throat. "Gods," she spluttered, wiping the back of her hand across her mouth as her eyes watered. "That's like something out of the poisons dungeon."

Thea winced. "And I thought fire extract was bad..."

Wren had come to appreciate the harsh taste of the amber liquid in the years after the war—a far cry from her first experience, when she'd spat a mouthful all over Ida—but the stuff from the drinks cart was lethal. Still, she couldn't help thinking of her friends, for a moment imagining them here with her and Thea like they had been for so many years before.

"What would they think of me now?" she asked quietly, as Thea laced up the back of her dress.

"Who?"

"Sam and Ida..." Wren sucked in a breath as the corset tightened around her midsection. "Do you think they would have laughed at the idea of me being a queen of the midrealms?"

"I think they would have been a damn sight more useful with these fucking laces," Thea gritted out as she nearly broke Wren's ribs with her ministrations.

"I won't argue that," Wren wheezed.

"But no, they wouldn't have laughed," Thea replied. "They would have been proud. They would have found a place in your court and never left your side."

Tears stung Wren's eyes. "You really think that?"

"I do." Thea squeezed her shoulder. "Now let's get you to the—"

"Wait," Wren interrupted, reaching for her belt. She popped a vial down her cleavage as she usually did, but then took her dagger as well. She felt Thea's eyes on her as she treated the blade with a coating of poison before returning it to its sheath and securing it around her thigh beneath her skirts.

Torj's warm words came back to her, soothing her like a balm over a wound.

"Have you ever heard of the warrior's second? It's the intake of breath before the slice of a blade, or the swing of a hammer... The warrior's second is where we make our actions count, make them worthy of legend..."

"Ready?" Thea prompted from the door.

Wren glanced longingly at the travel case that contained her alchemy tools and her work on the cure, desperate to plant herself at a desk and start. Instead, she scooped up a bundle of envelopes from her belongings and pushed them into Thea's hands. "Can you make sure these are sent? The addresses are all there."

"Who are they for?" her sister asked, brow furrowed as she skimmed the names. "More Master Alchemists?"

Wren shook her head. "No, they're letters to renowned rosarians."

Thea gave her a blank look.

"Rosarians," Wren repeated. "Experts on roses—people from all over the midrealms and beyond who have a reputation in caring for and cultivating them."

"I'll take your word for it." Thea pocketed the squares of parchment. "Now, are you ready?"

Wren lifted her chin and nodded. "As I'll ever be."

Lord Darian Devereux was waiting for her just outside her chambers, offering his arm. "You look breathtaking, love."

"Thank you," Wren replied stiffly as he led her down the corridor.

"And I look rather handsome, wouldn't you say?" he added, a gleam of amusement in his eyes.

"Dashing," Wren added blandly. "How long until we can talk numbers with the new Lord Briar? I want to be back at Drevenor as soon as possible."

"There are formalities to respect here, Elwren. And from what I hear, there have been issues with the supply lines to various allied forces in the midrealms. My father and his bannermen will want to discuss solutions as well."

"Over sparkling wine and roasted game?"

"Is there any other way?" Darian quipped as they descended the stairs, Thea close behind.

Lord and Lady Briar had indeed hosted an extravagant affair in their honor. The tables were adorned with silk linens and embroidered runners, silverware with pearl handles, and tiered displays of delicious delicacies. Musicians played in the corner of the large space, the light melodic notes drifting through air thick with perfume. Men and women circled the hall: courtiers, diplomats, nobles, all with spiced wines in hand, jewels glimmering on their fingers, and faces polished and powdered. Wren had never thought she'd miss Thezmarr again, but here she was, yearning for the mud of the Bloodwoods and the constant shouting of the shieldbearer training drills from the yard.

She became increasingly aware of how exposed the scar on her throat was, of the fine make of the fabric swishing about her legs, of the striking man at her side—who was right in every way but the way that mattered. She could hear the hushed whispers.

"What a handsome pair."

"Perhaps there's hope for the midrealms yet."

"Imagine their children—"

Bile rose in Wren's throat at that last comment. When they entered the formal banquet hall to applause, she accepted a flute of pale gold wine and tipped it back to wash out the taste.

Darian's arm snaked around her waist, drawing her close enough that she could feel the warmth of him through his finely tailored jacket. "Don't be shy now, future wife," he murmured, guiding her through yet another crowd.

I can damn well walk myself, she wanted to snap at him, but she bit the words back.

An unnerving presence dominated her other side, and she glanced across to see Lord Lucian flanking her right. "You should smile more," he whispered in her ear, his breath hot and sticky. "You won't win any favors with that scowl."

Wren swallowed an array of curses, tempted to deposit the contents of the vial in her cleavage down the nobleman's throat.

"And what about *our* exchange of favors, Lord Lucian?" she asked serenely instead. "I was promised methods and ingredients for the antidote to the Bear Slayer's poison...

and a direct line to your spies within the People's Vanguard."

"All in good time, Your Highness. You'll have what was promised when you're married. As agreed," he replied. "In the meantime, our first priority is the war efforts affecting the people of the midrealms, surely?"

"Surely," Wren replied.

"And I trust there will be no trouble from your warrior acquaintance when we see him again?" There was a smugness to Lucian's words that made Wren's skin itch, as though he was testing her control.

Control that she had to keep tightly leashed, lest she conjure a storm right then and there.

"There will be no trouble," she said. "There will be no need to see the Bear Slayer again once you deliver what was promised."

"We'll see about that, won't we, Your Highness. Though I do hope to call you *daughter* soon enough."

The sentiment made her feel as though she were sliding through oil, unable to scrape it from her skin. "Nothing would make me happier, my lord." Though she silently thought: *His time will come.*

When they were seated at the table, Wren surveyed the feast before them. The silver platters and crystal glasses were all courtesy of the man whose ring she wore and the alliance he offered her and her kingdom.

The man in question cleared his throat and raised his goblet. "A thousand thanks to our gracious hosts, Lord and Lady Briar. We are honored to be at your table tonight."

Was this what campaigning for allies meant? Pretty speeches and expensive wine? One display of wealth after another, indulging over and over? No wonder the common folk of the midrealms had been vulnerable to Silas' propaganda. Beneath the table, Wren picked at the skin around her fingernails.

But Darian wasn't done. "The noble house of Briar has been a friend of our family for as long as I can remember, and we have leaned on your support for many of our challenges throughout the years. My bride-to-be and I come here today to ask for that support again. Some of you may remember Delmira in its glory days... I'm told it was the most prosperous land the midrealms had ever seen. Now, it has the potential to reach those heights again, with one of the most valuable resources at its heart: the silvertide rose, strengthened by Elwren's storm magic. *That* is what we stand to gain with Elwren as queen, and me as her husband on the throne beside her."

Wren could see the greed glinting back at her, and a chill ran down her spine. Drawing attention to the importance of the roses felt wrong. They were meant to be protecting them, rallying the funds and army to help her harvest them to make the cure, not shouting about them from the rooftops.

But Darian was oblivious as he continued. "Silas the usurper stands for many false causes, but his biggest is the one you fear most—the threat to all that your families have built over the centuries. Your livelihoods, your wealth... Pledge your private armies to us, as you have done many a time before, and reap the rewards of our union when the war is won."

Darian nodded to his father, who rose next to speak.

"I have the first reports of the usurper's numbers," Lord

Lucian announced. The table fell silent around them. "Our corroborated estimate is that Silas' forces sit at around five thousand. A large bulk of the force is made up of those who call themselves the People's Vanguard, recruited from the common folk of all remaining kingdoms. I say we hit them with full force," he declared. "Squash them where they stand and watch their children scurry back to the hole they came from."

"Hear, hear." Lord Briar tapped his goblet on the table in solidarity.

"I disagree," Wren said loudly. "You are lumping an entire people in with the usurper, when in fact he has manipulated them into thinking he's fighting for them. The majority of them aren't violent traitors. They're misplaced and lost. They need our help."

"Of course, Your Highness." Lord Lucian bowed his head. "And should any of them prove to be innocent, we shall help them find their place once more. Your feminine rule is one of justice and mercy."

Darian's arm draped around Wren's shoulders as he laughed. "Why do you think I'm marrying her, Father? The midrealms need someone like Elwren Embervale at the helm."

Wren chewed the inside of her cheek to keep from stabbing the smug bastard with her poisoned hairpin. Instead, she cupped Darian's face with her palm. "Your faith means the world to me, my love."

The words tasted sickly sweet on her tongue, but Wren saw the nobility fawn at the intimate gesture. And so, she leaned into Darian, resting her head on his shoulder affectionately for a moment before gazing up at him with what she hoped looked like admiration.

"Tell me, if Lord Briar is generous enough to offer his support, what then?" She kept her tone light and bland. *A role*, she told herself. *This is a role you must play.*

"My father's own bannermen are a force of three hundred strong, and if Lord Briar obliges us, we will journey to Lord Pendelton next to request his assistance as well," Darian replied with a patronizing note. "It will then be a matter of rallying the royal armies of Aveum, Tver, Harenth, and Naarva to our cause and forming a battle plan. Tyranny threatens us all, and a usurper of one kingdom is a usurper of all."

Wren took a sip of wine as sounds of agreement echoed down the table. "I trust the issues with the supply lines have been remedied?" she asked. "I'd hate for any of our brave fighters to be left without..."

"Nothing to worry about, Your Highness," Lord Briar replied with another condescending smile. "A sizable force was sighted several leagues from Drevenor, not all too far from here. But they changed course, splitting into smaller groups and moving on. No challenge has been issued and our supply lines remain intact. The threat is no longer cause for concern."

Wren caught Kipp's eye. The strategist was thoughtfully tracing the rim of his goblet with a finger. "My intelligence suggests that Silas is avoiding direct conflict for now," he said. "That he's rallying and conserving his strength for a more focused attack, be that on Delmira's heartlands or somewhere else. But we cannot dismiss threats so easily. Whether he knows it yet or not, the silvertide roses are the key to either stopping or amplifying his shadow magic. We can't afford to underestimate his movements."

"My scouts have everything in hand," Lucian interjected testily. "Princess Elwren, you and your advisors shouldn't worry yourselves about these things."

Gentle fingers trailed down her cheek, causing her to start. Warm breath tickled the shell of her ear. "My father is an expert in these matters," Darian said. "Allow him the honor of aiding your cause."

Her skin crawling at his touch, Wren caught his hand and placed it on the table, covering it with hers, but managing to dig her nails into his skin. "Of course," she said placidly. But beneath her words, there was nothing placid about her.

Her lightning promised to lay siege to their corruption, as had her poison before.

CHAPTER 5
TORJ

"Throughout the midrealms, it is a sign of respect to raise three fingers to one's left shoulder in the presence of a Warsword."
—The Warsword's Way

"Shit," Cal said bluntly as he arrived at Torj and Wilder's sorry excuse for a camp between villages. "I didn't realize things were *this* bad."

"I thought you were sharper than that, Whitlock." Torj raised a brow and peered behind his former protégé, clapping eyes on Prince Zavier Terling.

"He's not half as sharp as he looks," Zavier quipped as he dismounted from his horse.

"Clearly, if he broke you out of confinement against orders," Wilder mused, though he didn't sound fazed.

"What the fuck, Cal?" Torj rounded on him. "He was in

official Thezmarrian custody. You've broken a dozen rules by springing him free."

Cal scoffed. "For your information, it was *Audra's* suggestion. She thought it was only a matter of time before someone tried to *remove* Zavier from the equation, given his affiliation with Silas."

Torj sighed and added another log to the fire. "Then you may as well sit down and tell us what you know about him. We need everything, Zavier. Anything that might give us an edge, help predict his plays, weaken him... Why does he want Wren's crown? Is it just the land he's after?"

"No," Zavier told them, warming his hands over the fire. "Silas blames the Embervale family for what happened to our own. Our mothers were close, but when Queen Brigh Embervale received intelligence about the darkness that was rising prior to the shadow war, she diverted resources to protect only Delmira's lands, deliberately abandoning Naarva despite her friendship with our mother. Despite the oath of mutual protection they'd shared."

"Is it true?" Torj asked. "Did Wren's family betray them?"

"I don't know, and I'm not even sure it matters. But it's what Silas believes," Zavier replied, heavy grief lacing his words.

"So, it's revenge..." Wilder said quietly.

"It started that way, yes," Zavier said. "Which was why I stupidly thought that if there was a way to bring our mother back, it would stop him going down this path. That he could be redeemed."

"And now?"

Zavier's shoulders caved inward. "Now... now there's no

saving him. He was the true alchemist of us Terling brothers. And I've watched him turn something he loved into the most corrupted version of itself."

"Wren says he's using shadow magic. Is that true?" Cal asked.

Zavier didn't look up, but he nodded. "Fragments left over from the previous war. Infused with royal blood to make targeting magic wielders possible... The brother I loved died long ago; I just didn't want to admit it." He drew a shaky breath before he continued. "If my parents could see him now... If the people of Naarva knew about him... I have to go with you, wherever you're going. I must help undo this."

A noise of frustration escaped Torj. "I think you've done enough. For all we know, it was *you* who tipped him off to target me to get to Wren. You could be the reason he knew to poison me."

It was Zavier's turn to scoff. "Your and Wren's relationship is the worst-kept secret in the midrealms. Silas is no fool. He was *there* at the battle of Drevenor. He saw with his own eyes what was between you two then, like every other man, woman, and child under the sun. The battle itself could have been a test—to provoke any magical connection... You tell us, Bear Slayer. Might he have seen something that day?"

Torj glared at the Naarvian prince. "I trust you about as much as I trust—"

"Torj," Wilder interjected. "I think the prince has a point."

Torj clenched his jaw and said nothing more.

Zavier forged on. "He's a summoner, like me. The

Embervales can wield lightning and thunder, whereas the Terling family can move objects with the power of our minds alone. Silas... Silas is the more powerful of us brothers, and ever since he attacked Drevenor at our graduation, he's been getting stronger. I don't know how. I've been trying to work it out for weeks."

"Does he know about the silvertide roses? That they're part of Wren's cure for his shadow alchemy?" Torj asked.

"I don't know," Zavier said. "If he doesn't, it's only a matter of time. There are so many more people involved now. Silas will have just as many spies as Lucian Devereux."

Torj was wrenched back to the final moments of that battle, where a pair of soulless eyes behind a horrifying mask stared back at him—

"Has he always worn a mask?" he asked abruptly, his gaze snapping back to Zavier.

Zavier frowned. "No... but he and I look quite similar. If he faced anyone who knew me, they would be able to tell we are kin. I just assumed it was to hide his identity."

"Is there any significance to its design? Does it mean anything to you?" Torj pressed.

But Zavier shook his head. "No. My guess would be that it's part of his intimidation tactics. A sea of masked men makes them somehow inhuman, doesn't it?"

"And what of his other tactics?" Wilder asked from across the fire. "The stories we've heard have been the same all over the outer villages—a stranger comes to town, breaks bread, and leaves. He pressures no one to join the People's Vanguard, simply shares information and then goes on his way. But then people go missing, others depart in the dark of night... Then there are the folk who suddenly start fights with their neighbors and friends, completely out of character, and things escalate to the point of death. Do you know anything of this?"

"I doubt it's Silas himself," Zavier said slowly. "But he has several trusted alchemists in his ranks ready to do his bidding. It could be some sort of elixir designed to amplify aggression, but from your description alone I can't be sure—"

A blur shot across the fire, and a startled shriek sounded from the darkness.

Wilder's swords were gleaming in the firelight and Torj had his hammer ready. The string of Cal's bow quivered as he nocked another arrow, his gaze fixed on something in the shadows.

"Will one of you Warswords tell me what's happening?" Zavier demanded, a hand pressed over his chest as he scanned the camp wildly.

"I come in peace!" a voice called from the forest.

"Then show yourself!" Torj shouted back.

"I would, but I'm now pinned to a tree," came the reply.

Torj nodded to Cal, who shouldered his bow and went to retrieve their new guest. Exchanging a wary look with Wilder, Torj waited.

The underbrush rustled as Cal emerged with a woman in tow. She carried herself well, her chin lifted, her back straight, though her eyes gave away her distrust.

"Who are you?" Wilder demanded.

Cal brought her into the light, dropping a large canvas sack at their feet—her belongings.

"My name is Senna Cross," she told them, eyeing their weapons with trepidation.

"You have my word that no harm will come to you while you say your piece here," Torj told her, equally apprehensive.

"I've lived in the midrealms long enough to know that promises from anyone mean nothing, let alone promises from strangers," Senna said, with a cool note of detachment.

Torj couldn't argue that. "Fair enough."

Senna dipped her head. "I was out in the fields when you came to my village," she explained. Her gaze darted over their small party, lingering on Zavier, but she continued, "I've been trying to find you since you left. But I couldn't take the main routes. They're not safe anymore."

"Because of the People's Vanguard?" Cal asked. "We know of their public floggings and hangings, and their witch hunts for outsiders..."

Senna's laugh held no humor. "If only it were that simple. The woman you spoke with? That was our village elder, but I'll wager she didn't tell you much."

"She told us of the stranger, and how those who broke bread with him were gone... or dead," Wilder allowed.

"Gone..." Senna repeated. "That's one word for it. And yes, there are plenty dead. The innkeeper's daughter whose throat was torn out two nights ago. The wheat farmer who was beaten to death with his own shovel... Whatever this enemy is doing, it goes beyond recruiting for a war."

"We know," Torj told her quietly. "He's using fragments of shadow magic from the previous war."

"If that's true—if he's delving into that kind of power..." Senna breathed. "Then who knows what he's capable of."

Zavier studied the woman with his arms folded over his

chest and a brow raised. "You followed us across dangerous lands to tell us this?"

"No," Senna replied, shaking her head. "I actually have something that might be of interest to you, Warswords." She reached for the bulky sack Cal had dropped at their feet.

"Allow me," Torj said, lifting it, though not expecting the weight—it was heavy. Almost as heavy as his war hammer. He felt a tremor start in his fingers, a bunching of the tendons in his hands, but he placed the item on the leaf-covered ground and pulled back the fabric.

Torj stared at the familiar weapon.

A mace.

Made of Naarvian steel.

"Where did you find this?" he demanded.

"In a small port town in the south of Harenth, along with more blood than I've ever seen. Something happened there. Something terrible."

Torj didn't take his eyes off the bludgeon.

"It belongs to a Warsword, doesn't it?" Senna asked over his shoulder.

Torj took in the recognizable spiked head, the runes carved into its grip. He'd seen it crush plates of armor and pulverize more warriors than he could count. "Not just any Warsword," he heard himself say. "That's Vernich the Bloodletter's mace."

CHAPTER 6
TORJ

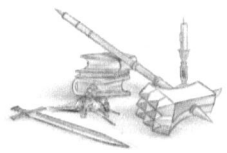

"A Warsword's Furies-gifted weapon is forged from steel mined from the Kingdom of Naarva, where the iron ore is the strongest in the midrealms, rumored to hold the power of the gods themselves."
—The Warsword's Way

"Y ou're sure this belongs to the Bloodletter?" Zavier asked. "Why take it?"

Senna scoffed. "That's Naarvian steel right there. Do you know how much that's worth? Our initial intention was to sell it."

"Why didn't you?"

"Because we found out who it belonged to... The Bloodletter. No amount of coin on a midrealms black market would cover such a prize. Not in these times."

"Who found it, exactly?" Torj asked.

Senna grimaced, as though she were recalling the scene vividly. "I did... It was a bloodbath. Bodies broken beyond recognition, severed limbs, caved-in skulls... It looked as though there had been some kind of raid. The place—a little shack by the coast—had been ransacked, no cupboard or corner left untouched. Whoever was there put up a fight. The blood was still thick on the walls when we got there a few days later, judging by the smell."

Torj pointed to the mace on the ground. "And this?"

"We found it in the sand just outside," Senna replied. "Seemed unlikely a Warsword of the Bloodletter's caliber would leave it behind. At least not on purpose." She scanned their faces. "I'm sorry for your loss."

No one spoke. Torj wondered if it was because the thought of Vernich the mighty Bloodletter no longer walking the midrealms was simply unbelievable. He was the first and eldest of the original three who had returned to Thezmarr all those years ago to train shieldbearers.

"There's more." Senna waved a small pouch at them. "You might want to hold your noses..."

Torj didn't register the words in time before Senna opened the little bag and tipped three severed fingers onto the ground.

The smell was instant—rotting flesh, pungent enough to make Torj's eyes water and force him to cover his nose and mouth with his hand. Zavier didn't fare so well; he darted away to dry heave into the bushes.

"What the fuck?" Cal exclaimed, pressing a kerchief to the lower half of his face with a grimace.

"They were found with the mace," Senna explained. "See the rings?"

Still pinching his nose, Torj forced himself to look at the severed digits. Sure enough, there were two rings on each of them: iron bands with delicate spikes, and no markings or sigils he recognized—

"Those rings belong to Warsword Graves," Cal said quietly. "And the fingers too, I'm guessing..."

"Who's Warsword Graves?" Zavier asked.

"Only one of the most brutal Warswords from the new cohort. Ashlyn Graves wore those rings to fuck people's faces up even more when she hit them," Cal replied. "I trained her briefly at Thezmarr before she was called for the Great Rite. She was reported missing shortly after Vernich disappeared. She was one of the Warswords sent to look for him."

Torj felt the shock ripple through the small group around him. Of their current company, there were three Warswords of the highest caliber, who had survived the Great Rite and the shadow war, only to find themselves here, with their fellow warriors being picked off one by one.

"We need to presume that they're dead," Wilder said stoically. "Vernich would never leave that mace behind willingly—"

"Well, I doubt Graves left her fingers behind willingly either, but that doesn't mean she's dead," Cal argued.

"All I'm saying is that we should assume we're another two Warswords down in this war," Wilder replied gently.

Torj flinched beside his brother-in-arms. If what Wren said about the poison in him was true, then Wilder was wrong.

The number was three.

They would be another *three* Warswords down in the war to come.

CHAPTER 7
WREN

"They're playing checkers when we're playing Dancing Alchemists."
—Elwren Embervale's notes and observations

"It's not as grand as our estate in Harenth, but with the right arrangements, it could make a stunning venue," Lady Briar told Wren, gesturing to the sweeping grounds of the manor before them.

"I'm not sure Darian and I are ready to view wedding locations just yet," Wren said stiffly. "We're only newly engaged, after all..."

Lady Briar waved her off. "Nonsense. If I know anything about the Devereux men, it's that they'll want this marriage squared away as soon as possible. Lord Briar and I would be happy to host the wedding here if you find it agreeable. The ceremony could be held down by the lake—there is a stunning arbor with climbing jasmine, and within a few weeks the gardens will be awash with tulips."

"You're too kind, Lady Briar. I'll ask Darian what he thinks. He may have a location in mind already..." During her time as the Poisoner, Wren had met enough nobility to learn how to mimic their language. In her experience, their type used a lot of words to say very little that mattered, which worked in her favor, given that she wasn't willing to give away any of the information she held close to her chest.

"How many times must I tell you to call me Agnes?" Lady Briar slapped her arm lightly in reprimand. "And the only location that man will be concerning himself with is the bedroom, if you catch my drift, Elwren."

Wren flushed. The forced touching and falsely sweet words exchanged with the dashing nobleman had already been enough to sicken her. So far, the nobility had upheld the custom of separate sleeping quarters for unwed couples, but if Lady Briar was making such comments, it was clear that Darian wasn't usually one to respect those boundaries. Sooner or later, people would expect him in her bed, and the thought alone made Wren want to gag.

Lady Briar watched Wren's expression and wiggled her eyebrows suggestively. Gods, Wren would gnaw off her own arm if it meant she could extract herself from this conversation. After breakfast, the men had excused themselves to Lord Briar's study, while Wren had been seized by Lady Briar to discuss "subjects more befitting of a woman of her noble standing." Which was how she had found herself arm in arm with Agnes now.

"I appreciate the generosity, truly, I do," Wren told her as they wandered the grounds. "But our main focus is the upcoming conflict, first and foremost."

"I suppose you do have a kingdom at stake," Lady Briar allowed.

"I do..." Wren replied slowly, feeling the hair on the nape of her neck rising. She glanced back toward the manor, spotting a familiar pair of eyes staring out at her.

Lucian.

The bastard had barely taken his eyes off her since the engagement had been announced. Wren could feel him monitoring her everywhere she went, studying not only her words, but her movements, her body language, ready to catch her out at any time.

So Wren tugged her companion a little closer, dipping her head as though confiding in a newly discovered best friend. "But once Delmira is secured, I would love to talk more about the wedding with you. I don't have many women acquaintances of your... social standing to guide me. I'd appreciate your insights, Agnes."

Lady Briar beamed. "It would be my pleasure, Elwren. You'll find me incredibly well connected with the best of the midrealms' cooks, florists, entertainers... It will be a lavish affair when we're done with it, to be sure."

Back at the manor, Lucian's shadow moved across the window.

"That sounds wonderful," Wren said, forcing a smile and steering them back toward the house.

"Doesn't it? Nothing would make me happier than seeing Darian marry a princess of the midrealms. If anyone was born to be a prince consort, it's him. He's got the pedigree and looks to match."

Wren had to stop herself from shuddering. "I couldn't agree more. Shall we freshen up before they serve morning tea on the terrace?"

"Of course."

Wren left Lady Briar in the foyer, but rather than heading for her guest chambers upstairs, she waited for Kipp outside Lord Briar's study.

"Lord Briar has pledged five hundred men to your cause," the strategist said by way of greeting as he ducked out of the room.

"And the catch?" Wren asked.

"They want land in Delmira when you've reclaimed the kingdom."

"Of course they do," Wren muttered, tugging her friend toward the stairs. She had to check on the potions she'd left bubbling on the windowsill. "As if they don't have enough wealth already. I'm assuming we agreed?"

"We did," Kipp replied with a grimace, following her. "He's also insisting that Lady Briar be one of your bridesmaids. They want it clear to the public from the start that they're close with the Delmirian royals."

"What did Thea have to say about that?" Wren mused, glancing behind them, wondering where her sister was.

"She made a convincing fuss about being your matron of honor, which was for the best. Had she said nothing it would have been suspicious. She's in there now, still arguing with Lucian about where to obtain the best weaponry for the new forces."

Ascending the grand staircase, Wren kept her voice low. "He was watching me from the windows..."

"I know," Kipp replied. "This agreement is precarious to say the least. You can't give him any reason to doubt the engagement. Torj—"

"Believe me, Kipp, I know what's at stake," she cut him off as they reached her chambers. "Do you think I'd remain silent and play the part of the demure wife-to-be for any other reason?"

"If this is you being demure..." he said wryly.

Wren rolled her eyes as she stepped inside and went straight to the alchemy she'd left brewing in her absence. With the window ajar, the steam drifted out into the estate grounds, but the faint scent of roses still lingered in her room.

It was easy to lose herself in the familiar tasks— crushing herbs between her fingers, testing their potency— but she yearned to shed the pretenses, to be able to focus on the real task at hand. Thoughts of Torj surged through her. Wren didn't remember unsheathing the dagger he had given her, but there it was in her hands, her fingertip running down the flat of the blade across the inscription, *Iron & Embers*. His vow to her. Their soul bond engraved in steel.

Kipp rested a comforting hand on her arm, but his words were anything but. "He'd rather die strong than live weak. We know that much about the Bear Slayer."

She pictured her Warsword out there, with poison coursing through his veins. The thought stole the breath from her lungs. He was hers to save. Hers to protect. And she would do exactly that if it was the last thing she ever did. She couldn't falter now.

In the distance, she could sense a storm brewing. She tasted rain on the tip of her tongue, felt the swell of promise in the air around her.

Wren steeled herself against Kipp's words. "Well, that's not his choice."

CHAPTER 8

TORJ

"Some orders are made to be disobeyed."
—Bear Slayer, Warsword of Thezmarr

Audra's orders took them across to a village in the Broken Isles, a directive that made Torj's blood boil. Every league of cold, unforgiving water between him and Wren felt like another betrayal. He'd argued with Cal and Wilder until his voice went hoarse and his fists clenched white-knuckled at his sides, ready to draw blood if necessary. Only Zavier had sided with him, but it meant nothing when Wilder—damn him to the icy dungeons of Aveum—was the sole keeper of Wren's location.

Torj *knew* that gathering information for the guild was important work, that it was vital for the war strategies to come, but their second agenda was as subtle as a war hammer: to keep him away from Wren and Darian. Each day without her was another cut to his heart. His hands ached to touch her face, to confirm she was real and not just a distant memory of a dream he had always yearned for. And beneath that longing, a darker thought festered—that at this very moment, she might be in Darian's arms, looking up at him with those willow-green eyes... The thought turned his stomach to acid, burning through his chest until he could barely breathe. It wasn't jealousy—it was terror that the bond they'd forged through blood and battle and ancient magic might weaken in his absence.

He dreamed of her every night—vivid, merciless visions where she reached for him across battlefields strewn with the fallen, her fingers always inches from his own before she dissolved into shadow. Then there were the dreams where he felt her softness against his body, the warmth of her palm cupping his face, the brush of her lips on his. By day, her voice haunted him, ghosting across his consciousness when the wind shifted just so. *Torj*, it would whisper, and he'd jerk his head up, muscles coiled tight, eyes scanning the horizon for a glimpse of her bronze hair.

It was happening again, her voice carrying on the breeze, when blood-curdling snarls sliced through his trance like a blade.

The noise was vicious and primal, but not... animal. The feral sounds echoing through the underbrush were distinctly *human*.

He signaled the others with a sharp gesture, then slid from Tucker's back and gripped his hammer, creeping closer. With each silent step forward, the sounds grew louder, more desperate. Through a veil of leaves, the village Audra had described came into view.

There, staked to the ground like a sacrifice, a man writhed in chains.

He thrashed against his restraints, the links rattling as white spittle flew from his mouth, not just foaming like a rabid dog but projecting with each guttural curse, each threat.

"I'll kill you all," he shouted. "I'll carve you up into little pieces. Let me go—"

Torj scanned the rest of the village, where a group of people were rummaging through a satchel, shaking their heads and murmuring among themselves.

"We've tried all of this before," an older woman said, pushing the bag back. "None of it works."

Torj watched a moment longer. There was no sign of the People's Vanguard's influence here, nor was Silas' sigil anywhere to be seen. These were no enemy soldiers or traitors to the midrealms... and so he signaled back to Wilder and shouldered his hammer, stepping out from the shadows, the others close behind.

"We're here to help," he told the villagers, his hands raised to show he meant no harm.

The bound man started cursing and pulling against his chains again. "Warsword filth, let me have him—"

Torj frowned. He'd met plenty of fools in his time who thought they could take on a Warsword, but they were usually bigger, and had at least some semblance of military training. This man was a simple farmer, by the look of him.

Torj turned to the small group. "What's going on here?"

Though the villagers looked wary, one man stepped forward. "I'm Jarros," he said, a tremor in his voice as he pointed to the chained man, who was still thrashing against his bonds. "And that there is my brother, Faulkner."

Torj folded his arms over his chest and surveyed the captive. "What's wrong with him?"

"Same as a lot of people who encountered the usurper. He's gone mad," an older woman replied. "He's become aggressive, violent."

Torj turned to study Faulkner, noting the hungry look in his bloodshot eyes, his straining muscles as he tried to claw his way toward the Warswords.

"It happened gradually," Jarros explained. "It started small, just him picking arguments with us. But then those fights became physical, and he seemed to enjoy them. Faulkner was never like that before—he was always gentle, good with animals and children... But he started talking about joining the People's Vanguard, where he could see real battle. As though fighting with us wasn't enough for him. It was like something came over him."

"We've tried everything to bring him out of the trance," the woman said. "But nothing works."

Torj passed a hand over his face before motioning to Zavier behind him. "This man is an alchemist; you need to tell him what you have tried so far. He may be able to help."

Zavier stepped forward without hesitating. "Are there others like Faulkner? Perhaps in different states to the one he's in now?"

"Not anymore," Jarros replied. "Many have answered the call of the People's Vanguard. Many wish to fight in Silas' war for Delmira."

"Shit," Wilder muttered, giving Torj a grim look. "Does this remind you of anything?"

Torj studied Faulkner, who looked more feral by the minute, still cursing and yelling, rattling his chains as he jerked violently. There was a familiarity there: the unhinged nature of him, the thirst for destruction... but Torj couldn't place it.

"The howlers." Cal stepped forward, not taking his eyes off the enraged prisoner. "He reminds me of the howlers from the shadow war."

As soon as Cal said the words, the realization hit Torj too. He was right. The same unnatural fury guided the man's movements, the same deranged darkness taking hold.

"But they were monsters," Jarros said slowly.

"They were once men," Cal corrected him gently. "But upon contact with shadow magic, they became mutilated, lost to themselves, mere instruments of violence."

Jarros shuddered. "Is that what's going to happen to Faulkner?"

"We don't know," Torj told him. "But from what you've told us and what we've learned from other villages... It sounds like Silas is building an army of madmen. Of people whose sole wish is to spill blood, no matter the cost. He's using shadow magic to instill a craving for violence in innocent people and calling them into his war."

Quiet fell as his words settled across the small group.

"Shit," Wilder breathed, but his curse was a distant noise to Torj.

Terror, pure and unfiltered, crashed through him. The shadow magic. The madness. Silas' army of corrupted souls. And somewhere out there—Wren. His soul-bonded. Trapped with the vipers, not knowing what was coming.

"Tell me where she is, Hawthorne." Torj was already at Tucker's side, his voice dangerously low. "Or Furies save me, I'll tear the midrealms apart to find her myself."

Cal stepped forward, placing a restraining hand on Torj's stallion. "Think, Torj. We have orders. Audra sent us here for—"

"Audra doesn't know about this," Torj cut him off, voice like gravel as he swung himself up into the saddle. "She doesn't know what Silas is creating, that we could be up against an army of fucking *howlers*."

"All the more reason to report back first," Cal insisted, his strained expression betraying his conflicting loyalties. "Thezmarr needs to prepare."

But it was to Wilder that Torj looked, the man who knew better than anyone what was at stake. "I won't ask you again, Hawthorne. Wren has to know."

"Three days' ride east once back on the mainland," he said quietly, reaching for his own reins. "And Elderbrock? We're coming with you."

CHAPTER 9

WREN

"A poisoner's mastery often boils down to the simple skill of attention to detail."
—The Poisoner's Handbook

With Lord Briar's bannermen secured, Wren rode with Darian and their guard to the Pendelton estate the next day. Thea kept close to her side, and Kipp did what Kipp did best: riding between the ranks and talking to the men, his stories often followed by loud bursts of laughter.

As they traveled, Wren was told a similar tale to the first —that Lord Pendelton originally hailed from Tver, but owned multiple properties across the midrealms and had been gracious enough to meet them at his manor in Naarva. Darian stressed to her several times that they were lucky

Lord Lucian's allies were being so accommodating with their schedules.

"I'm sure they're doing so out of the goodness of their hearts," Thea muttered dryly.

It had been a long while since Wren had done so much riding, and she was dismayed to find her thighs burning and her tailbone aching after several hours in the saddle. She missed riding with Torj at her back, the warmth of him surrounding her, the beat of his heart a steady rhythm against her spine while she breathed in his black-cedar-and-oakmoss scent.

She knew Audra had ordered him and Wilder to investigate Silas' reach to the local villages, but she didn't know *where* exactly. It felt like half a world away, wherever he was. They had spoken into each other's minds before, but perhaps now the distance was too great to reach one another... She could only hope that he wasn't feeling the effects of the poison yet, and that Wilder was looking out for him.

Wren could still sense the storm on the horizon, though it hadn't broken yet. A glance at her sister told her that Thea could feel it too. Neither Embervale called to it, but Wren felt her own magic dance at her fingertips as if in answer.

Her attention was snatched away as they turned a corner. Wren gaped at the verdant land that stretched before them, a private road cutting through the expanse of pristine grass and a sea of vibrant roses. It took an hour by carriage just to get to the front of the estate, which had been adorned with garlands of flowers in honor of their arrival.

A line of servants awaited, ready to take their luggage and offer them refreshments, but it was the elegant man and woman at the top of the stairs that caught Wren's attention. They were each beautifully dressed in colored silks that complemented the other, and both wore expressions of utter delight on their faces.

"Welcome, welcome!" the woman who could only be Lady Pendelton declared, her skirts swishing as she came forward to greet them.

Wren nearly recoiled as Lord Lucian took her hand and led her to their hosts. His fingers were cold and dry against hers, his grip harder than necessary, as though he were trying to bruise her bones.

"Lady Pendelton, Lord Pendelton, may I present my future daughter-in-law, Elwren Embervale, Princess of Delmira."

Wren kept her expression mild and pleasant as both nobles dipped into dignified bows.

"A pleasure to meet you both," she heard herself say. "Thank you for hosting us in your beautiful home. The roses on the way in are particularly stunning."

"The pleasure is all ours, Your Highness," Lord Pendelton said. "Perhaps my wife can show you the rest of our gardens."

"Oh, I'm sure she doesn't have time for my silly interests," Wren replied lightly. "I'd be happy if your groundskeeper showed me the way later."

Lord Pendelton gave her a strange look. "Braxton is hardly a common groundskeeper. He's one of the most revered horticulturists in Naarva."

Wren flashed a bland smile. "How wonderful."

At last, Lucian released her fingers, and she suppressed the urge to wipe them on her gown. But the unwanted touch was soon replaced by another, with Darian swooping in and sliding an arm around her waist as they were led inside. The crawling sensation along her skin told her that Lucian was close behind.

Wren longed for the quaint rooms of Drevenor with dried herbs strung up across the windows and crucibles bubbling on the workstations, but instead, she was greeted by yet another elaborate foyer, with enormous ceramic urns framing every doorway and half a dozen servants bustling through each room.

"We have prepared a wonderful dinner in celebration of your engagement," Lady Pendelton gushed. "So perhaps if you'd like to change, you can meet us in the dining hall in an hour? Our staff will show you to your quarters."

When Wren and Thea were escorted to their lavish guest chambers, Wren collapsed onto the bed with a heavy sigh.

"I don't know how much longer I can stomach this, Thee," she muttered, closing her eyes for a moment as she tried to summon her strength.

"Tell me about it," her sister groaned. "Lord Briar was insufferable in the previous meetings. Loves to hear himself talk. Now we're adding another nobleman to the fold, the meetings will be twice as long. Consider yourself lucky your time is spent doing more useful things."

Wren huffed. "Like what? Planning a wedding I want nothing to do with?"

"I meant your alchemy projects."

"I've hardly had a spare moment; they can't seem to fathom that a woman might want some time alone to pursue her own ambitions. Not even if those ambitions affect the state of the midrealms. It's all ceremony this, flowers that..."

"Ah, yes," Thea said dryly. "True women's work."

Reluctantly, Wren hauled herself upright. "I suppose I'd better change for whatever games await..."

"You can borrow my armor if you'd like," Thea ventured. Wren snorted.

Later that night, with another bridesmaid secured in Lady Pendelton, and a second offer to host the Embervale–Devereux wedding under her belt, Wren turned her attention firmly to the true matters at hand. The wine flowed freely and had already loosened several tongues, but she refused to retire for tea with the wives before saying her piece.

"I do not ask you to fight for a stranger's ambition, but for the rightful order of the midrealms," she told Lord Pendelton and his men. "With each day the usurper comes closer to taking my throne, our laws lose meaning and your own rights grow weaker... Your ancestors did not bow to tyrants. The blood of the brave flows through your veins. Will you let it be said that in your generation, courage finally failed?"

Darian gave a charming chuckle, covering her hand with his own. "What my beloved fiancée is saying is that those who march with us now, when victory is uncertain, will not find us forgetful when it is achieved. Lord Pendelton, your bannermen have been loyal to my house for seven generations. Lord Briar has already pledged his allegiance." Darian raised his glass to the man in question, who toasted him back with a smug grin.

It was clever to play them off one another, encouraging what Thea would call a *pissing contest*. But Darian was not finished.

"I did not choose to stand beside Wren for our love or her beauty—though both are formidable. I stand with her because she is the true heir of Delmira and I have seen how she treats her allies. That is the measure of a true ruler, and why you should pledge as many of your men to her cause as you can."

Lord Pendelton exchanged a glance with Lord Lucian before looking back to the betrothed couple. "We'll discuss it at length."

For two more days the negotiations continued, and what little time Wren stole for herself and her alchemy was interrupted by wedding planning. It seemed that more thoughts and funds were dedicated to her "big day" than to the upcoming war itself, and if that didn't showcase the values of Darian's connections, she didn't know what did.

That evening, their hosts had transformed a lady's dressing chamber into a modiste's workshop. The spacious room featured three deep alcoves along one wall, each curtained with heavy velvet for privacy during fittings. The opposite wall held floor-to-ceiling windows that overlooked the estate grounds, but the alcoves themselves remained well-shielded from outside view. Ornate screens, dress stands, and various furniture pieces cluttered the main space, creating natural dividers throughout the room. Wren went to one of the window seats, cushioned with velvet so an onlooker might be comfortable as they surveyed the world beneath with a sense of surreal removal. Removal she very much needed from the reality unfolding in the room behind her.

Wren was soon tugged back into the center of the room, where racks upon racks of gowns had been brought in for her perusal. She was shoved in front of strangers in little more than a shift as they forced her into gowns of varying degrees of ridiculousness.

Lady Briar, Lady Pendelton, their friends, and their team of dressmakers and seamstresses flocked to her, each clutching a flute of sparkling wine, exclaiming loudly about which fabrics suited Wren best and which jewels brought out the green in her eyes. Thea watched on from her station at the doorway, barely containing her grimace whenever Wren glanced her way.

It was all too much: the noise, the touching, the concept of marrying Darian Devereux when her heart was with a Warsword half a world away. Wren told herself to grin and bear it, to gush over the veils and lace with the same level of enthusiasm as the others, but a sadness leeched into her bones, and each effort left her increasingly drained.

She was tugged behind the modesty screen once more, her shift stripped away unceremoniously by Lady Pendelton's servants. They were careless with her body, with no thought for her privacy or vulnerability, her potions and dagger long since discovered and given to Thea for safekeeping. Wren hated being without them more than she hated her nakedness in front of the strangers. She was shoved into another gown; this one was fitted snugly, the bodice making it hard to breathe once its laces had been tightened.

Wren was paraded out by a seamstress, where the ladies, now thoroughly drunk, applauded and made suggestive comments as she was led toward the full-length mirror.

She nearly choked as she stared at her reflection. The dress was a beautiful creation, far simpler than the other designs that had nearly swallowed her in layers of tulle and lace. The silhouette suited her figure, hugging her curves and cinching her waist. But the pure white of the gown seemed to mock the darkness within...

Suddenly, her eyes stung with tears and panic burned up her throat as she struggled to get air into her lungs. She gripped the rack of dresses beside her, her knuckles turning bone-white as she braced herself. The longer she stared, the more the reflection before her became a stranger—a pristine lie.

The room seemed to shrink around her, the walls inching closer as her heartbeat quickened and a droplet of sweat traced down her spine. The bodice tightened like a vise. Had it been this constricting during the fitting? She tugged at the neckline, but the movement only seemed to make the fabric cling more desperately to her skin.

"Get out," she whispered, her voice almost inaudible amid the chatter.

Her reflection blurred as her vision tunneled, the edges darkening like parchment catching fire.

She yelled the words this time. "Get out!"

The women around her started, their gasps echoing across the gallery.

Thea swept in, ushering them out with gentle words. "The princess has been overcome with emotion. She needs a moment to gather herself."

But when only her sister remained, Wren motioned to the door. "You too, Thee..."

She didn't register the click of the door closing; she could only stare at the woman in the mirror. Her reflection was surreal, fragmenting like shattered glass, each piece revealing something she didn't recognize—or like. So many different versions of herself blinked back, none of them the right one.

She looked at the hem of the bridal gown, following the subtle lace pattern up the hourglass shape of her hips and the curves of her breasts to the sorrow shining in her eyes—

And then she froze as her gaze met a sea-blue stare in the reflection.

Torj Elderbrock stood behind her.

CHAPTER 10
TORJ

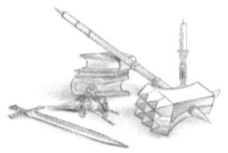

"A soul bond can be likened to an instinct of the most primal nature."
—Tethers and Magical Bonds Throughout History

"Torj," Wren whispered, turning to him from where she stood before the mirror.

With his name on her lips, he could only stare.

She was breathtaking in bridal white, the floor-length gown hugging her curves, the neckline plunging between her breasts. The silk gleamed in the candlelight as she moved toward him, her eyes red-rimmed.

Torj was in a trance. He had never allowed himself to envision Wren like this, as a bride. Some deep, dark part of him had always known that it would be pure torture, never fully believing it would come to pass. Only now, here she was, dressed for her wedding.

But it wasn't for him.

As her fingertips skated along his skin, he was suddenly young again, happening upon her in the Bloodwoods, her basket of herbs at her feet, a harvesting knife pointed at him. A ragged sound shuddered out of him then—relief, sorrow, longing, all tangled into one.

"You have no idea what you're doing to me," he murmured, cupping her face and drinking in every freckle, each shifting shade of green in her eyes.

"I'm sorry, I—"

"Why him?" he asked, voice cracking. "Tell me why it has to be *him*, after everything I told you."

"I've been trying to find the time to explain, but we can't be seen together. You can't—"

He knew he wasn't being rational, but the primal urge to wipe Darian's touches from her skin, to claim her as his own, as he was hers, was overpowering. Every principle he'd lived by warred against the need consuming him. She was promised to another—his sworn enemy, no less. But the bond between them was older than any vow, deeper than any moral code.

"Torj," she whispered, a plea.

There would be time for words later, but here and now?

Torj crushed his mouth to Wren's in a searing kiss.

He tasted the salt of her tears as she moaned against his lips, opening for him, the sound shooting straight to his cock. Desire surged forth, and he carried her to one of the alcoves, wrenching the thick curtain closed behind them.

He wasn't gentle. But nor was she. They matched each other's desperation and hunger, clawing at one another—

Wren broke away, her bright eyes piercing him down to his soul. "I love you."

"You say that now..." Torj let the hurt show, let her see how her plans had ruined him.

But Wren was fierce. "I'll say it every day until you know it's true, and forever after that." She pressed her palm to his chest, where lightning scars marred his inked skin. Her touch was not to push him away, but to center him, to command his full attention. "Look at me, Torj," she demanded. "I have never belonged to him. This is strategy, not a surrender. I belong to *you*."

"Then why can't we find some other way?"

"This part of the plan requires sacrifice," she said, and he heard what remained unspoken—that *she* was the sacrifice, offered up like a lamb to slaughter.

Torj didn't want to talk anymore. He wasn't sure he wanted to hear her answers. Instead, he wanted to remember the feel of her, the taste of her, the way she cried out *his* name when she came undone. She was his soul-bonded. *His.* And he would have her now, as the bond demanded.

Every fiber of his being longed to be united with her. And so he mapped the curves of her body with his hands, mesmerized as she arched into his touch like a woman starved. He savored every reaction to him: the tremor of a muscle, the soft sighs on her lips, the crease in her brow as he taunted and teased her body into a frenzy. A frenzy that only a soul-bonded could create.

With the curtains drawn, they were in their own world. He kissed her again, allowing his tongue to explore her mouth until she was whimpering and grinding herself against him in that beautiful white dress. A dress that Darian had given her.

"I want to tear this thing off you," he growled in her ear, fisting the fabric at her waist, his cock straining at the thought. He could feel moisture beading at the tip—so ready for her, always ready for her.

"Don't you dare, Bear Slayer," she hissed, tensing beneath his grip. But the brightness in her eyes betrayed her arousal, as did the rise and fall of her chest within the confines of her gown.

"I think you'd like it," he murmured against her neck, biting her gently so that she arched again. "You'd like it if I ripped this dress apart and fucked you for all the world to see. Tell me it's not true, Embers."

"Torj..." she warned, her tongue swiping across her lower lip.

"Don't worry," he told her, hiking the material up and bunching it around her thighs. "I'm not going to rip it off..."

Wren moaned as his fingers found her wet, bare center.

"But I *am* going to fuck you," he said, pushing two fingers inside her.

Her head hit the wall as it tipped back in ecstasy, and Torj bit the top of her breast to muffle a groan of his own. The heat of her was intoxicating, and he relished every stroke as he worked her until her legs were trembling around him. Where their skin touched, faint golden lines appeared, tracing patterns in a rhythm made for them and them alone—the physical manifestation of a bond written in fate.

He imagined the bliss of replacing his fingers with his

cock, that tight wet heat wrapping around the length of him. But not yet. First, he wanted his name on her lips.

Freeing her breasts from the bodice of her dress, he teased her nipples with tongue and teeth, while his hand dipped between her legs and circled her clit. Light patterns, building in pressure and speed, before he pinched.

The sight of her writhing for him was *almost* enough to stop him from realizing one very disturbing fact: she hadn't been wearing undergarments. Again.

With an open palm, he slapped her naked backside and Wren gasped, her eyes flying open in surprise. But her center grew even wetter as he pushed his fingers inside once more. He made a mental note of that for another time.

"You're bare beneath these skirts for him?" He didn't even recognize his own voice as it dipped to a growl.

"I—" she panted. "I can't wear them with a dress this tight—"

"You're mine, Embers." He gripped the swell of her backside hard enough to bruise, while he moved his fingers in punishing strokes. Through the bond, he could feel her heart racing to match his own, could sense her thoughts scattering like leaves in a storm. He knew she felt his rage, his jealousy, his desperate love—laid bare without words.

Wren watched him with a knowing glint in her eye. She spread her legs wider, holding up the skirts so that when he looked down, he could see his fingers glistening with her arousal as they moved in and out of her.

"Go on then, Bear Slayer," she taunted, riding his hand. "You said you were going to fuck me... so fuck me."

Torj met her challenging gaze and gave her a wicked smile. "You asked for it, Embers..."

He freed his cock from his leathers and lifted her, bracing her against the wall, Wren wrapping her legs around him for stability. Torj held his breath as he lined himself up with her entrance—

Wren jerked her hips and the tip of him slid inside.

"Fuck," he murmured against her lips. "That's cheating."

"You're taking too long—"

The curtains were suddenly ripped back.

"Not even a week engaged, and you make a cuckold of me," a familiar voice sounded.

CHAPTER 11
TORJ

"A Warsword's ability to adapt is often the difference between life and death."
—The Warsword's Way

"I'm not sure my heart can take it," Darian Devereux said dryly.

Heart hammering, Torj shielded Wren with his body, allowing her a moment to cover her exposed breasts and fix herself. He hurriedly tucked his erection back into his leathers and positioned his shirt to cover the clear outline.

Both his and Wren's cheeks flamed as they finally faced their unintended audience.

Darian was leaning against the side of the alcove, his arms folded over his chest, shaking his head as though disappointed. "You lovestruck fools need to control yourselves," he said, in that same wry tone. "At least until you're behind locked doors."

"What?" Torj managed. Whatever he had been expecting his nemesis to say, that hadn't been it.

Wren gripped his arm gently. "This is what I've been trying to tell you—"

Darian snorted. "Can't say it looked like there was much conversation happening in here..."

Torj opened and closed his mouth, struggling to understand what was unfolding before him. Wren turned his face to hers, her cheeks still flushed, her lips swollen.

"Darian isn't the man you think he is," she said firmly.

Torj's heart sank. He didn't know what the nobleman had told her, but Darian was lying. The bastard had used honeyed words and charmed her, convinced her—

Wren raised a brow. "You think I'm so easily hoodwinked?"

"No," Torj argued, increasingly aware of Darian's stare. "I just *know him*. I know—"

"Well, you're about to get firsthand insight, Bear Slayer," Darian said sharply. "Don't make a sound." He wrenched the curtains closed, his boots tapping across the marble floor as someone rapped on the far door.

The hinges creaked as it opened, and another pair of footsteps joined his.

"Father," Darian said by way of greeting.

Holding his breath, Torj peered through the thin gap between the curtains, instantly spotting both Devereux men by the hearth. The fire cast shadows that made Lord Lucian look monstrous, while illuminating Darian's perfect posture, but also the telltale twist of his signet ring—a tic he'd had since they were boys.

"I'd prefer to meet in your private quarters." Lord Lucian surveyed the racks of bridal gowns and array of cosmetics with a look of distaste.

"I think it wise to change locations here and there. You never know which chambermaid is listening in... Besides, I thought you'd like to witness our plans in motion before we retired to the library."

"If you think I have any interest in frilly dresses and gold wasted on ungrateful princesses, think again," Lord Lucian sneered.

"Fair enough." The clinking of glasses sounded. "Care for a drink?"

"You've done enough drinking today. I came here for information, not the Pendeltons' poor excuse for liquor or endless swathes of tulle."

"As you wish," Darian conceded.

"So, tell me, son, how goes the new bride-to-be?"

"She's malleable enough," Darian replied thoughtfully. "A life in a warrior's fortress does not a queen make... but there's potential. As soon as she's in my bed, I'll have her ear, among other things."

Torj's fists instantly clenched, but when he glanced at Wren, she didn't seem surprised or angered by the insult. She had heard it before, had perhaps even formed the wording herself. What had she said to him earlier?

This is strategy, not a surrender. He had assumed it was to get some sort of cure for him from Lucian... Never in his wildest dreams had he suspected Darian to be in on the plan.

"Good," Lord Lucian replied. "You will need to guide her to make the right decisions."

"Of course."

The clinking of glass sounded again as Lord Lucian made himself a drink after all. "And the Bear Slayer? Is he going to be an issue for us?"

"I shouldn't think so. You remember him, Father. All muscle, no brains."

"He watches too closely. And I saw how he looked at the storm wielder at Drevenor. His infatuation with her is plain for all to see."

"As it should be," Darian countered. "It makes her desirable, makes her a prize that even a Warsword cannot obtain. The fact that I have her hand, that she wears *our* ring, shows just how powerful the Devereuxs are."

Despite Wren's calmness at his side, Torj's blood was boiling as the two noblemen spoke of his soul-bonded as though she were nothing more than chattel.

"As we rightfully are," Lord Lucian was saying. "It's high time that the royals and Warswords' influence came to an end... I must admit, you've impressed me, Darian. First by dealing so swiftly with Perseus Graymoor and his underlings—"

Torj's gaze shot to Wren as he remembered the body being carried out of the ball at Lord Hullet's manor. The nobleman he'd accused Wren of poisoning.

Wren offered a satisfied smirk as if to say, *I told you so.*

"And now with the heir of Delmira... An inspired idea to marry into magic," Lord Lucian said as he sipped his drink.

"Perhaps I learned from the best after all, Father," Darian replied, still twisting his signet ring.

As ever, Lord Lucian withheld his full approval, always keeping his son on the hook. "We'll see if you pull it off yet. What are the next steps?"

Darian tucked his hands behind his back and started to pace. "With Lord Briar and Lord Pendelton's bannermen, we'll have ample incentive for the royal armies to join. We should meet them on the mainland and march on Delmira. The more swiftly we reclaim the kingdom, the better. Its resources will be ours, its lands ours to divide among whom we choose, and with Elwren's storms to defend it, Delmira will be the heart of a whole new era for the Devereux dynasty."

With his rage on the verge of choking him, only Wren's hand on Torj's arm stopped him from bursting through the curtains and strangling a Devereux bastard in each hand.

"I look forward to it," Lord Lucian said with a note of dismissal. "I'll expect updates along the way, with a full report upon your return."

"Of course," Darian replied smoothly. "Can I interest you in—"

"I'll see you when you're back," Lord Lucian cut him off, another trait that was familiar to Torj. Everything always ended on the older man's terms.

A moment later, the door clicked closed, and after another moment, the lock turned.

"That," came Darian's voice, "was incredibly stupid of you both."

It was Wren who pulled back the curtain first. "I know," she said. "I was reckless—"

But Torj surged past her, grabbing Darian by the throat

and lifting him bodily from the ground. "I told myself the next time I saw you I'd kill you—"

"Torj!" Wren hissed, pulling at his arm as the nobleman wheezed beneath his crushing grip. But Torj didn't want it to be over too quickly. He shoved Darian against the nearest wall, bracing his forearm against the prick's windpipe. He'd savor the bastard's death and then he'd smile down on his pulverized body—

"*Torj!*" Wren kept her voice down, but her urgency was palpable as she clawed at his arm. "Let him go!"

Torj would do no such thing. Not after all Darian had done. He wanted to watch the nobleman suffer. He wanted to—

He jerked back as lightning burst across his arm, the current sharp and insistent, causing him to drop Darian, who fell to the floor on his knees, coughing and spluttering. "Like I said," he rasped. "Reckless."

Torj's rage rose anew as Wren helped the nobleman to his feet. "I know," she said. "I'm sorry. I—"

"You both were," Darian interjected, though there was a note of amusement in his voice now. "Then again, I should have known better. The Bear Slayer has always had a voracious... appetite."

"*Enough.*" Torj was struggling to keep up with whatever was unfolding before him. Darian's only saving grace was that he'd kept them hidden from his father, that he'd known they were there, listening to every damning word, and he'd *let them*. But that didn't absolve him of everything he had done to Torj in the past, or in the present with Wren. "What the fuck is going on here?" he demanded. "I'm not leaving until I have answers this time."

"I would have thought it obvious, old friend," Darian drawled, fixing his doublet and brushing himself off. "The future Queen of Delmira and I are working together."

"After *everything* you've done, after all these years, you expect me to just accept that?" Torj felt the start of a tremor in his hand as he clenched his fists.

"No," came Wren's voice at his side, accompanied by a gentle touch on his arm. "But I expect you to trust me." She held out a scroll. "And this."

Torj took the parchment, but didn't unfurl it for fear of Wren seeing the trembling in his hand. "What is it?" he asked instead.

"She's alive," Wren said softly. "Your grandmother."

Torj could only stare at his soul-bonded, her words swinging between them like a pendulum.

Wren's expression softened. "Ever since you mentioned her, I've had Kipp investigating what happened to her. I wanted to give you closure, if anything, to know she was now at peace, only..."

"Only she's not at peace," Darian interjected. "Because she is very much alive in this festering pit we call the midrealms."

CHAPTER 12
TORJ

"The swing of a war hammer speaks volumes more than the silver tongue of a nobleman."
—Bear Slayer, Warsword of Thezmarr

Wren's hands were on his face, bringing him back to her as his pounding heart threatened to break through his chest. She forced his gaze to hers. "It was how I knew I could trust Darian, Torj," she said. "He saved her all those years ago. He got her away just in time."

"It's not possible." The words spilled from Torj's lips. For decades he had combed the midrealms for his grandmother before he had given up hope, had mourned her passing as he had his mother's—in a quiet rage that yearned to set the world ablaze.

Wren drew him to her and pressed a soft kiss against his lips. "Talk to Darian."

Torj lamented the loss of her touch instantly. He'd only just found her again. And there was so much he needed to tell her, so much still to say. As though sensing his turmoil, Wren turned to him when she reached the door.

"You've searched decades for the answers Darian has. You've waited long enough. Everything else will still be here when you're done."

"Thea should be waiting for you outside," Darian called after her. The sultry, flirty tone he usually used with Wren was completely stripped away. She gave him a nod of acknowledgment before she left.

When they were alone, Torj turned to Darian. "Talk fast, Devereux."

For the first time since he'd returned to Torj's life, the mask Darian wore so well slid free as he stared into the dying fire, his expression wary. His shoulders caved inward, and the brightness in his eyes had dulled. It was the look of defeat he'd worn as a boy, whenever he'd had dealings with his father.

"I did separate you from Grandmother Vara," Darian told him. "I *did* send her away—"

Torj gripped the back of a chair until the wood started to splinter.

"But not for the reasons you think," Darian continued. "She helped my mother escape... and that put her in more danger than you can know. My father knew it was Grandmother Vara who helped her, through the women's shelter. As soon as my mother was admitted for a broken arm, Vara refused to send her back to Lucian. After what happened to your mother, she swore she'd never bear witness to that kind of violence again."

Torj remained silent, the image of his own mother beaten to a bloody pulp flashing before his eyes, regret churning in his gut.

"I got your grandmother and my mother out of Tver before they could be caught," Darian explained. "My father has hunted them ever since. He's never stopped looking, never stopped cursing Vara's name for what she did."

Torj realized he was still holding the scroll Wren had given him. "And this?"

"That's her last known location, as discovered by your friend the strategist. It was one of his sources who uncovered the connection to me and reported it back to him, and then Wren."

"And you used your influence to send me out to deal with those cursed bears, why?" Torj said slowly, his voice dangerously low.

Darian sighed heavily. "I had to get you far away from it all. While I had your grandmother shipped off, while my father destroyed the shelter, while there was all manner of corrupt political dealings in the works. I knew if you got wind of even a fraction of what was going on, you'd never be safe. Either by his orders, or by your own recklessness." Darian cleared his throat as though to make a point. "You would have gone after him and gotten yourself killed in the process. Or worse, sent to the Scarlet Tower. My father knew guards at that place... I couldn't let you wind up there, Torj."

"I was a Warsword—"

"But not untouchable. Your friend Wilder Hawthorne proved that during the last war, didn't he?" Darian cut in fiercely. "I did what I had to do to keep the people I love safe. Haven't you ever had to keep a secret like that? It's been the hardest thing I've ever done, hiding this from you."

Torj remained standing by the chair, his knuckles white around the splintered wood. The scroll crumpled in his other hand. "So you decided for me? Just like that? You let me believe for decades that the only family I had left was gone?" His voice broke on the last word, and the rage that had been simmering beneath the surface threatened to boil over. The irony wasn't lost on him that not all that long ago, he had done the same thing to Wren.

"I did what I thought—"

"What you thought was best?" Torj laughed bitterly. "We've been here before, Devereux. You deciding what's best for me without my consent. You've always known better, haven't you? Even as a boy. Remember when you convinced me we could run away together? You got a stern lecture from your mother while I couldn't leave my bed for days after what my father did."

A flash of pain crossed Darian's face. "That's not fair, Torj. We were children."

"And now? What's your excuse now?" Torj demanded. "Do you have any idea what it was like? Searching for Vara year after year, clinging to some desperate hope that she was alive, only to eventually give her up for dead?"

Darian took a step toward him, but Torj raised a hand to stop him, staring at the scroll.

"She's truly alive? After all this time?"

"She's alive," Darian confirmed. "I've checked in over the years when I could, helped where I could. Mainly I encouraged her to move around as much as possible. She has only stayed away to protect my mother from my father. If he found her..."

Darian didn't need to finish that sentence. Torj knew exactly what Lucian Devereux was capable of—the same as his own father had been, only with more influence, more resources, more power.

"I'm truly sorry for all the pain I have caused you, for robbing you of the only family you had left." Darian's polished veneer cracked, revealing the weary, broken person beneath. "For what it's worth, I lost the only brother I'd ever had that same day."

It was the closest Darian had come to resembling the friend Torj had once known as a boy. Those were words he would have said back then, when they were young and trying to break free of both their fathers' holds.

Torj stared at him, trying to reconcile the boy he'd once called brother with the man who had kept such a devastating secret from him. The man who had let him grieve needlessly for years.

"So why now?" Torj asked roughly. "Why tell me now when you've kept this secret for decades?"

"I want a world without my father. Without men like him. The midrealms festers when they are at the helm, and I am tired of living in the poison they spread. I was born tired of it. But years ago, dear old Lucian started to suspect my wavering loyalty. He put conditions in place for my inheritance. Things that need... untangling."

"Like what?" Torj pressed.

"If you must know, there's a rather complex succession plan, with legal safeguards that would divert any inheritance from me if he died under suspicious circumstances... Then there's the required approval of his bannermen before I take over any of his land assets. The noble houses are all linked. Not to mention that there *may* be a piece of incriminating evidence or two that dear Lucian holds against me. I need those found and destroyed."

"And what does any of this have to do with Wren?"

"With Wren and her strategist's help, I've been able to consult with legal scholars who understand the intricacies of inheritance law. With our united visits to Houses Briar and Pendelton, we've positioned ourselves favorably with the bannermen. And the evidence... Well, that's being dealt with separately. When the time is right, Wren has promised to end Lucian for me."

"She means to poison him?" Torj guessed.

"It's her specialty, isn't it?" Darian replied with a hint of his usual smirk. "In the meantime, I'm also not opposed to helping her uncover whatever poison ails you, or Furies save us, she might add the lot of us to her ledger."

Torj tried to swallow the lump that had formed in his throat. "This engagement... What is it to you?"

"It's exactly what she told you it was—a means to an end." Darian's smile widened then. "Though watching you squirm has been an unexpected pleasure... It's like I've stolen your toys all over again."

"Still can't get your own toys, Devereux?" Torj said, but there was no bite in it. A ghost of a smile threatened the corner of his mouth.

Silence stretched between them, a reckoning of decades of grief and suppressed childhood memories.

Torj glanced down at the scroll in his hands once more,

struggling to comprehend the division between truth and reality, of all that he'd clung to over the years.

"You did all this to protect our families?" he said, finally taking a single step toward the hearth. "To protect me?"

Darian faced him, tentatively offering his hand. "What are brothers for?"

Torj stared at the outstretched hand for a long moment. The boy he once knew and the man before him blurred together.

"I'm... I'm not there yet, Darian," he said quietly. "But I'm grateful to you, for saving Vara. I want to see her. When it's safe. For now, we have one thing in common... I want to see Lucian Devereux fall."

He didn't take Darian's hand. Not yet. Instead, he moved to stand beside him at the hearth, both men facing the dying embers.

"Then we start there." Darian withdrew his hand. "The rest... the rest will take time."

Torj gave a single, curt nod. It wasn't forgiveness—not yet—but it was a beginning. The faintest glimmer of what once was, and what, perhaps, could be again.

CHAPTER 13
WREN

"The most impressive alchemist mind is that which stays curious."
—Drevenor Academy Handbook

"Some of these rose bushes are over a thousand years old," the horticulturist, Braxton, told Wren as they wandered across the breathtaking grounds of the Pendelton manor.

"I didn't realize they could live so long," Wren replied, reaching out to touch a silken red petal.

Braxton nodded. "There's a lot people don't know about roses. They're such a common bloom they're often overlooked."

"Do you have any silvertide in these gardens?" she asked.

"Only that which grows wild on the estate boundary.

It's much too ordinary for Lady Pendelton's prized garden beds."

"Can you take me to them?"

"The silvertide roses?" Braxton frowned.

"Yes. They're an interest of mine."

"An alchemist, aren't you?"

"I was," Wren replied quietly. "Not anymore, though."

"I imagine it's like being a gardener, though, eh? Once an alchemist, always an alchemist? This way, then."

Wren followed the horticulturist to the far edge of the property, which was quite some distance from the manor itself. She very much doubted that even Lucian's keen eyes could spy her out here. Against the stone wall climbed a dainty rose bush, its leaves dark green and its few flowers that familiar pearly white. It wasn't half as robust as the one by her cottage in Delmira, but it was certainly of the silvertide variety. She knew just from looking at these flowers that they wouldn't be as potent as the strain she needed for her cure, but they could help with comparisons and tests.

"Do you mind if I take some cuttings?" Wren asked her companion.

Braxton shrugged. "I don't see why not. They're nought but weeds to Her Ladyship. I'll get my pruning shears—"

"No need." Wren produced her own secateurs from her belt.

"You came prepared," he observed.

She leaned down to clip the first bloom for her supplies. "I always do, Master Braxton."

"If I'd known you were interested in getting samples, I would have brought you out at first light. Early morning is best for cuttings, when the plant is most hydrated. The flowers last longer then."

Wren blinked up at the horticulturist, stunned. "You know, in all my years of study, no Master Alchemist has ever told me that..."

Braxton shrugged again. "Lady Pendelton likes her flowers fresh. They keep for longer if I cut them in the morning for her vases."

Wren nodded, taking care of the thorns as she harvested another rose. "Well, thank you for sharing that. I'll keep it in mind." She raised a brow at him. "Any other gems of wisdom?"

"Depends."

"On what?"

"On why you want to know."

"Well, I'm not selling your trade secrets to the competition, if that's what you're thinking," she told him, wrapping her samples in fresh silkspore.

Braxton huffed a laugh. "What *are* you trying to do? Propagate? Make perfume? Garnish your drinks?"

Wren smiled. "I'll take any and all insights."

"Well, in that case, I'd tell you that sometimes hardwood cuttings taken in late autumn or winter have a higher rate of success than spring softwood cuttings, particularly with this variety... And in terms of more *creative* pursuits, the fruit that forms after flowering is often overlooked and underestimated."

"You mean rose hip?" Wren asked. "It has lots of medicinal purposes."

"Exactly," he said with a wink. "You may want to take a few samples of that too, eh?"

Wren found herself grinning. "You don't happen to have a greenhouse, do you, Braxton?"

~

"Vernich the Bloodletter is dead," Torj announced to the gathered nobility and bannermen.

Shocked whispers broke out across the Pendelton dining hall, and Wren herself sucked in a sharp breath from where she sat at the head of the table. She had spent much of the morning in Braxton's greenhouse, testing her silvertide cuttings from Delmira against those grown at the estate border. She had lost hours dissecting the rose hip from each and adding it to her experiments, testing its response to Torj's blood samples only to be dragged away from her work to the debriefing happening around her now.

"Vernich? You think Vernich is dead?" Thea repeated from behind her, flinching at the news.

Darian sat to Wren's right, his expression unreadable, and on her left Kipp said nothing, but she saw a muscle feather in his jaw.

Wren hadn't known the Bloodletter well, only that he'd had a bloody history with Thea, Cal, and Kipp from when they were shieldbearers. The eldest Warsword of the original cohort had some unorthodox methods that had often left his trainees in the infirmary. And yet, during the shadow war, Vernich Warner had shown them a different side of himself, and in the end, he had been celebrated as a hero alongside the rest. Which was why the news was so shocking.

"What else, Torj?" Thea called.

"Another Warsword, Ashlyn Graves, is also believed to be dead. Parts of her were found along with Vernich's mace. The amount of blood spilled there suggests none survived," Torj replied, bowing his head for a moment. "But it's with worse tidings than these that Hawthorne, Whitlock, and I rejoin you... Our orders took us to villages of the Broken Isles, where a new kind of devastation has impacted the people there. Silas is creating an army of followers similar to the monsters called howlers in the shadow war, if not a less developed form of the very same thing. They crave violence and are willing to join any cause in order to gain access to a bloodbath. That is who makes up much of his army. People who were once normal citizens of the midrealms, who are now lusting after violence of any kind and flocking to Silas' ranks."

Wren watched him, devastation washing over her in waves. It was just like the shadow war. The only difference was that she now knew the man who stood before them was her soul-bonded, and that he was dying. Even from where she sat, she could see the tremor he was trying to hide in his fingers—a symptom that was presenting far too early given what Lord Lucian had claimed about the poison being slow to release...

Was he somehow increasing Torj's rate of decline in order to force her hand with Darian sooner? Or had he lied? At Wren's request, Darian had attempted on several occasions to obtain the information from his father without raising suspicion, but to no avail. Either the senior Lord of Larkwood Valley kept his cards incredibly close to his chest, or he didn't trust his own son. Or both.

Wren stiffened as the veins in Torj's neck momentarily

darkened, a glimpse of the poison surging within. Darian squeezed her hand in warning and she averted her gaze from the Bear Slayer, turning instead to Lord Lucian, who had taken the floor.

"And what of the fact that you bring the Prince of Naarva with you?" the nobleman said, the edge in his voice clear for all to hear. "When the matter of his abdication remains unresolved and he was to remain confined in his residence at Drevenor?"

Zavier stood. "The Guild Master herself charged the Warswords with my protection. Not only did she have cause to fear for my life, but she also expected my expertise as an alchemist may be useful on the road. Which it has been. It was I who identified the dark alchemy and shadow magic being used to weaponize those poor souls into blood-thirsty creatures."

"So we have one wayward prince who garners the protection of not one, but *three* Warswords?" Lucian scoffed. "That doesn't support Silas' arguments at all."

"I didn't say I—"

But Lord Lucian didn't let the Prince of Naarva finish. "We thank you and the Warswords for the information." He turned to his fellow noblemen. "Lord Pendelton, Lord Briar, perhaps we should continue our discussion somewhere more private?"

Darian squeezed Wren's hand again. "That's my cue, my love."

"And mine," she replied, rising to her feet.

"*Darling.*" Darian's voice dropped slightly, a practiced skill to appear to whisper but to do so loud enough for others to still hear. "You know you can trust me to handle our military affairs. Go and catch up with the prince—I'm sure there's much to talk about." He dropped his voice to a true whisper then. "You know we're more likely to gain the numbers you require if it looks like a man is at the helm."

Wren stifled a cry of frustration, masking her rage with a pliant smile. "Take Kipp with you," she said calmly. "He knows the terrain of Delmira better than most."

Darian nodded and dropped her hand, walking ahead of his father.

As Lord Lucian rose, he brushed past Wren and murmured, "Remember what I said about making us look the fool..." His words were light, but the threat between them was anything but.

For a moment, Wren could feel the heat of Torj's gaze lingering on her as Lucian moved away. She could feel the Bear Slayer in the air around her, but she didn't so much as glance his way, not when Lord Lucian's menacing remark was still fresh in her ear.

Thankfully, Zavier approached. "It's good to see you, Wren," he said, sounding as tired as she felt.

"You too, Zave," she replied. "Was everything alright on the road?"

"You mean besides the madness of fury-inducing dark alchemy?"

"Yes, besides that."

"Then it was just grand," he told her dryly. "You want to show me what you've been working on?"

Wren had been heartened to see her friend with Torj and the others, though she found herself worrying for Dessa, who'd been left at the academy to guard her potions alone. It was Dessa who'd scarcely left her side since they'd met as novices, who had traveled with her to Delmira and seen the flourishing lands with her. Wren's stomach churned with unease. It felt wrong for them all to be here without her. But she showed Zavier to her quarters anyway, eager to talk with another alchemist. If the shadow war had taught her anything, it was that there was no such thing as too many medical supplies. With an extra pair of hands, she could start that afternoon. There was no doubt in her mind that they would need them all: fever reducers, pain relievers, sleeping drafts...

"I've been limited to what I could take on the road," she explained as Zavier surveyed her rudimentary set-up. "But along with some healing basics, I've been able to brew several doses of the cure I used on Queen Reyna during my opus."

"Can it be used as a preventative, or only an antidote?" Zavier asked.

"In its current form, only an antidote, but with more silvertide roses, I'll be able to adjust the formula so that it can be used to neutralize Silas' attacks. Finding more roses is crucial to our victory."

"Dessa was working on the same thing when I left," Zavier told her.

Wren sighed with relief. "Good. The more of us working on it the better."

Zavier went to wash his hands in the nearby basin. "If you show me what to do, I can start right now."

Wren desperately wanted to see Torj, to talk to him after they'd been interrupted the night before, but there was no way she could risk seeking him out so soon. She tried calling out to him with her mind, but all that came back to her was the echo of her own voice. And so she chose to distract herself with work, showing Zavier the first part of her method for creating the cure, noting that her remaining supplies of silvertide were dwindling.

It wasn't until Wren's vision blurred with exhaustion that she thought to retire to her bedroom. When she closed the door behind her and turned to face the canopy bed, she stopped in her tracks. There was a small, black box atop the silk sheets. Frowning, she stepped toward it. Thea had done the usual security sweep of her rooms before she and Zavier had entered, so whatever it was, her sister had deemed it safe to leave behind.

Wren tore open the box and lifted its rather intimate contents from the wrappings within, her mouth agape.

"Are these..." She dropped the box and examined the black lace with a shocked expression, the item hanging off her finger.

A note fluttered down from the fabric. And for the first time in weeks, Wren laughed. She laughed until her belly ached and tears tracked down her cheeks.

Wear some damn undergarments, Embers, the note read.

CHAPTER 14

TORJ

"A Warsword's strength represents that of the midrealms, and the favor of the Furies themselves."
—The Midrealms Chronicles

Torj told himself that he had only left the gift to make Wren laugh, not to stake his claim on her from afar. But as she entered the ballroom the next night, wearing another gown that hugged every inch of her curves, he knew she hadn't worn the undergarments, and the very thought drove him to the brink of insanity. For the briefest of seconds, her mask of indifference slipped, and she shot him a coy smile from across the room, one that sang with challenge, before she schooled her features back into a neutral expression.

He tried to avert his gaze, tried to keep his eyes off her, but she was mesmerizing, and she left him utterly unfocused, even from a distance.

"You shouldn't be here," Thea said at his side, catching him staring at her sister across the ballroom.

"Probably not," he agreed, feeling the bond grow restless in his chest.

"Lord Pendelton pledged his two hundred bannermen to Lucian this afternoon," Thea told him.

"You mean to Wren?" he asked, with a lift of his brow.

"To Lucian's cause, which currently aligns with our cause," she replied wryly.

Torj wasn't sure how much Thea knew of Lord Lucian and his history, so he simply said, "Sounds about right."

Thea made a noise of agreement. "So between Lucian, Lord Briar, and Lord Pendelton, we have one thousand bannermen to add to our ranks... It's not insignificant."

"No, it's not," Torj murmured, not taking his eyes off the dance floor. "Not when last I heard, some of the royal armies don't even amount to those numbers. Some because they lost so many in the last war, some because the people have a deep distrust for royal military... We need him."

"We do," Thea allowed. "But we don't need you here, watching this horseshit display. Why don't you go get some fresh air? Or better yet, some rest? You're looking a little peaky, Bear Slayer."

But Torj Elderbrock was a glutton for punishment, so instead of returning to his quarters like Thea wanted him to, he stayed.

And he watched.

Resplendent in a shimmering royal blue gown, Wren was dancing with Darian. Even knowing the whole story now, Torj couldn't breathe watching them. Each turn was a fresh knife between his ribs—her delicate hand lost in

Darian's grip, those aristocratic fingers possessively splayed across the small of her back, claiming territory that had once been Torj's alone.

His chest burned at the very sight, black spots swimming in his vision. The bond between them thrummed with a discord that set his teeth on edge.

He shouldn't have come. Furies save him, he shouldn't have come.

To watch his soul-bonded moving in perfect rhythm with another man was a special kind of torture. Darian's lips ghosted across the curve of her neck as he murmured something that made her shiver, and Torj tasted copper—he'd bitten through his cheek.

Green eyes snapped up, meeting his.

For just a heartbeat, something raw and desperate flickered in Wren's gaze before she turned away, pressing closer to Darian.

Torj could stand it no longer. He slipped away. He didn't know where he was going, only that he had to get out.

He found himself in the grounds shortly after, with Wilder and Cal, and the bannermen who had rallied at their lord's call. There were small groups from all over the midrealms and the scent of leather and sweat lingered in the night air. Some of the men ran drills while others were busy inspecting weapons, watching on warily as the trio of Warswords crossed the grass. Looking at those practicing in pairs, Torj was taken back to the first time he'd ever sparred with Wren. Trying to train her while she wore leggings that clung to every curve had been a cruel twist of fate.

"You're with me, Embervale."

"You can't be serious."

"I'm always serious."

"You really want me to spar with you?"

"Unless you'd rather someone else's hands all over you?"

A smile tugged at his mouth at the memory. They'd never stood a chance, had they?

"Come on, Bear Slayer," Wilder called out, shucking off his armor and twirling one of his swords. "Seems like you've got energy to burn..."

But Cal pushed him aside. "Allow me," his former protégé said. "I've been waiting for a chance to best him since the last time we sparred."

Torj bit back a sigh. He knew what his friends were doing, and it was a commendable effort. Usually, he'd launch himself straight into the distraction of physical exertion, but... he was tired. A word that was not normally in his vocabulary.

"What'll it be, Elderbrock?" Wilder teased. "Your former protégé or the Hand of Death?"

Feeling the interest from the other soldiers around them, Torj stripped away his armor, trying to ease the ache from his shoulders by rolling them before he picked up his hammer.

"I don't give a fuck which one of you I beat," he muttered. The familiar weight of the iron weapon should have been comforting—it had been the one constant in his decades as a warrior—but his grip felt wrong, unsteady. He flexed his fingers, willing them to still.

Cal moved to the center of a cleared space, spinning his sword in a showy way that reminded Torj of Zavier's fighting style. Any other day, Torj would have rolled his eyes at the younger Warsword's antics. Today, the display only heightened his irritation.

"Come on, then," Cal called, dropping into a ready stance. "Show me what you've got."

Torj didn't need the invitation. He lunged forward, putting more force behind his first strike than necessary. Cal parried, but the impact made him step back. Good. Fighting was simple. Fighting made sense. Each clash of their weapons drove thoughts of the betrothed couple in the hall further away—of what was happening there, of who was sitting beside whom, of hands touching across fine tablecloths—of a ring gleaming in the candlelight—

The flat of Cal's blade slapped Torj's exposed arm.

"Look alive, Bear Slayer!" Wilder called from the sidelines, not bothering to hide the note of surprise in his voice.

Torj tried to focus, but he felt dazed, as though the world around him were moving too fast and his reactions were too slow. He managed to block another of Cal's strikes, but his dominant arm seized beneath the weight of his hammer. The muscles locked, then spasmed, sending shooting pains up to his shoulder.

The war hammer clattered to the ground, and before he could recover his balance, his legs betrayed him too. He went down hard, the grass doing nothing to cushion the impact on his knees.

The grounds fell silent. He could feel every pair of eyes on him—the soldiers who had stopped their own practices to watch, the captain who'd arrived with a missive in his hand only moments before, and Wilder, who had been observing from close by. Torj's face burned. He'd rather take another dozen doses of whatever poison was working through his system than endure their stares for one more moment.

Wilder's boots appeared in his line of sight; a hand extended down to help him up. Torj's jaw clenched.

"I don't need—"

"I know you don't need it," Wilder cut him off, voice low enough that only Torj could hear. "Take it anyway."

For a moment, Torj considered stubbornly pushing himself up alone. But his arms were still trembling, and his damn pride had taken enough of a beating for one night. He clasped Wilder's forearm and let his friend pull him to his feet.

"Don't tell Wren," he murmured.

"What happens during training, stays in training," Wilder replied. "For now."

The captain with the scroll came forward then, looking flustered. "Warsword Elderbrock, Warsword Hawthorne, and Warsword Whitlock," he greeted them, touching three fingers to his shoulder in a respectful salute. "Lord Lucian's spies have intercepted enemy plans. Drevenor will be the next target of Silas' assault. He defers to Thezmarr for instruction—"

"And I *told him* the instruction," Wren snapped as she caught up to them from the manor, fire blazing in her green eyes. "We need to save Dessa and the silvertide roses. We need to return to the academy."

CHAPTER 15
WREN

"I am forevermore marked as a steward of this ancient art. And I will protect it and harness it, with all that I am and will be."
—Drevenor Academy Oath of Secrecy

"How many times has that happened?" Wren whispered to Cal as they readied their horses. "Torj falling like that?"

"That was the first time that I know of," Cal replied, voice low. "But he's not himself, and I don't think it's just you and Darian—"

"I know," Wren told him. What she didn't tell her friend was that she had to marry the nobleman soon if she was to have any chance of saving Torj—that time was not on her side, if it ever had been.

"So," Darian interrupted, striding toward them in his riding garb. "Looks like my father was wrong about the force that was near Drevenor earlier..." He offered Wren a leg-up onto her horse. Now clad in her own riding leathers instead of a stupid silk ballgown, she accepted his help as Cal drifted into the background, his brows knitted together in concern.

"They marched on Drevenor as soon as our attention was elsewhere," she observed.

"So it seems," Darian agreed.

Wren had hoped to have more time in Braxton's greenhouse with her work on Torj's cure, but time was of the essence now. She would have to hope that the rosarians she had written to responded; meanwhile, she had to get to Drevenor. Thanks to the noblemen, their bannermen had rallied quickly and were now ready to ride to the academy's aid.

What if it's too late? Fear clenched her heart in an unforgiving fist, but she didn't voice the words aloud. Instead, Wren guided her horse to the head of the company where Thea, Wilder, Torj, and Cal were waiting impatiently.

"You should ride ahead," Wren told them. "Your stallions are faster, and I can't bear the thought of Dessa alone if Silas' men reach the academy before us."

"She's not alone," Thea replied. "Audra and a unit of Thezmarr's Guardians are stationed there, plus Drevenor's own security. It is not defenseless."

"All the same," Wren pressed. "Please, Thea. I can't lose another friend. I can't lose Dessa too—"

"You won't," her sister vowed, guiding her horse away from the company. "I'll meet you there."

Wren shot her a grateful look and watched as Thea

urged her stallion into a hard gallop and rode through the estate gates, leaving the bannermen in her wake.

It wasn't long before Darian had rallied the rest of their small force, but it felt like an age to Wren. With each moment, Silas drew closer and closer to Drevenor with who knew how many men at his disposal.

At last, they rode out, heading west, the crescent moon looming overhead. The food Wren had eaten earlier curdled in her stomach as the hours passed and understanding washed over her. Her work on the cure to dark alchemy, the crop of silvertide roses, the remaining shadow artifacts from the war—they were all ripe for Silas' taking. He only needed to reach out his hand.

Wren glanced across to where Torj sat atop his stallion, looking as fierce as ever. Only she knew differently. She had seen the tremors in his hands. She had seen him fall in the sparring session against Cal. The poison was taking hold of him, much sooner than Lucian had implied, and here they were, riding straight into more danger. If the Bear Slayer could sense her gaze on him, he ignored it. His focus was straight ahead, and soon, Wren saw why.

A familiar cart lay upturned on the side of the road—

"Roderick!" Zavier shouted, his horse breaking into a canter beneath him as he surged toward the site.

Wren broke away from the group as well, her heart pounding. She followed her friend to find the man who had taken them from the academy to Highguard clutching a wound in his abdomen. Torchlight revealed the blood flowing between his fingers as he struggled to catch his breath. Wren swung down from her saddle and crouched by Roderick's side. She had seen many wounds like his in her time, and she knew what it meant. From Roderick's tired expression, he knew it as well.

"It's alright," Zavier assured him, jumping down from his horse and gripping Roderick's shoulder. "You'll be fine, you'll—"

"Don't start lying to me now, Prince," the man wheezed. "There was already fighting at the gates when I passed Drevenor. They came after me shortly after. You need to go."

"I'm not leaving you," Zavier argued.

"No, you're not." Roderick coughed blood down his shirt. "Looks like I'll be leaving first."

The poor man's choking intensified, spraying blood across Zavier's doublet, but Zavier didn't release his hand.

"Good luck, my friend," Roderick rasped.

They could only watch as the light faded from his eyes and he took his final breath, the rise and fall of his chest ceasing.

Torj rested a hand on Zavier's shoulder. "There will be time to mourn your friend later, Prince. But right now, another friend of yours is somewhere in there."

Wren's gaze snapped to where Torj pointed, seeing now the smoke that billowed into the air from a distance. With a cry of panic, she scrambled back onto her horse and squeezed its sides until she was flying into a gallop. She heard the thunderous sound of hooves beside her, and knew it was Torj and the others.

Dust drifted from the road ahead, and soon, Thea rode toward them. "They've breached the walls," she shouted, rounding her horse back into their formation. "All the guards around the perimeter are dead. The gates are no more, and the road to the main building is a bloodbath."

Panic gripped Wren's throat, but she didn't slow her pace toward the academy. "What of Audra? Dessa?"

"There's still fighting going on inside," Thea told her as they rode, glancing behind at the bannermen. "Wren, if we fight now, you'll lose half your men, maybe more. You'll be sending them to their deaths, leaving you with no one to fight for you in Delmira."

"Dessa's in there, Thee."

"I know. Leave Lord Pendelton's archers on the perimeter. Take a small force of us inside to get Dessa; get your work and anything else that can't fall into enemy hands. Then we live to fight another day."

It was her decision, Wren knew that. But she had made decisions like this before, decisions that she couldn't take back, and they festered within her now like an old wound. Regret and guilt entwined in a harrowing onslaught of images: people she had loved and lost, people who'd been hurt because of her.

But they were running out of time. The smoke that plumed from the grounds was not the natural gray of ordinary fire, but tinted with a sickly green hue, twisting into serpentine shapes against the starless sky, a telltale sign of alchemy corrupted with shadow magic.

"We need orders," came the captain's gruff voice behind them.

A strangled noise escaped Wren as they reached the broken gates, and she saw dozens of bodies scattered beneath the wrought iron. She could hear the clash of conflict from within the academy walls now—the distinct sound of steel against steel, the shouts of pain and fear from the people inside.

Bracing herself, Wren turned to Darian. "Leave your archers behind, as Thea said," she told him. "Take the rest of the bannermen to the port. We'll meet you there."

Darian startled. "Are you sure—?"

"Go!" Wren told him, already turning toward the Warswords and Zavier. "We get Dessa, we take whatever artifacts we can get our hands on, and we get out, understood?"

No one argued. Instead, they unsheathed their weapons and rode for the entrance, while the Pendelton archers readied their bows and guarded their backs.

The foyer had been taken. Ribbons of smoke and chemical vapor drifted up through the branches of the great tree that graced the center of the academy, and screams echoed through the galleries. That tree had stood there for hundreds of years, its roots delving deep into the academy's foundations. Its leaves curled inward like burning parchment, blackening from the edges, while the bark blistered and wept amber sap that hissed when it hit the floor. Centuries of growth undone in moments.

Inside, the masters of Drevenor fought back-to-back with Audra and her remaining Thezmarrians. Audra's face was a map of determination carved in blood—a gash above her eye sent crimson rivulets down her temple and cheek. She moved like water, her blade singing through the air before connecting with her opponent's throat. The steel bit deep, opening a second mouth that gushed dark red, the man's scream becoming nothing but a wet wheeze as he clawed futilely at the wound before he stilled.

Farissa and the other masters were fighting with a combination of weapons and alchemy. Strange mists and vapors drifted from shattered glass vials, and several discarded bodies showed signs of violent poisoning.

"Farissa!" Wren shouted, charging forward, her lightning kissing her fingertips before striking a man down. "Have you seen Dessa?"

"Residences! She was in your quarters last!" Farissa called back, not even glancing her way as she blew a handful of powder across a trio of men.

"Warswords!" Audra's voice bellowed. "If we're separated, you know where we meet."

"Go get Dessa." Wilder motioned to the blood-stained staircase. "I'll help Audra here and will be right behind you."

From the corner of her eye, Wren saw Thea press a hard kiss to the Warsword's lips, but that was where she left them. She didn't wait a moment longer; she rushed toward the stairs with Torj and the others on her heels—smoke escaped from beneath the doors there too. The acrid scent made her eyes water. This wasn't regular smoke. It clung to the skin like oil, leaving a film that itched. The fumes caught in the back of her throat—metallic and sweet at first, then transforming into something that reeked of burnt hair. Each breath felt like swallowing needles, her lungs protesting as the traces of corrupted alchemy infiltrated her body. Her eyes watered so severely that the world blurred into streaks of flame and shadow, tears cutting clean tracks down her soot-stained cheeks.

No, she thought, her heart rate spiking. She couldn't be dragged back there, couldn't—

"It's not wraiths," Torj murmured in her ear, seeming to sense her freezing up beside him.

"But it is some form of that magic. I can taste it..."

A crash from below made them all jump. Before Wren could even process the danger, Torj had pulled her against the solid wall of his chest. His heartbeat thundered against her cheek, steady despite the chaos, a rhythm her own heart had come to recognize as safety. His arms formed a fortress around her, and for one suspended moment amid the madness, she allowed herself to sink into that protection, to draw strength from the way their bodies remembered each other even when their minds were consumed by thoughts of survival. This—what existed between them—was worth fighting for with everything she had.

The sounds of conflict were getting closer—boots on stone, the clash of steel, screams cut terrifyingly short. Wren's mind raced as she took the stairs two at a time toward Dessa. The enemy wasn't just attacking—they were methodically taking control of Drevenor's assets. The coveted ingredients in the storage vaults. The records of rare alchemy in the workshops. The experimental weapons in the foundry. And soon, the forbidden texts in the archives and the remnants from the shadow war. Everything they had would now be used against them.

"Dessa!" Wren began shouting her friend's name long before her door was in sight, but as they rounded the corner, her heart seized.

Three masked men were trying to break the door down.

"Allow me," Torj said, swinging his war hammer in anticipation. The enemy didn't even see him coming. Any hint of weakness in the Bear Slayer was gone and he brought the trio down within seconds of one another. They fell like sacks of grain, their blood spilling across the stone floor.

"Dessa!" Wren screamed. "It's Wren, are you in there?"

"I'm here," came her voice from within. "But I welded the door shut..."

"Stand back," Torj called. The sound of splintering timber followed as the Bear Slayer broke down the door with a single kick.

Wren rushed past him, spying Dessa immediately. Her friend's eyes were wide with fear, but otherwise, she seemed unharmed. She shoved a satchel into Wren's chest.

"Here," she said hoarsely. "It's your notes on the cure. I took everything I could—"

A whimper sounded and Wren's gaze snapped to her sister, whose eyes were fixed on a figure filling the door frame.

"Wilder," Thea croaked, surging for him.

The Hand of Death staggered toward them, covered in blood, more crimson dripping from his silver blades—

"It's not mine, Princess," he insisted to Thea, who was running her hands over him in search of an injury. He cupped her face and pressed a kiss to her mouth before breaking away. "I swear."

"He'll be alright," Torj said gently. "Furies know if the Scarlet Tower didn't kill him, nothing can."

After pressing his forehead to Thea's and murmuring something in her ear that made her grip his arms tighter, Wilder turned to Wren and the others. "We're trapped," he told them grimly. "Fucked if I know how Silas managed to rally this many to his cause, but he's got the academy thoroughly infiltrated, and many in his ranks seem to possess extra strength. They're not ordinary men."

"Neither are we," Cal said, nocking an arrow to his bow.

"Now's not the time for heroics, Whitlock," Torj said, peering out the window, where flames licked across the grounds. "We all need to get the fuck out of this building."

"But what about the shadow artifacts? And all the advanced alchemy created by the masters?" Wren managed. "We can't let them take it."

"No, we can't." Torj's expression was grim as the building shook with another explosion from below. "But you're not going to like my suggestion."

Wren looked around desperately, shoving the last of her potions in her cloak pockets. "What is it?"

"We have to take it away before they get hold of it," Torj said. "We have to destroy Drevenor."

CHAPTER 16

WREN

"I will delve into the dark abyss of knowledge and guard the secrets entrusted to me."
—Drevenor Academy Oath of Secrecy

As Torj's words hung in the air between them, something inside Wren crumbled. The truth of it settled in her chest like a stone—cold, immovable, and agonizingly right. Silas the Kingsbane had already wielded dark alchemy against them; they couldn't afford for him to gain access to anything else.

Knowledge is the victor over fate. The mind is a blade. The academy's familiar scent of fragrant herbs had been swallowed by the harsh reek of metal and blood. Wren's throat tightened as she scanned her room one final time, fingertips ghosting over belongings that weren't just possessions, but milestones. Each piece told a story: the mortar and pestle worn smooth from countless hours of grinding ingredients, the crucible where she'd first mastered the cure... Even her workbench was a map of her journey from novice to sage, her fingers tracing the burn marks and stains. But wrapped up in it all was Torj. It was the place they'd come together, the place where they'd finally let themselves fall...

But she found herself nodding, a plan formulating in her mind. "You're right," she told Torj. "We have a responsibility. Everything within these walls—the experiments, the weapons, the research—we can't let them have it. Master Crawford's dungeons are full of elixirs and ingredients that will fuel a fire. We have enough experiments and stores to set off a chain reaction of fires and explosions."

"We need to get out of here first," Kipp said, grimacing as he peered out her door. "The enemy is making their way up the levels as we speak."

"So, you're saying the only way out is through a fucking window at this height?" Cal asked.

"Something like that," Kipp replied.

"We've been in worse situations," Thea ventured, though she winced.

But Wren grabbed her sister's arm, a memory sparking. "When you were shieldbearers, how did you escape the Chained Islands? In the initiation trial?"

Thea's gaze shot to Cal. "That would be the work of Callahan the Flaming Arrow... He shot an arrow with a rope across the cliffs and we used our belts to glide down the line."

Wren nodded; she remembered Thea telling her about it

years ago. "Then that's how we get out of here. Break a window, use a—"

Glass shattered as Torj kicked a window in, fragments falling onto the enemy below. Several soldiers looked up, pointing and shouting. He was already motioning to Cal. "If you can get an arrow in that support beam over there, it should hold—"

Several men from the People's Vanguard burst into the room and attacked, and Wren found herself surrounded and protected by Warswords, with Kipp, Dessa, and Zavier pressed close to her as well. The clash of steel, the cries of pain were all too familiar, as was the claustrophobic feeling of being jostled among sweaty bodies, but Cal was now tying a length of rope to an arrow.

"The weight will change the dynamic of the—" Torj started.

"I know, Bear Slayer," Cal reminded him gently. "I'm not a shieldbearer anymore."

"No, you're Callahan the Flaming fucking Arrow," Kipp said, clapping a hand on his shoulder. "Aim true, or we're all fucked."

Cal rolled his eyes at Wren as he handed Torj one end of the rope to tie around a pillar behind them, his bow creaking as he notched the arrow to the string. "No pressure."

But Wren was too anxious to offer a smile back.

Her friend's arrow soared, embedding deep into the untouched healer's workshop facade in the far corner. After testing the taut strength of the rope, Cal looped his belt over it and climbed up onto the windowsill. "See you down there," he said, before launching himself into the night.

Dessa screamed, but she was soon being lifted by Kipp.

"Shouldn't a Warsword take her?" Thea called.

Kipp only grinned. "I know I've been a shell of my former self since the beautiful Dessa left me, but she knows from plenty of experience that I can handle her—"

"I didn't *leave you.*" Dessa slapped his arm, the height before her suddenly forgotten. "We *mutually agreed* that our time together had run its course. Actually, those were *your* exact words."

"Semantics, dear Dessa. Did you truly think my heart would not be bruised by our separation?"

"The only thing that's bruised is your head from walking into that pole at the Mortar and Pestle," Dessa replied with a snort.

"*That's* what that's from?" Kipp exclaimed before he looped her arms around his neck. "Better hang on." That was all the warning he gave before he leapt from the window, his belt hooked over the rope, Dessa plastered to his side as they flew through the air.

"Poor girl," Thea mused quietly. "Wren, you're up."

Wren looked at her own belt of potions. "I can't use this—"

Before she could finish her sentence, she was swept up into a pair of warm, strong arms.

"You're with me, Embers." Torj's voice vibrated through her, low and intimate despite the mayhem around them. His arms tightened, a silent promise in their strength, and she curled into him instinctively, one hand splaying across his chest, his lightning scars seeming to sing beneath her touch. Their eyes met briefly—a thousand words passing between them in that glance—before he lifted them both to the windowsill. In that moment, with death pressing close from all sides, the fierce tenderness in his gaze nearly undid her.

Wren's gasp died on her lips as they launched into nothingness. Her stomach lurched violently, left somewhere behind as gravity seized them. The cold whipped her face and bit her skin through her clothes. The scent of chemicals tangling with smoke stung her nostrils, along with the smell of burning rope coming from Torj's belt. But something else caught her attention.

A flaming arrow carving through the dark of night. Setting ablaze the gardens where she'd brought so many wildflowers to life with her storm magic. In seconds, fire consumed all that she had achieved there.

After everything they had fought for in the shadow war, after the battle they'd won on her graduation day, it had come to this...?

The ground rushed toward them with terrifying speed, the world tilting as Torj's boots hit the grass below, but he held her steady as he found his footing, placing her carefully on solid earth.

"Cal's got the crops and conservatory. He's got the Pendelton archers under his command—those who are left, anyway," Kipp said. "Any ideas on how to trigger the kind of devastation you'll need to obliterate any remaining shadow magic?"

"One," Wren replied, allowing lightning to surge at her fingers, but movement at the forefront of the building caught her eye.

Through the writhing smoke, a masked figure emerged.

Their movements were *wrong*—too fluid, too fast.

Behind them, the stone of the building itself blackened and cracked, the very air rippling around them like heat above a forge. But instead of warmth, a preternatural cold radiated outward, and Wren's breath frosted before her face despite the nearby flames. The ground where the figure trod withered, grass becoming ash without passing through fire.

"That's Silas..." Zavier rasped, landing behind them. "He's here."

Without thinking, Wren gathered her power, feeling the familiar crackle of storm magic dance across her skin and culminate at her fingertips. She hurled it at Silas, expecting to see him dive for cover.

Instead, he simply... stood there. The lightning that should have struck him dead dissipated like morning mist.

"Something's wrong," Wren told the others, watching her lightning vanish harmlessly around Silas. "He's not just blocking it, he's..."

She recognized the telltale signs of shadow alchemy at work—the faint residue in the air, the way her royal magic seemed to dissolve like salt in water. It was alchemy twisted into something unnatural, something that made her stomach turn.

Torj was at her side, peering over her shoulder.

"Look at his skin," she told the Bear Slayer, horror dawning as she understood. Where her magic touched Silas, there was a reaction she'd never seen before—not like this. His flesh rippled like disturbed water, revealing a network of veins that should have been blue but instead writhed black beneath the surface. They pulsed obscenely, swelling as they drank in her power, mapping his body with strange, elaborate patterns.

The air between them vibrated with wrongness, the natural order perverted as her storm—a force meant to destroy him—instead fed the very enemy it targeted.

Wren tasted blood on her tongue, felt it drip from her nose as she struggled to fill her lungs with air. "He's not just stopping my magic," she said hoarsely. "He's consuming it."

CHAPTER 17

TORJ

"Warswords were originally trained to fight alone, but as the shadow war erupted across the midrealms and the world became rife with monsters, working in teams was deemed the more effective tactic."
—A History of Thezmarr

"**W**ren!" Torj leapt in front of her, dragging her away from Silas' line of fire. Every report they'd received had told them the Kingsbane was in Delmira, and yet here he was, that strange power rippling off him.

Wren moved to strike again, but Torj gripped her wrists.

"You have to stop. You're only fueling him and hurting yourself."

Dazed, she touched her fingers to the blood leaking from her nose, her green eyes widening as she stared at the crimson on her fingertips.

"How?" she croaked, trying to peer over his shoulder to where their enemy stood, stronger than before.

"I don't know, Embers, but we have to deal with Drevenor before he—"

Thea skidded to a stop beside them, staring at Silas, her mouth agape. "What the fuck *was* that?"

"He's *absorbing* the storm magic," Torj told her, keeping his voice measured, though he was anything but calm inside. "Anything you and Wren throw at him could be thrown right back at us. You need to destroy the building and everything inside it—the alchemy, the secrets, the books, the shadow artifacts, *anything* he could use to grow stronger. You need to *bring the academy down.*"

Thea shot Wren a look of disbelief, but Wren nodded in confirmation. "He's right. We saw it with our own eyes, Thea. I don't understand it, but he's right."

Without hesitation, Torj swung his war hammer in a deadly arc and called, "Hawthorne, Whitlock, you're with me!"

He didn't need to glance beside him to know his fellow Warswords had fallen into formation. One of Cal's arrows whistled through the air, shooting straight for Silas, who deflected it with his shield.

"We need to buy Wren and Thea as much time as we can," Torj told them as they closed in on the Kingsbane. "If Silas gets his hands on whatever's inside the academy, this war is over before it has begun. Masks up."

"Understood," Wilder said gruffly, unsheathing his dual swords.

They pulled swaths of fabric over the lower halves of their faces and charged toward Silas. Torj saw a blur of movement in his periphery—Wren and Thea breaking away from their small party, moving in perfect synchronization, their lightning blazing paths through the enemy ranks. Thea cut down any who dared attack them directly while Wren ran in her wake, throwing bolts of brilliant white-like spears toward the academy. Across the grounds, their movements flowed like a deadly dance, each anticipating the other's needs without a word, all the while channeling their storm magic into the great tree that still towered through the heart of the building.

Cal gave a sudden shout as another of his arrows ricocheted off Silas' shield and a unit of three dozen masked men appeared behind their leader from the swirling mist. Torj had barely a second to register the arrival of Silas' reinforcements before they surged forward, their darkened armor a stark contrast against the lightning-lit battlefield.

A glass orb shattered between Torj and a masked opponent, and he whirled around to see Dessa pulling vials from her pockets and launching them at the enemy. Torj dove just in time before the orb exploded, showering Silas' men with a horrifying sickly green liquid that had them screaming.

Smoke erupted around them, thick and acrid, clawing at Torj's lungs as he swung his hammer into an attacker's breastplate. The metal caved in, along with his sternum. Torj fought his way toward Silas, ducking and weaving between enemy alchemists and Cal's latest volley of arrows.

Too late, he saw an opponent reach for a potion, but Wilder was there, slicing clean through the enemy's wrist before he could throw the vial.

"Thanks," Torj grunted as he swung his hammer with so

much force that it crushed the head right off a masked man's shoulders.

Behind the first wave of soldiers were those akin to the howlers from the shadow war—not quite as mutilated as the monsters that had come before, but just as blood-thirsty and violent.

"To me!" Torj shouted.

The three Warswords moved as one, a triangle of deadly precision, as the next wave of Silas' men crashed against them. Torj's hammer carved devastating arcs, each impact sending men flying backward with crushed armor and broken bones. Cal had abandoned his bow for twin daggers, his movements a blur as he sliced through vulnerable points in their enemies' defenses. Wilder roared with each swing of his swords, cutting down two men at once with a cross-slash that left them crumpling to the ground.

Silas remained untouched, watching them intensely. His shield shimmered, absorbing every fragment of energy and magic that flickered around him, while the air crackled with residual storm power.

Torj caught glimpses of Wren and Thea through the chaos. They had reached the academy's main entrance, lightning coalescing around their joined hands as they worked in tandem, feeding their storm magic into the ancient tree that had grown throughout the building's existence. The branches sprouting above the academy's spires began to glow with an eerie teal light, vibrating with barely contained power.

"They need more time!" Torj shouted, blocking a sword strike with his hammer's haft before delivering a punishing blow to his attacker's chest.

"Stop them!" Silas screamed through the fray, and instantly a unit broke away from the main fighting, sprinting toward the Embervale sisters.

"Cal!" Wilder called out.

Cal's signature flaming arrows carved through the air once more, each hitting a target, causing them to drop one by one. The youngest Warsword then dropped back so he could pick off any of Silas' men who attempted to attack Wren and Thea.

Now, lightning struck the tree's massive frame, setting the academy's interior ablaze with blue-white fire that not only consumed the building, but devoured the very shadows within.

Silas himself turned to the Embervale sisters, reaching for their magic. The air between them distorted as he attempted to siphon their power, even from afar, but Torj threw himself between the Kingsbane and the storm wielders.

"No," he said through gritted teeth. He could feel his strength ebbing, the tremors starting up again in his hands as he gripped his war hammer.

"The loyal Warsword," Silas mocked, sounding eerily like Zavier. "So keen to die for others."

Torj circled warily, keeping himself between Silas and the sisters. "Not planning on dying today."

"But soon, yes?" There was a smile in Silas' voice now. "I hear you know of the parting gift I left you with when you rescued poor Reyna. How hard that must be for you and your storm queen—to share such a bond, only to be torn apart..."

Torj ignored his words, didn't give Silas the satisfaction

of seeing him flinch. It was just an expression, wasn't it? Silas couldn't know of their soul bond, could he?

Torj swung his hammer, only to see a curved blade materialize in Silas' hand beside his shield, coated in a familiar alchemical sheen.

They clashed in a furious exchange of blows, Torj's Furies-given strength coursing through him, but ebbing away faster than ever before. And Silas moved like smoke, impossible to pin down. The alchemy-treated blade left trails of darkness in the air, and where it struck Torj's hammer, the metal hissed and blackened.

"You can't stop what's coming," Silas hissed, pressing his advantage as Torj defended. "I made sure of it."

In the distance, Torj could hear Wilder and Cal fighting their way toward him, leaving a trail of bodies in their wake. Behind them, the academy shuddered violently. The great oak had become a conduit for pure storm energy, its branches reaching to the clouds above, drawing down lightning in continuous streams. A sudden blast shattered all the remaining windows and the building's walls began to collapse inward as the lightning and flames coursed through the tree's roots, tearing through the foundation.

Even with the distance between them, Torj felt Wren's cry of anguish in his bones, her lightning causing the earth to rumble beneath their very boots. Fire engulfed everything in its path, consuming all the knowledge that Drevenor housed, the knowledge that had been the victor over fate. In moments, decades of work were gone. The last samples of the silvertide rose, Wren's carefully documented experiments, every breakthrough she had made—all of it dissolved into ash, and Torj grieved for her.

Silas struck with his shield, and Torj staggered backward. He landed hard, the breath knocked from his lungs, tremors wracking not only his hands but his body as well. Through blurred vision, he saw Silas rise to his feet. The energy he'd absorbed was swirling around him in a maelstrom, his mask shimmering with alchemy now as well.

"The old world is dying, Warsword," the Kingsbane said. "I'm the future now."

Torj's arms burned with effort, his hammer buckling as he blocked another blow from Silas' otherworldly weapon. "The future," he rasped, spotting Wren from the corner of his eye, "doesn't belong to men like you."

Torj felt her power surge through their bond, and in the distance, the academy gave one final, tremendous groan before collapsing entirely.

And then, lightning blinded them all.

CHAPTER 18

WREN

*"Resilience is humanity's oldest alchemy—transforming
suffering into strength."*
—Transformative Arts of Alchemy

"I hereby pledge myself to Drevenor," Wren murmured in reverence as the academy went up in flames.

They fled on horseback as it burned, with Silas claiming its ashes as his own. Wren and Thea's lightning had temporarily stunned them all, leaving them with just enough time to run before Silas could take the power for himself, before a fresh wave of incensed People's Vanguard soldiers descended on the burning academy grounds.

The Kingsbane didn't pursue them, which told Wren that despite their efforts and all the destruction, he had what he wanted, and he would face them at full power in Delmira.

Wren's chest constricted and an ache pulsed in her throat as she struggled to swallow the lump that formed there. Another home destroyed; another piece of her gone. Even knowing it was necessary, even having chosen this, the devastation was absolute. Wiping the blood from her nose, she didn't speak as they raced through the night, the air thick with smoke around them. She didn't trust herself to keep her composure.

During the madness of the fight, Wren had glimpsed small groups of remaining students fleeing into the forest under the guidance of Drevenor's faculty. Master Crawford had organized an evacuation route months ago—a contingency they'd hoped never to use. Wren could only hope that they'd made it out safely, and that they were making their way toward the safe houses established throughout Naarva.

The road to the seaside port town was a blur as shock settled over Wren. Drevenor was no more. The gardens, the workshops, the conservatory, the poisons dungeon... All nothing but rubble now. The academic institution had survived the brutality of the shadow war only to succumb to another form of darkness.

As they rode, Wren's mind wandered to the half-finished experiments she'd left behind in the alchemy workshop—projects she'd never complete. The gleaming Master Alchemist medallion she'd imagined hanging around her neck seemed like a child's fantasy now. Despite everything, some small, stubborn part of her had clung to the possibility of returning someday to finish what she'd started at Drevenor. To earn her mastery, to take her place among the great alchemists whose work she'd studied so diligently. That fragile hope had burned with the academy. There would be no graduation ceremony, no quiet afternoons in the workshop perfecting formulas. The path she'd once envisioned for herself had vanished completely, replaced by the road to war.

Wren's teeth were chattering, and she realized distantly that she was cold. She could feel Torj's worried gaze on her, but she couldn't meet it. If she did, she would fall apart.

Soon, weathered stone buildings with salt-encrusted facades came into view as the road descended toward the harbor, the settlement awash with the glow of street lanterns. The briny sea air hit Wren's face, catching on the tears she couldn't recall shedding, the salt scent mingling with those of fish, tar, and chimney smoke. Gulls circled overhead, while townsfolk eyed them suspiciously as they followed the winding street toward the heart of the port town.

"If you're looking for that party of rich pricks, they're at the Salt and Barrel, three crossroads down," came a scratchy voice from a nearby cart.

Wren's head snapped toward the sound, spotting a withered old man gutting fish on the side of the road.

"Thank you," Thea replied, and the man's eyes widened at the sight of her.

He put three bloody fingers to his shoulder in salute. "Meant no offense," he added.

Wren urged her horse on, but heard Thea snort behind her. "None taken," her sister said. "They *are* a bunch of rich pricks."

The Salt and Barrel sat right on the edge of the town, its glass windows thick and warped, distorting the view of the merriment within. The cheerful notes of a fiddle drifted through the door. Darian stood by a trough outside, sipping from a tankard. His eyes widened when he spotted them. "Do I need to send the rest of the men—?"

Torj's husky voice cut through the night. "Drevenor has fallen. Your bride needs a healer. And rest. See to it that she gets it, Lord Devereux."

"While I appreciate the sentiment, I don't take orders from Warswords," Darian replied smoothly.

"You will if you know what's good for you," the Bear Slayer warned, before stalking off, not into the inn, but toward the harbormaster's tower.

Gentle hands helped Wren down from her horse. "Are you alright?" Cal murmured.

Numb, she nodded as she was ushered inside. A low-ceilinged common room with blackened wooden beams greeted her, full of mismatched furniture positioned around a large hearth and bar.

"Now this is my kind of place," she heard Kipp declare somewhere behind her, but a chill raked down her spine as her gaze went straight to Lord Lucian. He was seated at a table in the far corner with Lord Briar and Lord Pendelton, surveying her disheveled state, his eyes narrowing as he searched the faces around her. An arm fell around her shoulders and Lucian's attention lingered a moment longer before he returned to the conversation around him.

"Torj did well to make himself scarce," Darian whispered as he steered her through the rabble toward a narrow staircase. "My father's watching everything. Always."

Wren swallowed the sob that threatened to burst from

her lips. She knew it was safer for her soul-bonded to keep his distance, but it didn't stop her longing for his presence, for the comfort of his touch.

"This way. I booked a room for you," Darian told her.

"Silas was at Drevenor," Wren managed as she climbed the stairs with him. "Not just a unit of his men, but him too. In the flesh."

"I know," Darian replied. "My father's spies met us here with their report, as did some of Drevenor's evacuated students. The academy wasn't at full capacity. Most made it out. But it was too late for us to come after you—"

"It would have made no difference. He's stronger than we knew. The fact that he's not running us down with his army now tells me that he's got much more up his sleeve."

When they reached the top of the stairs, Darian guided her down the hallway and stopped at the last door. "Do you really need a healer?" he asked, fitting a key to the lock. "I doubt we'll find one better than you, Dessa, or Zavier in this cesspit."

Wren shook her head. "I'm not hurt."

"Are you sure? Because it's my head beneath the war hammer if the Bear Slayer finds out otherwise."

Wren huffed a weak laugh. "I'm sure. I just need to wash this soot off."

Darian nodded. "There's hot water waiting for you inside. I brought your pack up as well, so you should have everything you need. Here's the key." He pressed it into her palm. "My father has booked us passage on the first ship out in the morning. It leaves for Harenth at dawn. From there, it's up to you where we go."

The fresh image of cinders settling across the grounds of

Drevenor came to her then, along with a truth that stirred within—one she had learned in the wake of the last war...

Sometimes, the most resilient blooms were the ones that grew from the ashes.

She could sense the dark clouds gathering overhead, could feel the thunder rolling in answer to her resolve. This time, when her storm broke, it would show Silas the Kingsbane exactly what grew from scorched earth and thorns.

Wren met Darian's gaze and named a place she'd hoped never to return to again. "First we ride to Thezmarr," she told him. "Then, to war."

CHAPTER 19
WREN

"A queen's reign is not defined by the absence of storms, but her ability to continue sailing through them."
—The Midrealms Chronicles

T he tub was small, but the water within was steaming, as Darian had promised. With shaking hands, Wren used a dropper to infuse the bath with the last of her lavender oil, hoping it would calm her rising panic.

At last, she submerged herself completely, lingering beneath the surface for as long as her lungs would allow. The lavender and hot water had the desired effect, quietening her racing thoughts and heart. Drevenor was gone, but it lived on in her, and in her friends. This was *not* the end.

Wren scrubbed the grime from her skin with a newfound determination. The destruction of the academy had been necessary, regardless of what Silas may or may not have gained, for Wren knew what he was capable of now. She could prepare to defend Delmira with everything she had.

Knowledge is the victor over fate. The mind is a blade, she chanted to herself as she lathered the soap through her hair.

When she was clean and dry, Wren went to her pack and pulled out the little black box Torj had given her. Smiling to herself, she slipped into the lace undergarments before donning her usual linen dress and apron.

There was no workbench in the room, but there was a dresser that would do. Wren gathered her notebook and potion belt and went to work. Even here it was easy to lose herself in alchemy, in the precious, precarious balance of chemistry and magic. She took the last of her silvertide roses from the silkspore wrappings and methodically removed the thorns. She cast the thought of the burning gardens aside and instead chose to look forward, to where more roses awaited her in her kingdom. They were her salvation now, her hidden hand against Lucian, should he fail to provide the information she needed about Torj's poison.

Hours passed as she simmered the beginnings of her cure over the fire. Without all her tools from the workshop, her usual formulas required adjusting, but there was a freedom in that. What once had taken precise measurements now needed intuition and a thorough understanding of how elements might interact, rather than the rigid rules of a laboratory.

Just as she finished stirring the mixture and returned the lid to the pot, she felt him.

"You shouldn't be here," she said, her voice raw as she slowly turned.

The Bear Slayer closed the door behind him. "I know."

Wren sucked in a breath, her heart hammering. "What about Lucian? He's downstairs. What if he saw you? Or if someone reports this to him, you visiting my chambers like this?"

"Lucian's busy."

Wren didn't ask with what. She took a disbelieving step toward the Warsword, taking in the broad expanse of his chest, the fire in his eyes.

"I had to be here for you," Torj said, his voice pained. "I had to make sure you're alright."

"I'm alright," she told him, fighting every instinct in her body to reach for him. If she did, she knew it would be the end of her. Instead, she turned back to the dresser, trying to busy her hands with replacing the vials in her potion belt.

"That's it?"

Wren's fingers stilled as she whispered, "You can't be here. If Lucian—"

"He's occupied. And I don't want to hear his name again."

Wren could feel him drawing nearer, could feel his gaze searing every part of her.

"I can't concentrate when you look at me like that," she murmured, not tearing her eyes away from her task as heat flushed her cheeks.

"Like what, Embers?"

"Like you want to devour me."

Torj caged her against the dresser, where he leaned in

and ran his nose along the side of her neck, grazing the soft skin there with his teeth. "That's exactly what I want to do."

"Torj..." she warned. She wasn't sure how much more of this she could take. Heat bloomed between her thighs, and her nipples ached against the rough fabric of her gown.

"You needed me. So I came." Torj slipped a hand around her waist and pulled her flush against him. "We need each other, Embers. Feel what you do to me," he said low in her ear, pressing his granite length against her backside.

Wren dropped her belt with a dull thud and spun around to face him, already breathless. She stared into the deep-sea blue of his eyes before gripping his hand and guiding it up her skirt. "Feel what you do to me," she whispered against his lips.

With fabric bunching around his wrist, Torj groaned as his fingertips brushed lace and he blinked slowly. "Are you wearing what I bought you, Embers?"

CHAPTER 20
TORJ

"Only in shadow can we appreciate light's persistence."
—Bear Slayer, Warsword of Thezmarr

"You'd like to think that, wouldn't you?" Wren's words were low and sultry.

"I would." It came out as a growl, the sound rumbling between them. An irrational, primal sense of satisfaction surged through Torj as he glimpsed the black lace Wren was struggling to cover. The undergarments *he'd* bought for her. Taking in the flush across the top of her chest, and her lip caught between her teeth, Torj was nothing but a blaze of longing.

"These new undergarments..." He slid his hand to her thigh beneath her skirts. "Are they wet?"

Wren spread her legs a little wider, and he bit back a moan. His cock had its own pulse, throbbing almost painfully against his leathers. Gods, he wanted to take her right there, right on the floor atop the potions and papers.

"Why don't you find out?" Wren challenged, her gaze full of fire.

The tight leash Torj had on himself threatened to snap. It was impossible not to move toward her, impossible not to lean into that dark frenzy of need rising within.

Bracing himself over her now, backing her against the dresser, he skated his hand over the curve of her backside, the fabric of her skirts rustling over his touch before he gripped the back of her thigh and hoisted one leg up.

Wren was watching him with hooded eyes, and a soft moan broke from her lips as his fingers skimmed higher, hitting the outer seam of lace. He wasn't sure he was breathing. She was so warm, so silken beneath the circles he drew with his thumb.

"Torj..." she whimpered.

Gods, he knew they shouldn't, he knew what was at stake if they were caught, but his self-restraint was wafer-thin after all they had been through, after seeing her with Darian these past few weeks. It was Torj's life on the line. But he knew that holding himself in check wouldn't last. He had created a whirlpool of desire between them. And in that moment, he decided that feeling Wren writhe beneath him was a worthy cause to die for.

She moaned again as he inched toward where she wanted him and he clapped a hand over her mouth, quietening the noise lest someone hear from the hallway outside.

Between her legs, his fingertips brushed against damp —no, *soaked*—fabric.

And gods, he'd never stood a chance.

Torj's voice dropped low with his own need. "Is this for me, Embers?"

Wren pulled away from the hand gagging her, pushing her hips toward him, demanding more friction. "Yes," she murmured, the word thick with lust. "You know it is, damn you."

Smug pride bloomed in his chest as he grazed her clit over her wet undergarments. "What are we going to do about it?"

Wren was panting now. "Please."

The note of desperation made his cock twitch, and he was tempted to draw this out for hours, tempted to make her beg. But they didn't have the luxury of time, and the needy roll of her hips beneath his touch, the way she opened her legs for him, had him caving. Furies save him, he would always cave for her, no matter the cost.

"Torj—" Her hand shot out to grab his forearm, her nails digging into his muscles.

He slid the undergarments to the side and stroked her bare skin, her breath catching at the contact. Anyone could walk in on them like this, and there would be no denying what was going on, not with both of them flushed and panting, with his hands all over her. A sick part of him *wanted* someone to see, so that the whole world would know who Wren truly belonged to.

But that couldn't happen, and so he whispered, "Are you going to stay quiet for me, Embers?"

He wanted to inflict as much pleasure upon his soul-bonded as possible. He wanted her drunk on him. He wanted her knees quaking and his name on her lips.

Torj lifted her skirts.

And saw black lace against luscious skin.

Wren followed his gaze. "Admiring your choice?"

Torj felt as though the wind had been knocked out of him. Only a scrap of lace covered the most intimate part of her.

He shook his head in wonder. "Admiring *you*," he murmured. "Every. Fucking. Inch. Of. You."

He dropped a hand back down to her hip, fisting the lace, that wet fabric the only thing blocking his path to pure erotic bliss. In one swift jerk of his hand, he tore the garment from her skin.

Wren gasped, but he swallowed the sound with a fierce kiss, and pushed two fingers inside her. Her walls clamped around him instantly and she rocked against him, her expression hazy, her head tipping back as he hit that spot deep within.

Torj's vision blurred as he imagined driving his cock into her wet heat, pumping his fingers in long, torturous strokes. "We shouldn't be doing this," he ground out.

"No, we shouldn't," Wren managed as she rode his hand. "But I can't stop."

He slid his fingers in and out of her, spreading her wetness over her clit, swallowing another moan with a kiss.

Wren broke away. "What if we're caught?"

"Would you like that, Embers?" The thought sent a thrill right to his cock, as he once again pictured someone bursting in on them, his name on Wren's lips in ecstasy.

Wren was writhing against his fingers. "I... I need more."

"Remember, you'll have to be quiet," he told her, still toying with her.

"I can—"

Torj reached for the discarded scrap of lace and put it to her lips. "I think you'll need some help with that."

Eyes wide, cheeks flushed, Wren allowed him to push the fabric into her mouth. As his fingers traced her collarbone, the sensation echoed on his own skin, the soul bond reflecting each touch, each ripple of need, until he could scarcely tell where his body ended and hers began.

"Bend over the dresser for me, Embers."

A muffled whimper sounded, but Wren did as he bid. He placed a flat palm against her lower back and pushed her down, so that her chest was flush with the dresser's surface. He bunched her skirts up over her backside and groaned at the sight.

"Spread your legs," he ordered. "*Wider*. Show me everything."

Torj was rock fucking hard as he freed himself, sliding the length of his cock through her desire. He'd go mad if he didn't get inside her. He didn't care about the flimsy walls, or the Devereux bannermen down the hall... His soul-bonded *needed* him, and he'd be damned if he didn't deliver.

A guttural moan escaped Torj as he pushed the head of his cock into her tight heat. How was she this perfect? Wren Embervale was fucking *made* for him. He pulsed there for a moment, savoring the sweet sounds of desperation Wren was making around the undergarments stuffed in her mouth.

And then she angled her hips backward, and Torj slid home.

"Fuck..." he groaned as she clenched around him.

He kept one hand on her lower back, the other spearing

through her hair, mindful of the poison-tipped pin. He gripped her tresses hard and she moaned, and that was all the encouragement he needed to start fucking her in earnest.

He lost himself in her. "Gods, you're addictive," he grunted as he thrust, relishing the soft curve of her backside hitting his pelvis. He prayed there would come a time where he could take her slowly, building her to the brink over and over before he let her explode. But that was not what she needed now. No, he could read her body as if it were his own, and the way she met every hard thrust with a demanding tilt of her hips told him she needed the Warsword as well as the man—rough and primal instincts taking hold.

When she wriggled on the dresser, freeing a hand to reach between her legs, he fucked her harder, and he felt her thighs tremble as her climax started to unravel.

"Yes," she moaned around the material still in her mouth, grinding back against him.

At the sound of her, Torj felt himself spiraling out of control, the buildup becoming too much to bear.

That familiar thread of gold flickered to life between them, and he thanked the Furies—for it was the only thing in this gods-forsaken world he was certain of.

Wren moved beneath him, knocking a bottle off the dresser as the peak of her orgasm hit. The way she felt, the way she rolled her body—it tipped Torj over the edge, his own release tearing through him like a storm. He came inside her, biting back a shout as his whole body shuddered.

Panting, he collapsed over her back, kissing the length

of her spine over her dress. "Was that what you needed?" he asked huskily, his body still trembling in the aftermath.

Wren removed the undergarments from her mouth. "Gods, yes," she managed, resting her brow against the dresser.

Smiling against her neck, Torj slid from her body, running a gentle hand over the curve of her backside. "Wait there."

Wren gaped at him in disbelief. "Like this?"

But Torj only moved a few steps to a nearby pitcher of water and took a strip of fresh linen from the supplies. Wetting it, he brought it back to Wren and gently washed between her thighs, wiping away the evidence of what they'd done.

"Was I too rough?" he asked, pulling her skirts down and tossing the rag aside.

"You were perfect," she replied as he gathered her into his arms.

He kissed her soundly then, savoring the taste and feel of her before breaking away to rest his brow against hers. "Worshiping your body is my honor," he told her. "My fucking privilege."

She cupped his face with her palm, smiling softly. "The feeling is mutual, Bear Slayer. Gods, I've missed you."

Torj pressed a gentle kiss to her lips before tidying the dresser while Wren righted her clothes, her cheeks stained pink. She looked so beautiful, so full of life and fire that it almost hurt. He *was* hurting, Torj realized. At the thought that all of this was temporary, that they may never get the tomorrows that went hand-in-hand with a soul bond. With the poison coursing through him and the midrealms, there was no promise of anything other than the now, and all the while they had to pretend they meant nothing to one another.

As the afterglow faded, sadness continued to weigh him down. He hated that this brief pocket of time together was a mere interlude. He wanted more for her, for *them*. But life had dictated otherwise, and the injustice of it hit him like a club.

As though sensing his melancholy, Wren flung something at him—the torn scrap of lace.

She grinned. "You owe me another pair of undergarments, by the way..."

Torj caught it against his chest and felt the still-damp fabric between his fingers, a smile tugging at the corner of his mouth. "Is that so?"

"Yes," Wren replied.

Torj's cock was hardening again beneath her heated stare, her eyes trailing over his chest, his abdomen, and the V above his hips.

He pocketed the lace, flashing her a devious grin of his own. "Then I'll be keeping these," he told her as he slipped from her room.

CHAPTER 21
WREN

*"The 'assassin's teapot,' also known as 'the Ladies' Luncheon,'
has been one of the most innovative creations to emerge from the
alchemy workshops of Thezmarr since the repurposing of dried
iruseed."*
—A History of Thezmarr

Wren woke before dawn, alone but sated, with a pleasant soreness between her legs. She hated that the bed was empty beside her, but she was grateful for the brief time they'd stolen for themselves the night before. She had needed her soul-bonded, and he'd come for her, no matter the cost.

The potential consequences of their actions made her stomach squirm as she readied herself for the day. But she trusted Torj with her life, and so she cast her worries aside, at least for the time being.

A soft knock sounded at the door, and a familiar voice called out, "It's me."

Wren pulled Dessa inside and into a tight hug. "I'm so sorry I haven't seen you until now—"

Dessa waved her off. "Don't be ridiculous. I brought food." She held out a piece of bread lathered in honey. "Thought you might need something sweet."

Wren closed the door behind them and took a bite, almost moaning. She hadn't realized how hungry she was. "Thank you."

She studied her friend for a moment, awash with gratitude at her ongoing support. They had come a long way since they'd been tasked with finding antidotes to poison in the Evermere Forest. Wren had thought Dessa too chipper then, too bright against her own darkness, but Dessa had endured. She had as much backbone as any of them, and to see what she had seen and still have a gentle heart and a smile on her face? That was more than admirable.

"I'm sorry about Drevenor," Wren told her. "I'm sorry you never got to finish your opus, to help your father..."

Dessa gave a sad smile. "Master Nyella approved my designs before the attack. It was going to work."

Wren felt as though she'd been punched in the gut. "I'm so sorry."

"It's not your fault, Wren. I sent my designs home. There's an inventor there. He's no alchemist, but he'll do his best. If he has no luck, he has promised to hold on to the designs until I can return."

"And your father?"

"He has good days and bad—more bad than good lately,

so I'm told... But if I can bring his memory back, I want the world around him to be one he recognizes. That's why my place is here with you, Wren. Only with you can we achieve the world I want him to remember."

Words failed Wren then, so instead, she took her friend's hand in her own. She knew she could make no promises, that the world Dessa wished for might never exist again, if it ever had at all... but Wren would try. That was all she could offer; that was all she could do.

Dessa squeezed her hand in return. "Did the Bear Slayer find you last night?"

Wren's heart seized. "What do you mean?"

But Dessa gave her a sly smile. "I was charged with occupying Lord Lucian—"

"Oh, Dessa, I'm so sorry. I hate the idea of you being forced to spend even a minute with that bastard—"

"It wasn't so bad." Dessa laughed. "He was unconscious, after all."

Wren stared at her. "What?"

Dessa simply shrugged. "I thought it was high time I took a leaf out of your book, so to speak. I didn't have a teapot on hand, but you can drug a bottle of wine just as easily... I used the pollen of a vale lotus."

"The water lily?" Wren blinked.

Dessa nodded keenly. "Master Norlander told us about it. It dissolves completely, and any lingering herbal aroma can be mistaken for an expensive vintage's complexity. It works gradually, so it's perfect for adding to liquor, as it simply amplifies the effects of increasing drowsiness as the subject drinks more... Eventually, they succumb to sleep like the rest of the drunks around them."

A hoarse sound escaped Wren. Laughter of her own. "Dessa..." she wheezed. "You're mad."

"I learned from the best," Dessa replied with a grin. "Besides, we're about to board a ship with very close quarters... Thought you might need—"

"Alright, I see your point," Wren said quickly, deciding to change tack. "How did your work go while we were gone?"

Dessa sighed. "I drew the same conclusions as you. The poison is complex, a mixture of alchemy and shadow magic, just like what Silas used on Queen Reyna. But it's reacting differently with Torj. Likely because he's not only a Warsword, but the sovereign magic inside him is *yours*. We know from our experiments with Thea in the gardens that yours is different, but you managed to test the original cure on yourself and it worked... so there's hope."

"I did. But I don't have Furies-given Warsword power, do I?" Wren replied. "There are too many unknown variables within Torj's power. It's why I need the information from Lucian... but if he doesn't hold up his end of the bargain, I'll find another way. I'll get the silvertide roses from Delmira and cure him myself, one way or another."

"You have the talent, and you have Zavier and me, however we can help," Dessa told her. "Do you think it's releasing faster than expected? Has Torj talked to you about an increase in symptoms?"

"He hasn't talked about it... but I've seen it for myself. Tremors, muscle spasms..."

"You're the poison expert," Dessa said gently. "Is that one of the earlier or later stages of exposure?"

"Later." Wren caught her bottom lip between her teeth as her mind churned through every scenario she could think of. Was it possible that Torj hadn't been honest with her? That his symptoms were far more advanced than he'd admitted?

"I had Thea send those letters to the rosarians... Did you receive any response at Drevenor?" she asked.

Dessa shook her head.

"Shit... I listed Drevenor's rookery as the point of contact," Wren muttered, cursing herself as she dropped her head in her hands, despair thick in her throat. She blinked back her tears and tried to compose herself.

Dessa spoke again, sadness lacing her voice this time. "You don't have to pretend with me. I thought you knew that by now."

"I—"

"I know I'll never be the other friends you had. I'm not trying to replace them, not ever. But I want you to know: I can handle this. Whatever tormented thoughts you have, I have them too. And in my experience, they hold a lot less power over you when they're shared."

"I know, Dess," Wren replied, offering a tired but genuine smile this time. "I appreciate you and everything you do for me."

"The feeling is mutual," Dessa said. "Now, we need to get moving. The others are already making their way to the docks."

"We have a problem," Kipp said as they prepared to board *The Furies' Will* to travel to the mainland of the midrealms.

"I can't say I'm all that fond of those words," Wren replied, folding her arms over her chest as she waited for the bad tidings.

"Lord Briar has been asking questions about you," Kipp ventured. "Specifically regarding what you did in the years after the shadow war, and why no one really heard from you."

"Why would he be asking about that now?"

"My guess?" Kipp took a sip from his flask while the bannermen guided the horses into the hold. "That someone tipped him off. Someone who wanted to put the pressure on you to... remain compliant."

"Lucian," Wren breathed. "But wouldn't that reflect badly on him if it came to light?"

"He'd feign ignorance, as all good politicians do," Kipp replied.

"How long?" Wren asked, toying with one of the vials in her belt. "How long do you think we have until the truth is out?"

"Not long enough. You need to get ahead of it while you can. Change the perception of who Wren Embervale is."

"How can I change the perception when it's *true*? The midrealms knows I executed Osiris for his treason in the shadow war. As for the deaths of those who helped fund and aid the conflict, I *am* responsible." She drew a trembling breath. "I took justice into my own hands and delivered it as I saw fit."

"You don't regret it, then?" There was no judgment in Kipp's tone, only curiosity.

"No. The only thing I regret is that it now risks the plan we've laid out, that it puts Torj in jeopardy. I regret that one nobleman has the power to alter the tides of the upcoming war with one piece of a larger truth."

"So tell them your whole truth," Kipp said.

Wren scoffed. "Oh, it's that easy, is it?"

Kipp shrugged. "One thing that has always struck me about the politics of the midrealms is that things are so often done behind closed doors. As you said, battles are planned over sparkling wine and feasts, not accessible to the common folk—the folk who are impacted the most. Perhaps it's time you spoke directly to the people."

"And how do you propose I do that?"

"The same way Silas did. *Write to them.* Have posters put up in every town, every tavern. I think we know someone who may be able to help with that, don't you?" Kipp raised an amused brow.

"You don't think it's too late for that?" she asked.

"It's never too late for the truth."

Wren inhaled the salty sea air as the breeze picked up around them, closing her eyes for a moment. "It would be a half-truth, though, wouldn't it? To tell the people my story as the Poisoner, while still pretending I'm engaged to Darian."

When she opened her eyes, Wren had never seen Kipp look as earnest as he did now, placing both hands gently on her shoulders. "Only you can decide what to tell them, Wren. It's your truth to tell."

CHAPTER 22
TORJ

"Since the founding of the warrior guild, Warswords have journeyed across the midrealms and beyond, but inevitably, they always return to Thezmarr, as surely as the river finds the sea."
—The Warsword's Way

Torj knew the last place Wren wanted to go was Thezmarr. He'd *seen* her nightmares. The rivers of blood, the lashing shadows, the acrid scent of burning hair... He knew what that place did to her—what it did to *him*, if he was honest. Where Wren remembered her friends' heads on spikes and her eldest sister dying in the courtyard, he remembered *her*. The ferocity etched across her face and the lightning she commanded with her fingertips. But most of all, he remembered her scream. Not the sound she made as Anya died, nor as the talon of a wraith tore through her skin, but as he leapt toward that vortex of darkness, praying that he could put something—*anything*—in between her and the end of all that was good. He never wanted to hear that sound again.

A spray of sea water up on deck wrenched him from his thoughts. They were a long way from Thezmarr yet, far from any semblance of peace, but they would fight again. What other choice did they have? Torj looked to the choppy waves on the darkening horizon, the crisp, briny air whipping around him, the sails taut above. He couldn't make sense of how they'd got here. How, after everything that had happened during and after the shadow war, this was the precipice upon which they stood. Flashes of Silas' taunts came to him, and regret surged in a wave of nausea. In another life, he could have pummeled that smug bastard to death with one swing of his hammer, but in his poisoned body... he was weak, and he had failed them all.

He didn't know why he had kept Vernich's mace, but he held it now against the rail as he looked out to the expanse of white-tipped sea.

"We should hold a funeral while we can," Kipp said as he approached, nodding at the weapon Torj clung to. "For the Bloodletter and Ashlyn Graves. Our ancestors used to do such rites out at sea."

"It seems like a needless formality among all of this." Torj motioned to where the bannermen were setting up hammocks on deck.

But Kipp simply grasped his shoulder. "They were Warswords of Thezmarr. They deserve to be honored."

Perhaps it was because Torj was facing his own mortality that he threw himself into helping Kipp organize the Bloodletter's farewell at sea. Truth be told, he relished having a task to distract him from the unpredictability that now plagued his body. The tremor he'd grappled with was no longer contained to his fingers. Both hands shook, and often. He'd done his best to hide it, but he knew Wren had noticed, even from afar. It was only a matter of time before she confronted him about it, Lucian be damned—or worse still, before she forged ahead and actually went through with the ruse of marrying Darian.

With the help of Cal, Kipp, and Wilder, Torj built a raft that they would lower into the sea. He placed Vernich's mace atop the kindling, while Cal added a jar containing the preserved fingers of Ashlyn Graves. The raft was only small, not nearly large enough to resemble the life either dead Warsword had led, but it was all they could give them.

Kipp had boarded *The Furies' Will* prepared, and with his supplies, the alchemists made wreaths of red leaves and set them alongside the other tokens the bannermen had given as a show of respect.

Torj looked away as the raft was lowered into the water, still not quite able to fathom that this was Vernich Warner's farewell. He was witnessing the whittling down of a symbol that had sustained the midrealms for centuries, that had seen them survive the shadow war.

With Vernich gone, Torj was the oldest Warsword who remained.

No, you're not. Wren's voice bloomed gently through the bond, and he glanced around to see her standing a few feet away, with Darian at her side.

Torj wasn't sure he'd ever get used to the bond between them—this living tether that opened not only his heart and soul to Wren, but his mind as well. Perhaps he'd never understand it completely, perhaps that was part of its magic, but it was hard to marvel at that now as the makeshift funeral pyre for the Bloodletter drifted unlit across the sea beneath the cloudless sky.

Embers, without Vernich, it's just me and Wilder left from the original cohort, he told her.

A small smile tugged at the corner of her mouth, though she kept her gaze ahead. *I think you're forgetting someone, Bear Slayer...*

Movement at the stern caught Torj's attention as a figure seemed to drop down on deck out of nowhere. The man was broad, tall, and imposing, with sun-kissed olive skin, his dark hair threaded with silver, pulled back into a knot. Behind his back, membranous red-and-black wings were folded neatly.

Talemir Starling.

A lifetime ago, the legendary Warsword had been Wilder's mentor, and the best friend of Wilder's older brother, Malik. Torj had grown up training under their command at Thezmarr, in awe of their warrior prowess when he himself was a mere Guardian of the fortress. Before the main conflict of the shadow war, Talemir had made history by leaving the Warsword way of life behind to marry Drue Emmerson, a Naarvian ranger. What the midrealms hadn't known was that they were fighting a secret battle against the shadow wraiths in Naarva, and that they were preparing for the war to come. It was during those years that Talemir's moniker, the Prince of Hearts, had changed to the name by which he was now known: the Shadow Prince.

Now, here he was, in the flesh. The older Warsword strode toward Torj, his shadow-touched wings tucked behind his back, his gaze flitting between Darian and Wren before settling on the Bear Slayer.

"Good to see you, Elderbrock," he said, dipping his head in greeting.

Thea shoved her way through the crowd, surging forward on her tip-toes and pulling Talemir into a hard hug. "Tal! You made it!"

The Shadow Prince smiled, returning her embrace before breaking away and hauling Torj into one as well.

Mindful of his friend's wings, Torj clapped Tal on the shoulder before surveying him with a grin. The years had been good to Talemir Starling; he only looked more roguishly handsome, even with the fine lines around his eyes.

Soon, Wilder joined them too, wrapping his arms around his former mentor without hesitation. "Fatherhood still suits you."

"I was about to say the same," Torj offered.

Talemir made a noise of disbelief and motioned to the prominent gray streaks in his hair. "This isn't from wielding lightning in a war like yours, brother. *This* is from dealing with my menace of a son on a daily basis."

Wilder chuckled. "So no plans on having a second, then?"

Talemir looked horrified. "And giving him an ally? Gods, no."

Beside Torj, Thea was smiling, and he missed Wren's

presence even more as she asked, "How is Ryland? And Drue?"

Talemir returned the smile. "They're good. There are a handful of other shadow-touched children in Ciraun now, so Ry has plenty of playmates... though I wish they'd just *play*. Right now, they're in their fly-into-anything-solid-and-require-sutures phase. We've got our work cut out for us." He shook his head fondly. "Drue was appointed commander of the city guard as soon as we moved to the capital, and of course, she's a fucking natural." The pride in his voice was crystal clear.

They stood on the deck, watching the raft carrying all that remained of Vernich drift further out to sea. But Torj couldn't stop his gaze from sliding once more to Wren, who remained at Darian's side.

"I heard she's engaged," Talemir said, following his stare.

Torj grunted in confirmation. He didn't bother to explain that it was a ruse for information and allies, that it was part of a broader plan to save his life and defeat Silas.

"To that pompous prick there, no less..." Tal pushed.

"If you're trying to piss me off, mission accomplished, Shadow Prince."

Wilder snorted from where he leaned against the railing with one arm slung around Thea's shoulders. Torj shot him a glare.

But Tal shrugged. "I'm just wondering what the fuck happened. You were meant to figure that out years ago."

"Consider it figured out," Torj bit back, lowering his voice. "I love her. I can't have her, not in the way that I want. End of story."

"What a shit story."

Torj gave a dark laugh. "Tell me about it."

"It's not the end," Tal told him with a knowing grin. "No romance ends like that. Trust me, I've read hundreds."

Torj shook his head. "You and your damn books."

"I'll send you some. You could learn a thing or two," Tal replied with a wink. "If my heart can handle the talon of a shadow wraith, then you can handle whatever poison courses through you, Bear Slayer. Trust me on that."

Torj stared at his friend. "Who told you about that?"

"Wren did. She wrote to Drue about obtaining sun orchid essence—what we used in the war against the wraiths... She told us what happened and that she needed to experiment with different cures."

"Then you have my thanks," Torj replied. "You and Drue both."

Talemir nodded. "For what it's worth, you have my support in any upcoming conflict. But the shadow-touched... As I told Wren and Thea, I can make no promises. I can only ask."

"Do you still see Dratos?" Torj asked, remembering the other shadow-touched warrior who had fought in the war alongside them.

"Not often," Talemir replied. "He doesn't stay in one place too long these days. He took Anya's death hard, blamed himself..."

"He wasn't the only one who blamed themselves," Torj muttered.

"Blame always goes hand in hand with death," Talemir said thoughtfully, before his gaze fell to the raft floating in the distance. "It's been a long time since I attended a death rite for a Warsword..."

"I know," Torj managed. "I never thought it would be Vernich next. Even though he was the oldest, the bastard seemed like he was built to live forever."

"Can't disagree with you there," Talemir chuckled before calling out to Cal, who stood in the crow's nest. "Shall we give him a proper sendoff, then?"

Above them, Cal nocked a flaming arrow to his bow and shot it into the sky.

CHAPTER 23

TORJ

"Traditionally, upon his death, the life of a Warsword is honored upon the Plains of Orax at Thezmarr."
—The Warsword's Way

Callahan the Flaming Arrow did not miss, and the Warswords, alchemists, bannermen, and crew gathered to watch Vernich and Graves' raft catch alight. The fire burned bright on the horizon, the plume of smoke catching in the briny wind as they bid the Bloodletter a final farewell.

Torj found himself with Wilder and Talemir as night gathered and the last of the rite's flames flickered out. "Where are Thea and Cal?" he asked, glancing around for his fellow Warswords.

Wilder gestured vaguely below deck. "We asked them to stay, but Thea said if we were going to toast the end of our kind, she wanted no part in it. I told her it was simply the end of another era, but she wasn't interested. I don't think she's accepted his death yet. She was oddly fond of him, after the war."

"Understandable." Torj remembered the Bloodletter in all his gruesome glory, the most vicious of them all. "I can't believe the mean old bastard is gone."

"Nor I." Talemir raised a flask. "To Vernich, the grumpiest prick who ever lived." He took a generous swig and poured a splash overboard.

Wilder reached for the liquor next. "To Vernich... I'll never forgive you for that stunt you pulled when Thea was a shieldbearer. But you took every hit from me like a legend."

Torj accepted the flask last and raised it to the sky. "To the Bloodletter. For being there when it counted most, in the end."

The burn of the fire extract down his throat was a welcome momentary distraction. Afterward, Torj pressed the flask back into Talemir's waiting hand and made his excuses. Leaving his brothers in arms behind, he tried not to rush as he made his way below deck to the hold, praying to the Furies that besides the horses and cargo, it would be empty. A tremor that had started in his fingers and toyed with his knees was taking hold in a much bigger way, and he needed to be out of sight, needed to face it without the concerned stares of his friends. The weight of his war hammer across his back was suddenly almost too much to bear, as though it wanted to drag him through the keel of the ship and into the depths of the sea below.

Heart pounding, Torj staggered toward the narrow stairs past the cabins that still felt so far away. He had always been strong, even before his Furies-given power. This weakness was not who he was—he wouldn't allow it.

But as he stumbled into the first stall in the hold and his vision swam with black spots, the armor he wore against his regrets cracked.

"Embers," he heard himself mutter. How could they have been given such a gift, only to lose it so soon? There was not enough time. But then, he supposed there would never be enough time, not when it came to her.

A blurred but familiar face came into view.

"Don't tell Wren," Torj managed, before he lost consciousness.

The air was crisper when Torj awoke in the same stall, and the guttering light from the lanterns told him he'd been out for a while. Hay straws poked into him at sharp angles, and his mouth felt dry.

With a groan, he sat up, distantly wondering if he'd hit his head.

"Needed a little cat nap in your old age, I see," Darian observed from where he sat a few feet away on a hay bale, toying with something between his fingers that Torj couldn't see. "If you keep scowling like that you'll get wrinkles," the nobleman added, his voice smooth. "Or *more* wrinkles, I should say."

Darian's smile was as smug as ever. He'd perfected it from the age of sixteen and had been wielding it against men and women alike ever since.

Torj rolled his eyes and sat up with a groan. "Don't you ever get sick of yourself?"

"Why would I when I'm such excellent company?" Darian quipped.

"You haven't changed."

The nobleman laughed. "You don't mess with perfection, brother."

"That's not what I'd call it," Torj grunted in reply as he tried to dust himself off. "What are you doing here?"

"Well, someone had to break your fall. I can only imagine the damage I'd be billed for if your thick skull cracked the ship floor," Darian replied with a smirk.

"Do you ever stop?" Torj muttered.

The smirk widened into a grin. "Not if I can help it. So, what's with you collapsing?"

Torj ground his teeth. "I didn't *collapse*."

"Then you swooned in my presence? I'm touched." But there was an edge to Darian's voice now. "What's going on? What happened to you?"

"Nothing—"

"Don't insult my intelligence, Bear Slayer," Darian snapped. "Tell me what's going on—or do I need to get my betrothed involved?"

Torj stared daggers at him. He knew the prick was just using the term to aggravate him; the problem was... *it worked*. Every. Fucking. Time.

Darian pocketed whatever he was fidgeting with and got to his feet. "So be it. I'll call my wife-to-be and she can deal with you—"

"She's *not* your wife." Torj hated the bastard. Hated him.

"You know what the problem is, anyway. I've been poisoned, remember?"

"But that shouldn't be affecting you this badly yet." Darian surged for the stall door. "I'll get Wren—"

"There's nothing to be done right now."

"Then why did you ask me not to tell her?" Darian demanded.

"I just don't want her to see me like this."

"If she's ever woken up next to you in the morning, I assure you, the states are almost identical—"

The Bear Slayer growled. "Devereux."

"Elderbrock."

Torj wanted to get up, wanted to show Darian that there was nothing wrong with him, but his limbs felt heavy, and his mind was full of fog. He needed a moment, just a moment, to get his bearings.

Darian returned to the hay bale and sat down with a sigh. "I thought things were good between us, brother..."

Torj glanced up. "Just because I found out you helped my grandmother doesn't mean I have to like your highborn bullshit."

Darian laughed. Actually *laughed*. "Well, I for one could do without the brooding warrior attitude. You really know how to kill a mood, you know that? We used to have fun, Elderbrock. Don't you remember?" The nobleman stretched out his legs, crossing them at the ankles. "The drinking games... The maidens watching us spar... The—"

"There's none of that anymore," Torj muttered, closing his eyes against the ache forming behind them.

"True," Darian said. "They weren't maidens for long—"

"Darian," Torj snapped. "What do you want?"

168

"Besides the pleasure of your company after all this time?"

A familiar quiet settled between their barbs. A silence that hung heavy with the echo of beatings and verbal lashings long past. When they had been boys, there had always been a strange sense of calm after such things—a sick sense of relief that the worst had happened, and at last the waiting was over, at least for a little while. Slowly, they would come back to themselves with a smart-ass quip or a bad joke while they tried to suspend their reality for just a moment longer.

"When we were boys," Torj said quietly. "At your father's estate, training in the yard with wooden swords..."

Darian tensed beside him. "I remember."

"You told me you wanted to study music, not politics."

"Look how that turned out, eh?" Darian said wryly.

"And he punished you by punishing me," Torj ventured as the memory came back to him. While they trained, Darian had disarmed Torj, but Lord Lucian had forced his son to keep attacking, to keep striking while he was down.

"Well, bruises on the local riff-raff were no concern of his. He couldn't very well have his blue-blooded son sporting black eyes, now could he?" Darian's words were flat and devoid of emotion, but his gaze was steel.

Torj remembered how Darian's young face had turned ash-white while Lord Lucian surveyed them from the balcony above. "A true noble swordsman shows no mercy, right?"

"That's what he said, yes."

Torj swallowed the lump in his throat. "I think that day hurt you more than it did me."

"The blood and stitches you needed said otherwise," Darian replied. "I should have gone against him. Life might have been different."

"It might have been. You might have wound up dead. I understood, you know... even then. What it meant to disobey a father like yours. I never held it against you." Torj's hand drifted to his throat, where every now and then, he could still feel the imprint of his own father's hands. "Do you think we should have told someone about them? Our fathers?"

Darian gave a dark laugh. "Told who?"

"Anyone."

Shaking his head, the nobleman sighed. "They would have killed us."

Torj nodded. "Mine killed my mother instead."

"That wasn't your fault, brother," Darian murmured. "It never was."

Torj glanced behind them to make sure he wasn't going to be overheard. "Perhaps it was out of my control then... but it's not now."

"What are you talking about?" Darian looked genuinely puzzled.

"Wren." Torj braced himself against the wall, sucking in a lungful of the musty air, desperation clawing at his insides. "You'll look after her, won't you? Protect her from Lucian?"

"I thought we'd discussed this." Darian adopted a condescending tone. "Unfortunately, my engagement to the love of your life is fake. Though I daresay I'll miss our repartee."

"Don't play the fool, Darian. It doesn't suit you."

"Did the mighty Bear Slayer just compliment me?"

Torj scoffed. "That's a stretch."

"Then tell me, what *are* you saying, brother?"

Torj forged on. "She'll want a workroom for her alchemy, and a library. A big one. The biggest you can afford, which should be sizable—"

"You *know* I'm not *actually* marrying—"

"And a garden," Torj continued. "With the best herbs you can find from all over the realms. She'll want to tend to it herself and—"

"Elderbrock. *Stop*."

Torj blinked. "What?"

"Stop making plans for when you're gone. I won't have it. And most importantly, *she* won't have it. Furies save you, have you *met* her?"

"I just..."

"Just *what*?" Darian demanded.

Torj's breath rattled in his chest. "I want her to have everything."

Darian turned to him then, incredulous. "Everything is nothing without you."

"She'll move on. She'll—"

Darian cut him off. "Would *you*?"

Torj froze. Gods, he hated that Darian—Darian fucking Devereux—had a point. *The* point. They were soul bonded. Equals. And yet he was still behaving like a gods-damned child.

"You're right," he said, hanging his head.

Darian blinked, cupping his ear in disbelief. "What was that?"

"Don't be a smug bastard. I won't say it twice."

"Should have got it in writing," Darian retorted.

"You should have."

"She *loves* you," Darian said more seriously. "Anyone with eyes can see it. The way she looks at you—it's how my aunt used to look at my uncle before they died..." He trailed off. "Don't waste it."

"I'm a dying Warsword. She's to be queen."

Darian scoffed. "And I'm a highborn lord conspiring against his own father." He got to his feet again and offered Torj his hand. "The old rules are fading, brother. Maybe it's time we wrote new ones."

The word "brother" hung between them again—an olive branch, a recognition of what they once were to each other.

Torj considered the outstretched hand, his heart still heavy. "Men like me don't write the rules. We follow them."

"What a load of bullshit," Darian retorted. "Queen. Alchemist. Poisoner. Warsword. Man. One day we'll live in a world where it doesn't fucking matter. Now take my damn hand and let me help your pathetic ass up."

Torj snorted at that. The old Darian was definitely still in there, and so he grasped his friend's hand.

"Besides," Darian added, lighter now that he'd hauled Torj up, "can you imagine anyone telling Wren she can't have what she wants? I've seen her in action. She makes the Bear Slayer look like a stuffed animal. The woman's terrifying."

That startled a laugh from Torj. "You have no idea."

As the two men left the hold and stepped out onto the deck, something had shifted. The air was clearer between them, old wounds beginning to knit closed. Ever cautious of his father, Darian looked around carefully before he pulled something from his pocket and held it out for Torj to see beneath the moonlight.

"Your grandmother gave this to me," he said quietly, handing it to Torj. "It was once hers, then it belonged to your mother."

Torj stopped walking.

Darian gripped his shoulder, forcing him to take his eyes off the delicate circle of silver and meet his friend's determined gaze. "Don't let anyone tell you that you're not worthy of her. Not even yourself."

Torj speared his fingers through his hair. "And what does that matter, given your impending marriage to her?"

The nobleman's eyes flickered to the distance, his voice dropping low. "A lot can happen between now and when we get to an altar... and there are many reasons why weddings don't go ahead. Think on it, brother."

Darian's words lingered long after he had left to speak with Kipp. They echoed through Torj like a chord struck over and over.

He hadn't moved on from Elwren Embervale in nearly thirteen years, and he never would. They were fucking *soul bonded*. Perhaps, at long last, it was time he stopped fighting it, fighting himself, and started fighting for *her* instead.

And suddenly, the answer was clear.

Torj reached for her through the bond. *Embers, I need to talk to you.*

CHAPTER 24
WREN

"It is a wise alchemist indeed who knows that while answers may light the path forward, it is the right questions that reveal which path to take."
—Alchemy Unbound

Wren needed somewhere private to think, to write, to tinker with her experiments on the cure away from Lucian's prying eyes. Kipp had suggested the compartment where the ship's anchor chain was stored as they sailed—the chain locker.

It was a relatively small space, accessed through a small hatch in the bow of *The Furies' Will*. It smelled of rope and metal, and it was dark but for the lantern Kipp had given her. Thankfully, though, the area was kept dry to prevent the chains from excessive rusting. For a place that seemed rarely visited by the main crew, it was strangely equipped for her purposes, which meant it wasn't the first time Kipp had made use of the space.

Wren could hear the others upstairs, enjoying the gentle breeze and the sun as it bore down upon the deck. She knew the opportunities to do so would become few and far between as the weeks ahead unfolded, but after boarding *The Furies' Will*, her advisor's words weighed heavily on her mind.

The truth.

Wren wasn't even sure she knew it herself anymore. She had played too many roles, worn too many masks, and sometimes she didn't recognize the person staring back at her in the mirror. Now, sequestered away in the chain locker, she stared at the blank sheet of parchment before her, willing the answers to come.

She could confess to the people of the midrealms who she truly was—poisoner *and* heir, or she could deny it altogether. She could write a mix of falsehoods and facts, blending the two together into something more palatable. Or she could lie. Just like Silas had. None of the options felt right; none of them gave her any semblance of peace. Wren doubted she'd ever experience that particular feeling again.

Ink dripped from the tip of her quill onto the page, seeping into the parchment like blood. It wouldn't be long before she was writing orders for armies, before real blood was spilled in her name.

But then, she was called by another name, through the bond between her and the Bear Slayer: *Embers, I need to talk to you.*

Wren allowed his voice to soak into her, husky and rich, providing solace amid the turmoil. *Do you know where the*

175

chain locker is? she replied. *Below the main deck in the forecastle area?*

What in the midrealms are you doing there? came his response.

Do you know it? she pressed.

I know it.

Wren placed the quill back in the ink pot and dropped her head into her hands. She felt so lost amid the tangled web she had woven for herself, the feeling threatening to become a spiraling mass of darkness within.

She felt him before he spoke, that sturdy, reassuring presence that brought warmth to her chest even in the deepest throes of anxiety.

"We shouldn't be taking this risk," she whispered. But she couldn't bring herself to regret it, even as she said, "Lucian has spies everywhere."

"Darian practically told me to come here himself," Torj said, a large palm circling her back. "Are you alright?"

"Kipp thinks I should write to the people of the midrealms..." She swallowed the lump in her throat and looked up at the beautiful man gilded by the lantern beside her, praying that he'd have some answers for her.

"And what do you think?" he asked.

"I think that whenever I make a decision, people get hurt," she told him, glancing at his trembling hands.

He followed her gaze down. "This is not your fault, Embers." He covered the tremor with a tug of his sleeve.

"Don't do that," she said quietly.

He looked up, feigning ignorance. "Do what?"

"Hide things from me. I saw your hand. I know the poison is working its way through your system faster than we anticipated. I can't help you if I don't know what's going on."

"I'm fine," he said. "Or do I need to prove it to you?" he added suggestively.

Ignoring the innuendo, Wren took his weakened hand in hers. He tried to snatch it back, but she held firm, shooting him a warning look before she started to examine it.

"How long?" she asked.

"Not—"

"I won't ask you again, Bear Slayer."

He had the good sense to look sheepish. "A while..."

"I figured," she said. "I'm working on getting the information about it from Lucian, and I have Zavier and Dessa working around the clock here—"

"There are more important things, Embers," he started gently.

"More important than you?" she demanded. "Imagine if I had said those words to you. Don't cast your worth aside, not to me. You are *everything*, and I will not let this happen to you. There is no scenario in which you do not survive this, do you understand me?"

"Always so bossy, Embers." A smile sounded in his voice.

"Someone's got to be with you Warswords. So stubborn." She turned his hand over in hers, looking for any additional outward signs. "Anything else you need to tell me?"

Torj sighed. "There was a moment, in the sparring ring, with Cal. My muscles locked up, and..."

"And?" she pressed. She had seen it with her own eyes, but she needed to know the cause, the symptoms.

Torj's cheeks flushed. "I fell. I had no control. And before I sent word to you just now, I fainted."

Wren hated the shame she saw in his gaze, that he didn't want to share this part of himself with her.

"Darian helped me, and I feel fine now. But..." He didn't need to say that he was embarrassed. Torj Elderbrock did not fall, not from his horse, not from anything. He'd told her so several times himself.

So Wren simply nodded. "Thank you for telling me."

"We should assign you more guards once we get to the mainland," he said slowly. "In case it happens again. In case I can't—"

"There is no 'in case,'" she told him. "I have all the guards and protection I need. As long as I have you, I'll be fine. Are you ready for what lies ahead at Thezmarr?"

Torj looked like he wanted to argue, but instead, he reached for her. "I'm always ready."

Warmth bloomed in Wren's chest at that. She cupped his face, smiling softly. "There's the Bear Slayer I know and love. Now, what were you saying about proving it to me? Or do you have more hard truths you need to get off your chest?"

"Hard truths? No." Torj tucked her hair behind her ear with a soft smile. "My truth, the only truth that matters, is that you are *everything* to me. My friend. My lover. My soul-bonded... My *queen*. My truth is that I love you more and more every day, if that's even possible after the last thirteen years of loving you. If life has taught me anything, Embers, it's that not much can stand in the way of that."

"That's quite a speech, Bear Slayer..." she murmured, ignoring the sting of welling tears.

"You think?" He fitted himself between her legs, still smiling. "In that case, there's something I need to ask you, Embers..."

Heat radiated from his torso against her legs, and she breathed in his black-cedar-and-oakmoss scent. "So ask."

CHAPTER 25
TORJ

"A soul bond is too strong to be broken by an individual."
—Tethers and Magical Bonds Throughout History

Torj's whole body was alight with need, his cock was rock-hard against his leathers, and his fists were clenched in desperation at his sides as Wren palmed him through his clothes. He wanted nothing more than to throw her down and fuck her into the floor.

"I need to speak to the captain, and here you are, pushing me again, Embers... Tempting me. I won't be responsible for what happens if you keep going."

"After what you just asked?" Wren countered. "Perhaps you need to be pushed."

His hands coasted up her leg, beneath her skirts, and sure enough—

"No undergarments again, you vixen..."

"Someone destroyed my last pair."

"You made sure of it," he growled as longing barreled through him. Dozens of images, some from the past, some imagined, flooded his mind. Every moment he'd wanted her before, every moment he'd want her forever after...

Wren's nostrils flared, as though she could sense his thoughts, could see the very things he was picturing. And there it was again: that glimmer of gold between them. Wren danced her fingers through it, letting the thread coil around her fingers.

"It's beautiful, isn't it?" she sighed.

"That's not what I'm appreciating right now," he said gruffly, his hands tracing up her sides, from her hips and waist to the curve of her breasts.

"We shouldn't," she protested, but there was little conviction in her voice.

"No, we shouldn't..." And then he crashed his mouth to hers.

The kiss was hungry and desperate. As soon as her mouth was on his he realized how tightly wound he'd been, how much he'd craved her, even in the short time between now and the inn. But all thoughts emptied from Torj's mind as Wren caught his lip between her teeth and demanded more. He explored her tongue with his, deepening the kiss, delving into her and tasting all that was his, Wren making needy noises beneath him.

He broke away to say against her lips, "As much as I want to take my time with you, Embers—"

"There is none, I know," she panted. "So fuck me, Bear Slayer. Make it quick and hard. Just help me get rid of this gods-forsaken ache."

He walked her backward so she was flush against the coil of chains, his hands already exploring her. "That I can do."

As much as he wished to tear her clothes off and worship her naked body, Torj confined himself to hiking her skirts up around her thighs, baring her to him.

"Torj..." Wren murmured as he dragged two fingers down the wet center of her.

"You're soaked, Embers..."

Wren reached for his laces and undid them roughly, freeing his hard cock. "Of course I am," she muttered. "Do you know how much I've been wanting you? *Needing* you?"

Torj didn't wait a second longer. He lined himself up with her entrance and sheathed himself inside her with one powerful thrust.

Wren cried out, but he swallowed the sound with a passionate kiss, almost blacking out at the feel of her tight and wet around him. He allowed her a moment to adjust to the size of him, but when she tilted her hips eagerly, he unleashed himself on her.

Caging her against the wall of the anchor's chains, her skirts bunched between them, he fucked her hard. Every glide inside of her had him groaning into the crook of her neck, biting the sensitive skin there. He set a punishing pace of long, hard strokes, pistoning his hips to hit that spot inside her that had her clawing at his shoulders. Gods, there was so much he wanted to do, so much he wanted to show her, but there was never any fucking time.

"Harder," Wren commanded against his lips. "This is the last chance we'll get for a while, Bear Slayer. You'd best make it count."

It was in his nature to want to drag things out, to wring multiple orgasms from her before he found his own release, but she was right. He slammed into her with enough force that the ink pot on the nearby table rattled, and he moaned her name into her heated skin.

The rhythm of his thrusts was relentless, and when he saw Wren's eyes start to flutter closed, he reached between their bodies.

"Look at me when you come apart," he growled, pressing his thumb to her clit.

"Fuck," she cried, her hips rolling with his. "Torj—"

"That's it, Embers." He circled her clit again and again, her eyes going wide as she clenched around him. "Tell me, tell me when you're there—"

He had to clap a hand over her scream as her climax hit. He knew when, for she tightened around him and dragged him over the edge with her. Pleasure cascaded through him and a primal noise broke from his throat as he spilled himself inside her, his vision blurring. The force of it was so powerful that his knees buckled, and he had to brace himself against the wooden planking.

Torj looked up, noting the pink flush across Wren's cheeks, and the way she bit her lower lip. Her chest was heaving, as was his as they looked down between them, his release leaking from between her thighs.

"Fuck..." he groaned at the sight. In that moment, there was no denying who she belonged to, no pretending. His claim was right there for them to see, and it made him want to take her again and again.

Wren Embervale was his.

CHAPTER 26
WREN

"Of an alchemist's prized tools, the finest magnifying lens is crafted not from glass, but from study that dissolves the barrier between what we perceive and what truly is."
—Drevenor Academy Handbook

It was nightfall by the time they finished talking and Torj slipped from the compartment to find the captain, but Wren was more alert, more alive than she'd been in a long time when she reached for her quill.

Now, she knew exactly what to write.

She stayed in the chain locker for as long as she could bear it before she staged a visit to Darian in front of Lucian and then returned to her cabin to continue scribbling away. She only paused to push the parchment into Kipp's hands and take whatever food he brought her. All concept of time was lost to her as she poured herself into the pages before her, her hand cramping from the endless hours of use. She couldn't remember the last time she'd felt the sun on her face. Cracking her knuckles and rubbing her bleary eyes, she retrieved a new leaf of parchment with a sigh—

"We're dropping anchor," Kipp's voice sounded from the door. "Time to go. Tal's flown back to Naarva to speak with the shadow-touched."

Surprised, Wren rolled her aching shoulders and dropped her head into her hands, instantly regretting that she hadn't slept ahead of the hard ride to Thezmarr. "Surely it'll be hours before we can actually disembark—"

"No, we're first off. I called in a favor."

Wren gave a tired laugh. "Of course you did. No doubt you want to use the newfound time to stop by the Fox?"

"Not this time," Kipp replied, his expression unreadable.

A chill ran down her spine. "What is it? It's not like you to—"

"I can't be sure yet," Kipp told her quietly. "But the sooner we leave, the better."

Seeing Kipp serious was unnerving to say the least, and so Wren got to her feet, quickly packing away her things in her oilskin satchel and securing her belt of potions around her waist.

Up on deck, several members of the crew were releasing the mechanisms and controlling the drop of the anchor into the dark waters below, feeding the rope through the hawsehole. A loud scraping noise filled the air as the thick hemp scraped against the wooden hull, followed by a tremendous splash as the iron hit the water.

Kipp fidgeted beside Wren. She had traveled by ship with him enough times by now to know that he was not usually a nervous voyager, and yet he peered beyond the docks with narrowed eyes, shifting from foot to foot.

"What is it?" Thea asked as she joined them, noting the same anxious movements in their friend.

"Settler's Port is quiet," Kipp replied, not taking his eyes off the docks below.

Wren followed his gaze. The markets, usually buzzing with activity, were empty of patrons and vendors alike. There were no stalls, no traders hawking their wares...

She risked a glance across the deck to where Torj stood rigid beside Wilder, surveying the quiet port below, his brow furrowed, a muscle twitching beneath the stubble of his jaw.

"Must be something going on in the capital," Lord Lucian offered as the crew began securing the remaining rope to the bollards. "Regent Liora is known to love her festivals."

Wren shot Thea a look of disbelief, only to find her sister's expression mirroring her own.

It wasn't long before they disembarked, and were met with an unnatural silence looming like a heavy cloud. No gulls squawking, no insects buzzing around the market scraps, and certainly not the hum of a prosperous city beyond...

With their horses being led out from the hold, Darian sent scouts ahead while the Warswords and a skeleton company followed in their wake. Wren refused to be left behind, as did Dessa, Zavier, and Kipp, who all trailed after the warriors. Unease settled over Wren as they moved into the outskirts of the capital, her nape prickling, her palms growing clammy. This was an outlying residential area, she realized, taking in the withered plants in the windowsills, the lines of laundry hanging above.

Ahead of her, Torj took his war hammer in his hands, and beside him, Thea and Wilder unsheathed their swords. The telltale creak of Cal's bow sounded from nearby as well.

Torj's voice came to her. *Stay close, Embers.*

But she didn't need to be a Warsword to sense the danger ahead. Wren gnawed on her lip, a faint yet familiar floral scent tickling her nostrils.

"My lord!" one of Darian's scouts cried, running toward them.

"What is it?" Darian demanded.

"You have to see it for yourself," the scout said, his voice wavering.

But the nobleman didn't move a muscle. Instead, he surveyed his man critically. "We have royals among us. Is it safe for them to enter the town?"

"Everyone's dead."

Darian blinked, his only tell the tightening of his grip on the pommel of his sword. "Very well. Lead on."

Their company moved forward, and no one said a word. Wren's heart was in her throat as they walked into the outer town square, that strange sense of *wrongness* still humming around them.

She gasped.

Not at the prominent gallows erected in the heart of the place, but at the dozens of bodies littered across the ground. Men, women, and children of all ages lay lifeless in the dirt.

"Furies save us..." Dessa breathed nearby.

Wren darted to the closest body.

HELEN SCHEUERER

"Wren, no—" Thea called out. But she was already there, searching for a pulse.

She found none. Not on the first body, or the second, or the rest that came after.

The scout was right—everyone was dead.

Wren had seen bodies piled like this before, during the shadow war, but it had always been after a battle, where blood had raged as hot as the fires that burst from her potions, and weapons had clashed with the song of violence. This was different.

These deaths were quiet, calculated.

It had been a mass execution.

Wren sought Darian. The nobleman was walking around the bodies like her, staring at them in disbelief.

"This town was governed by one of Lord Briar's relatives," he said, glancing back toward the port, where the lord remained oblivious to the slaughter.

Wren's gaze fell to the well before the gallows. Stepping over the dead, she approached it. Its bucket was raised and swaying in the gentle breeze as though someone had paused mid-task. She reached for the ladle and peered into the water. There was nothing to be seen; the water was clear, but that faint scent nagged at her.

"Is it some form of dark alchemy?" Dessa asked, staring into the bucket beside her.

"There are no signs of struggle," Cal called out as he searched the corpses for clues. "No injuries that I can see..."

Wren looked at the devastation before her, recognizing the subtle sweet fragrance at last. Oleander.

"Because they weren't slain by blades," she ventured slowly. "They were poisoned."

CHAPTER 27
TORJ

"It is often argued that when denied the sword, women learned that the vial was the deadlier weapon—patient, precise, and impossible to trace. Which is why many claim that poison is the weapon of womenfolk."
—The Midrealms Chronicles

"Shit." Torj's gaze settled on Wren as the realization dawned in all its ugly glory.

Poison, not dark alchemy, had been used here.

There was no trace of Silas, nor of his shadow-infused power, nothing to implicate the Kingsbane or his army of blood-thirsty soldiers.

A well had been poisoned. And poison, as the midrealms knew, was a woman's weapon.

"We need to send a message to Regent Liora," Wren was

saying to Darian. "She may not yet be aware this has happened."

The nobleman motioned to one of his scouts, who was already retrieving a parchment and quill from his supplies—

"Devereux," Torj heard himself say. "Perhaps it's best this is kept quiet for now? We don't want anyone getting the wrong idea, given who was first on the scene... Given Lord Briar's past experience with... poison."

Darian glanced back toward the docks, brow furrowing before he turned to Wren. "What do you think?"

Wren gave a pointed glance at the scouts. "I think we have nothing to hide," she said. "Covering this up in any way will make us look guilty. Not to mention it's a disrespect to the poor people who died here. We will report this to both Regent Liora and Lord Briar, then we will carry on to Thezmarr as planned."

"So be it," Darian said with a nod.

Only the presence of the messenger stopped Torj from going straight to Wren and taking her hands in his to implore her. There was no way to know which men in the Devereux employ they could trust, and so he spoke through their bond instead.

Silas knows your past—that you were the Poisoner, Embers.

I know, she replied calmly. *He means for me to take the fall for this slaughter after proving I was responsible for the deaths of the nobles after the war.*

Then why are you allowing Darian to place us here? Torj argued. *You should be far, far away from this.*

Wren didn't so much as glance his way, but her voice filled his mind. *It's too late for that, Bear Slayer. There is no hiding from this. Lord Briar has already been asking questions. It's clever on Silas' part... Part of a broader scheme to sow the seeds of suspicion before revealing me to the midrealms. By targeting a poorer community like this, he immediately isolates anyone who may have sympathized with my original vendetta against the rich and corrupt.*

And you're letting him? Torj had to stop himself from charging over to her and shaking her by the shoulders. He speared his fingers through his hair, looking to the rest of their company. What would the allies they'd amassed do if they found out that the queen they followed was a killer? Any nuance would be lost as the news rippled through the midrealms, causing waves of confusion and misinformation.

With the messenger on his way to the palace, Darian took the lead back toward the docks, while Torj fell back.

His body jerked as he was tugged into an alleyway.

"I don't regret it," Wren said, holding her chin high, meeting his gaze as they hid in the shadows. "Not for a second."

"If you hadn't—"

"Then those vile men would still be walking the midrealms, spreading poison of their own throughout the kingdoms. I did what I could at the time to cut the rot out of this place. That's all any of us can ever do."

"I was going to say," Torj replied gently, "that if you hadn't, the world may have found itself cloaked in darkness again much sooner."

Wren stared at him, and he understood her shock. It was the first time he hadn't fought her on the subject. For five years after the shadow war, he'd more than objected to

191

her self-assigned role as the Poisoner. His code as a warrior of Thezmarr hadn't allowed him to understand why she had needed to seek retribution—but now...

Torj reached out, his thumb tracing the line of her jaw and ghosting over her bottom lip. "You did what you could —what you thought you had to at the time. I will not begrudge you that. Not now. Not *ever* again."

CHAPTER 28
WREN

"We are all daughters of darkness... We were born into a world of it, a place that would dictate the way in which we defend ourselves, the way we live our lives. No more. That world is no longer. And the next one will be what we make it."
—Audra Delaney, Guild Master of Thezmarr

Everyone always said that Thezmarr sat at the edge of the world—a fortress amid a wild landscape, made of cold, sharp lines. It was hemmed in by rugged black mountains and a seemingly endless sea, whose waves were so tall they seemed to collide with the clouds. In Wren's youth, it had all seemed so imposing, larger than life... and then after the war, it had been a territory of scorched earth, a place of nightmares, leaking with shadow and darkness.

Now, Wren paused at the fortress gates. She thought she had ridden through them for the last time almost a year ago. And yet, here she was. At the end of one war and the beginning of another.

The late autumn wind carried the scent of salt from the sea, mingling with woodsmoke from the new guardhouses. New flags snapped in the breeze—not the blood-red standards she remembered from the war, but deep purple pennants proudly displaying the three crossed swords of the Warsword totem.

She waited for her lungs to constrict, for panic to grip her by the throat, for the scent of burnt hair to fill her nostrils. The anticipation had her straight-backed in her saddle, but the familiar terror didn't take hold.

Exhaling shakily, Wren looked to the towering walls. Plain stone greeted her. Nothing more. And for the first time, the sight didn't send her into a vivid flashback of her friends' heads spiked atop the walls.

What did that mean? That she was forgetting them and their suffering? Surely that was the cost of her survival—to carry them with her always? To never forget?

They're at peace now, Torj's voice said into her mind. He was riding somewhere toward the rear of the company, but he knew her, knew what haunted her dreams and what triggered those visceral returns to the past.

I hope so, she replied as she passed beneath the gates.

His presence brushed against her consciousness again, gentle and reassuring. *The past doesn't own us, Embers.*

Wren allowed herself a small smile at that.

Next, the courtyard opened up before her, and her eyes fell immediately to where Anya had taken her last breath, to where she'd gifted her storm magic to her younger sisters— her final sacrifice for the good of the midrealms, despite being painted as the villain for so long. Wren's heart still ached for her. Just like Sam and Ida, Anya's life had been cut short, and the injustice of it would never fade.

"Do you know what she said to me before the end?" Thea spoke suddenly from beside her, the words sounding loud in the empty cobblestone square.

Wren looked to her sister, who sat proudly atop her Tverrian stallion— something else Anya hadn't lived to see. "What?"

Thea took a deep breath, her gaze still lingering on the spot where their sister had died. "We knew she wasn't going to make it... so I asked her not to leave us without any hope for the world." Her voice wavered. "She told me that she had wanted to scorch the earth with her fury, but that there was still hope left... and then she looked at you."

Tears stung Wren's eyes, and for once, she didn't fight them. "Really?" she managed, the word thick in her throat.

Thea nodded. "She knew you were the future, even then."

"But—"

Thea gave a sad laugh, shaking her head. "You can't argue with Anya, not even in death."

The last time Wren had visited the fortress, parts of the structure had still been covered in scaffolding. That was no longer the case. Under Audra's command, the home of the realm's protectors had been rebuilt, with much improvement. Even the sound was different—where once there had been the clash of steel and cries for help, and then eerie silence, now came the ordinary bustle of daily life: the ring of a blacksmith's hammer, voices calling across the courtyard, the scrape of cart wheels on stone. It was all so different... and when Wren entered the great hall, she gasped.

For at the heart of the grand space towered three giant stone sculptures.

A breathtaking monument to the Furies, replacing the one that had been destroyed during the war. Instead of swords that pierced the hall's ceiling, the new tribute showed the Furies as they truly were: protectors, warriors, goddesses—women who had carried the weight of the realm on their shoulders. Wren's throat tightened as she admired Audra's decision to portray the original Warswords in all their glory, as women of flesh and blood, of strength and sacrifice. Their faces held both power and compassion, showing everything the Furies embodied in their purest form, everything Anya had been beneath her rage.

The old monument had been about fear; this one spoke of hope.

Thea held out a dagger and nodded to the plinth of the monument. "I told Anya she was just as much a hero as any Thezmarrian. I promised I'd carve her name there."

"Then that's what we'll do," Wren murmured, taking the blade.

Together, she and Thea etched Anya's name into the stone, as was tradition to acknowledge a warrior's sacrifice to the midrealms. The scrape of metal rang out in the vast space, each stroke a reminder of what they'd lost—and what they'd gained despite it all. Sisterhood. Understanding.

Thea traced over their carving with her fingers. "To Anya... a mosaic of contradictions," she said, echoing the words Wren had spoken during the funeral rites nearly six years ago now. *A mosaic of contradictions, a blend of darkness and light, and as such, she mirrored the very heart of humanity...* Perhaps that could be said of all the Embervales.

Wren placed her hand over Thea's and said a final farewell to Anya. "Rest now, sister." The words felt different this time—less like goodbye and more like permission. Permission to look toward tomorrow, to do what needed to be done.

A layer of dust coated the workbenches within the alchemy workshop of Thezmarr. Without the laws preventing women from wielding blades, without Farissa's formidable presence, alchemy had been all but abandoned at the fortress. From the state of the room, Wren wasn't sure when it had last been used. There was something liberating about that, though, and as she wiped down the surfaces and opened her travel case, she breathed her first easy breath in a while.

It wasn't long before the desk was covered in her notebooks and equipment, in her various vials and pouches of herbs, the chaos a familiar comfort to her. Gods, how she wished Sam and Ida were there with her, as they had been so many times before, brainstorming the problems of a particular tincture, or discussing the optimum measurements of a potion. She could use their wisdom now.

The poison inside Torj was gaining ground, and though she was making progress on her cure, she wasn't moving fast enough. There had been no word from the rosarians she'd contacted, and she didn't expect any help from them now, even after sending additional ravens detailing her change in location. For this, she was on her own. And so she worked, hunched over her shallow glass dishes brimming with blood and silvertide roses, praying to the Furies that she'd find the cure to save her soul-bonded.

CHAPTER 29
TORJ

"Thezmarr was, and always will be, the home of the protectors of the midrealms."
—A History of Thezmarr

Torj had lost count of how many times he had sat in Thezmarr's war room over the years. First as a young shieldbearer taking meeting notes, then as a Guardian relaying messages from abroad, and eventually as a Warsword strategizing for battle himself. But only one moment in this room stood out to him in a sea of others...

"Where's Wren?"

Gods, he'd been bound to her even then. He remembered the day as though it were yesterday: stuck in another post-war council, debating the state of the midrealms, when he'd realized she was no longer at the table. He'd known instantly where she'd gone, and what she'd gone to do. For all his Furies-given power, he hadn't been fast enough to stop her. He'd raced through the corridors to find her in the alchemy workshop with the imprisoned former Guild Master, a teapot sitting innocently between them.

Now, he gazed upon a replica of that same teapot sitting proudly on a shelf, and across the table from him, Wren gave him a gentle smile.

Any regrets, Bear Slayer? she asked into his mind.

He bit back his answering grin. *Not one, Embers.*

"Alright," Audra called from the head of the table. "Now that everyone has gathered, we need to make our positions clear as to the upcoming conflict."

Torj looked around to find an array of familiar faces looking to the Guild Master: Wren, Wilder, Thea, Cal, and Kipp, who had all been here before, as well as Zavier, Dessa, and Darian.

"For my part," Audra continued, "Delmira has the full support of Thezmarr behind it. We do not suffer tyrants, and will not stand by as another attempts to usurp a trueborn heir of the midrealms. Our forces stand at one thousand strong."

Torj said nothing, but he felt the unease ripple through the room. Lucian's spies had relayed the enemy numbers, and by all accounts Silas' army was cited at five thousand— possibly more, depending on how many poor folks had succumbed to the howler-like state of bloodlust. Wren would need a lot more support if they were to stand a fighting chance, even with Lucian's bannermen and Thezmarr's best among them.

"How many will join the march from Thezmarr to Delmira?" Torj asked.

Audra bowed her head in acknowledgment. "Our Guardians make up three hundred of our total numbers and are stationed across the midrealms, so they will gather and meet us in Delmira. However, we have seven hundred shieldbearers either here at Thezmarr or within a day's ride —this is the force that will leave from the fortress with you."

"Shieldbearers..." Darian said slowly. "Aren't they your novices? Your amateurs? I mean no disrespect, Guild Master, but we need *warriors*, not students, in this war."

"A Thezmarrian shieldbearer may be young or inexperienced," Thea cut in, "but they would still be far more battle-trained than the average foot soldier within the People's Vanguard or Silas' army of howlers. They can hold their own."

Audra nodded. "Exactly. And you'll find that the shieldbearers under my tutelage are a breed of their own," she added proudly.

"What about the Warswords?" Darian asked. "How many do we have and where are they?"

"With the deaths of Cahira, Vernich the Bloodletter, and Ashlyn Graves, we now have ten Warswords remaining, which is far more than we had in the previous war," Audra replied. "And I will say this... Graves was widely known as the backbone of the new era of Warswords. Her loyalty to the guild and its warriors was second to none. Thezmarr wants blood for her death, and for the deaths of Vernich and Cahira. My warriors are ready to fight."

That seemed to satisfy Darian. "Good."

"What of the other kingdoms?" Torj interjected. "What do they bring to the conflict?"

"As you know, Aveum suffered great losses during the shadow war, with one of the final battles fought on their doorstep. Even so, Queen Reyna has pledged seven hundred men to come to Delmira's defense. They march from the winter kingdom as we speak. Harenth is in a similar position in that it sustained great losses in the war, but there is also an understandable reluctance to trust a royal military after what King Artos did. As such, it has lost a great many to the efforts of the People's Vanguard. Regent Liora cites their army at one thousand, and vows that besides a small unit left behind to guard the capital, her men are on standby to march as soon as we establish a base in Delmira. She has also expressed her thanks for alerting her to the poisoning of the townsfolk of outer Hailford. It is being investigated as we speak."

"And what of King Leiko? Do we suspect any resistance from him?" Wren asked. "He hasn't exactly been forthcoming..."

Audra grimaced. "King Leiko has his own scars from the shadow war that make him difficult to work with, I'll admit. However, I received word from him yesterday that his army of twelve hundred will come to our aid. They, too, march as we speak."

Darian cleared his throat. "And with the newly forged alliances that Elwren and I have made in celebration of our union, we have one thousand men to offer to the cause."

Kipp looked up from the notes he'd been taking. "Which leaves our allied forces at just under five thousand to Silas' five... Not bad, considering the odds we've had in the past."

"Agreed," Thea said. "And having a bunch of angry Warswords on our side helps."

"And angry alchemists," Wren added.

"I think we can agree that *everyone's* fucking angry." Wilder huffed a hoarse laugh. "What about Talemir? And the shadow-touched? He said he'd send word."

Audra tensed. "I was brought a message by Drue's hawk the day before last. Despite their efforts, they have only managed to gather a force of thirty volunteers."

Torj's chest seized. He remembered Talemir's warning aboard *The Furies' Will* that he could make no promises, but... "Only thirty?" he asked quietly.

With a sigh, Audra stood. "Their kind was vilified badly during the last war. They were taken prisoner, tortured, experimented on... and still they fought for us at the end. Talemir tells me that since the shadow war, their kind has not been accepted anywhere except within their own communities. Common folk of the midrealms still associate them with evil. Most want nothing to do with the broader world now. I can't say I blame them."

Resigned silence fell across the table, and Torj felt like a prize idiot for not seeing it more clearly sooner. Talemir had protected an entire people from darkness for years, only to be treated like dirt after fighting for the midrealms. He had a shadow-touched son to protect from the world, too.

"Shit," Torj muttered.

Audra nodded. "An apt summary. From here it's a matter of logistics—which travel routes for which forces; gathering any final information on Silas' battalions, as well as supplies not only for the journey, but the garrisons we need to set up along the way. We'll reconvene on that tomorrow."

Wren caught his eye. *Thea said she wants to talk to me. I'll see you later?*

If we can manage to sneak away, that sounds good, Embers.

As everyone stood and made for the door, Wilder approached Torj. "Did you know it was that bad with the shadow-touched?" he asked.

Torj shook his head. "No. I knew they kept to themselves, but I just thought it was because that's what they've always done. He never said anything to you?"

"Not a word," Wilder said. "I was going to write to him tonight anyway. I'll talk to him, see if there's anything we can do."

"Thanks," Torj replied, dipping his chin to Wilder as his friend clapped him on the shoulder and left.

Poor Tal, Torj thought, rubbing his aching temples. The Warsword once known as the Prince of Hearts had given everything to protect the midrealms, becoming part wraith himself in one of the earlier battles, and continued to fight against the darkness ever since. With his shadow-touched airborne units, he'd been instrumental in the war, as had his wife Drue, whose knowledge of the sun orchids had helped defeat the monsters. And this was how the midrealms repaid him? Gods, when was the last time they had seen true justice done?

Torj's gaze fell to the unassuming teapot on the shelf, and for the first time since setting foot back on Thezmarr soil, he laughed.

CHAPTER 30
WREN

"Herb lore teaches us that power resides not in what is loudly proclaimed, but in what is quietly understood."
—From Root to Petal: Understanding Plants and Their Properties

"*What?*" Wren stared at her sister, convinced she'd misheard her. The word echoed off the stone walls of the dining hall, bouncing between the towering monuments. But Thea was smiling, and there was a light in her eyes Wren hadn't seen since before the world had grown dark again.

"Wilder proposed," she repeated, her expression faltering. She rubbed the scars on the backs of her hands, a habit she'd had since childhood.

Wren felt fresh tears track down her cheeks as she

hauled Thea into her arms, squeezing her hard. "He finally did it," she mumbled into Thea's braid. "At long last."

"You knew?" Thea exclaimed.

Wren pulled back from the embrace, grinning like a lunatic. "Of course I knew. He's been telling anyone who will listen for half a decade that you'd be his wife one day." She hugged her sister again. "I'm so happy for you, Thea. Congratulations."

"I'm sorry it's come at such a shit time—"

"Don't you *dare* be sorry for this. It's wonderful. It's a light in the dark. It's a promise of a future. Something to fight for." The words tumbled from her lips uncontrollably, but Wren meant every single one.

"But everything is so up in the air. And you've got your stupid charade with Darian, and—"

"Don't *ever* be sorry. Don't let anything stand in the way of the happiness that you deserve, sister."

Wren hugged her again, and when she drew back, silver lined Thea's eyes.

Nudging her with an elbow to lighten the mood, Wren asked, "What about the whole *Warswords don't have wives* thing?"

The sisters ambled to where the rest of their company was gathered around a buffet spread.

"Fuck it." Thea grinned, grabbing a plate. "Who's gonna stop us?"

Wren had been convinced that Thezmarr would never be home to a happy memory again, but Thea and Wilder's news swept through the fortress like wildfire, and with it came an infectious energy that Wren hadn't experienced since before the shadow war.

The marriage of two Warswords, two heroes of the midrealms, was all anyone could talk about. Even though the days were taken up with council meetings, correspondence, and managing weaponry supplies and rations, Wren felt lighter than she had in a long time, and the quiet moments in between battle planning were beautiful. Thea was *happy*. And if nothing else, that was something good in the world.

"We want to get married here," Thea declared over breakfast one morning.

Wren wasn't surprised. Thezmarr had always been special to her sister. "When?" she asked, bringing her cup to her lips.

"The day after next—"

Wren spat her tea across her plate, choking. "What? *Are you mad?*"

Thea gave her a sheepish smile. "You're not the first person to ask that, but no. I want to be his wife, Wren. I don't want to waste any more time. Another war is upon us... This might be the only chance we get."

"Thea—" Wren started to protest.

But Thea shook her head. "Don't deny it. Besides, it's very *us*, isn't it? Getting married at a warrior fortress before a battle?"

A laugh bubbled from Wren's lips. "That's true..."

"You haven't heard the best part," Kipp interjected, turning from his conversation with Cal on the opposite side of the table. He put a hand on his chest proudly. "I get to perform the ceremony."

"You *what?*" Wilder barked from the far end.

Thea grimaced, shooting her husband-to-be an apologetic look. "I *may* have lost a bet with him a few years ago..."

Wilder stared at her in disbelief, shaking his head, but Wren burst out laughing. Her sister and the Hand of Death were getting married. And Kipp would be the one to do it. It was perfect.

The ludicrous joyful feeling lasted for most of the day, even as Wren sat in meeting after meeting with Darian, discussing Silas' supposed inner circle of influence.

"It's made up of alchemists and military commanders he brought with him from beyond the former Veil border. That is where his warfare tactics stem from, and it is these men, of whom there are fifty or so, who organize the rest of his forces," the nobleman told her, reading from a letter stamped with the Devereux sigil.

But when Darian suggested yet another gathering in the war room, Wren finally lost her patience, and instead of justifying her decisions, she found herself retracing an old, familiar path to the herb garden in the Bloodwoods.

There, she fell into old habits, crouching down in the dirt and gathering supplies. The familiar scents of rosemary and sage filled her nostrils, mingling with the aroma of fresh sap from the trees that gave the Bloodwoods their name. Her fingers remembered the patterns—which stems to pinch, which leaves to pluck, what foliage needed the keen blade of her harvesting knife. Healing herbs, fighting herbs, herbs for sleep and strength and clarity of mind. They would need them all before long.

All the alchemists were gone from Thezmarr, and so the garden was wilder now, far less tended than in her memories. Chamomile had spread beyond its beds, tiny white flowers dotting the path like stars fallen to earth. Nightshade and wolfsbane twisted together in dark corners —beautiful and deadly, just like the women who had once cared for this place. Sam and Ida, even Thea for a time.

"I thought I'd find you here," Torj called out as he strode into the clearing. The late afternoon light caught his silver hair and the iron of his hammer, and for a moment, Wren was reliving the first time they'd met in these very woods. Her heart lifted at the sight of him. It felt like an age since they'd shared a private moment together, even just a quiet aside. Gods, she missed him. She missed his sturdy presence, his gentle words, his lightning-kissed touch. The garden seemed to hold its breath, remembering other meetings, other touches.

But he wasn't on his own. Zavier and Dessa followed close behind him, their boots crushing herbs and releasing bursts of fragrance into the air.

When Torj reached her, he didn't touch her—though everything in her ached for it. Instead, he simply said quietly, "Even if I can't be with you, I didn't want you to be alone."

Zavier dropped to his knees beside her, immediately identifying some of the herbs she'd gathered. "Bloodroot and feverfew," he said, examining her pile. "Planning for the worst?"

"Always." Wren managed a wry smile. "Though I was thinking we might need something more festive first..." She held up a sprig of rosemary.

"Isn't that rosemary?" Torj interjected with a frown.

Wren fought the smile tempting her lips. "Someone's been studying."

"In case you haven't noticed, I've spent the better part of a year at an alchemy academy," Torj replied dryly. "Not that I'm complaining," he added.

Wren did smile then. "Long ago, rosemary was often woven into bridal crowns... A symbol of fidelity and remembrance."

Dessa nodded enthusiastically. "My mother sewed it into her veil..." She paused. "I don't think Thea will have a veil, do you?"

Wren snorted. "No, I don't think that's likely, Dess."

"What about this?" Torj held out a stem of lavender, its purple floret bright and aromatic. "Does this have a meaning?"

"Some say it signifies love and devotion," she told him quietly.

His throat bobbed. "Right."

"A warrior's wedding needs a warrior's garland," Dessa declared, settling on Wren's other side. She pulled a leatherbound book from her satchel—one Wren recognized from Thezmarr's library; one she had studied as a girl. It made her heart seize. She'd thought everything in the library had been destroyed in the final battle. It was oddly moving to her that this, of all things, had been the item to survive.

Dessa forged on. "Your sister should have all of it—protection, strength, victory..."

"And love," Torj added softly, offering the alchemists the lavender he had gathered. "She should have that too."

Wren took it, her gaze falling to where the Warsword had placed a single sprig in the laces of his jerkin.

He watched them for a moment, his expression softening. "I'll leave you to your gardening, then." He turned to go, then paused. "Just... try not to poison anyone before the ceremony?"

"Wouldn't dream of it," Wren retorted, but Torj was already striding away.

As Wren returned to her harvesting, Dessa spread the book open between them. The pages were covered in flowing script, recipes and warnings intermingled with personal observations. "Look," she said, pointing to a particular entry. "A blessing wreath. We could adapt it..."

They worked in comfortable silence for a while, gathering, sorting, and weaving. It felt good to lose herself in the familiar rhythms, to let her hands remember what her mind sometimes wanted to forget.

"You know," Zavier said eventually, "there's something fitting about this. Collecting healing supplies and making a bridal crown in the same breath."

Wren looked up at the darkening sky, where the first stars were beginning to appear. "That's what we fought for last time," she replied softly. "Not just survival. The right to have moments like this, even in the dark."

CHAPTER 31
TORJ

"The strongest bonds between Warswords are forged not when standing shoulder to shoulder in triumph, but when lifting each other from the dust of defeat."
—The Warsword's Way

A message was waiting for Torj back at the fortress: *Northern training arena. Bring liquor.*

Beneath the scratchy handwriting was a sketch of a fox's head.

The strategist had a set of balls on him, alright. He was probably the only person Torj knew who would leave orders for a Warsword concerning drinks amid planning for battle.

"Fuck it." Torj stuffed the piece of parchment in his pocket before turning toward the steps to the cellar.

Soon after, he emerged with two bottles of wine in each hand and a flagon of fire extract wedged under his arm. If he knew anything about Kipp, it was that it was always better to be oversupplied. The fortress' private stock would have to do—and if anyone had complaints about him raiding it, they could take it up with his hammer.

The walk to the northern arena gave him too much time to think. About the war councils that morning. About *her*. About how fucking complicated everything had become. The bottles clinked with each step, a steady rhythm that matched the pounding in his head.

As he approached the arena, sounds carried on the wind —the clash of steel, grunts of exertion, and barked commands from below. *Shieldbearers*. He'd forgotten about the evening training sessions. The sound transported him back to his own days as a newcomer to the fortress, before titles and soul bonds and the weight of impossible choices. It was also where he had trained Cal, Kipp, and Thea in their early days... The unlikely trio had always been intent on getting into trouble.

The arena stood at the base of the black mountains, not just a clearing, but a space designed for watching bloody victories and defeats from above. It was surreal, standing at the vantage point and surveying the next generation of Thezmarrian warriors. There was one noticeable difference in this cohort... Women. For the first time in a long while, Torj saw how many women fighters there were in the ranks. Gone were the days of laws against women wielding blades; here they swung them with deadly precision and pride. Thea would be proud. In fact, she was probably down there somewhere amid the chaos. He made to step into view when a pebble struck his shoulder.

"Elderbrock, get your ass over here," came Kipp's whisper from a cluster of bushes above the training ground.

Torj ducked into the shadows, bottles clinking. "What in the midrealms are you doing up here hiding like a—"

The words died in his throat as he registered who exactly was huddled in the underbrush. Wilder sat cross-legged on a fallen log, his usual stern expression cracked by a lazy smile. And beside him, Talemir Starling lounged against a boulder, his wings draped out behind him, looking far too amused for a man of his status.

"Didn't think I'd miss my apprentice's wedding, did you?" he said with a grin.

Even Wilder's brother Malik was there, his dog Dax sprawled at his feet. And Cal, who, to Torj's knowledge, was *supposed* to be inspecting Thezmarr's long-range weapons supply, was sitting on the ground, scratching calculations in the dirt with a stick.

"Surprise," Kipp declared, reaching for one of the bottles. "The Hand of Death is getting married."

"I'm aware..." Torj handed over the wine, his gaze fixed on Wilder. "Though I didn't expect to be celebrating it while crouched in the bushes like common thieves."

"Those are baby shieldbearers down there," Talemir said, nodding toward the arena. "Wouldn't do for them to see their superiors drunk on duty."

"We're not *on duty*," Wilder protested, but there was no heat in it. Just that same stupid, happy smile that looked foreign on his battle-hardened face.

"Speak for yourself," Cal muttered, still focused on whatever he was scratching in the dirt. "The bloody

214

weapons master has some of us calculating catapult trajectories."

Malik reached over and carefully, deliberately, drew his boot through Cal's calculations.

"You utter—" Cal started, but Kipp shoved a bottle into his hands.

"Tonight," he announced, "we're not strategists or Warswords or whatever the fuck else. Tonight, we're just..." He waved his hand vaguely, searching for the word.

"A bunch of idiots getting drunk?" Torj finished for him, his knees clicking as he bent to take a place beside Malik with a groan.

Kipp's grin only widened. "Exactly!"

"I'll drink to that," Talemir said, lifting a flagon.

"You'll drink to anything," Wilder quipped.

Talemir smirked. "Here's to you, apprentice."

"You don't think you could let that lie for one evening?" Wilder rolled his eyes and accepted a bottle of wine from Torj.

"Not a chance. Not as my not-so-young-anymore apprentice readies for his big day," the winged Warsword teased.

Wilder gave Talemir a flat look and drank straight from the bottle. "I rescind your invitation."

Torj laughed, the sound startling Dax, the dog at Malik's feet. It had been years since Torj had seen him and his owner last... Dax had gray whiskers around his maw now, and Malik had similar streaks of silver through his otherwise dark hair.

"How are you, Mal?" Torj asked quietly.

As always, Malik simply smiled. He had been non-verbal

for decades now, ever since he was injured during a wraith battle in Naarva. He had been known as Malik the Shieldbreaker before then, Wilder's indomitable older brother, a giant among men.

"He's causing as much trouble as always," Talemir answered with a fond smile at his friend. "He's managed to come out to Ciraun once or twice, mainly to cause chaos with Ryland and leave Drue and me to pick up the pieces."

Wilder laughed into his drink. "What are friends for?"

Torj surveyed the group of men with affection and took a sip of fire extract. "I think we're focusing on the wrong Warsword, given the point of this... celebration."

Wilder groaned. "Can we not make a big deal—"

But his protests only encouraged Torj. "Is it true that when you first met Thea, you shot an arrow at her head?"

Talemir choked on his drink. "What?"

"Ah, yes," Kipp said fondly, taking a swig from his half-empty bottle. "How every sweeping love story begins..."

"She still agreed to marry me," Wilder replied smugly.

"Only after she knocked you on your ass several times during the years in between," Kipp added gleefully.

Wilder shrugged. "And what a privilege it was."

Cal made a retching sound as he scanned the grinning faces of Wilder, Torj, and Talemir. "You're all insufferable."

Kipp shot him a look of outrage. "How dare you—"

"Not you, you prick. All the lovestruck warriors!" Cal exclaimed.

Torj didn't have the heart to point out that the woman he loved was currently publicly engaged to another man.

"It's my wedding tomorrow. I'm supposed to be lovestruck," Wilder argued.

But Kipp put a soothing hand on Cal's shoulder, nodding sagely. "I'm right there with you, Flaming Arrow. But we're free men! The world is at our feet—"

"Then why don't you head down there and show the shieldbearers a thing or two?" Torj interjected, motioning to the drills underway in the arena below.

Kipp appeared scandalized. "Are you suggesting that we interrupt the invaluable training of those beautiful women down there?"

"No," Torj told him evenly, masking any note of amusement that might slip through. "I'm suggesting that you take your griping and turn it into something productive by contributing to their education. And they're not all women, though it shows who you're paying attention to."

"I think he's trying to get rid of us," Cal muttered.

"That too," Torj replied.

But Kipp dismissed him with a wave, already tugging Cal down the hill. "Come on, Callahan, let's leave the old men to reminisce. Isn't that Emilia from the kitchens down there? Who knew she could swing a sword!"

Torj shook his head with a huff of laughter, glancing at Wilder. "Sometimes, it's like no time at all has passed with those two."

Wilder rested back on his elbows. "I can't work out if they make me feel younger or older."

"Older," Torj replied. "*Definitely* older."

From below came the sound of Kipp's distinctive laugh, followed by Cal's outraged cry. Torj didn't need to look to know they were already causing chaos among the shieldbearers.

"To think," Talemir mused, his gaze settling on his

217

former apprentice, "the great Hand of Death has been tamed at last."

Malik's shoulders shook in silent laughter, but Wilder just smiled that same peaceful smile. "Not tamed. Just... found something worth fighting for beyond the blade. Someone."

The words hit Torj like a physical blow. He took another drink of fire extract, letting it burn away the image of Wren dressed in Devereux finery, standing beside his childhood friend. Instead he pictured her in her own splendor as a crown was placed atop her head.

"Speaking of fighting." Talemir's wings rustled as he straightened, suddenly serious. "Tomorrow you'll be married, but the day after..."

"The day after, we face whatever comes," Wilder finished firmly. "As we always have: together."

Malik reached over and gripped his brother's shoulder. Even without words, his meaning was clear: *always*.

As the crescent moon glowed above the black mountains, casting long shadows across the torchlit training grounds below, Torj thought about how some bonds—whether forged in battle, brotherhood, or love— ran deeper than any darkness that tried to break them.

And so, he raised his bottle. "To whatever comes, then."

"To whatever comes," his brothers echoed.

CHAPTER 32
WREN

"It has always been rumored that upon the completion of the Great Rite, the Furies required the Warswords to vow never to marry. This has always been hearsay."
—A History of Thezmarr

"S top fidgeting," Wren hissed at her sister as they stood in front of a mirror in Farissa's old quarters.

"I'm not fidgeting," Thea bit back, dropping her hands by her sides, only to pick them up again and wring her fingers a moment later. "Do you think the braid is too..."

"Too what?" Wren asked, amused. "Too warrior-like? Too Althea Embervale?" She reached for the flowers they'd threaded through her sister's bronze hair. "The braid is perfect. *You're* perfect."

Thea sighed as Wren tied the laces of her dress. A familiar gesture made strange by circumstance—quiet moments like these had always been shared before battles, not weddings.

It was a thought Thea seemed to share as she asked, "Why in the midrealms did I let Dessa talk me into wearing this? A Warsword in white? It feels wrong."

Wren snorted. "Like a poisoner wearing a crown?"

Thea grinned at that. "We're breaking all kinds of rules, aren't we?"

"I've never known you to follow a rule in your life, Thee."

Her sister barked a laugh. "True enough."

It was just the pair of them getting ready for the ceremony, as Thea had requested. Wren had been surprised that she hadn't wanted Cal and Kipp there, but Thea insisted that she'd see enough of them, especially Kipp, as he presided smugly over her and Wilder's vows.

It was only when Thea spoke again that Wren realized why she hadn't wanted her other friends present.

"What if I can't be both? A wife and a Warsword?" she asked quietly, glancing up at Wren with a rare vulnerability shining in her celadon eyes.

"Thea," Wren said gently. "You're the one who taught me we don't have to choose. Woman, warrior... Warsword, lightning wielder—"

"But—"

Wren gripped her sister by the shoulders. "You are allowed to be happy. You are allowed to revel in joy, even when all else is uncertain," she told her. "*Especially* when all else is uncertain."

Thea stared at her, and Wren took the opportunity to reach for the gift she'd brought, wrapped in plain linen. She pressed it into Thea's hands.

"What's this?" Thea blinked at the small bundle, brow furrowed.

Wren laughed. "Well, you've got something old..." She tugged on the leather strap tying the end of Thea's braid. "Something borrowed..." She gestured to the dress. "And now... for something deadly." She winked.

Thea unwrapped the fabric, and her eyes widened at the delicate piece of steel she found.

"Wren..." she breathed, astonishment etched across her face.

It was an ornate throwing star, made of the finest Naarvian steel.

"I treated the points with my strongest incapacitating potion," Wren explained. "There's also a pouch for it, made from the leather of your first sword grip."

Thea shook her head in disbelief. "How did you...?"

"Kipp helped. Don't ask how he got it. I'm not sure either of us want to know, but you didn't exactly give us much notice."

"It's beautiful," Thea murmured, testing the star's weight between her fingers. "Thank you."

"Well..." Wren blinked back unexpected tears. "You are the Shadow of Death, after all. We figured you needed something to represent that part of you on your wedding day."

Thea laughed, the sound catching slightly in her throat. "When did you become so wise, little sister?"

"I've *always* been wise," Wren told her. "Someone had to balance out your recklessness, remember?" She straightened Thea's dress one final time. "Ready?"

Thea sheathed the throwing star and secured it beneath her skirts before she squared her shoulders and nodded. "Ready."

Thea had chosen the spot: the clifftops of Thezmarr, where she had first clapped eyes on Wilder Hawthorne so many years ago, where she had ended the shadow war with him at her side.

Wren knew its meaning, and she felt nothing but pride as Malik escorted her sister down the makeshift aisle. The Shieldbreaker moved slowly, supporting himself with a cane on one side, while Thea looped her arm through his on the other, but he was beaming.

"Classic Mal." Talemir grinned beside Wren. "He loves a good wedding."

Wren couldn't stop the lump forming in her throat at the sight of her sister in a wedding gown, a retired Warsword on one side, his aging canine on the other. Dax seemed just as proud as his master, trotting at Thea's feet, his tail wagging hard.

When they reached Wilder, Malik hugged his brother, and a few muffled laughs sounded from the small crowd as he practically dwarfed Wilder. When he hugged Thea, he lifted her bodily from the ground, which only resulted in more laughter.

Talemir chuckled and stepped forward, taking Malik's free arm and guiding him to the seat they'd brought for him. Wren blinked back her tears at the tenderness between the two men.

At last, Wilder took Thea's hands in his and smiled. Wren's heart seized at that smile—not begrudging Thea her happiness, not for a second, but... in the light of such love, she wished that she could give the Warsword at her own side the same public acknowledgment. That it wasn't another man's ring on her finger.

Kipp clearing his throat brought her out of her thoughts. "I'm sure I'm not the only one who is relieved to find themselves here at last," he said with a smile. "Finally, we get to witness the union of Wilder Hawthorne, the Hand of Death, and Althea Embervale, the Shadow of Death. They have asked me to keep this short and sweet—and devoid of my usual charming humor..."

A laugh bubbled from Wren's lips—a tall order for Kipp indeed.

"So, I will simply say this," Kipp continued, his smile warm and genuine as he looked from Wilder to Thea. "It's been an honor and a privilege witnessing you both fall in love, watching you overcome adversity, both in wartime and in times of peace. The Furies made you for one another, and what an absolute joy it is to be here at your wedding today."

Wren wished that she could give Torj the same sort of celebration, the celebration he deserved.

"Wilder, your vows, if you please?" Kipp said.

It was like the rest of the world did not exist for the Hand of Death. He had eyes only for Thea as he spoke. "I had a vision of you when I was held prisoner in the Scarlet Tower all those years ago..." He drew a shaky breath. "It was not of darkness and torment, or the war that was unfolding around us at the time. It was of *this*." He took a ring from his pocket and held it out. "It was a vision of slipping a simple silver band over your finger, of calling you my wife."

Wren saw Thea's lip quiver, but Wilder continued.

"Thea, no amount of time with you will ever be enough. Am I worthy of you? No. But I will spend the rest of my days trying to be, with everything that I have. We have belonged together ever since you spied on me atop these very cliffs. I have longed for the day I could call you my wife, and now you are... I love you, and I always will."

Wren's tears spilled as Thea's did, and the sniffling around her told her she wasn't the only one feeling the onslaught of emotions.

Wilder slid the ring on Thea's finger and smiled. "You're up, Princess."

Thea's answering smile was radiant. "Ever since I met you, life has been one giant adventure. As your apprentice, as your friend, as your enemy, as your lover, there hasn't been a dull moment. We have been through so much together, and apart, not to mention when I hunted you across the midrealms for a year... But my world does not exist unless you're in it. I love you with all my heart, from the depths of my soul, and promise that I always will, until the last of my days."

Thea slipped a larger version of the same silver band onto Wilder's finger, and they beamed at one another.

"Well, not that I haven't already seen enough of this, but... you may now kiss the bride!" Kipp declared.

Wilder swept Thea up in his arms, oblivious to the rose petals that were being thrown around them, and kissed her soundly.

As Wren palmed away her tears, a warm presence

pressed against her left side. The familiar scent of black cedar and oakmoss wrapped around her senses, and a large hand covered hers, just for a moment.

And then the Bear Slayer was gone, off to congratulate the happy couple.

CHAPTER 33
TORJ

"A warrior's second can count for everything."
—Bear Slayer, Warsword of Thezmarr

It was just like Wilder and Thea to get married on the brink of war, and Torj loved them all the more for it. As Kipp had said, they were made for each other—steel meeting steel in a fiery blaze. They moved together through the throng of well-wishers, fluid like one body of water through the valleys of the realms. They were always touching, always together, speaking a silent language only the two of them understood. Radiating joy, they laughed and kissed and embraced their loved ones with absolute certainty. Torj only wished he could be so bold, so resilient in the face of all that loomed ahead.

He had watched the tears stream down Wren's face as the Warswords exchanged vows, unable to draw her into his arms, unable to press a kiss to her brow. Gods, had it made him ache. And amid the festivities of a real wedding, it was impossible not to think back to when he and Wren had played the role of husband and wife. It hadn't mattered that it was all just a ruse; laying claim to her with that word for the world to see had felt so right.

He gripped his goblet to keep the tremor in his hand at bay and stayed to the edges of the celebrations, not wanting to detract from the happy couple. Wilder was right... This was something to fight for.

The scent of spring rain and jasmine came to life around him as the crowd parted, allowing Wren through, that intoxicating fragrance thoroughly tormenting him as she drew nearer.

What are you doing, Embers? he called to her through their bond.

The corner of her mouth twitched as she replied, *Coming to talk to you, Bear Slayer.*

As much as Torj wanted to be with her, they couldn't risk Lucian's wrath—not now, not when they had come this far. *That's not a good idea. Lucian—*

There's nothing untoward about two old friends chatting at a wedding, she dismissed him.

Torj didn't take his eyes off the happy couples swaying to the music before him. *Old friends... Is that what we are?*

You know exactly what we are, came her answer as she stood beside him.

"Dancing on a clifftop..." Wren mused aloud with a shake of her head. "It's a very Thea thing to do."

"You've been known to jump into danger every now and

then, too," Torj told her quietly. "Perhaps it's an Embervale thing."

Wren chuckled. "Along with a proclivity for Warswords, apparently..."

Tensing, Torj glanced around for Devereux Senior and his lackeys. No doubt someone had their eyes on them already. "Don't let anyone else hear you say that."

They continued to watch the couples dancing, Torj sipping from his drink and trying to hide the shaking in his hand again. His attention drifted to Thea and Wilder once more. Their arms were around each other, Wilder lifting Thea from the ground. "They look happy," he said softly.

"They deserve it." Wren had followed his gaze to where they moved together, their warrior's grace and agility just as suited to dancing as to battle.

Wren's fingers brushed his arm, her words blooming in his mind.

Meet me before dawn. There's a stream past the alchemist's grove in the Bloodwoods.

We can't, he told her, fixing his stare anywhere but on her. *We won't get away with Dessa drugging Lucian twice.*

Who said anything about that? she asked. *Meet me.*

It's too dangerous, Torj told her. *Don't make this harder than it has to be, Embers.*

From across the crowd, Darian was motioning to her, a charming smile gracing his handsome face, and beside him Lord Lucian and Lord Briar were deep in conversation.

The next words Torj spoke aloud were gentle, but firm. "You should go. Your fiancé needs you."

Wren didn't say goodbye as she was swallowed up by the festive crowd, as though she had merely exchanged a few polite words with a man who was once her guard before returning to her future husband.

She didn't look back as Darian slid an arm around her waist when she reached him. Torj could see why people were smitten with the match; the Delmirian princess and the Lord of Larkwood Valley made a handsome, impressive couple.

And just as he was about to descend into a spiral of dark thoughts, Wren's voice came back to him through the soul bond.

You'd best meet me by the stream come morning, Bear Slayer, or I'll be all alone...

Though he couldn't risk meeting her gaze while she danced with Darian, he knew Wren was smiling—not for the nobleman, but for him.

You wicked woman, he replied.

My poor Torj... You have no idea.

CHAPTER 34
WREN

"A true soul bond manifests not as possibility but as inevitability
—as certain as the dawn following the night."
—Tethers and Magical Bonds Throughout History

"What in the midrealms are you doing?" Torj's angry voice hissed over the sound of the babbling stream.

The pre-dawn air was crisp as Wren crouched beside the water, dragging a wet washcloth over her neck. Beyond the Bloodwoods, the bannermen were camped in the Plains of Orax, but around her, the grass was shrouded in early morning mist, and a cluster of ancient willows with curtain-like branches swept down to the brook. They provided privacy from the nearby camp, while moss-covered boulders created natural walls, enclosing the area.

Taking a steadying breath, Wren rinsed the scrap of

material and brought it to her throat and collarbone this time.

"Wren?" Torj clearly wasn't happy. "I said, what are you doing?"

"Bathing," she replied bluntly, dragging the cloth over her chest. "What's it look like, Bear Slayer?"

"Alone? Unguarded?"

Wren made a show of shrugging. "I told you to meet me. You are my protector, after all..."

Her words had the desired effect.

"Have you lost your wits, woman?" Torj stormed toward her, his heavy boots crushing the damp leaf litter, his nostrils flaring as his gaze dropped to her shift, where her hard nipples showed through the thin fabric. "And in nothing but a slip?" His voice carried the commanding authority he'd shown back in the war room, but underneath it, she heard the fear—not of her inability to defend herself, but of losing her. It made her want to both soothe him and challenge him further, to remind him that she was no delicate flower to be protected. She was his match in every way that mattered.

Wren bunched the hem of the garment to reveal her thigh, where his dagger was firmly secured. "Well, not just a slip..."

Torj swore. "You're going to kill me long before this damn poison does, Embers. Get back to the fortress before I do something stupid." Even angry, his movements weren't as swift as they should be—the poison's work already showing in the slight stiffness of his stride. It made her heart clench, made her need to touch him, to prove he was still here, still hers.

"Perhaps I want you to do something stupid," she teased lightly.

The warrior licked his lips as he surveyed her, his gaze darkening as he drank in the sight of her bare legs and taut nipples. "Believe me, my blood's sure as fuck not pumping to my brain right now, so it's inevitable if you don't move that beautiful ass..."

Wren squeezed the washcloth, allowing water to run down her front, turning her shift transparent. "You seem to have a thing for my ass, Warsword."

Cursing again, the Bear Slayer ran his fingers through his hair. "You haven't tormented me enough?" he rasped. "I'm hanging on by a thread here."

Wren closed the gap between them and palmed him through his leathers. "I don't want you to hang on," she told him. "I want you to let go. You *need* to let go."

Torj jerked beneath her touch, his cheeks turning pink. "You know what I need, do you, Embers?"

"Yes," she said simply, and she freed his cock.

"Fuck," he groaned as her hand wrapped around him. "This is a bad idea..."

Above them, the willow branches swayed, creating shifting patterns of shadow and light across his face as he watched her with darkened eyes. The stream's constant rhythm matched their ragged breathing.

"It's the best idea I've had all week, Bear Slayer," she quipped, before she fell to her knees in the damp soil.

She had seen how tightly wound he was, had seen how his dark gaze had followed her and Darian yesterday. The way his jaw clenched when the nobleman touched her arm or danced with her, the raw possession in his eyes that sent heat pooling in her belly. She needed him to remember that the games of royal politics didn't change what they shared. Didn't undo the words they'd said to one another. That beneath the titles of heir and Warsword was something primal and unshakeable: they were soul bonded, and would be until their final breaths.

"I want to remind you who you belong to, Warsword," she told him, blowing a stream of cool air over the wet tip of his shaft.

"There's no question of that," he replied hoarsely.

"Good." Wren kissed the tip of his cock. "I'm going to need you to come hard and fast for me, then..."

"As my queen commands," he managed, his voice rough but still carrying that note of deference that made her pulse quicken. Even like this, with his cock on her lips and his control slipping, he acknowledged her power over him—not just as a ruler, but as the woman who held his heart.

Wren ran her tongue from base to tip, before she swallowed him down.

The Warsword towering above her stifled a moan as she took the full length of him in her mouth, and she could feel his powerful thighs trembling. Her hand reached between them to cup his balls, massaging them gently as she swirled her tongue over the crown of him.

"Fuck," he muttered. "Fuck, Wren—"

She hummed around him, and his hands shot into her hair, guiding her motions over him. The cool air against her wet shift made her shiver, a counterpoint to the heat of him on her tongue. Somewhere above, a morning bird began its song, but she was lost to everything except the taste of him, the sounds escaping him competing with the stream's endless murmur.

"Furies save me, Embers... You take me so well."

His praise sent a bolt of desire straight to her clit, and she moved her hand between her legs to ease the ache there.

"Gods," Torj managed. "You're perfect. You're the most beautiful thing I've ever seen. I fucking love watching you touch yourself. I love *you*."

His tumbling words washed over Wren as she took him deep in her throat, her heart clenching at the raw note in his voice. He gave her everything—his vulnerability, his strength, his complete devotion. She moaned around him, trying to pour all her feelings into the way she pleasured him, into the bond that linked them. How many more times would she hear those words? How many more dawns would they share? The poison flowing through Torj's veins haunted her waking moments—an hourglass counting down their remaining time together. They only had the moments they stole for themselves, and when each hour felt like sand slipping through her fingers, she would take advantage of every single one.

A low rumble of need escaped Torj, and the sound had her spreading her legs beneath her, increasing the pressure on her clit at the same time, the sensation building from the base of her spine and rippling through her entire being.

"I'm going to come, Embers, I'm—" Torj's words were cut short as he shuddered, gripping her hair by the roots and emptying into her throat.

Wren moaned, swallowing the Warsword's climax down and seeing stars as her own orgasm hit her. With the taste of him on her lips, she cried out, not quite completely sated, because what she longed for most was to have him inside her, filling her, claiming her—

Torj eased himself from her mouth, panting as he tucked himself away and helped her to her feet, shaking his head in wonderment. "You are something else, Embers..."

"I'm *yours*," she told him fiercely as she turned back to the fortress. "And don't you dare forget it."

CHAPTER 35

TORJ

"The archives of every kingdom tell the same story: war ends only long enough for the banners to change, and for its people to forget the scars of their forefathers."
—The Midrealms Chronicles

War waited for no one, which meant as dawn broke over Thezmarr, their company was saddled and ready to depart. The morning air was brisk, the dew-kissed grass surrounding the corral sparkled beneath the early morning sun, and for a moment, Torj was reminded of a far simpler time. A time where he woke at the same hour every day, where he trained until his shirt was drenched in sweat, where he tended to horses in that same corral, and ran through drills with shieldbearers over and over. There had been a rhythm to life back then, one that he missed in the face of all this unknown.

Talemir grasped his hand in a firm shake, his wings

spread behind him, ready to take flight. "I'll see you in Delmira, Bear Slayer. I'm sorry I can't offer more support."

"You're doing everything you can, Tal. You've given so much already. We're lucky to have you at all," Torj replied. "Fly safe."

The Shadow Prince nodded. "Send me your position as soon as you have it."

"Will do."

A second later, a powerful gust of wind blasted through their ranks as Talemir took to the skies, his large wings casting shadows along the cliffs.

Audra brought her horse up alongside Torj's stallion. "You're in command," she told him, with no room for compromise in her tone. "I want you to set up garrisons along the way, establish patrol routes—"

"We don't have the numbers to do that," Torj replied. "If we leave behind units to oversee the crossroads and create defense perimeters, we won't have enough in our core force."

Audra folded her arms over her chest. "We're yet to be joined by Aveum, Harenth, and Tver's armies."

Torj shook his head. "Something tells me the aid we receive from King Leiko will be underwhelming. From what I understand, he's not pleased with the recent turn of events..." He glanced at Wren and Darian, who were mounting their own horses.

"His Majesty forgets he owes his life and crown to Elwren. And before her, to the Warswords and Guardians of Thezmarr coming to his defense during the attack on his castle. I'll make sure he remembers," Audra said. "I'll rejoin you in Delmira. Send word to Harenth when you establish a stronghold."

Torj nodded stiffly. "We intend to gather at Wren's old cottage and wait for the rest of the Devereux connections and rulers' armies to answer our call there. It's where the supply of silvertide roses is, and Wren knows the lay of the land well there."

"What then?" Audra asked.

"Once all our forces are joined and we have accurate reports on Silas' movements, we'll march on the capital."

Audra studied him for a moment before she said quietly, "I don't need to remind you that you're the unofficial queen's guard, do I?"

"Queen or not, I'll always protect her," he told the Guild Master.

"Good. Then you know what to do." With that, Audra turned her horse to address the company that had gathered in their wake. "Warsword Torj Elderbrock will be leading this campaign," she called out, her voice echoing down the ranks. "He has the full weight of Thezmarr behind him as we attack to unseat the usurper, Silas the Kingsbane, and return the Delmirian throne to its rightful heir, Elwren Embervale. Our loyalty is to the midrealms, *always*. We will not see another tyrant drag us into darkness. Ride well, Thezmarrians. Do our guild proud."

A cheer erupted from the throng as Audra pressed three fingers to her shoulder and dipped her head to Torj.

"See you in Delmira, Elderbrock," she said, before urging her horse toward the Mourner's Trail.

Wilder and Thea approached him on horseback, matching silver bands adorning their fourth fingers.

"Not exactly what I'd call a honeymoon," Torj said as they started down the trail.

Thea laughed. "It's *exactly* what I'd call a honeymoon. Adventure. Sleeping beneath the stars. Killing a tyrant or two..."

"That's my wife," Wilder murmured with a smile.

Torj rolled his eyes. "So in marriage you'll be even more insufferable?"

"We're a fucking delight, Bear Slayer," Wilder retorted. "But no, I came bearing shortcuts. There's a narrow mountain tunnel to the north that leads to Delmira. You don't have to take the Wesford Road."

Torj's brows shot up. "Since when?"

"Since always," Wilder replied. "I just never told anyone but Thea about it. We used it when she was still my apprentice. Silas won't know of it, and he'll be expecting us to travel across the main route."

Torj turned to their company behind him. Seven hundred shieldbearers and Lucian's three hundred bannermen... "Can it take us?"

"We'll have to go in single file for some parts, but yes," Thea answered. "It shouldn't be a problem unless Wren loses control of her magic between the mountains."

"You know that from experience?" Torj asked.

Thea shrugged. "A certain Warsword was being particularly frustrating during my last journey through there, but no mountains were brought down. Luckily."

Torj glanced over his shoulder, back to where Wren sat atop her mare. Dessa rode beside her and the two women were talking animatedly. He liked seeing her like that. There had been a time where he'd worried for her—so intent on isolating herself from the rest of the world, her heartbreak over Ida and Sam preventing her from developing new friendships... She had Dessa and Zavier now, as well as Thea, Wilder, Cal, and Kipp. No matter what happened to him, she'd always have them.

"It's going to be alright, Bear Slayer," Thea said quietly beside him.

"I didn't say it wouldn't be," he grunted.

"You didn't have to. Your face is like an open book," she replied.

"I don't believe that for a second," he argued. "I'm a seasoned Warsword, I can mask my—"

A snort sounded on his other side as Darian appeared on his thoroughbred stallion, likely worth Torj's weight in gold. "You mask nothing, brother," the nobleman said with an infuriating grin. "You wear your big heart on your sleeve. You always have."

"Have not," Torj muttered.

"I think the posh git is right," Thea declared.

Darian shot her a look of annoyance. "Glad to hear that's catching on."

"Not as glad as I am," Torj quipped. "Now, can we pick up the pace? I want to reach Delmira before the next century."

Thea laughed. "After you, Bear Slayer. We'll tell you when to turn off the trail."

And so, Torj led them north, to war.

CHAPTER 36
WREN

"Delmira was once the most fertile kingdom in all the midrealms. No one knew why, and yet when it fell to the darkness, some rejoiced."
—The Midrealms Chronicles

W ren's magic crackled in her veins as the unit moved into single file through the narrow mountain pass. She blamed Thea, who had warned her so incessantly about not using magic that now it was all she could think about. Things were already so on edge, so unstable within her, that it felt like walking a tightrope... One false move and instead of tumbling from the wire, she'd bring an entire mountain down around them.

No pressure, she thought darkly.

Voices echoed up the cavernous walls, and it smelled of damp. Wren rested her hand on the grip of the dagger Torj had given her. She didn't have him by her side to ground her, to tether her to the present, but something that had belonged to him was the next best thing.

Easy, Embers, his gravelly voice bloomed in her mind. *I can feel your magic simmering around us...*

I can't help it, she replied, squinting through the dark, trying to make out his broad shoulders ahead, his hammer strapped across his back.

You have more control, more strength than you realize, came his answer.

And how do you know that, Bear Slayer? she asked.

Because I know you.

I miss you. The words tumbled from her mind into his before she could stop them, and as they drifted down that tether between them, she felt the truth of them, the weight of them in her chest. Had it only been in the dark and early hours of that very morning that they'd been together by the stream? It felt like a lifetime ago. *Gods, I miss you.*

And I miss you, *Embers. You have no idea the torture it has been not to claim you for all to see. You're mine. Mind, body, and soul, and yet...*

And yet here we are, she finished for him. *Together but apart.*

For a moment, there was nothing but silence through the bond, and Wren worried that she'd said too much, been too hopeless—until his voice caused a shiver to wash across her skin.

How can I make it better? How can I serve you, my queen?

She relished the sound of him, her toes curling in her boots at the title on his tongue. He said it with reverence, and the promise of pleasure. *I need a distraction,* she told him.

Wren swore she could hear his laugh echo somewhere. *Shall I tell you a story? Or paint you a picture, Embers?*

Wren's grip tightened on her reins. *Paint me a picture.*

As my queen commands, he replied, his inner voice low and sultry now.

Wren didn't know how he did it, but suddenly he was there, as clear as day in her mind. He was naked, in all his war-honed glory—the bulging muscles shifting in his back, his sculpted backside clenching as he thrust...

Torj was showing her *them*. He had her bent over a table, and he was driving into her. She arched beneath him, lifting her hips to meet every stroke.

Wren watched them as though she were an outsider looking in, her heart hammering and her breath catching as Torj's massive hands spread her open, his thumb brushing an incredibly intimate part of her...

Has anyone ever touched you here, Embers?

No... She nearly moaned the word aloud.

Then I'll be the first. He circled her back entrance with the pad of his thumb as he pounded into her. *And the last.*

Wren realized she was on the verge of grinding into her saddle, and she was suddenly grateful for the dark, for she knew her cheeks were flushed.

Was that distraction enough for you? A note of amusement laced Torj's voice.

Wren didn't reply straight away; she was too busy trying to compose herself. She could feel the dampness between her legs, and her whole body was throbbing with need. *Will that...* She swallowed. *Will that feel as good as I think it will?*

She could hear the smile in her Bear Slayer's words. *Guess we'll have to find out... Does it interest you, Embers?*

Everything with you interests me.

Then the possibilities are endless, he replied. *But I'll have to politely retreat now. Riding with a cock as hard as stone and balls fit to burst isn't exactly comfortable...*

Wren suppressed a laugh. *I thought I took care of you this morning. But apologies for the inconvenience, Warsword.*

Once is never enough with you. And I don't want your apologies. I want you to think about how good the pressure might feel there, how my cock—

Wren managed to close her mind before Torj could paint the next picture, and she heard him laugh up ahead. Who knew her Warsword was so filthy? And apparently... so was she.

But the interlude with the Bear Slayer had done the trick. Though she was coiled tight with unmet need, her magic had quietened, and she was no longer at risk of bringing the mountain down on their heads as they navigated the narrow pass.

She didn't know how long they rode for. Without sunlight filtering through, there was little way to tell the passage of time. All she knew was that her legs ached and her back was painfully stiff. Wren had never taken this route to Delmira; according to Thea, only she and Wilder knew of it—and Kipp, by his own admission. She wasn't surprised at the latter. He had a way of navigating the midrealms that hardly anyone understood. Underground passageways between taverns, endless connections... A mountain pass was probably child's play to the strategist.

At last, Wren spotted the faint rays of light illuminating the end of the tunnel and silently thanked the Furies. As she exited, she took in a deep breath of fresh air and looked to the stretch of land before her. Gilded in the burnt orange hues of dawn or dusk—she didn't know which—was Delmira.

"Holy shit," she heard Thea exclaim nearby.

Sloping hills covered in verdant grass and vibrant wildflowers paved the way into the kingdom, and a sapphire-blue lake glimmered on the horizon.

"The view's beautiful, isn't it?" Wren turned, searching for her sister, but met the sea-storm gaze of Torj beside her instead.

"Yes," he said, not taking his eyes off her. "It is."

Her cheeks grew hot beneath the intensity of his stare, her traitorous mind taking her back to those images he'd shown her. His lips twitched upward, as though he knew *exactly* what she was thinking about.

"Made an impression on you, did it?" he asked quietly. "That's good to know, Embers. *Very* good to know."

Before she could reply, Torj was riding to the head of the army, addressing the company that had gathered at the foot of the mountain. "We'll camp here tonight and establish our first garrison. When we depart tomorrow, we'll leave a skeleton unit of shieldbearers behind until we can afford to send reinforcements."

Wren watched as the Bear Slayer moved through their forces with authority, directing his fellow Warswords and soldiers to set up tents and create defensive perimeters.

"We can use the mountain tunnel as a supply route from

Thezmarr," she heard him tell one of the commanders. "But it needs constant patrols."

No one questioned him. Here, Torj Elderbrock was in his element. The most senior Warsword remaining among them, more than familiar with the challenges of unknown territory, limited resources, and the threat of attack. It was what he had been trained for all his life. Had Wren forgotten that somewhere along the way? That he was more than a protector?

As she and Dessa set up the medical tent, she kept stealing glances at him. Commanding, disciplined, and efficient, Torj had everyone marching to the beat of his drum, and there was something incredibly... *powerful* about it, something erotic. Wren blamed the Bear Slayer for the way her thoughts kept coming back to the physical side of things. His offered distraction had a lasting effect, resulting in an ache that had settled low in her belly.

"He's quite impressive, isn't he?" Dessa commented, following her gaze across the camp to where Torj was using his war hammer to secure a tent to the ground.

"He is," Wren agreed. "I was just thinking... We've seen him fight, we've seen him defend, but this..."

Dessa nodded. "We haven't seen him lead. Was this what he was like in the war?"

"I suppose he was," Wren replied. "Though it's not the thing I remember most."

"Oh? What do you remember?"

"How he irritated me to no end. How he was overprotective. How he gave me my first proper pair of secateurs. How he walked into a tent pole at the sight of me in armor for the first time. It's the little things I remember..."

Wren sighed heavily as Darian approached them, and she saw Torj's shoulders tense, even from afar. "What can I do for you?" she asked the nobleman.

Darian motioned to the forces building campfires. "I thought the question was what I could do for you."

"You know I am grateful for your support," Wren told him. "How are you progressing with the legalities and paperwork on your end?"

"More complications, I'm afraid," he said, glancing across to where Lord Lucian held court with Lord Briar and Lord Pendelton. "My father proves to be three steps ahead when it comes to my inheritance, as always."

"Well, when you're ready, I'm a woman of my word," Wren assured him.

"Of that I have no doubt," the nobleman replied. "In the meantime, I think it's best we mingle with our supporters, don't you?"

Wren nodded stiffly. "I suppose you're right."

Darian offered his arm. "There will come a time where all of this is behind us. But for now, we need to present a united front. We need to woo them, assure them they will have our favor as a royal house when the war is done."

Wren accepted his arm and whispered, "And when they discover this has all been a ruse?"

"You will have won them a war, and it won't matter," Darian told her.

"I'm not sure they'll see it like that."

"Probably not," Darian admitted. "But that's all we've got for the moment. If they're not supporting us and our union, there's every chance they'll go to Silas."

"Well, we can't have that," Wren muttered.

Darian gave a dark laugh. "No, we certainly can't. Perhaps some wine will dull the pain?"

"There's not enough wine in the world," Wren told him.

CHAPTER 37
TORJ

"No battle unfolds according to design."
—The Warsword's Way

Whether she was aware of it or not, as they traveled deeper into the heart of Delmira, Wren was getting stronger. Torj could feel her magic surging through the soul bond, could feel her storm power coming back to her in waves. She was a force to be reckoned with, one that Silas the Kingsbane should fear with every fiber of his being —for the Poisoner was coming for him, and she would not be stopped. Torj only hoped he'd be there to see it.

His condition ebbed and flowed, often in proximity to Wren. When he felt close to her, he was the capable Warsword he'd always been; when there was distance between them, his fingers were wracked with tremors, his muscles spasmed unexpectedly, and fatigue hit him out of nowhere. He was doing everything Dessa instructed, taking every vile concoction she brewed for him, and yet it didn't seem to make a difference. One moment his skin was singing with the memory of Wren's touch, the next he was having to brace himself against his saddle horn.

As planned, they left a skeleton unit to guard the mountain tunnel and the garrison, with the bulk of their forces riding into Delmira just after dawn. Everyone besides himself, Wren, Kipp, and Dessa were unnerved by the newfound state of the kingdom around them. He rode with the three of them at the front of the company, Kipp making observations for his battle planning as they went.

"See those?" he called out over the noise of the horses, pointing to a fork in the nearby river. "Those are freshly formed waterways—they'll be unpredictable, prone to flooding." He turned to Wren. "Remember how we utilized flooding in the shadow war?"

"I'm not forgetting anytime soon, Kipp," she said dryly. "What else?"

He pointed to the closest tree line. "The forests are all full of new growth—they're dense, but easy enough to move through. Good for cover if we're wanting to move with any measure of stealth. And those meadowlands over there? Perfect for cavalry."

"You've got a decent eye, Snowden," Torj muttered with reluctant approval. "I'll give you that. Make sure we identify the best water sources along the way and map them for subsequent forces."

"Already in the works, Bear Slayer," Kipp replied with a grin.

They rode north, where they came upon old roads that

had been swallowed by new growth. In the distance there were villages that had been reclaimed by nature, the seemingly endless heather and wild thyme dancing in the breeze.

As they passed the ruins of old watchtowers and fortifications, a strange sense of uneasiness washed over Torj. He had been here in his younger years as a shieldbearer and as a Guardian. Even then it had been a land of ruins. It was as though for decades, time had stood still in Delmira, that it had always been and always would be this way—lost to the darkness past.

But that wasn't right. For it was teeming with life.

Vibrant flowers bloomed in the cracks of broken bridges. Trees towered where there had been none before. Roads long abandoned and in disrepair were overgrown with greenery.

"Those are natural choke points there. See where the old route is overrun—"

"I see them, Kipp," Torj cut him off. "But we need to establish our base first. We need to send out scouts to see what parts of the territory Silas is occupying, what his numbers look like..."

"Of course, of course," Kipp waved him off.

If Torj had had his way, their army would have assembled outside of Delmira and marched on the kingdom as one united front. But with their force consisting of so many different factions, they couldn't simply lie in wait. Lord Briar and Lord Pendelton had assured him that the remaining units of their bannermen would join them as soon as they could. Which made Torj all the more uneasy. He wouldn't have a solid idea of their numbers and resources until they were in the heart of the territory, where Wren's alchemist's cottage stood abandoned and in disrepair. It wasn't an ideal destination by any means, but Wren needed the silvertide roses for her counter-alchemy, so there was little choice in the matter.

They pressed on through the afternoon, the landscape growing wilder and more vibrant with each league. Torj dispatched small scouting parties at regular intervals, watching them disappear into the rampant greenery with a growing sense of unease. The new growth worked both for and against them—it provided cover, yes, but it also meant their forces were more spread out than he'd like, more vulnerable to ambush.

A muscle spasmed in his thigh, and he shifted in his saddle, trying to hide his discomfort. Wren glanced his way, her eyes narrowing. The soul bond thrummed between them, and for a moment the pain eased.

By sunset, they'd covered more ground than expected and the first scouts were returning with their reports: no signs of Silas' forces yet, but plenty of evidence that people had passed through recently. Broken branches. Disturbed earth. The remnants of campfires.

Delmira was no longer a secret.

Wren had dismounted some time ago to gather herbs from the underbrush and hadn't looked up since, but her fingers worked with quick, nervous energy as her words reached Torj through the soul bond.

I can't believe it recovered after all this time... Only for us to bring war right back to its doorstep.

At long last, they arrived at the place Wren had called home for half a decade. As Torj clapped eyes on the ramshackle cottage overgrown with ivy, regret lanced through him. For five years she had grieved alone here, in this isolated place. He should have been here with her. They could have had that time together.

Steeling himself, Torj swung down from his saddle and suppressed a groan at his aching body. He felt as though he'd been sparring with Vernich fucking Warner for several rounds, or the cursed bears he'd slain all those years ago. Then he remembered both of those opponents were dead, a thought that made that time in his life feel very far away.

"We'll make your cottage a makeshift alchemy workshop," he heard Thea tell Wren, but he was already stumbling away, determined not to let any of their forces see him like this—so suddenly weak, so useless—

A strong arm looped through his, pulling him upright.

Only a Warsword could lift him like that.

"I've got you."

Cal.

Torj could feel prying eyes on him as his former protégé guided him through the trees to some semblance of privacy. His surroundings were no more than a passing blur as he struggled to keep his feet underneath him.

Torj didn't know how much time had passed, only coming back to himself as Cal spoke again. "Almost there."

It wasn't long before Torj was blinking up at a ceiling made of canvas, something soft beneath his head.

"In here, Dessa!" Cal called from close by, and the rustling of the tent flap sounded.

Something cool was pressed to Torj's lips—a vial—but

the taste on his tongue was bitter, and he turned his head away in protest.

"It's a tonic made of dried iruseed." Dessa's voice sounded from somewhere above as gentle hands tried to coax his head to turn back toward the vial. "It'll just keep you conscious—"

"I don't want to be conscious," Torj muttered, turning away again.

"I can't help you if I can't talk to you. I need to find out what hurts," Dessa pleaded.

Torj drew a trembling breath. "Everything," he croaked, and then he passed out.

CHAPTER 38
TORJ

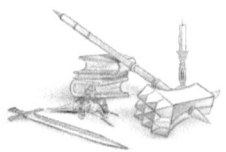

"For the soul-bonded, a glimpse across time's veil reveals not just what was, but what is, and what always will be."
—Tethers and Magical Bonds Throughout History

He dreamed of her. Of *them.*

A younger Torj Elderbrock strode through the corridors of Thezmarr, his hammer strapped to his back, his hand resting on the hilt of his sword, following the shieldbearer Sebastos Barlowe. Ever since Thezmarr had accepted a woman into its training program, Barlowe had been causing all kinds of trouble among the lower ranks. Torj was about ready to drag him before the Guild Master to answer for his horseshit hazing.

But just as he was about to bark out a command for Barlowe to halt, the shieldbearer paused outside the open door of an alchemy workshop, a sneer etched on his face.

Torj softened his steps and hung back, curious to see what the little prick was up to. Barlowe lingered in the doorway, leering at someone within.

"Your sister says hello from combat practice," he taunted. "Though her bloody lip might shut her up for a bit."

Torj's skin prickled instantly, his fists curling at his sides. He recognized that sick note of reverence, the one that relished the idea of a woman hurt. He took a step forward. Forget the Guild Master. He'd show Barlowe the meaning of pain—

A voice sounded from inside the workshop, but Torj couldn't make out her words. Whatever she'd said, it only seemed to rile Barlowe further. The shieldbearer stepped inside, a menacing gleam in his eyes now. "That prank you pulled had me in the infirmary for three days, bitch."

Torj was at the door to the workshop in seconds, peering into the room.

His breath caught.

There she was.

Wren Zoltaire.

She stood at a bench in her simple linen gown and apron, not bothering to look up as she tied bushels of mixed herbs together. Gods, she was more beautiful than he remembered. It had been four years since he'd met her in the Bloodwoods and she'd stitched him up. Four years of stealing glances at her whenever he was at Thezmarr, of finding excuses to pass the alchemy workshops and the library, of taking the detour past the herb gardens... But his Warsword duties had kept him from the fortress of late. It had been six months since he'd seen her last, and Furies knew that every day without her in his sight was a day wasted.

"Did you hear me?" Barlowe spat at her now. "Three fucking days in—"

"Perhaps you should have made better choices," came Wren's clear reply, and still she didn't deign to look up from her work.

A snarl escaped Barlowe. "I'll teach you about better choices—"

"Oh?" Wren sounded genuinely surprised. "You didn't learn your lesson the first time, then?"

Torj could—and couldn't—believe that she was goading Sebastos Barlowe. Everyone knew he was a cruel, violent prick with a tendency to lash out, especially at women. It was a miracle Torj hadn't wrung his neck already, but the lad proved once again that gold trumped honor in some circles. Peering through the crack in the door, Torj watched as Barlowe stalked toward the young alchemist, glaring at her as though she were no more than dirt.

"Who the fuck do you think you are?" he demanded, crowding her, his intent clear. Torj pressed his fingers to the door. He'd let this go on long enough. The only thing that had given him pause was the complete lack of fear in Wren's discerning gaze, but he'd be damned if he let the bastard get any closer to her—

Just as he was about to intervene, Wren *smiled*.

And gods, was it a terrifyingly beautiful sight.

Barlowe tensed like he had a blade to his bollocks. Only it wasn't a blade.

It was a long, sharp silver pin.

Delicate. Dainty. *Deadly.*

Just like Wren Zoltaire.

A *hairpin*, Torj realized as he watched Wren's bronze tresses fall loose around her face. She was still smiling as she said with pure confidence, "I'm Wren Zoltaire. Who the fuck are you?"

Desire surged through Torj. This woman was a storm incarnate, and gods, did he relish seeing her rage. Furies save them all from the damage she could do. Behind the unassuming facade was a ruthless vixen, and he fucking loved it.

Barlowe blanched, his knees visibly quaking. He opened and closed his mouth several times before blustering, "You—"

"If a bit of powder can land you in the infirmary for three days, imagine what a sharp object to your balls might do." She twisted the pin for emphasis, and Torj heard the spineless prick whimper.

"If you touch my sister..." Wren murmured, her voice laced with the promise of violence. "If you so much as lay a finger on her... I'll make this seem like child's play."

Her icy words jogged Torj's memory. Her sister... Wren was *Thea's sister*... and apparently, the taste for vengeance ran in the family.

With a satisfied smirk, Torj watched as Wren allowed Barlowe to scurry away like the scared rat he was, in such a panic that he didn't even pause as he passed Torj on the other side of the door.

After a moment, the Warsword couldn't resist another glance inside. A soft smile played on Wren's lips while she twirled her hairpin between her fingers. His heart pounded at the sight of her.

She didn't look up when she spoke again. "Are you going to watch from the shadows, Bear Slayer? Or are you going to come in and say hello?"

CHAPTER 39
WREN

"The alchemist knows that the most valuable elements require the strongest vessels—not to contain their essence, but to preserve it."
—Arcane Alchemy: Unveiling the Mysteries of Matter

"I have to go to him, Thee," Wren hissed, fighting against her sister's hold as Cal finished telling her what had happened to Torj.

"Not yet." Thea braced her forearm across Wren's chest to stop her from rushing from the tent. "Lucian's out there sniffing around. If he sees you running across camp to be at the Bear Slayer's bedside, this will all have been for nothing."

"I don't care." Wren pushed against the immovable force that was Thea's Furies-given strength. "He *needs me*."

"He will when he wakes," Thea said. "But he's sleeping

now. Dessa's with him. There's nothing you can do for him now."

Wren stepped back from her sister and passed a hand over her face, her chest constricting with every moment she wasn't with her soul-bonded as he suffered. "I should have killed Lucian the moment he told me about the poison, not gone along with this horseshit."

"No arguments from me there," Thea replied. "But you didn't, and this is where we are now. You need to show your face in front of the bannermen, show your unity with the Devereuxs. Then, when everyone is drunk and passed out, we'll cover you while you visit Torj."

Wren shook her head, fighting back tears of despair. "I hate this," she murmured.

"I know," Thea said gently, tugging on her hand. "Come sit by the fire with me and Wilder. We're going to sharpen our swords."

"Is that some sort of warrior couple innuendo?" Wren asked weakly.

Thea snorted. "No. We take the care of our blades rather seriously."

With that, Wren allowed her sister to lead her from the tent and guide her to one of the campfires, where Wilder was waiting. As she sat, Wren unsheathed the dagger at her thigh and pulled it into her lap.

Thea let out a low, appreciative whistle. "Naarvian steel..."

"Torj had it altered for me," Wren said quietly.

Wilder glanced up at that. "He not only gave you a Naarvian steel blade, but had it altered from the Furies' chosen form?"

261

"Yes." Wren balanced the weapon on her fingertip, showing how the weight suited her perfectly. "Will you teach me how to care for it?"

"Here." Thea offered her whetstone. "You want a coarser stone to begin with, for repairs and major sharpening."

Wren took the rough object and waited.

"You can use water or oil to wet the stone before you start. I prefer water. Then you hold the blade at a consistent angle, like this." Thea pointed to where Wilder was holding his sword against his own whetstone. "Then you draw the blade across the rough surface in smooth strokes, from base to tip—"

Wilder snorted. "Something you're rather familiar with, Princess..."

Wren's mouth twitched. "I remember when you were a serious warrior, Wilder. Good to see how thoroughly Thea's corrupted you."

"I never stood a chance," he replied. "My mind was always filthy when it came to her."

"I'm well aware," Wren said dryly before turning back to her sister. "You were saying?"

"You need to maintain even pressure and repeat the motion on both sides until it's sharp. Then, you can use a finer stone for a razor edge."

Wren dragged her dagger over the whetstone. "Like this?"

"Make the angle a touch sharper," Thea told her. "Yes, like that."

Wren repeated the motion, and when she looked up for Thea's approval, she saw that her sister had started on another blade with a rag this time. Without a word, Wilder handed Thea the oil she needed before she could ask. Her sister's fingers brushed his as she took it, a touch that lingered just a heartbeat too long to be casual, even after all these years. Every small gesture between them made Wren ache for Torj—the way Wilder shifted to block the wind when Thea shivered, how Thea absently brushed the fire's ash from his shirt while reaching for another whetstone.

The cool night air was filled with the soft scrape of steel on stone and the crackle of the fire. Wren had hoped the repetitive task would quieten her mind, but it only made the thoughts churn faster. What if she and Torj never got the years her sister and Wilder had? What if they had squandered their chance? The thought of poison coursing through the Bear Slayer's veins made Wren nauseous.

Wilder's voice cut through her thoughts. "I've been where you are."

Wren looked up to see the Hand of Death watching her with a pained expression.

"Remember when we thought that fate stone belonged to Thea?" he asked. "We all thought that she would only live until she turned twenty-seven."

"I'm not likely to forget it," Wren said. "It belonged to Anya instead..."

Wilder dipped his head. "It did. But we didn't know that until the end. For the entire first chapter of our time together, I thought I would lose her..."

"But Torj... Torj *is* dying," Wren whispered, finally saying the words she'd been too afraid to say aloud before this moment. "The poison is moving faster than we anticipated, and I am no closer to saving him. Even if Lucian gives me what I need, there may not be enough time. How do I know that and not..."

"Break?" Thea finished. "You don't. You break a little every day. But you keep going, because that's what warriors do—we fight anyway."

"And I'm a warrior..." Wren said slowly.

"You are." Thea nodded. "You always have been."

"She's right," Wilder agreed. "You and Torj both. And you'll find a way through it, no matter what."

The words hit home. Wren drew her blade across the whetstone one final time, testing its edge with her thumb. It was sharp enough to cut. Something that had to be maintained carefully, deliberately, with the right balance of pressure and restraint...

"Thank you," she said, first meeting her sister's eyes, then Wilder's. "For showing me how."

From across the camp, she saw Cal signal to her, and so Wren rose from her place by the fire and slipped into the darkness, leaving Thea and Wilder to their quiet companionship.

Wren slipped into the Bear Slayer's darkened tent and between his sheets with the stealth of a Warsword herself.

"What are you doing?" Torj murmured, his voice thick with exhaustion. "We can't—"

"You needed me. So I came."

"I'm fine—"

Wren pressed her index finger to his lips to silence him

before sweeping her nightshirt up over her head and pressing her naked body against the hard heat of his muscular chest. She traced the web of scarring over his inked heart—the mark she'd made with lightning when she'd refused to let him go all those years ago.

"The others told me how you collapsed," she said quietly.

"Traitors," he muttered.

"They're trying to keep you alive. As am I." Wren threw a leg over his thick thighs and pulled herself on top of him, her bare skin sliding over his.

"Is that so?" The Bear Slayer's trembling hands were already tracing her curves. "'Cause it feels like you're trying to kill me, Embers..."

Wren brought a glass vial to his lips. "Drink this, you stubborn Warsword."

He let her tip the liquid into his mouth without protesting. "What is it?"

"A strengthening potion of sorts. It's not nearly as strong as I'd like it to be, but we've had limited time to brew it and increase its potency," she replied, noting that the tremors wracking the hand resting on her hip were abating.

"So, this is how you save me?" he murmured, trailing circles across her bare skin. She could feel him growing hard beneath her and bit back a smile. Wren rolled her hips and clapped a hand over Torj's mouth as he swore. "You need *rest*, Bear Slayer."

"I'll rest when I'm dead."

"You'll rest when I tell you to." Wren slid off him to the empty space beside. On the few occasions when they'd had

HELEN SCHEUERER

the freedom to share a bed, Torj had always covered her body with his, cocooning himself around her, always her shield against the world. But this time, Wren wanted to hold him.

Gently, she pushed him onto his side and wrapped herself around him from behind, feeling the heat of his back seep into her.

"I love you," she whispered against his spine.

Torj guided her hand around his ribs and clutched it to his scarred chest. "I love you too, Embers... but I'm not sure even that is enough to stop this. How do you plan on keeping me here?"

Wren pressed her hand over his heart. "By showing you what you'd be missing if you left this world without me."

"Believe me, I'm aware," he replied thickly.

"Do you know what my deepest fear is?" she asked him, threading her fingers through his. "It's not failing as queen, or letting the midrealms down... It's not a second war, or my role in it. It's losing you. I can't lose you, Torj. Not you."

She could feel the steady rhythm of his heart beating against her palm as he said, "My deepest fear is leaving you unprotected... or that I'll become part of the reason you're no longer safe." He kissed her knuckles. "The poison... It's getting worse, Wren."

"I know," she whispered. Her eyes burned as hot tears slipped free, tracking down her cheeks.

He turned to face her, gently catching her tears with his thumb. "I'm not afraid of dying, Embers... I never have been. Truth be told, I thought I'd die long before now."

Wren let him see her emotions; she didn't hide as she

lifted her gaze to his. "I used to think dying for someone would be the ultimate act of love, but... *living* for someone—that's the ultimate act. I need you to live for me, Bear Slayer. Because together, we can change the world."

CHAPTER 40
WREN

*"Certain combinations of elements create resonance—
amplifying properties that remain dormant when separated. The
same can be said for the company alchemists keep."*
—Drevenor Academy Handbook

"*There is no 'always' for people like us...*" Torj had said it
to her in the gardens of Drevenor, right after tearing
their bond apart. Heading to the cottage now, Wren refused
to believe it. She would not, could not, give up.

"How did it go?" Dessa looked up from where she was
de-thorning a silvertide rose. She had the bloom upright on
its stem and was dragging her harvesting knife down
through the foliage and thorns, just as Wren had shown her
earlier.

Wren pulled on a pair of gloves herself and began to
gather the severed thorns. "Torj is putting on a brave face,

but he's struggling. Badly. The poison is taking hold much faster than we anticipated. And I don't know how to help him. I'm no closer to obtaining the information Lucian promised me, and I have no idea how to counter what's sapping his strength."

Dessa must have heard the note of desperation in her voice. She set down her rose and walked around the bench to Wren. Without another word, the alchemist embraced her.

For a moment, Wren stood rigid in her friend's arms. But when Dessa didn't let go, Wren's whole body sagged, and a quiet sob broke from her lips. Dessa rubbed soothing circles across her back and said nothing, allowing her the space to talk through her feelings.

"I don't know what to do," Wren whispered, finally allowing her tears to flow freely. "There isn't enough *time*. Between the war, the countermeasure against the shadow alchemy, and Torj's poisoning, I don't know how to do it all. I can't..." She drew a trembling breath and clung to Dessa. "I keep thinking... I shouldn't be queen."

"Why not?" Dessa asked softly.

Wren pulled back from her friend and palmed the tears from her eyes. For the first time since she'd agreed to take the Delmirian throne, she spoke her truest fear aloud. "Because I'd let the midrealms burn to save him."

The weight of her words settled in her chest, along with her soul bond and the heaviness of her impending crown. She couldn't bring herself to be ashamed, not with the bond still thrumming between her and the Bear Slayer.

"I think it's time I accepted my fate," she told her friend. "I think I need to marry Darian."

Dessa shook her head, her expression taut with horror. "You *can't*, Wren—"

"It's the lesser of any of the other evils. I'd do anything to save him, and we're out of time."

Wren knew the magnitude of her confession; she could feel the weight of it like a block of lead around her heart. She had been strong for the Bear Slayer in the safe bubble of his tent, but as she crept from his bed in the hours before dawn, leaving him sleeping soundly, she had nearly gone straight to Lucian to beg the nobleman, to pledge herself to Darian right then and there.

"Time?" Dessa said, squeezing her hands. "That's what you need?"

Wren blinked at her in surprise. She wasn't sure what she had expected Dessa's response to be, but this hadn't been it. "Among other things," she said slowly.

Dessa was nodding, more to herself than to Wren. "If time is what you need, then time is what I'll get you."

Wren gave her a sad smile. "But Dess... how?"

Dessa gave her fingers a final squeeze of encouragement before she released them and headed to the door. "Leave it with me, alright?"

Wren didn't see that she had a choice. "Alright."

As the hours passed in strange waves, Wren spent them hunched over the workbench in her cottage, working on the cure. Her fingers were bleeding even through her gloves as she de-thorned the roses and ground ingredients, her nostrils filled with the scent of dried herbs and simmering potions. When her vision started to blur and her growling stomach forced her away from her work, she stood in the doorway, eating an apple from a nearby tree and surveying the preparations for the war ahead.

Outside, Darian was overseeing the management of the supplies and logistics, calling out orders to quartermasters who were frantically organizing wagons of preserved foods and grain for the horses, all brought in from Thezmarr. In the distance, Wren could see Cal inspecting weapons at the field forge, where the clang of metal rang out across the camp.

"Walk with me," Kipp said, appearing at her side and thrusting his chin toward the surrounding forest.

Wren fell into step with her friend easily, and together, they wove through the trees in the direction of the silvertide roses she'd found there months before.

"I've dispatched scouts to gauge any enemy movements ahead, and to assess the terrain between here and Dorinth," Kipp told her thoughtfully. "I've had an idea for something... A decoy camp. Which I'll need your help with, by the way."

"My help?" Wren didn't hide her surprise.

Kipp made a noise of amusement. "Rumor has it that you're good with poisons, Your Queenliness..."

"I've been known to dabble," she replied as she moved through the underbrush. "Aren't we meeting with the council soon? Why are you telling me now?"

"Because for the moment, only you, myself, and Cal know. And that's how I'd like to keep it."

"Any particular reason?" she prompted.

Kipp shrugged. "I like the element of surprise."

271

"So I've heard." Wren parted the bushes before her, the grasses brushing against her skirts as they moved through the flourishing forest. "Do you think we're ready for this?" she asked her friend.

"Ready? I'm not sure anyone's ever ready for war," Kipp said. "But we're doing everything we can to be prepared. You did well to keep stockpiling the healers' supplies while we were on the road."

"I would have done better were the masters with us," she replied. "Have you heard from Farissa and the others? I had hoped they'd join us at Thezmarr after what happened at Drevenor."

Kipp sighed. "I've heard nothing through my usual channels, but with the exception of your former mentor, the other masters weren't here for the shadow war. I see no reason they would stay in the midrealms for the next."

"Because it's a war of alchemy. Because their *home* was destroyed. Because—"

"I'm not saying there aren't valid reasons," Kipp interrupted. "I'm only saying I wouldn't count on their support."

Wren's reply died on her lips as they reached the small crop of roses. The silvery petals shivered in the breeze, glimmering like pearls against the deep greenery and thorns.

"There's even less than I remember," she murmured.

"We took a lot with us last time..." Kipp crouched down and surveyed the blooms. "It's not enough, is it?"

Wren unsheathed her harvesting knife and severed a single rose from the bush, twirling it between her tender fingers, the silvery white petals seeming to taunt her now. "Not even close."

"Wren," Kipp said, his tone serious. "I can plan as many battles as you need, I can come up with all the strategies under the sun, but... without the counter-alchemy, it will all be for nothing. *This* is where I need you to tell me what to do."

Wren swallowed the hard lump that had been forming in her throat. "I need you to get a map," she heard herself say. "I'm going to mark some locations, and then you're going to send the Bear Slayer, along with your most trusted men among us, right to them."

CHAPTER 41
WREN

"Transformation requires precision, not abundance."
—Alchemy Unbound

Lord Lucian's eyes tracked Wren as she entered the makeshift command tent that afternoon with Kipp at her side. Her stomach churned with unease, but she told herself that there was no way anyone had seen her slip from Torj's tent in the dark before dawn.

"This tent is far too small for so many egos," she muttered to her friend.

Kipp chuckled beside her. "You're not wrong there."

Along with Lord Briar and Lord Pendelton, there were at least half a dozen noblemen that Wren didn't recognize. She scanned their fancy doublets, the weapons that had likely never seen a day's combat gleaming at their hips, and the familiar exchanges between them all. Every chair around the table was full but for the one next to Darian. In addition to his allies, there were Zavier and Thea, while Wilder and Cal stood behind them.

"Where's Elderbrock?" the latter asked, adjusting his bow over his shoulder.

"He's indisposed," Wren replied in a tone that invited no further questioning. If her friends were surprised that Audra's own appointed Warsword wasn't present, they didn't show it.

"And Dessa?" Thea said.

"In the cottage. She agreed to watch over the potions brewing," Wren told her sister quickly before returning her attention to the gathered company.

"There she is!" Darian rose from his chair, a charming grin plastered on his face. "My future wife, as radiant as ever."

Wren didn't know how, but she managed not to grimace at the greeting. She forced herself to return Darian's enthusiasm and took his offered hand with a smile. "I hope I'm not late. I was tending to some of the warriors in the healer's station."

"That's my Elwren," Darian said fondly, showing her to her seat at the table. "A heart of gold. Always putting others before herself. You're right on time, my love."

"An honorable trait in a woman," someone said from the far end.

Schooling her features into an impenetrable mask, Wren silently relished the crackle of storm magic in her veins and the clinking vials of poison at her belt. *Let them think you're demure and unambitious. Let them believe you are just another pawn in their games. It will make what lies ahead all the more satisfying.*

Thea met her gaze from across the table, a similar glint in her celadon eyes. If there was one thing the Embervale sisters agreed on, it was that old men had no place telling women what traits made them honorable.

Speaking of which... The nape of Wren's neck prickled, and her eyes were drawn to Lord Briar, who was staring daggers at her. His hand rested on a crumpled letter atop the table, his knuckles whitening as his fingers curled around the parchment. The tension hung thick in the air, palpable enough that Kipp shifted closer behind her chair.

"I see the ravens have been busy," Wren remarked coolly, taking note of the identical letters before several of the noblemen.

Lord Pendelton cleared his throat. "Your Highness, there are... concerning rumors circulating." He gestured to the letter before him. "Rumors that you're responsible for certain... incidents."

Wren tried not to visibly stiffen in her seat. She had known news of her letters to the common folk would travel fast, but she had underestimated the speed of the reports back to the nobles, who usually had little concern for those beneath their station.

"Rumors are just that—rumors, Lord Pendelton," Darian interjected smoothly. "You know that well enough, being the victim of so many yourself."

The nobleman flushed a deep crimson. "That's not what we're discussing."

"No, we're discussing the incidents attached to the Princess of Delmira," Lord Briar said sharply, eyes narrowed with suspicion. "This letter"—he tapped the parchment with a ringed finger—"claims you are the assassin known as the Poisoner. That half a dozen noble houses lost their patriarchs to your... handiwork. Myself included."

A flutter of whispers swept through the tent. Wren watched their faces, cataloging each reaction carefully. Lord Lucian's expression was unreadable and he was uncharacteristically quiet.

"Consider who benefits from such rumors, my lords. Who would seek to destabilize our already precarious alliance as we begin our campaign?" She let her gaze drift meaningfully toward the tent flap. "Our enemy has spies everywhere, as we all know too well."

"The correspondence in question bears your seal, according to our sources," Lord Briar insisted.

"Seals can be forged," Darian cut in, reaching for Wren's hand. "My father's has been in the past. Yours too, Lord Pendelton, if you'll recall those dreadful accusations from that maid of yours."

Lord Pendelton flushed again.

"It seems that you yourself have been a victim of similar schemes," Wren said, her voice deliberately gentle. "What matters now is reclaiming Delmira. Unless you believe these rumors more important than defeating Silas and his dark alchemy?"

Lord Pendelton glanced at his companions, and then to Lord Briar in particular. The latter gave a stiff nod.

"Very well," Lord Pendelton replied at last. "But this matter is not settled, Princess."

"Few matters ever are in times of war, my lord," Wren

replied, her spine as strong as steel. "Now, shall we continue our meeting?"

The noblemen exchanged glances, their disapproval evident, but their ambition stronger. None were willing to abandon their chance at influence in a restored Delmira.

Clearing his throat, Darian shifted his and Wren's joined hands on the table for all to see, Wren's engagement ring glinting in the candlelight. "I believe we need to talk of the coronation?"

It was by no means a question—it was a directive, one that his allies followed immediately.

"Ancient law states that any coronation of a Delmirian royal must be performed *inside* the city of Dorinth," Lord Pendelton declared, peering over a large tome as he chewed on the end of a pipe.

"But there *is* no city of Dorinth," Zavier countered, his dark brows knitting together. "The capital fell. It's nothing but the ruins and rubble the enemy has built their fortress upon."

"I can't change the law, Your Highness," the older nobleman replied. "In fact, it's the very same one you adhered to when you were crowned in Ciraun, the capital of your kingdom."

"I don't care if Wren gets crowned in the ruins or here in the army camp. She's the rightful queen and deserves her crown," the prince told them boldly.

"And as touching as that vote of confidence is for the princess, this is the kingdom of Delmira, not Naarva. Your vote does not carry much weight here," Lord Briar replied.

"Watch your tongue, Lord Briar," Darian interjected. "Prince Zavier may be a guest here, but he is *our* guest. The guest of *Princess* Elwren and myself. He will be treated with respect."

Lord Briar flushed and bowed his head. "Yes, my lord."

"Is a coronation truly a priority right now?" Thea asked as she picked at her fingernails with her dagger. "What difference does it make if Wren has a crown or not until we win this war?"

"While I agree with the sentiment," Darian said, "many noble houses of the midrealms will only answer to the summons of a king or queen. Without the proper title, oaths can remain unfulfilled, and people will be too unsure of the succession to pick a side."

"The side without the tyrant surely suffices," Thea retorted.

"You'd think," Wilder snorted.

While Wren agreed with her sister and new brother-in-law, their observations were hardly helpful in this scenario. There was more than one reason this tactic was being pushed...

She turned to Kipp. "I'm guessing there is another reason for us taking back the capital?"

"Naturally," Kipp replied. "The ruins of the capital are one of the most strategic military positions in all of Delmira. It's one of Silas' most advantageous strongholds. The clifftops are an excellent vantage point for incoming attack, the ruins themselves provide ample coverage, and my personal favorite... the tavern—"

A unified groan from all who knew Kipp sounded across the tent.

"Rude," he chastised them, before looking to the noblemen, likely spying their bulging coin purses in their pockets. "The tavern, the Flying Stag, is linked to an underground network, just like its sister locations throughout the midrealms, which means—"

"We can smuggle supplies and reinforcements in, right under their noses," Cal said with a shake of his head. "I don't know why I'm surprised."

"Nor do I," Kipp mused. "You've known me long enough by now, Callahan—I'm brilliant."

"That's one word for it," Cal muttered, folding his arms over his chest.

"And why weren't these networks made known to us before?" Lord Briar called. "We spent *a week* traipsing over enemy ground in full view, when we could have—"

"Alerted them to the card up our sleeve?" Kipp interjected. "I wasn't going to risk *that*, my good man. And there are spies all over—"

The nobleman went red as he blustered, "Are you calling me a spy?"

Kipp raised a brow. "*Are* you a spy?"

"Kipp!" Wren snapped. "Not helping."

But the strategist simply shrugged. "In my professional opinion—"

"And *what*, exactly, qualifies you to give your so-called professional opinion?" Lord Ethel, another nobleman, cut in aggressively. Clearly a nerve had been struck.

Kipp surveyed him with a cool, unaffected expression. "Only that I was the lead strategist in the shadow war. That as a result of my careful planning and input, countless lives were saved. Including yours." He glanced at Wren. "Am I missing something?"

"That's the gist of it," Wren agreed, trying to suppress the smug note in her voice. "Continue, please."

She didn't think she'd ever seen a man turn as red as Ethel.

Kipp didn't gloat as she expected; instead, he turned to the rest of the table. "As I was saying, I believe that laying siege to this particular post is the best option. We rally as many allies as we can here, gather as much intelligence on Silas and the People's Vanguard as possible, and have Princess Elwren and her potion-inclined allies work on our alchemical defense. Then, we march on Dorinth. From the outskirts, I suggest we set up a decoy camp and draw the enemy out, then take the high ground for ourselves."

Across from Wren, Cal folded his arms over his chest and looked to Zavier. "You know Silas best... What do you think? Will he anticipate this?"

Zavier tapped his fingers against the table. "He seems to know more than we think... His presence at Drevenor proves that, as did the stunt at Harenth with the townsfolk. But my gut feeling is that he would be surprised if our forces instigated an attack. I assume he thinks we'll be working from a defensive standpoint, that we're scared of him and his dark alchemy."

"Aren't we?" one of the noblemen said.

"No," Wren replied firmly. "We have been here before and came out the other side. We will do so again."

"But that's what I'm saying," Zavier continued. "Silas' followers are not driven by loyalty or love, or even a common cause... They are motivated by fear. Perhaps there is something we can do to show them that? To crack the foundations of his support?"

Kipp was nodding. "I already have something in motion, Prince."

Lord Ethel rose to his feet and addressed Kipp, this time with a respectful dip of his head. "When do we leave, then, Snowden?"

"Three days from now," Kipp replied. "The rest of the Devereux forces are due to join us by tomorrow, with the units from Aveum, Harenth, and Tver to meet us on the way."

"Very well," Lord Pendelton said. "I'll inform our men."

Lord Lucian's scrutinizing stare swept over them and Wren trained her eyes on him, refusing to look away, to yield to the challenge in his glower. His expression was utterly clear this time: her reputation had almost cost him dearly, and he wasn't pleased. But he dipped his head in a show of respect. "Until our next meeting," he offered stiffly, before he took his leave.

The other noblemen followed with similar farewells, leaving Kipp and Wren behind with Zavier, Darian, Thea, Wilder, and Cal, the Warswords collapsing into the newly vacated seats.

Thea's head dropped into her hands. "There isn't a tea strong enough in the midrealms for how I'm feeling right now. There's so much dick-swinging it's insufferable. Didn't we put an end to all that during the last war? Remember when Anya kicked all of them out of the war tent and the women did the planning? I much preferred that."

"Same here." Wren huffed a tired laugh before she turned to Darian. "Your father is growing impatient..."

Darian grimaced. "He is. He's determined to see us married before your coronation, so there can be no doubt of the role the Devereux name played in the reclaiming of the most prosperous kingdom in the midrealms..."

"Do you think he's encouraging allies not to pledge to us until after we're wed?" she asked.

"I wouldn't put it past him. One of his many mottos is about seeing the ink dry on the parchment before fulfilling a deal." Darian took a deep breath, as though trying to compose himself. "And from what I understand, our time is running out regarding the other matter at hand?"

Wren nodded.

The nobleman swore under his breath. "It wasn't supposed to happen like this. I thought it was slow-releasing. That's what my father said..."

"I know," Wren said, sounding far calmer than she felt. "The thing is, I don't even think he's lying. I believe it was *supposed* to be slow-releasing, but something is accelerating its symptoms."

Darian glanced around the tent, despair etched across his features. "If I ask about it again, it will only make my father suspicious."

Wren shook her head. "He won't tell you anyway. You've played your part well so far—don't throw it all away now. If it comes to it, I'll marry you, Darian." She ignored the sounds of shock from her friends. "But for now, we bide our time. Does that mean we have no solid allies? Not even in the men sworn to you personally?"

"We have allies," Darian argued. "Certainly more than when we started this farce."

"But enough to take Dorinth? Enough to lay siege to an enemy stronghold?" Wren bit back.

The nobleman sighed. "My father is a cunning man. He

may be starting to suspect there's more to my end of the bargain than meets the eye."

"Then perhaps it's time I held up my end of our deal... I could handle him as discussed."

Darian blinked at her. "It's too soon."

Wren could feel her friends' eyes on them, assessing their dynamic, all of them on edge. Only Kipp and Torj knew what she had promised the Lord of Larkwood Valley in exchange for his help with her campaign.

"But if he's... no longer an obstacle, the Devereux connections will look to you for leadership. If you summon their banners, they will come."

"It's not that simple," Darian said, his voice low. "There are restrictions in place for this very reason, legal ramifications if things take a certain turn."

"Are you having second thoughts?" she asked.

The laugh that burst from Darian was dark. "Do you know what it's like to smile at someone who has caused you harm? Who drove the most important person in your life away?"

Wren gave him a flat look. "I've got a fair idea, yes. For as long as I can remember, I've smiled for men who would sooner lock me away in a kitchen than hear my thoughts. For many years, I pretended I was less than I am to survive." She leaned back in her chair. "Say the word and it will be done."

"I appreciate it." Darian's relief was palpable. "Now, where is the Bear Slayer?"

CHAPTER 42
TORJ

"The wisest warriors know when to break formation."
—The Warsword's Way

Torj could feel her anguish through the soul bond, and it damn near destroyed him. Guilt festered alongside the poison in his veins as he swept his beeswax-covered cloth over his armor. He was failing Wren in every way imaginable. He had promised her *always*, and yet he was dying. He had said *together* with every fiber of his being, but he was leaving her on her own...

A tremor wracked his hand, and he dropped the cloth in the dirt, cursing under his breath—

"Are you the Bear Slayer?" a youthful voice asked from the flap of the armory tent as he reached down to retrieve the scrap of fabric.

I was, he thought bitterly.

"Who's asking?" He looked up to see three young shieldbearers standing before him, clutching their own armor.

The girl on the end elbowed the boy in the middle and pointed to the totem on his right arm, and the war hammer resting against the table a few feet away. "It *is* him!"

The boy on the end shot them a mortified look.

"What can I do for you, Thezmarrians?" Torj asked, realizing that the trio reminded him of Cal, Kipp, and Thea when they were as green as the grass beyond the camp.

"Can you show us how to..." The girl motioned to his armor. "Do what you're doing?"

He stared at them for a moment, and suddenly they seemed impossibly young, *too young* to be marching off to war. They were in their late teens or early twenties, but the gulf between them and his battle-worn self seemed endless. Outside, he could hear the bustle of preparation, the shouts accompanying the training drills, the rattling wheels of the supply carts... Wren was out there too, likely elbow-deep in potions and cursing his name. Her calls through the bond had gone quiet, and he didn't know if he was terrified or relieved by that.

"Bear Slayer?" one of the shieldbearers prompted, shifting nervously from foot to foot.

Yes, they reminded him of Cal, Kipp, and Thea, alright, and it made his stomach drop. Part of him couldn't believe they were back here, on the brink of another colossal fight for survival. The war would happen with or without him; the least he could do was show these poor shieldbearers how to tend to their armor.

He sighed and reached for a clean piece of material.

"First, you need to wipe the leather thoroughly with a damp cloth to remove dirt, sweat, and any mold," he began, amused by their rapt attention. "Do you know why you need to oil your armor?"

They shook their heads.

"What the fuck is Esyllt teaching you back there?" he muttered. "You need to oil your armor regularly to maintain its flexibility and stop it from cracking. You need to be able to move well in it—it shouldn't restrict you in any way. If it cracks, it might leave you vulnerable, and it's much harder to repair."

"What oil are you using?" the girl asked. She was wearing her hair in a side braid, just like Thea, Torj noticed, and she was already mimicking his motions over the shoulder piece in her lap.

"I'm using beeswax because it doesn't have an odor, but you can use tallow, lanolin... I'd advise against fish oil," he told them.

As he demonstrated, more shieldbearers filled the tent, and he suddenly found himself giving the lesson Esyllt the weapons master had given him back at the fortress, decades ago.

"Pay special attention to the creases where the leather flexes, and areas exposed to regular friction—"

"What about the stitching and the buckles?" someone called out.

"Those too," he replied. "When you're done, leave it to dry so the oil can fully penetrate. Somewhere out of direct sunlight."

When he looked up next, he saw Dessa lingering by the entrance of the tent. The red-haired alchemist was pacing impatiently, and as soon as she noticed his attention, she motioned wildly for him to join her.

Leaving the shieldbearers to their own devices, he went to her. "What's wrong, Dessa? Is it Wren? Is she alright?"

"You'd know if you spoke to her," she said tersely.

It was like a punch to the gut. "I deserve that," he muttered, hanging his head.

"Yes, you do," Dessa replied frankly. "But that's not why I'm here."

Torj realized he was grinding his teeth. "Why *are* you here?"

"To give you time," Dessa told him.

In the privacy of Zavier's tent, Torj stared at the dropper full of liquid while Dessa held the concoction out to him eagerly.

"What is it, exactly?" Torj asked her, glancing between the two alchemists suspiciously. "Wren already gave me something."

"This is a more powerful mixture than that... Significantly so. It's actually a rather illegal strengthening draft," she replied in complete seriousness.

"Illegal?" Torj scoffed. "Surely we're a bit beyond that these days...?"

Dessa gave a small shrug. "Well, it would have been banned at Drevenor, is what I mean."

"Why?" Torj pressed.

"Because it mixes a lot of potent ingredients that could be abused in order to surpass the competition in, say, a setting like the Gauntlet," Zavier answered. "It's not something that should be taken lightly, or used long term, for that matter."

At last, Torj took the dropper from Dessa and studied the seemingly innocent substance within. Though spending months on end at an academy for alchemists had told him that there was rarely such a thing as an *innocent* concoction. "And how is this going to give me more time?"

"It will give you your strength and energy back, allowing your Furies-given power to fight the poison in your system, at least until Wren adapts her cure for you," Dessa told him. "It contains dry iruseed, which you're familiar with."

Torj dipped his head in confirmation. Back in the day, all Warswords had carried around a small supply in case they needed to stay conscious after being wounded. After the shadow war it became less common, chiefly due to the shortage of supplies and alchemists.

"What else?" he asked.

"Peppered broadleaf," Zavier chimed in. "Usually used as a kind of smelling salt."

Torj studied the two alchemists, rolling the dropper between his fingers. "Are you going to list every ingredient before you share the one you're most concerned about?"

Dessa actually winced. "We didn't know how you'd feel about it."

"As long as it lets me wield a hammer in this war and protect Wren, I have no feelings about it but gratitude."

"We know *Wren* certainly won't like it," Dessa added.

That didn't deter Torj, not after everything Wren had said to him. "If this gives me the chance to contribute anything to her fight, then just tell me how much to take and when to take it."

"You should know what you're dealing with." Zavier paced the small space of his tent. "We took inspiration from the alchemy Silas used in the initial attack on Drevenor..."

Torj froze.

"Remember how he seemed to get stronger at one point?" Zavier forged on. "He ingested something, and you could actually see it work through his body?"

Torj wasn't likely to forget. He could still see it now: the force of the tonic racing beneath the masked enemy's skin, his stature seeming to grow, his stare glowing with an unnatural power...

Dessa was watching him. "We've only tested it on each other—"

"You *what?*" he blurted.

"We—"

"I heard you." He shook his head in disbelief and dragged a hand through his unkempt hair. "I just had no idea you were *that* foolish! Really, Dessa? Taking inspiration from dark alchemy and testing it on yourself, and the Prince of Naarva, no less?"

"We're not here to talk about us," Zavier snapped, his expression suddenly dark. "We're here because of a mistake *I* made. We are in this mess *because of me*. You were poisoned *because of me*. Meanwhile, Wren is *drowning*. Dessa and I... Our specialties aren't poisons and cures. We can't do what Wren does. But as Dessa said: we *can* buy her some time. That's what this draft does, Bear Slayer. It gives you back your strength so you can fight another day, and another, until *she* can save you."

Torj's gaze fell to the dropper once more. "Alchemists..." he muttered. "You're all mad, the lot of you."

"True enough," Zavier huffed. "We've made a decent supply that should last for the next week. If you take it in small doses, you should be able to maintain your usual stamina and strength."

"I'll be able to fight and ride? Everything as good as before?" Torj pressed.

"Yes, that's the idea," Dessa replied.

"Good." Torj was already moving, reaching for the map Kipp had brought him earlier. "Then I know what I have to do."

CHAPTER 43

WREN

"The curious paradox of dreams: they can flourish in the most toxic soil, drawing strength from the very poisons meant to destroy them."
—Elwren Embervale's notes and observations

The staggered arrival of their allies caused chaos to sweep across the camp. There was no uniformity—an array of banners and sigils dotted the tents with color, and Wren had no idea which units belonged to whom. Among all the movement and madness, with the land beside her old cottage now brimming with warriors, there was one notable missing figure.

"Where is he?" Lord Lucian demanded as he strode through the ranks. "According to your Guild Master, the Bear Slayer was meant to be leading this campaign, and we're due to leave!"

Wren blinked at the enraged man. "I haven't a clue, Lord Lucian. Perhaps the other Warswords can help..."

Lucian crowded her, his stance wide, clearly trying to intimidate her. "Don't play games with me, girl. You may be marrying my son, but that doesn't mean you get to act coy—"

"I simply answered your question. And may I remind you that you're the one cautioning me to stay away from him? I'm merely following your instructions." Wren rested a hand on her belt of potions and lifted her chin. "I suggest you rethink the way in which you speak to me, my lord. You may be of a noble house, but I am a ruler of the midrealms."

His nostrils flared, as though he couldn't fathom a woman challenging him in such a way. "Not yet, Princess Elwren. Not yet."

Wren lowered her voice. "Is that a threat?"

"I would never threaten my future daughter-in-law." The meaning was cleverly laced between his words. No, Lord Lucian wouldn't threaten his son's wife, but anyone who didn't hold that title? He'd have no qualms putting them in harm's way.

"I'm glad to hear it," Wren told him, glancing over to where Thea was shooting her a questioning look. "I suggest that we move out as planned, with or without the Bear Slayer. Don't you agree?"

The smile that graced Lord Lucian's face was almost serpentine. "Absolutely. I see no reason to delay. I'm eager to see the crown upon your head, Elwren, and my son standing proudly as your husband at your side."

Wren wished she could say that it was the first time she'd mounted a horse at the head of a war force, but it wasn't. It was, however, the first time she'd been a part of one without the Bear Slayer. Her heart was lodged in her throat as she looked around, scanning the iron-clad warriors for his silver hair and piercing gaze.

Fitting her boot to her stirrup, she pulled herself up into the saddle, her fingers numb on the reins. She hadn't seen Torj since that night in his tent, the night she'd practically begged him to live for her... She'd sent her orders through Kipp, not sure she would be able to face him without breaking. She had told him she loved him countless times, and now, instead of saying the words, she poured that feeling through the bond, hoping that it reached him, wherever he was. The connection between them, usually a warm presence at the edge of her consciousness, now felt stretched thin like a thread about to snap. There was a hollowness where he should be, an echo chamber where the essence of him had anchored her. Wren found herself reaching for him through that invisible tether, only to grasp at emptiness.

Behind her, Dessa and Zavier were overseeing the transport of the last remaining silvertide in their saddlebags. There was little hope Wren would be able to distill more of the cure while they were on the road, and the dwindling supplies left fewer options in any case.

All too soon, Wilder called for them to move out, and the blossoming landscape ahead blurred as Wren blinked hard, fighting back tears. *"He'd rather die strong than live weak..."* Kipp's words both haunted her and steeled her. She wasn't going to let that happen. Not in her lifetime.

As they rode across her kingdom, Wren remembered sharing the saddle with Torj during those first few months at Drevenor. Gods, how he'd infuriated her. But even then, the rhythmic beat of the Warsword's heart at her back had been a comfort, his body surrounding her with his strength and his fierce determination. Back then, she had fought him every step of the way, and now... now she wished for nothing more than his solid presence behind her, the war-drum beat of his heart against her spine, promising retribution.

Thea's horse pushed up alongside Wren's, her sister's presence offering her some reprieve from her thoughts.

"Lord Lucian's a piece of work," Thea muttered with a glare in the nobleman's direction.

"What's he done now?" Wren asked.

"Existed. Shared his narrow beliefs. Been himself," Thea retorted. "That's enough, right? You've met the man."

"Unfortunately."

"I hate that he's got us over a barrel," Thea said under her breath. "Not just with the Bear Slayer's situation, but with the allies too..."

"You and me both," Wren admitted. "Kipp and I have been working on something—"

"The letters?" Thea asked. "He told me. I think it's as good an idea as any."

Wren sighed. "I thought so too at first. But who am I to demand the common folk hear my story? Who am I to ask for understanding from those who have suffered the most since the last war?"

"You're one of them," Thea said unexpectedly. "Or at least, you were. Was it so long ago that you were a simple alchemist of Thezmarr? An orphan with no more to her name than the tools at her belt and the skills at her fingertips?"

"I was one of many." Wren adjusted her grip on the reins, flexing the ache from her hands.

"So?" Thea pressed. "It doesn't make your experience any less."

"I don't like asking for help..."

Thea snorted. "Shocking."

"You're one to talk," Wren shot back before she sighed. "Honestly, I hate it. I hate to ask anyone."

"Again, sister... that's not exactly new information to me," Thea said gently. "Though it might help if you told me why."

Wren shifted in her saddle, her posture growing rigid as her scalp prickled. "It was me who asked Sam and Ida to stay back at Thezmarr while I left. It was *my* idea that they remain behind and make more of the sun orchid essence. I thought we could use more of it at the fortress. I asked them to do that. It's my fault they were captured. My fault they're dead."

"Oh, Wren," Thea murmured, her voice pained. "That wasn't your doing."

Wren forced the words out. "If I hadn't asked them to stay back—"

"You think if you hadn't asked for their help, they wouldn't have died?" Thea finished for her. "There's no way you can know that. They could have just as easily died in the battles! It was *their choice* to stay at Thezmarr, to continue their work. You can't let what happened to them stop you from seeking help, from asking for support when you need it. You can't go through life like that."

"I haven't... I wrote the letters like Kipp told me to. I have asked for allies where I could. I even sent Torj away to—"

"You're doing all that you can," her sister cut her off. "I think Kipp's right. You should keep writing the letters. Silas got his platform; you should do the same. If people are going to choose sides, let them know what you stand for."

Wren tried to cling to Thea's resolve, and as they continued to ride across Delmira, she tried to remain stoic about the fate she and Torj now faced. Under different circumstances, they had been apart before, and she had survived. But now, knowing what they were to one another...

The hollow ache in her chest whispered that she wouldn't survive a second time, nor would she want to.

A shadow fell across her face. She looked up, expecting to see storm clouds gathering in answer to her turmoil.

But it was a familiar set of broad shoulders that blocked out the sun. Torj Elderbrock sat tall in his saddle before her, his hammer across his back, determination gleaming in his eyes.

Wren's heart stuttered, then raced, her breath catching painfully in her lungs. The world around her—the army, Thea, even Lucian's schemes—all faded away. Her fingers trembled on the reins, and she fought the desperate urge to fling herself from her horse to his.

He didn't reach for her; he didn't address her, not aloud. But the bond between them, so empty just moments before, now hummed with his presence—stronger and clearer than she had felt in weeks.

Torj guided his horse into the ranks, and it was only

then that she saw his stallion pulled a cart behind him. A cart gleaming with pearly white blooms.

With silvertide roses.

And then, Torj's words echoed through their golden bond and into her mind.

I want to live, Embers. For you. Always for you.

CHAPTER 44
TORJ

"Hope and poison share one critical property: dosage determines outcome. Too little of one or too much of the other can be equally fatal."
—The Poisoner's Handbook

Torj spoke those words to Wren soul-to-soul, with all the reverence and love he could muster, and the relief in her eyes threatened to unravel him completely. Despite the roses he delivered, the news he brought with him was not good, and he hated that her reprieve would only last mere moments.

You're a sight for sore eyes, Embers, he told her.

Wren's gaze moved over him methodically, studying him. *You look better...*

I am. Dessa and Zavier gave me something to help.

Wren's eyes twinkled. *Do I even want to know?*

Probably not, he allowed. *But the important thing is that I'm here with you. And will be, for as long as you need me.*

I'll never not need you, Bear Slayer.

That's not true, Embers. But you have me all the same.

Wren's attention slid to the cart behind him. *Why do I get the sense there is more to this tale?*

As if in answer, a distant rumble of thunder rolled across the verdant fields.

Because there is, Torj told her grimly, before guiding Tucker to the head of the force where Wilder was waiting, Wren following on their heels.

Wilder gaped at the supply of silvertide when Torj reached him. "Where did those come from?"

He wasn't the only one. Torj's arrival had caught the attention of Lucian and Darian, as well as Lord Briar and Lord Pendelton, who insisted on stopping, drawing their company to an abrupt halt so they could gather around the Bear Slayer.

Shifting uneasily in his saddle, Torj retrieved the map from his pocket and passed it across to Wilder. "When Wren was studying for her opus at Drevenor, she discovered that places where she'd used her storm magic flourished in ways that regular land didn't. When she first arrived in Delmira after the shadow war, she poured her power into the land in her grief. Those places are marked on that map, and over the last few days, I rode to the closest locations to our base. I sent scouts to the others."

"And?" Wilder pressed hopefully.

Torj didn't dare look in Wren's direction, not with

300

Lucian watching like a hawk, not when the words about to spill from his lips were so wretched.

"Silvertide did grow in those locations," he said slowly. "But everywhere I went, it was burned to a crisp."

"What?" Wren breathed. "It's gone? All of it?"

Torj dipped his head in confirmation. "I salvaged what I could from the outskirts of every field I visited. But... it has been destroyed. My scouts reported the same from their locations."

Wilder cursed.

"This confirms it, then," Wren murmured. "Silas knows about the roses and what they mean to us, what they can do... that they threaten the advantage he has over us."

Torj nodded. "I think that's a safe bet. My scouts will return with what little they were able to recover, but it won't be much."

"How much of the cure can you produce with the silvertide we have?" Darian asked, scanning the cart's supplies critically.

"I don't know," Wren replied. "It depends on the state of the roses themselves. Even if they look intact, they could be damaged by smoke or ash. As soon as we establish another base, I can work on more. But we need to preserve these stores with silkspore until then." She fiddled with her belt of potions before speaking again. "There is one more place, not marked on the map... It may have what we need."

Torj frowned, looking down at the locations he'd systematically checked off at her request. Why had she not trusted him with one more?

"Where?" he asked.

Wren pointed to the map. "If we take a slight detour

before the ravine here, this area *might* have some of the roses we need. Then we can make camp, and hopefully the other alchemists and I can brew more of the cure by night."

"Sounds like a good plan," Wilder allowed as Torj folded up his map and returned it to his pocket.

"Sounds like the only plan," Torj muttered.

Over the next two days, as they journeyed toward the ravine, Torj and his fellow Warswords were vigilant about sending out patrols—they needed to be aware of their surroundings at all times. Everyone, even the shieldbearers, knew what a risk it was to move such a large company out in the open, but it was a necessity.

On the third morning, Torj assessed their reports. "Where are the scouts who went south?" he asked Darian, scanning the handful of warriors who had arrived at dawn and were now tending to their sweaty horses. "There were two..."

But no answer came.

"Doesn't look like they've returned yet," Kipp said with a frown.

"They should be back by now," Torj replied. "They should have been the first to arrive. Who did we send ahead?"

"Wilder and Thea," Kipp told him, his voice low.

Torj signaled for their company to halt. "Then we wait for their report. If the southern scouts aren't back by then, we have to assume they're dead."

Kipp nodded grimly. "I think you're right."

Torj addressed the company. "We'll make camp tonight when we find suitable grounds. For now, water your horses, see to your needs. As soon as we're rejoined by Warswords Hawthorne and Embervale, we'll ride hard. Be prepared."

"Someone is watching us," Darian remarked from his saddle.

Torj had felt it too—eyes on them from somewhere in the distance. But no attack came. No challenge. Just the weight of observation, growing heavier with each league. "I know."

Stay close, Embers, he said through the bond, and her lightning flickered back in response.

Another hour passed before Kipp called out, "They're back!"

Torj whirled around to see the married Warsword couple ride into the clearing, their cheeks flushed with exertion.

"Well?" he prompted when he reached them, with Wren and Darian close behind.

"No enemy scouts or forces that we could see," Thea told them. "What have the rest reported?"

"Our southern scouts haven't returned," Torj replied.

"So they're dead," Thea surmised.

"I'd say so," Torj agreed, his voice heavy with regret.

"The good news is that you were right about what was on the map," Wilder said, lacing the words with meaning. "There's also a decent flat area for camping, and the ravine is just beyond. An old trade route used to run through it, by the looks of things. Narrow passage."

Thea chimed in. "You should see it, Torj—there's

303

enough there for Wren to make every kingdom its own batch of the cure—"

"And what? It's just sitting there, unguarded, untouched?" he challenged.

"As far as we could see," Wilder offered.

Torj turned to Wren. "Then that's where we go. We move now."

CHAPTER 45
WREN

*"The tree that cannot bend with strong winds will be uprooted.
The tree that can bow and twist with the seasons survives."*
—The Green Apothecary: A Guide to Medicinal Plants

The river roared ahead of them, swollen with the healthy rainfall that now blessed Delmira's lands. Even from the bank, Wren could feel the spray on her face, could see how the water churned and foamed over hidden rocks. Her horse shifted beneath her, ears pinned back, clearly sharing her unease.

She had traveled this stretch of land before, only when she had last been here, the riverbed had been no more than a cracked depression in the earth, with not even a trickle of water to speak of... Now, it was a force that could sweep them away.

"Zavier and I crossed here," Cal shouted, pointing to a

dip in the river's flow. "We were up to our waists, but it seems to be the shallowest point." His shirt was still soaked through from his previous crossing scouting the terrain ahead, but he didn't hesitate as he guided his stallion back to the surging current.

"Keep your horse's head pointed slightly upstream," Torj called to their bannermen over the rush of water. "Let them find their own footing. If they start to swim, give them their head and keep your feet free of the stirrups. Trust in their strength, in their instincts—they want to be on solid ground as much as you do."

Wren watched as the first riders entered the water after Cal. The horses' hooves disappeared beneath the surface, then their legs, their riders lifting their feet as the frigid water rose around them. Some of the mounts snorted and balked, but their training held. The current pushed at them, trying to sweep them downstream, but they fought against it, muscles straining.

After you, Embers. Torj motioned for her to start crossing next.

Wren braced herself for the icy impact. The moment her horse stepped into the river, the cold hit her like a physical blow. The current was stronger than it looked, tugging at her mount's legs, making each step treacherous. Water splashed up around them, soaking through her boots, her breeches, stealing her breath.

Halfway across, her mare lost its footing on the slick riverbed. For one heart-stopping moment, they were swimming, the current threatening to pull them under. She forced herself to stay calm, to keep her grip on the reins light as her mount fought to regain its balance. Water swelled around them, and Wren realized that no storm magic or alchemy could save her from drowning. It was her and her horse at the mercy of the current, and she had to close her eyes briefly, handing over her fate to the mare beneath her.

Finally, mercifully, her horse's hooves found purchase on the far bank. They scrambled up, water streaming from her clothes and tack, both of them trembling from cold and exertion. Wren was already dreading the second crossing on the way back.

More water sprayed as Torj's stallion leapt up onto the shore. The Warsword's gaze went straight to her, assessing her.

You're alright?

Cold, but in one piece, she replied. *You?*

My blood always runs hot with you around anyway. His lips curved in a suggestive smile.

Wren's heart lifted. Even soaked to the bone, it was good to see him joke. If she could keep him in decent spirits while she figured out a solution, it would help keep her mind fresh.

So she answered through their bond with a smug smile of her own. *I'm well aware... but control yourself, Warsword. We're on a mission.*

They paused on the far bank only long enough to wring out their cloaks and check their weapons hadn't been compromised by the water. Wren's teeth chattered as she tipped half the river from her boots and checked the potions at her belt. Thankfully, all of her vials were airtight by design.

Torj gave her one last heated look. *The things I'd do to get you out of those wet clothes and into a warm bed,* he murmured into her mind before he urged his horse forward. "Cal," he called. "Lead the way."

Cal pointed ahead. "There," he said quietly. "There's a good place to set up camp just beyond that rise."

Even with the changes, Wren recognized the land. She had sat on that very ridge, sharing her rations with her horse because there was no grass for grazing. Only parched, yellowed fields had stretched out before her, echoing her loneliness and grief back to her. It hadn't been the first time she'd cried after the war, but it had been one of the more significant outpourings of her sorrow.

The piercing sound of her own scream came back to her, carving through all else, followed by the near-deafening clap of thunder. Her storm had raged all night, washing her tears into the earth, striking lightning so hard into the ground that smoke drifted in ribbons from the soil. Yes, she knew this place like she knew the shape of the pain in her own chest.

The others reached the crest in the land before she did, and she heard their murmurs of surprise.

Dessa was the first to turn back to her. "Wren..." she croaked, her voice thick with emotion.

Still shivering from the cold, Wren urged her horse to close the gap, and before she knew it, the plains were there —but they were not the same.

Silvertide roses dotted the land before them, their luminescent petals dancing in the gentle breeze. For a moment, all Wren could do was stare. She'd spent so long cultivating pots of these flowers back at Drevenor, carefully tending to each bloom. But this...

"I can't believe it," she murmured to Dessa, shaking her head at the scattered flowers.

"Nor can I," Dessa replied, tears lining her eyes. "This is going to help us win. I... I didn't know if we could."

Wren reached across and squeezed her friend's icy hand. "We did it once before. We can do it again. And now..." She motioned to the modest crop of roses, words failing her.

Zavier brought his horse up alongside hers and spoke to Dessa, motioning to their group of chosen harvesters. "Are you sure about the method you taught them? That they're capable?"

Cal brandished his dagger in a show of confidence, reciting Dessa's instructions: "Cut at the second node, leave the roots intact. Work in pairs—one cuts while the other gathers and packs."

"That's it," Dessa said encouragingly. "Right, Wren?"

Wren nodded, but her attention had landed on Torj, who now stood with his stallion slightly apart from the group, his hands flexing and unflexing at his sides.

At last, Wren dismounted and slipped into the crop with the other harvesters, unsheathing her knife. She worked alongside Dessa. Cut, gather, pack. The rhythm of it was almost hypnotic, especially when the rest of their group moved with the precision Dessa had drilled into them during their forced march here.

"They would make the Master of Lifelore proud," Wren told her friend.

Dessa gave a sad smile. "And yet, Drevenor is no more... Lifelore, warfare, healing, design... What will become of those pillars of alchemy now? Of the alchemists who wanted to learn?"

"Perhaps you will teach them," Wren said gently, flicking her knife across another stem, careful of the thorns.

They harvested all that they could before moving on to flatter terrain. There, they set up camp, including a makeshift alchemy workshop for Wren and the others. It wasn't long before they were de-thorning the silvertide roses and starting new batches of Wren's cure for the dark alchemy.

"I wish you didn't have to do this tonight," Torj said quietly, coming to stand beside her. "You need rest."

She said nothing, continuing the intricate work at hand. She longed for him to wrap his arms around her waist, to bury his face in the crook of her neck and kiss her, but... regardless of whether they trusted their current company or not, she was still publicly engaged to another man. A man whose father held the key to her soul-bonded's life, who had allies she needed to win over if she wanted to stand any chance of winning this war.

Zavier and Dessa made their excuses—something flimsy about collecting more water when a fresh bucket stood at Wren's feet. But she didn't protest as they left. Instead, she inhaled the familiar scent of her Warsword and fought every instinct to throw herself into his arms.

"You take on too much," he ventured, his fingers grazing hers as he reached for a bundle of dried herbs, mimicking her actions and crushing it thoroughly.

Wren glanced around to check that Lord Lucian was

nowhere in sight. "I'm afraid that's a trait we share, Bear Slayer."

The Warsword drew closer. She could feel the heat radiating from his powerful body. "Then I can't hold it against you, can I?"

The bond crackled between them, full of lightning and Furies-given strength—a joining of both their magics, a promise that linked them, soul to soul.

Wren's breath hitched with the force of their connection. The Bear Slayer tensed beside her, and she knew he felt the same sensations coursing through his own being. A symphony of desire and love danced across their shared bond, drawing them to one another with a power almost beyond their control.

Torj leaned in so that his words tickled the shell of her ear. "Is it wrong that after this gods-forsaken day, all I want to do is take you to my tent and taste every inch of you?"

The sultry promise in his words had Wren biting back a whimper. She was well versed in what the Warsword's mouth could do to her, and it made her knees buckle. His scent wrapped around her—it was all she could do not to lean in. She glanced at the others, who were busy over a crucible, but far too close for her liking.

"We can't..." she murmured, though the images had already started to flood her mind—Torj's teasing touch, the slow torture of him peeling her clothes away, piece by piece, the trail of his tongue along her skin... The push of his hard cock inside her—

Torj gave a low groan. "You're killing me, Embers."

Wren glanced up to find the Bear Slayer biting his lip as he studied her with a heated gaze. "You... you saw all that?"

"Saw?" Torj loosed a tense breath. "Embers, I fucking *felt* it."

Wren gaped at him.

He offered an amused shrug before twisting his body to reveal his lower half. "Believe me now?" The thick, hard outline of his erection was clearly visible, straining against his leathers.

The sight had heat blooming between her thighs, had her nipples tightening against the rough fabric of her bodice. It took all the willpower Wren had to stop herself from grabbing a fistful of the Bear Slayer's shirt and hauling his mouth down to hers—

"It's a damn good thing I'm not the jealous type," Darian observed as he entered the makeshift alchemy station. "And for Furies' sake, Elderbrock, show some decorum. Not all of us want to see your monster cock multiple times in the space of a few weeks."

A laugh burst from Wren as Torj adjusted himself, the tips of his ears turning red. But the Warsword clicked his tongue with annoyance. "It's not my fault you're always showing up where you're not welcome."

"I'm never not welcome," Darian quipped.

"Consider this a first, then," Torj replied gruffly.

Amusement gleamed in the nobleman's eyes before he fixed them with a serious look, his tone full of warning. "I could have been anyone just now."

"I know," Wren muttered, hanging her head.

"Do you?" Darian challenged. "Because what I've just walked in on makes a mockery of our engagement. You were lucky it was only me, but what if it had been my father? Or any one of his bannermen or spies? Any alliances you hope to make would have been quashed before they began. And whatever information he has about Torj's poisoning would go up in smoke." He studied them, his expression softening. "The people of the midrealms, the people we love, depend on your discretion. I don't say this to be cruel. I say it out of necessity." His gaze landed on Torj. "I hope you know that, brother."

Before either of them could respond, Darian walked back toward the tents.

Wren sighed. "I'm sorry," she told the Bear Slayer. "I'm sorry I've made such a mess of all this."

"It's not your fault. You can only play the hand you're dealt as best you can."

She faltered. "I'm trying..."

"I know," he replied. "And I'll be here. Every step of the way, just as I promised."

Wren felt the ghost of his touch on her skin, a whisper of pleasure to come, someday, before he went back to the heart of the camp. A deep pulse of longing settled low in her belly as she watched her Warsword walk away.

It made her ache.

"We could split up," Kipp suggested before dawn the next morning. "The bulk of our forces can continue on to the meeting point, while a smaller unit lures the enemy after us into the ravine..."

"And the roses? Who takes that supply?" Wren asked.

"We split it between the two, so we're not completely

without should anything happen," Cal ventured. "We are playing the bait, after all..."

Wren watched as Torj weighed up his options and the advice of his friends.

"Lord Lucian," he said at last, turning to the man he despised above all else. "Take our forces and continue on the planned route. Make it look like that's still our primary objective." Next, his gaze found his childhood friend. "Lord Darian, you'd best come with us, to ensure your bride's safety. I'll lead our small party through the ravine."

"Absolutely not. Elwren comes with us," Lord Lucian said. "I will not have my future daughter-in-law used as bait like a worm on a hook."

"I'm afraid we need the storm wielders at our disposal, Lord Lucian," Kipp interjected smoothly. "If we mean to eliminate the force behind us, we'll need their power, as I'm sure you understand."

A vein pulsed in Lucian's temple as he glared at the strategist, before Darian led him away, following Torj's orders.

The smaller company moved forward at a steady pace while they waited for Cal and Zavier to return from their scouting mission. Wren kept glancing back the way they'd come, trying not to think about what would happen if her friends didn't make it back.

It wasn't until hours later that Cal's voice carried ahead of him. "Incoming!" He and Zavier drove their horses hard toward the company, faces grim. "At least a hundred soldiers on our tail, well-armed, moving in formation," Cal reported.

Wren tried to gauge the Warswords' reactions. A hundred men against their fifty... She was no military expert, but at a guess, she'd say they were at a disadvantage.

"How far?" Torj demanded.

"Quarter of a league, maybe less," Zavier replied, pulling his mount up beside Wren's. "They're not trying to hide anymore."

"Any sign of our scouts?" Wren asked.

Cal shook his head. "None."

"Shit," Torj muttered, his jaw tightening. "I was hoping to avoid conflict so soon, but if we can eliminate even one portion of Silas' force, we should take the opportunity. The ravine is the best option. We'll be able to draw them into the narrows and pick them off one by one. They have the numbers, but the location is perfect, and we have Warswords and alchemists among us."

It felt wrong to move at the same unhurried pace as before when they knew there was an enemy plot in motion behind them. But they had to act as though they were unaware, as though they were simply marching toward the capital, relying on the prestige of their force as a deterrent.

"Do you think they plan to attack?" Wren asked Torj. "Would *you*, in their position? They'll want to take advantage of us being outnumbered, won't they?"

"We are outnumbered, yes," the Warsword said. "But with a smaller force like ours, we have the ability to move faster, adapt, change formations... We got our supply wagons, heavy siege weaponry, and half the silvertide away

315

from the fight." Torj looked thoughtful. "We have no idea what sort of skill set the unit behind us has. They could be seasoned warriors, or simply farmers who were recruited into the People's Vanguard. Something tells me Silas would have no issue sacrificing either."

"You're right about that," Zavier interjected, his expression grim. "And Silas' tactics are as much about mind games as combat maneuvers. He knew the value of emotional warfare even as a child."

"How so?" Wren asked, watching her friend's shoulders cave inward.

"When we were young, it was always me, Silas, and our friend Otis. We did everything together—played, attended my mother's lessons, and Otis' father taught us how to fence... He even gifted us matching wooden swords. We were only little, and one day Silas came down with a fever, as children do, leaving me to play with Otis for the week. We thought nothing of it, only that we missed our friend and that three was the perfect number for so many of our games. But when Silas recovered and returned to us, he was different —surly. Not long after, my wooden sword was found splintered into pieces... Silas told me that Otis had done it."

"And you believed him?" Wren said.

"I was a child. And he was my brother," Zavier replied sadly.

Wren wanted to hug her friend. She could hear the pain in his voice. "What happened to Otis?"

"I told my parents what he'd supposedly done. They told his parents... and his father beat the daylights out of him in the street." Zavier's voice was hoarse. "Of course, it wasn't until much later that I realized it had been Silas. That he'd done it out of jealousy. And that he'd stood by, watching Otis' thrashing without a care in the world."

A shiver raked down Wren's spine. "Gods..."

"So yes." Zavier straightened in his saddle. "Silas knows how to use people's emotions against them. And he's more than willing to sit back and watch people destroy one another."

"Does he care about anything? Beyond power and control? Any*one*?" Torj prompted from the other side of Wren.

"I thought he cared about me," Zavier replied. "But I think those days are long gone."

"I'm sorry," Wren said.

"I truly thought I could help him."

Wren sighed. "I know you did, Zave—"

She was cut off by the arrival of Thea, who looked as fierce as ever, ready for battle. Her sister's attention went straight to Torj. "Wilder and I are concerned that we're being herded into a trap," she said without preamble. "It's all well and good to utilize the ravine, Bear Slayer, but what if more waits for us on the other side?"

"The area has been secured. Kipp assures me that there are no access points within the ravine but for the entrance and exit. I've had ten scouts ride ahead to ensure there's no secondary People's Vanguard force waiting for us on the other side as well."

"A man after my own heart," Kipp declared. "But it's true—everything is in order."

"Good." Thea nodded, seemingly placated now.

HELEN SCHEUERER

"It's settled, then," Torj said. "Let's lure those fuckers to their deaths."

Wren couldn't help but admire the sight of Torj Elderbrock atop his Tverrian stallion against the backdrop of the Delmirian landscape. He looked every bit a Warsword of Thezmarr, strapped into his armor with his war hammer slung across his broad shoulders.

Behind him, the kingdom—*her* kingdom—was thriving, oblivious to the promise of violence that marched across its ground. Endless plains and rolling hills of emerald green swept to the horizon, while flocks of humming sparrows danced in formation across the cloudless sky. The breeze was warm on Wren's face, and were it not for the rattling of metal breastplates and chain mail behind her, she could have believed it was a peaceful summer's day.

In all her life, she had never enjoyed one of those... not in the way she'd read about in books—with blankets laid across soft grass and wildflowers, baskets of food and drink, surrounded by laughter.

What are you thinking of? Torj's voice spoke into her mind.

Peace, she replied. *Or at least what I imagine it to be. Even after the war, I had nothing like it. Though the shadows had gone, there was still so much darkness in the world around me, and within myself... Sometimes I wonder about the person I would be in a time of peace. And if I'd be able to sustain myself on something so good after all this time.*

It was easier, somehow, not saying the words aloud, but pouring them into Torj through their bond. An unspoken secret between them, something she could say only to him, only in the deepest parts of their minds and souls.

318

Her Warsword's eyes gleamed. *Of course you could be sustained by good.* You *are good.*

She muffled her sad laugh. *You are biased,* she said, trying for a light tone, before turning the conversation to him. *What about you? What does peace look like for the mighty Bear Slayer of Thezmarr?*

A smile tugged at the corner of his mouth. *Freedom,* he replied. *Freedom to court you. To take our time. To have you on my arm for all to see. To not be worried for our safety, but instead for our only concern to be which beautiful place to travel next...*

Wren's heart sank a little. She doubted her new life as a queen would be one of voyages and adventure. *I'm afraid my only travels for a good few years will be in the name of diplomatic relations.*

It doesn't matter. I'll go anywhere as long as it's with you, Embers.

They came to a stop outside the ravine, which towered before them, its ancient stone worn smooth by time and water, an open maw to the dark, narrow fissure beyond.

Anywhere? Wren asked silently. *Even back into the shadows?* Her magic thrummed beneath her skin in anticipation.

If that's where you're going, that's where I go too.

And so Wren took a deep breath, and urged her horse into the dark.

CHAPTER 46
TORJ

"The seasoned Warsword understands that every battle plan is merely the first compromise in a day that will demand many more."
—The Warsword's Way

Torj had never been fond of enclosed spaces, likely a result of his father locking him in the kitchen cupboards when he was younger. He had always preferred the sweeping, tussock-covered valleys of Tver. There, the land stretched out as far as the sky, open and inviting, full of rushing rivers and herds of wild horses running free.

The ravine with fifty warriors who hadn't washed in several days was far from his ideal location, especially as it forced them close together, almost in single file over jagged rocks and scree. There was a certain kind of tension that came with knowingly making oneself vulnerable, and it made Torj's skin prickle as they edged deeper into the ravine, solid rock towering on both sides.

Sound traveled differently here, following the twisting narrow path and echoing upward. While Torj was confident atop his Tverrian stallion, other riders weren't so lucky. The terrain and the strange noises made some horses skittish, while others struggled to keep their footing across the uneven ground.

As they made their way through, Torj saw the challenge of maintaining proper spacing between their forces to avoid bunching, or worse—dangerous gaps. The metallic sound of armor and hoofbeats against rock created an unsettling chorus around his wandering thoughts.

The nape of his neck prickled, and sensing his unease, Tucker shifted too. What if the poison had affected Torj's mind? What if it had led him to make a rash decision? To risk their entire force? The nagging sensation didn't leave him as they continued their trek, and beside him, he could feel Wren's storm magic growing restless.

I don't like this, she said into his mind. *Something's not right.*

I know, Torj replied, scanning behind them for any sign of the enemy. They should have been entering the ravine by now—

"Torj." Wren spoke aloud this time, pointing ahead.

At the front of their force, dust drifted into the air.

Torj started toward it. "What in the midrealms—"

There was a ripple of panic traveling over the column of soldiers, and suddenly, people were instinctively trying to turn their horses around in the confined space.

"What is it?" Torj called, unable to see what had caused the commotion.

A scream sounded, and Torj's stomach leapt into his throat as he saw seemingly solid sections of the ravine floor begin to shift.

Horses reared. Soldiers fell from their saddles, their formation breaking instantly.

The enemy was lying in wait, in hidden trenches below.

"We have to retreat," Darian called from nearby.

But Torj's heart seized as he turned back. "We can't."

For the enemy force they'd lured after them had arrived, hemming them in between two solid walls of rock and an enemy force on either end of the ravine.

"Fuck," Torj hissed. It was a tactical nightmare, being attacked from below and forced back, as well as the confined space—there was nowhere to retreat, and no space to move into defensive formations. A trap.

They were being forced together, horses almost trampling one another. No one had swung a blade yet, but it was only a matter of time, and in such close quarters, it would be a bloodbath.

Wren, he called. *Do you have anything in your belt that could get us out of this?*

Not without risking our own soldiers, came the reply, though he could almost hear her wracking her mind for other options. But there were none.

He'd made a mistake. A big one.

And it would cost them everything.

Torj reached for his hammer. There was no other way this would end.

Get behind me if you can, Embers. He sent the instruction

through their bond, hoping that despite the tight quarters, she'd be able to maneuver closer to him.

Something whistled through the air—an arrow, brushing against Torj's shoulder before it pierced the chest of a soldier behind him. A soft gasp of shock left the poor bastard's lips before he looked down at the projectile protruding from his heart. And then he slid from the saddle, hitting the ground with a thud, dead.

"Attack!" Torj bellowed, for it was all they could do.

The clash of steel amplified tenfold in the narrow passage, along with the screams and the horses' panic. The sound was overwhelming, threatening to swallow them all whole.

Torj swung his hammer blindly as smoke and dust became trapped in the ravine, the visibility growing poorer with each passing moment. But all he could think was that it was his fault—his mistake that had led them to this deadly precipice, and he had no idea how the fuck he was going to get them out.

He could feel Wren behind him, her magic illuminating the dark with flashes of lightning, but he knew she wouldn't risk something more for fear of bringing the stone walls down upon them all.

Torj carved his way through the force that had emerged from the hidden trench, bone crunching beneath the iron head of his hammer as he went. But the chaos only escalated, and with a bitter pang of regret, he realized how outnumbered they truly were. He scanned the bedlam for Wren—she was with Thea, the two storm wielders striking out with small, precise bolts of lightning, while Wilder and Cal defended them from attack. Torj leapt from his stallion's back and launched himself toward them, as much as the cramped space would allow. He brought down half a dozen enemy soldiers as he did, but they continued to swarm, blocking Torj's forces inside the ravine to be picked off one by one—

A near-deafening roar of rage shook the passage, debris tumbling from the sides. And through the haze, a spiked club plunged through the air.

Cries of terror echoed up the passage as the rusted barbs tore through the enemy commander's throat, painting the rocks with death.

And through the crimson mist stepped Vernich the fucking Bloodletter.

CHAPTER 47

TORJ

"Many a great warrior of the midrealms measures his worth by the weapon he wields, until he discovers that which he cannot defend against. The heart, once pierced by love, renders even Naarvian steel obsolete."
—The Warsword's Way

"Where the fuck is my mace?" Vernich growled, jerking his club free from the commander's neck, fresh blood splattering at his boots.

No one spoke as the Warsword they'd all thought long dead emerged from the shadows, crushing enemy skulls with his bare hands, their faces turning to pulp as he threw them against the stone. There was no mistake. It was him. Larger than life, violence incarnate, vicious to the bone. His clothes and armor were weathered, his skin smudged with grime and gore that did not belong to him.

Vernich swung his club again, and this time struck the side of the ravine—once, twice, three times, in the exact same spot.

A deep, resonant rumble grew into a near-deafening roar as rock began to tumble from above. Desperate screams were cut short, the vibrating ground beneath them now violently shaking.

Rock cascaded, the thunderous deluge crashing down the ravine. Sharp fragments of debris stung Torj's exposed skin, and a suffocating cloud of dust billowed around them. Grit coated his tongue and teeth as he flung himself toward Wren, trying to shield her from the avalanche of stone.

It obliterated the enemy behind Torj and his company.

And when the dust settled, Vernich stalked toward them.

He stopped in front of Torj and Wilder, scowling. The last time Torj had seen the Bloodletter had been at the one-year memorial of the shadow war at Thezmarr, and though Torj wasn't sure how it was possible, the years in between had hardened the older Warsword even more. He didn't know the Bloodletter's age; he'd never thought—or dared —to ask, but the warrior's face was lined with deep creases around his eyes, and his graying beard and hair were unkempt.

"Elderbrock. Hawthorne," Vernich grunted, his rough voice unchanged by time. "I knew you'd try to take them in the ravine. Fools. Now, I'll only ask this once more... Where. Is. My. Fucking. Mace?"

"We burned it in a funeral rite," Wilder replied, stunned. "We thought you were dead."

"Do I look fucking dead to you?" Vernich's bloodshot

eyes were wide, the rage that had been simmering beneath the surface rising and rising—

"*They* thought you were dead." Kipp came forward, tugging his horse along behind him. "I, however, suspected that killing the likes of you might be harder than the enemy expected."

Vernich's eyes narrowed as he took in the sight of the strategist, who reached for his saddle blanket and lifted the fabric.

There, strapped to his horse, was the Bloodletter's mace.

Everyone, including Torj, stared. They had burned the weapon atop the funeral pyre, hadn't they? He'd seen it go up in flames himself.

And yet the weapon was there, unmarked—cared for, even. Not a clump of flesh or hair in sight. It was in the best condition Torj had ever seen it in.

Kipp shrugged. "Kept it, just in case."

"You..." Vernich blinked at him, dumbfounded.

"Are full of surprises, I know." Kipp winked. "You're welcome, by the way."

Vernich tossed his spiked club aside and pulled his legendary mace from the horse's back, looking unnervingly dazed. "I always liked you," he grunted.

Kipp answered with a grin. "Now, shall we get the fuck out of here?"

"Thought you'd never ask," Cal muttered as he hesitated before the older Warsword. Slowly, he offered his hand. "Good to have you back, Bloodletter."

Vernich froze, like he'd never seen a handshake before. Torj nudged him with an elbow to the side and he lurched forward, clasping Cal's hand in his.

"Good to be back, Whitlock."

Torj stifled a laugh as a look of shock passed over Cal's face. He was likely surprised that Vernich knew his name and had deigned to use it.

But there had been enough dithering. Torj looked to his elder. "I assume you have a base?"

Straightening, Vernich gave a nod. "I've got a hidden settlement just beyond the hills to the north. We can debrief there."

Torj exchanged a look of disbelief with Wren. *Vernich the Savior... Who knew?*

A subtle smile played on her lips. *We need as many of those as we can get, Bear Slayer.*

It was no wonder they hadn't found any trace of a force on the other side of the ravine. The rolling hills had seemed empty, unassuming—exactly as they were meant to seem.

Torj, Wren, Kipp, Cal, Zavier, Dessa, Wilder, Thea, and Darian rode in Vernich's wake, the Warsword having taken the horse of one of the fallen warriors. The rest of their company would meet them in three days' time, where they would be joined by the incoming forces.

Midway up a grassy hill, Vernich signaled for them to halt. Torj watched in disbelief as the massive warrior hopped from one seemingly innocent stone to the next in a deliberate sequence, each step precise and practiced. The stones themselves looked weathered, unremarkable—just the kind of detail most eyes would skip right over.

A mechanical groan sounded from beneath his boots,

followed by the whisper of hidden gears. To Torj's shock, the grass and soil parted like a pair of doors, earth and roots drawing back in a perfect seam to reveal stone steps descending into the shadowed hillside.

"How the fuck is this possible?" Torj breathed as the Bloodletter stepped aside and motioned for them to enter.

"Counterweight mechanism," Vernich replied gruffly.

Torj didn't bother to hide his surprise. "You built this?"

Vernich snorted. "No, this was already here. Hand your horses over to our horse master there, he'll make sure they're looked after. We can't have them in the main sector."

"Main sector?" Wren murmured in awe as she passed her reins over to a man who had emerged from the opening in the hillside.

"You'll see," Vernich said, motioning for them to follow.

With their horses led away, Torj found himself walking alongside Wilder and Cal, his fellow Warswords wearing similar expressions of bewilderment. It took a moment for his eyes to adjust to the dim lighting, but when they did, he couldn't help but gasp.

Torches lined the walls of what could only be described as an underground shelter. The inside of the hill had been hollowed out, and a wide, winding staircase seemed to wrap around multiple levels.

They followed Vernich down, further beneath the hillside, passing a vast underground well system, complete with an array of pulleys and buckets. As they delved deeper into the hollow, several people slipped by them on the stairs. Not warriors clad in armor and weapons, Torj noticed, but regular people... Children, even.

"In here," Vernich grunted, holding a door open for them.

Inside was a gathering space of sorts, with vaulted ceilings supported by stone columns. In the center were several logs, which Vernich waved toward.

"Take a seat," he said, studying their faces. "I looked much the same when I found this place..."

When they had all sat down on the stumps of timber, Torj rested his hammer across his thighs and looked up at the Bloodletter. "And what exactly is this place?"

Vernich pulled a scrap of fabric from his pocket and passed it over his face, attempting to scrub away some of the dirt and dried blood. "The Warren," he replied. "They call it the Warren. It's been here since before the original fall of Delmira decades ago. It was where many of the common people fled when the first wave of shadow magic hit this kingdom."

"Amazing. How does it work?" Kipp was already craning his neck and squinting at the ceiling.

"You haven't got any ideas?" Vernich mused. "The light comes from hidden skylights disguised as rocky outcrops on the outside. Ventilation comes from shafts camouflaged as small surface caves or natural fissures. It's an entire network, not too dissimilar to your tavern passageways."

Kipp looked thrilled.

"How did you find it?" Torj asked.

"I knew it was here from long ago. You forget, I was around when Delmira fell. I didn't know if this place would still be in use, or if it was abandoned. Turned out, not so abandoned," the older Warsword said with a note of amusement. "Over the years, people have come here, waiting for Delmira to be claimed... Waiting for their homeland to be rebuilt."

"Who's here?" Darian demanded. "Who—"

"Who the fuck are you?" Vernich snapped.

"He's a posh git from Tver," Kipp answered helpfully. "But he's got his uses. It's largely his forces we've got trailing behind us. And it's his coin we're using."

"Thanks for that," Darian muttered with a roll of his eyes.

Vernich's hardened expression didn't abate, his lip curling as he surveyed Darian's fine clothes and polished boots.

"Vernich," Wilder intervened. "Who else is here? How many?"

With a muscle twitching in his jaw, the older Warsword tore his gaze away from the nobleman and returned his attention to the group. "About two hundred people, give or take—"

"*Two hundred?*" Wren exclaimed, clapping her hand over her mouth as though surprised by her own outburst.

Vernich nodded. "It's become a haven of sorts, for people from all over the midrealms who needed to go into hiding. There are Guardians of Thezmarr here too, warriors we found injured and healed as best we could, who then stayed on to defend the Warren if need be. For the past few months, I've been recruiting too... There are many here who would be willing to fight, for the right leader."

Torj tried not to let himself hope. Vernich had already saved their asses once—he couldn't possibly have gathered an army for them. Could he?

"What happened to you?" he asked his fellow Warsword

instead. "We were told you were killed. That's how we found your mace—"

"Along with these." Kipp produced something from his pack. Thankfully, the alchemists had thought to preserve them in a small jar, rather than let them rot: the three fingers they'd found with Vernich's weapon.

"For fuck's sake, Kipp! You took those off the fucking pyre too?" Cal snapped, his whole face scrunching in disgust. "That's just foul—"

"I thought whoever they belong to might want them back," the strategist shrugged, still holding up the glass vessel, the severed digits floating inside.

Thankfully, Vernich snatched them from him and examined them through the glass. His nose wrinkled before he tossed the jar back. "I doubt they'll be of much use to Graves now. But yes. We were attacked and captured just outside of my village. So much for fishing and fucking retirement," he muttered. "They used some sort of poison on us—me and two other Warswords. We managed to escape a few days later. But the blade they'd used on Graves had been contaminated. She was in bad shape. I brought us here in the hopes that there might be some supplies left in the place... We found a whole settlement instead."

Torj couldn't believe it. All this time in Delmira, there had been life beneath the ashes... All that time Wren had roamed her own ruined kingdom, there were people here after all.

"Why let us believe you were dead?" Torj asked. "What have you been doing all this time?"

"The usurper has spies everywhere, Elderbrock. If Thezmarr believed me dead, so would he. Better he underestimates your Warsword numbers. As for what we've been doing here... We've been waiting, preparing."

"How many are in fighting shape?" Darian asked. Torj could practically see the calculations whirring in his mind. The nobleman had always been good at understanding the advantage and making the most of it, which was exactly what he was trying to do now, though it wasn't going down all too well. Vernich's eyes narrowed again, but Darian pressed on. "We need as many in our army as possible, and as we're fighting for the survival of the midrealms, it stands to reason that the people here partake as well..."

Beside Torj, Wren flinched. "We can't just come here and ask them to fight for us."

"Why not? They're people of the midrealms too. They've seen what Silas is capable of, or they wouldn't be here," Darian argued.

"Ask them whatever you like," Vernich interjected, his tone flat. "Just don't count on their numbers. Some came here for safety, not more violence. Though I assure you there are plenty among us who have a taste for revenge."

Wren shot the older Warsword a grateful look and Torj fought the urge to take her hand in his, to soothe the magic he could feel rolling off her in waves. Instead, he addressed Vernich again. "How long did you spend in captivity? What can you tell us of Silas?"

The Bloodletter's fists clenched at his sides. "Too long. And I can tell you that he's more monster than any of those fucking wraiths we fought in the last war..."

"How so?" Thea asked. "We need every piece of information we can get our hands on if we mean to defeat him."

At last, Vernich took a seat on one of the logs. "From what I understand, Silas started out wanting to suppress certain types of magic... The strength of the Warswords, the power of each of the rulers. Where we were being held, we heard many conversations about it, saw the alchemy at work for ourselves. My full strength has only just returned recently after my time as a prisoner."

The Bloodletter's words were steeped in fury, and Torj was no stranger to the note of self-loathing there too. His fellow Warsword blamed himself; that much was clear.

"He's using shadow magic, too," Vernich continued, shaking his head. "Collecting remnants from the previous war and somehow harvesting what little darkness remains. It seems he can extract it—from bones, from the horns and talons of the monsters... It's not what it was, not lashing cords of power, but it's enough to corrupt other things. Alchemy, men, and by the looks of things... his own magic."

"We know, but how does that manifest?" Zavier called out.

Vernich's gaze fell to the young man with the same discerning look he'd given Darian. "Another posh git?"

"To a certain extent." Zavier shrugged. "Zavier Terling. Crown Prince of Naarva."

Vernich blinked at him several times before looking to Torj for confirmation, disbelief etched on his face.

"It's true," Torj confirmed.

"Figures," Vernich grunted. "I'm guessing he's your brother, then, given how similar you look and the fact that he's got Naarvian summoner magic?"

"Unfortunately," Zavier replied.

"Unfortunate doesn't even cover it," Vernich spat. "Least he covers that smug face with a damn mask."

"Do you know anything about the masks, Vernich?" Wren asked, getting to her feet and stepping forward. "It's not just Silas who wears one, and I was wondering if there was anything more to them... Did you notice anything about them when you were—"

"Can do you one better than tell you about it," Vernich grunted. "I can show you. In our last skirmish I got hold of one. Really enjoyed tearing it off the smug prick's face. I'll have it brought to the workroom for you."

"Workroom?" Wren echoed, the word surprising Torj just as much.

But Vernich simply frowned. "You're an alchemist, aren't you? The people of the Warren have been preparing a space for you since you claimed the throne."

Wren's mouth dropped open, and Torj could hardly blame her. "Oh."

The door swung inward, and the Warswords, Torj included, shot to their feet, weapons raised.

A striking young woman entered the room without flinching at the sight of them, the totem of three crossed swords on her arm marking her as one of them. Torj hadn't seen her before, and he would have remembered her, given the unique style of her blonde hair. She was tall and muscular, and the sides of her head were closely shorn, creating a stark contrast with the flowing length that remained braided down the middle. A series of elaborate plaits were woven like a thorny crown, twisted tight against her scalp.

She reminds me of Anya, Wren murmured into his mind.

Whoever she was, she strode into the space with every confidence, a hand with only two fingers resting against the pommel of her sword. "Bloodletter," she addressed Vernich. "The others are growing restless. They want news."

Vernich gave a nod. "On my way."

The Warsword didn't so much as glance in their direction as she swept from the room, her golden braid gleaming.

There was a scraping sound, and Torj turned to see Kipp pushing the log beneath him back and standing in a daze. He opened and closed his mouth several times before he could actually speak.

"I think I've died and seen one of the Furies for the first time in the flesh," he breathed, his gaze fixed on the door. "For the love of sour mead and the Laughing Fox, someone tell me... *Who* in the midrealms was *that?*"

"Ashlyn Graves," Cal answered at the same time as Vernich leapt to his feet with a snarl on his lips.

The Bloodletter snatched the front of Kipp's shirt in his fist, the fabric tearing. "*That,*" he growled, "*is my daughter.*"

CHAPTER 48
WREN

"The people of the Warren will abide by the laws of the midrealms."
—The Accords of the Warren

Wren was so taken aback she almost lost her balance. Torj's hand shot out to steady her before she tumbled from the makeshift seat.

But no one was more shocked than Kipp. "*Daughter?*" he spluttered.

"Yes," Vernich hissed. "*Daughter.*"

Kipp's gaze darted to the door. "But it's only been six years since the war, and she's—"

Wren could see the tendons in Vernich's neck straining as he answered, "Thirty-four years old... You think I was a virgin for the first thirty fucking years of my life, Snowden?"

"Your own daughter calls you Bloodletter?" Kipp managed. "Do you call her Graves?"

The vein in Vernich's neck was about to pop—

A deep chuckle sounded. "Let him down, Vernich," Wilder said, rising to his feet and clapping the Bloodletter on the shoulder.

"Would *you* want this menace drooling over *your* daughter?" Vernich snapped.

Wren rolled her eyes and stood, dusting herself off. "Your daughter looks *more* than capable of looking after herself," she interjected. "And Kipp didn't know."

At last, Vernich released Kipp's shirt. "He does now."

Kipp backed away sheepishly. "Heard you loud and clear, Bloodletter. No hard feelings..."

Vernich's face was still red. "If you so much as *look* in her direction—"

Torj nudged the older Warsword toward the door. "How come you never told us about her?" he asked quietly.

"Didn't know she existed, did I?" Vernich replied, sounding suddenly calmer. "Wasn't until after she passed the Great Rite that she came to find me. It was only then that she told me who she was."

"And she's a Warsword..." Wilder murmured.

"Course she is," Vernich retorted, the pride clear as day in his voice as he led them from the gathering space.

Kipp fell into step beside Wren, cheeks flushed, eyes bright while he rummaged for something in his pocket.

Wren recognized that expression all too well. "What?"

Kipp grinned, pulling out the jar. "Do you think she wants her fingers back?"

The piece of metal was distorted—warped by flames and alchemy, if the lingering scent was anything to go by. Wren used a pair of tongs to turn it over on the bench, drawing her lantern closer for better light.

"It's definitely part of a mask?" she asked Vernich the Bloodletter, who stood just behind her, peering over her shoulder.

"Pulled it off the bastard's face myself," he grunted, pointing to a foul-looking clump on the inside. "That there's part of his brow."

Wren's stomach rolled with a wave of nausea. Rotting flesh. That also accounted for the stench. "And how long have you had this?"

Vernich shrugged. "Few weeks? A month? I can't exactly remember when we escaped that shithole."

"You haven't done anything to it? Washed it? Tried to burn it?"

The gruff Warsword snorted. "Does it look like it's been fucking washed? And no. We just took what we could. There are a few amateur alchemists among the people of the Warren—we figured they'd look into it."

"And?" Zavier chimed in from the door, striding forward to the bench to get a better look.

"And they're amateurs. They didn't understand what they were looking at," Vernich replied flatly. "So what *are* we looking at?"

Wren stared at the scrap of metal, noting the obsidian color of the front, before turning it over once more. At a guess, the piece was from the part of the mask that covered the top of the nose and brow, but there wasn't enough of it to truly examine. However, one minor detail caught her eye.

"See this pattern here?" She pointed to the inside of the mask, where a series of dense grooves had been carved.

"I see it," Zavier said, while Vernich grunted in confirmation.

"In design, Master Mercer taught us that patterns like this are often used to create more adhesion between the piece and the alchemy. This wasn't used on the manacles Silas adapted. This is a new element, used only on the masks..."

"So what? The alchemy is more effective for longer?" Zavier asked.

"That would be my guess, but without a complete mask, we can't really draw any definitive conclusions," Wren replied.

"Well, I don't know shit about alchemy," Vernich muttered from behind them. "But I'll gladly rip another mask off an enemy's face for you."

Wren smiled. "That would be appreciated, thank you, Vernich."

The Bloodletter nodded and strode off.

"He's growing on me," Zavier said with a note of amusement.

"Same here," Wren agreed. "If he can get us a complete mask... I just have a feeling that it will help make sense of things."

Zavier shrugged. "I meant what I said back at Drevenor. Silas looks like me—if we were to be recognized as brothers, it would bring his entire reason for this war into question. A royal fighting the power of other royals, because a former royal got too power-hungry? He's protecting his identity, Wren."

"It can't help to investigate."

"Because you've got so much free time already," Zavier quipped.

Wren's patience wore thin. "If you're not going to help, get out. I need to focus."

Zavier lifted his hands in surrender and went after Vernich.

Wren worked into the early hours of the morning in the Warren's workroom. At some point in the night, Dessa had joined her, and the pair had hunched over the benches, distilling as much of the dark alchemy cure as possible. Wren even managed to amend her formula so that the liquid could be taken as a preventative rather than an antidote. The silvertide roses needed to be used in a higher concentration for that particular elixir, though, and so there was only so much they could create with the bulk of the supplies Torj had found with their forces somewhere beyond the stronghold.

She also had several dishes of Torj's blood out for examination, testing them with various antidotes she had brewed. *The difference between poison and cure is simply a matter of dose,* she told herself as she worked. As soon as she dissected *what* the poison was, the cure would be within reach.

A knock sounded at the door, and Zavier peeked inside. "Need help?"

"Always." Wren wiped the sweat from her brow and tended to the flames beneath one of the bubbling crucibles.

"About time," Dessa quipped from her corner of the room.

"Good," Zavier replied, stepping forward to reveal a dozen other faces behind him. "I brought some..."

Wren's brow furrowed. "Zave... are you going to explain?"

Zavier entered the room, his eyes brighter than she'd seen them in a long while. "Everyone here has a skill we can use," he told her. "They may not be alchemists trained at Drevenor, but... a former cook with extraordinary knife skills? A gardener with knowledge of herbs and poisonous plants? Oh, and there's a man who brews beer somewhere back there..."

"Don't introduce him to Kipp, whatever you do," Wren replied with a wry smile.

"Duly noted," Zavier said. "But what do you think? I can set them up with stations to prepare the different ingredients and tasks, and you and Dessa can do all the actual alchemy?"

Wren met her friend's gaze, and then those of the eager faces behind him. They had come here to help her, to help Delmira.

And so she grinned. "Let's do it."

CHAPTER 49
TORJ

"Remnants of the past often serve as a means to illuminate the path to the future."
—Arcane Alchemy: Unveiling the Mysteries of Matter

Torj spotted her in the workroom instantly, her hair falling into her eyes as she handed out pouches of herbs to the people of the Warren. The makeshift alchemy space had caused quite the stir in the underground stronghold, with many volunteering to help the future Queen of Delmira, and others coming to her for assistance of their own.

Instinctively, Torj moved toward her, the connection between them tugging him closer, needing her nearer. Extra lanterns had been lit within the cavernous space and the flickering flames caught the bronze in Wren's hair. Her usually sharp expression was softened by the questions the people asked about her remedies. She handed out supplies as though she hadn't spent hours upon hours preparing them.

Wren was teaching them how to make the counter-alchemy as well, with different benches set up for different purposes. Some were finely chopping herbs, some were monitoring the fires beneath the cauldrons, and others—

"No, like this," Wren patiently demonstrated to one of the women, showing her how to properly distill the concoction. "See how the color changes? That's when you know it's ready for the next step."

Perhaps it was her hope that for every person who understood true alchemy, it would be one less who could be tempted by Silas' corrupted form.

"She's something, isn't she?" Thea stood in the doorway, following his line of sight to her sister among the bustle.

"That's an understatement, and both you and I know it," Torj huffed.

"So why aren't you in there, standing by her side?" Thea asked.

"Because it's a privilege to watch her. She doesn't need me casting a shadow over her while she does what only she can do."

Thea surveyed him. "You poor bastard. You've got it bad."

"No shit."

She laughed. "As you should. She's the best of us."

"You don't think I know that?"

"I think you know it all too well," Thea replied with a shrug.

"What's that supposed to mean?"

"It means you're like Wilder. You don't think you deserve it, but you do. You are also one of the best of us—"

Torj opened his mouth to argue, but Thea silenced him with a look.

"Haven't you learned not to argue with an Embervale sister yet?"

With a scoff, Torj shook his head. "Just because I'll lose doesn't stop me from trying."

Thea grinned. "Atta boy."

At that, Torj couldn't help but laugh.

It had been three days since Torj had taken a dose of Dessa and Zavier's strengthening potion. He was trying to make it last, trying to go without for as long as possible before he needed to top up. But sitting in the weapons room of the Warren with his war hammer heavy across his lap, he realized he had hit that limit. His hand trembled as he tipped Wren's cleaning aid to the scrap of fabric, and it felt as though his thighs were bruising under the weight of the weapon.

"Fuck's sake," he muttered, shifting uncomfortably, ignoring the nagging worry that he soon might not be able to lift the hammer at all.

As he was agonizing over his failings, the door swung open and in strolled Wilder, Vernich, Cal, Thea, and Kipp— four Warswords and a strategist, all here to witness his undoing.

Great, Torj thought darkly.

But they nodded in greeting, Thea letting out a low whistle at the sight of the weapon-covered walls. "Not bad, Bloodletter... not bad at all."

"It's no Naarvian steel, but it'll slice traitors open all the same," Vernich replied. "We've been doing some guerilla warfare across Silas' known bases. A lot of this weaponry is his."

"Impressive," Thea replied. "Have you sent word to Audra?"

Vernich shook his head. "Too dangerous. Can't afford to have this place discovered."

Torj turned his attention back to his hammer, his hand trembling more violently as he tried to clean the dried blood from its runes—

Suddenly the hammer lifted from his lap, and he looked up to see Vernich pulling it onto his own, taking the cleaning aid and cloth as well without so much as a word.

"What are you doing?" Torj hissed, his face heating.

"Arranging flowers for your funeral," Vernich said bluntly. "What's it look like I'm fucking doing?"

The Bloodletter guided the cloth over the carved iron with a smooth, practiced hand, giving it as much care as he might his own prized weapon. He seemed to admire the way the concoction cut right through the grime and gore in the runes, examining the bottle with a hum of approval before putting it down.

"Want to know why I switched from sword to mace?" he asked suddenly.

Torj's brows shot up. He hadn't known that the older Warsword had ever wielded anything *but* the mace. "Alright."

Vernich paused his work to roll up the sleeve of his shirt, revealing a thick scar along the length of his right forearm. "Managed to cop a slice right through the tendon here," he said, his voice rough with the memory as he pointed to the marred flesh. "Wasn't even a Guardian yet, but sparring got a little heated in the arena. I couldn't work a sword properly after that, not at the level I needed, to pass the initiation test. According to the healers, the injury compromised my finger dexterity and fine wrist control."

"I didn't know that," Wilder murmured beside Torj.

"Why would you?" Vernich replied gruffly. "Anyway, I was told I wouldn't be able to master the precise sword techniques needed to become one of Thezmarr's best. Thought my life as a warrior was over..." He grinned, the sight somewhat unhinged. "And then Esyllt gave me a mace. Said I might not have the wrist dexterity anymore, but I could end just as many lives by crushing rather than slicing."

Kipp snorted. "Sounds about right."

But Torj didn't take his eyes off the Bloodletter, his stomach roiling with unease. "Why are you telling me this?"

"Because I adapted," Vernich replied. "And that's what you need to do now."

Torj shook his head. "The day I can't lift this hammer is the day I'll no longer be a Warsword."

"What a load of shit," Thea declared from where she was sharpening her own blade. "A Warsword's strength isn't limited to the swing of their arm."

"No?" Torj laughed darkly. "Would you want a Warsword who couldn't wield a weapon guarding your flank?"

But Thea's gaze was angry, and unyielding. "If you think my sister is going to let you die, you've got another thing coming, Bear Slayer."

There was a murmur of agreement around him.

"How's the potion Dessa and Zavier made?" Wilder asked.

"It helps," Torj replied. "But I don't want to become dependent on it. It's similar to the alchemy Silas used during the first attack on Drevenor, and who knows what darkness fed that? We don't know its lasting effects yet."

"Maybe it's time you considered a lighter weapon? If the Bloodletter can adapt, so can you..." Cal said tentatively, as though waiting for Torj to bite his head off.

Was that who he was becoming? Someone people didn't want to share their true thoughts with for fear of being rebuked?

"Our oath is to protect," Wilder said gently. "Nothing says we have to do it alone."

Torj sighed. "Can we talk about something else?"

"Like the fact that Vernich Warner the Bloodletter has a *daughter*?" Kipp offered up quickly.

"A *Warsword* daughter, no less," Thea agreed.

"*The* Warsword, according to Audra," Kipp added. "Ashlyn Graves is a legend among the newer cohort."

Vernich glared at them both, and Torj fought back a smile. The older man had been horrible to the pair of them during their shieldbearer training, so despite the fact that Vernich was a better man now, it still brought Torj joy to see him riled up.

"We should definitely talk about that. How'd it happen, anyway?" Wilder asked.

Vernich's nostrils flared. "I'd have thought you'd be familiar with the act, Hawthorne. You're a married man now, after all."

Wilder rolled his eyes. "You know what I mean."

"Of course he does," Thea interjected. "Where's her mother, Vernich? *Who's* her mother?"

"None of your fucking business," the Bloodletter snapped. But his brusque attitude didn't have the fear-inducing effect it once had, and seeing their expectant expressions, Vernich threw up his hands in surrender. "Fine. Her mother was a woman I met on the road a long time ago. We spent some time together and parted ways. I didn't know Graves existed until she came to find me. She was explaining who she was when we were attacked and captured. That's the story."

"So you *do* call her Graves!" Kipp exclaimed with glee. "I'm sure you left out some details along the way, but it's a start. Who knew that a lump like you could have a daughter as beautiful as her—"

"You." Vernich was on his feet in an instant, a thick finger pointed inches from Kipp's face. "You stay the fuck away from her."

Kipp had the audacity to wink at him.

"Furies save us," Torj muttered, standing up. "Try not to kill each other before the war."

CHAPTER 50
WREN

"Even the most illustrious lineages throughout history bear the scars of lessons dearly purchased."
—The Midrealms Chronicles

"Shit!" Thea exclaimed as the dagger landed between her feet, just shy of one of her toes. She looked up at Wren in disbelief. "What are you playing at?"

"I would have thought you'd recognize a game of Dancing Alchemists when you saw it," Wren said from her workbench. "That's what you get for sneaking up on someone who's already on edge."

A smile broke across her sister's face. "If you want to play, we'll play."

Wren huffed a tired laugh and motioned to the array of ingredients and tools strewn across the table's surface. "Perhaps another time."

"So you got a shot in for free?"

"You didn't lose any digits," Wren offered as Thea yanked the dagger from the timber floor and offered it to her, grip first. She took it and re-sheathed the blade at her hip.

"I still can't believe he altered his own Naarvian steel for you." Thea was still looking at the dagger in question. "Then again, he'd do just about anything for you, so..." She swung herself up onto the bench so her legs were dangling over the side. From there, she surveyed the mess of potions and tinctures. "You don't ever stop, do you?"

"How can I?" Wren replied. "We need as much of the counter-alchemy as possible, and there's still Torj's cure to solve. There aren't enough hours in the day, particularly as we're about to be on the move again. It's hard setting this up every time we stop to make camp."

"As soon as we take the capital, we'll set you up a proper workspace," Thea said.

"You say that like it's so simple."

"I know," Thea admitted. "But what else is there? I won't talk in measures of defeat before the war has even begun."

"It began long ago, Thea. Perhaps it was never truly over."

Thea sighed. "I sometimes think the same thing. What if we had done things differently back then...?"

"We'll never know," Wren told her. "All we can do is work with what we have now, and do our best to make sure that history doesn't repeat itself."

"You say that like it's so simple," Thea echoed back to her, a small smile tugging at the corner of her mouth.

HELEN SCHEUERER

Wren laughed and stirred the bubbling liquid in the crucible, feeling her sister's gaze still on her.

"Did you ever think we'd end up here?" Thea asked quietly. "Two orphaned girls from Thezmarr..."

"That we'd be in some underground shelter in our own kingdom? That we'd be on the brink of another war?"

"More so who we've become," Thea replied, pulling her own dagger from its sheath and starting to carve into the workbench, brows knitting together in concentration.

"You, I could see. You were destined to be a warrior from the moment you were able to pick up a stick and pretend it was a sword," Wren told her. "But me? The alchemist poisoner becoming queen? No... I didn't see that coming. I still find it hard to believe."

"I don't," Thea said firmly. "You were born to lead, Wren. I have always thought that."

Wren snorted. "That's ridiculous."

"Is it?" Thea challenged, still carving into the timber of the bench with her dagger. "You know what I remember most about Thezmarr? Not the cold or the hunger when we were growing up. I remember you stealing extra blankets for me. Making medicines when I was sick. Treating my wounds when I was injured. You were taking care of people long before there was a crown in question. Sam and Ida would agree with me. And Anya knew all along. That's the kind of ruler people need."

Hearing their names aloud was like a punch to Wren's gut, and for a second, she could smell burnt hair in the air, and hear the echoes of screams.

Crucible. Harvesting knife. Lavender. Rose thorns. She

clung to each object as she brought herself back to the present, looking up at her sister through the grief.

"Don't you wonder who we'll lose this time?" she asked quietly. "Every night I wonder who I've spoken to for the last time, and what those words might have been."

"I won't promise that everyone we love will be safe," Thea ventured. "But I can promise that if we do nothing, the midrealms as we know it will be done for. So we have no choice. We have to fight."

Wren poured the steaming liquid from the crucible into the waiting vial. "I know."

Thea blew the timber shavings from where she'd been carving into the bench and Wren glanced over, curious as to what she had deemed worthy of defacing property that wasn't theirs.

T & W, the carving read, followed by a lightning bolt.

"Ah, how sweet," Wren mused. "Thea and Wilder... I'm surprised you haven't drawn a massive sword next to it."

Thea laughed. "It's not for me and Wilder."

"No?"

"No." Thea traced the letters. "It's for me and you, you fool. Thea and Wren."

"Oh."

"We Embervales have to stick together," Thea told her. "I won't lose you as well."

A wave of grief washed over Wren, her eyes stinging with unshed tears. "Nor I you."

Thea elbowed her. "Glad we got that settled, then."

But Wren couldn't stop the rising feeling of dread inching its way up her throat. "Am I making a mistake, Thee? Claiming the throne? Taking this on?"

Thea's features softened and she reached out to grasp Wren's shoulder. "I think you're going to have to make hard decisions again and again in this life... The only thing that's going to help you live with them is if you decide based on your own beliefs, your own truth." Thea released her. "And that's what you did, isn't it?"

Slowly, Wren nodded.

"Then no, I don't think you made a mistake, Wren," her sister told her.

"Gods, I hope you're right."

CHAPTER 51
TORJ

"A force divided in purpose is already half-defeated before the first arrow flies."
—The Warsword's Way

Vernich and one hundred and fifty brave souls from the Warren led them out of the underground labyrinth. Kipp had shown the Bloodletter where they were meeting the rest of their forces and the older Warsword had moved quickly. Retired or not, he hadn't lost his touch. The incline told Torj that they were moving straight for the capital, Dorinth, which sat on a cliff's edge, or had, once upon a time.

When they emerged from the Warren, they were greeted by crumpled pillars and piles of broken stone. The remnants of the fallen kingdom had been overrun by nature—long vibrant grasses, wildflowers, and trees.

"This is what's left of the outer city wall and watchtowers," Vernich explained, pointing to the stone and rubble amid the undergrowth. "The old city gates are a few leagues south, but Silas will have guards posted there. You can see the capital—"

Torj's breath caught in his throat. His hand shot out, gripping Vernich's arm with enough force to make the man wince.

"Furies above," Torj whispered, his awestruck voice barely audible over the sudden pounding of his heart.

Between them and Dorinth stretched a field of pearly white—a sea of silvertide roses swaying in the gentle morning breeze, their iridescent petals catching the sunlight like fragments of glass. The flowers carpeted the entire expanse, as far as the eye could see, creating a luminous barrier between their small force and the capital they meant to take.

"Wren..." Her name escaped his lips like a prayer.

She guided her horse forward, stopping alongside him. "What is it?" But as she followed his gaze, the words died on her tongue and she blinked rapidly. "Silvertide," she breathed, her voice cracking. She gripped her reins so tightly her knuckles turned white. "It's... impossible. There's so much of it."

Behind them, Zavier swore softly and looked to Torj. "I thought you said it was all gone?"

"I thought it was. Every spot marked on the map was burned. For the locations I couldn't get to, my scouts confirmed it. Silas had them all destroyed. Except for the wild roses we came across before Vernich arrived."

"And except for this field at the foot of his stronghold," Thea ventured dryly.

"Except for that," Torj agreed, his words quiet with disbelief as he shared a glance with Wren. In her eyes he saw the same wild hope that had seized his own chest. "This wasn't marked on the map..."

"I didn't want you venturing this close to Silas on your own," Wren replied quietly, tears brimming. "And after you returned with the news of the ruined fields... I didn't dare to dream that this would have survived Silas' claiming of the capital."

"But this is it, Wren," he said, unable to stop the note of relief in his voice. "We have enough for a whole army. This is our chance. To stop Silas, to... to cure me."

But Wren's expression was unreadable, and though he reached for her through the bond, she was keeping her emotions guarded. "We can't harvest it now. Dorinth, along with a good portion of Silas' armed forces, sits right behind it—we'd be slaughtered before we gathered enough."

"And if we attempt take the capital first..." Zavier trailed off.

"Then this miraculous field might be destroyed in the battle to come," Torj finished for him with a nod. "We need to rejoin our company. Then we'll figure out how to do both —take the capital and secure the silvertide." He looked at each of their faces in turn before his gaze settled on Wren. "This changes everything."

At last, they crested the final ridge to behold Lord Lucian's encampment sprawled across the valley floor. Hope flared in Torj's chest—the banners of Harenth snapped in the wind alongside their own, and he thanked the Furies for their mercy. The royal force had arrived and set up camp right alongside the shieldbearers of Thezmarr, as well as the Devereux, Briar, and Pendelton bannermen. Now, their numbers resembled that of an actual army, with Regent Liora's company of one thousand bolstering not only their size, but their morale as well—though he could see no sign of the armies from Aveum or Tver, and that realization curdled uncomfortably in the pit of his stomach.

"What took you so long?" Lord Lucian demanded, stepping out of his command tent and pinning them with a scrutinizing stare.

Torj was a second away from snapping when Vernich's voice rumbled behind him.

"What's this? Another rich prick trying to tell us how to do our jobs?" the Bloodletter grunted, swinging down from his saddle. "Brought you reinforcements. You'd be wise to welcome us graciously."

Torj had to stifle a snort of amusement when Lucian actually *blanched* as the older Warsword towered over him.

"I was told you had died," Lucian managed delicately.

"Do I look fucking dead to you?" Vernich all but snarled.

Lucian's eyes narrowed. "Do you know who I am, Bloodletter?"

"Your name doesn't matter," Vernich scoffed. "I've known plenty of men like you, and you're all the fucking same. Damn waste of space if you ask me—"

"Who are we expecting?" Wilder interjected suddenly,

turning to the south, where a cloud of dust rose in the distance.

Lucian tensed as the horses closed in. "We haven't received word from King Leiko, and Aveum's army isn't due to arrive until—"

"It's not a whole force," Torj observed. "Four, maybe five riders?"

Wilder was already unsheathing his swords. "Let's go."

Gripping his hammer, Torj jogged with Wilder to the outer perimeter of their company, to see five hooded figures on horseback cantering toward them.

"Archers," Cal bellowed from their ranks.

The telltale creak of a dozen bows sounded at his command.

"Hold!" Torj ordered as the riders slowed upon approach.

"Bear Slayer," called a familiar voice. Farissa lowered her hood. "I bring the Master Alchemists of Drevenor," she announced. "We've come to join the fight."

One by one, the masters dismounted and lowered their hoods: the Master of Lifelore, Hardim Norlander; the Master of Warfare, Landis Crawford; the Master of Design, Nyella Mercer; and the High Chancellor of Drevenor himself, Remington Belcourt.

Behind them, Torj now noticed a smaller group of riders —a handful of determined-looking students in travel-worn cloaks, their faces set with the same grim resolve as their masters. Part of Drevenor's surviving cohort, come to fight alongside their teachers, and their peers.

"We've come to assist," the High Chancellor said. "In any way that we can."

Torj would never like the man after everything his leadership at Drevenor had put Wren through, but they weren't exactly in a position to be turning away help—the help of Master Alchemists, no less. "How did you find us?"

"A man in Harenth," Farissa answered. "He had been a spy for the People's Vanguard for a time, but apparently Elwren helped him on her previous trip to Delmira... His daughter was ill and she gave him the means to cure her."

Wren came forward then, brow furrowed. "I remember him. Paden was the name he gave us."

Farissa nodded. "That was him. His daughter made a full recovery, and he decided to switch sides. He's working for Regent Liora now. When he heard us asking after you, he told us where you were."

Thea clapped Wren on the back and laughed with a note of disbelief. "Sister, you knew what you were doing, even then..."

"Hardly," Wren murmured before addressing Kipp. "Now, shall we talk strategy?"

Torj looked to where Kipp was standing by his horse, his expression deadly serious. "Absolutely."

In Lucian's war tent, they gathered around a map and Kipp pointed to three locations. "Silas has divided his forces —here, here, and here. Intelligence reports that the bulk of his army fortifies the capital ruins, giving them both elevation and natural defenses. But what was already our most challenging target now presents an additional complication..."

Kipp's gaze swept across them all.

"The silvertide roses. A field of unprecedented size stands between us and Dorinth. Make no mistake—we need both. The capital secures our military advantage and legitimizes Wren's claim through a proper coronation. The roses provide our only hope of countering the Kingsbane's dark alchemy."

"So what do you suggest?" Lord Lucian asked, eyeing the strategist with keen interest.

"We need to lure them away from the capital," Kipp replied. "If we can draw a significant portion of his forces away from both the city and the fields..."

"We can fight them on our terms," Wren finished.

"Better yet—we might not have to fight them at all." Kipp's eyes gleamed. "Wren's poisoning skills give us an advantage. If we can lure them to a camp we've prepared..."

"We eliminate a chunk of their army without risking our own," Thea said.

"And create a gap in their defenses," Torj added cautiously. "But the bait has to be convincing."

Wren met his eyes. "Who better to serve as bait than the very queen they're hunting?"

"Absolutely fucking not." The words were out before Torj could stop them, sounding more like a growl than a complete sentence. Wren's eyes flashed to where the poison had darkened the veins in his arms.

"Tell us how you really feel, Bear Slayer," Kipp muttered.

There was a tinge of red to Torj's vision as he stared down the strategist, fists clenched at his sides. "You're insane if you think—"

"This is happening, Elderbrock," Wren snapped, her tone all business. "I'll lure them out with storm magic— Silas won't be able to resist trying to capture that power for himself. He'll send a decent force, which we can obliterate.

It's more than worth the risk, especially as we're yet to be joined by Tver and Aveum's forces."

Torj's body was tense, his fists clenching at his sides. *It's not worth risking you*, he argued through the bond.

But Wren didn't spare him another look; her gaze was fixed on Lucian Devereux. "I can't ask others to risk their lives for me if I'm not willing to do the same for them."

"For once, Princess Elwren, we are in agreement," Lucian replied.

"What happened to not risking your future daughter-in-law?" Torj bit back. "It wasn't all that long ago you were against using her 'like a worm on a hook'—wasn't that the phrase?"

Darian shot Torj a warning glance before reproaching his father. "Do we really think sending my bride-to-be out on her own like this is a good idea, Father?"

"Yes," Lucian replied. "It shows your allies that she is willing to put their lives first, that she is not afraid to rise to a challenge. When I want your opinion, Darian, I'll damn well ask for it."

Torj's heart hammered against his sternum as he scanned the group desperately for someone who was willing to speak up. But no one did. And he could say no more without risking the ruse between Wren and Darian.

Wren continued smoothly. "Zavier and Dessa can continue work on the cure in my absence. And I won't be on my own. Kipp and Cal will accompany me."

"Not to state the obvious," Cal said slowly. "But you're suggesting that only three of us take on an entire unit of Silas' army? How?"

"A brilliant observation, Callahan," Kipp said with a winning smile. "You leave that to Wren and me."

"This seems ambitious, Snowden," Wilder interjected. "Even for you."

"I'll take that as a compliment," Kipp replied.

"I don't think it was meant as one," Torj told him.

But to his dismay, murmurs of agreement sounded all around him, and before he knew it, he was watching as Wren mounted her horse and looked out onto the lands before them. She took his breath away, fierce and fearless in her armor, the jagged scar at her throat peeking out from beneath. Her belt of potions and poisons was secured around her waist, while her hands were steady on the reins, her chin held high.

Alchemist. Poisoner. Queen.

"Bear Slayer," she commanded, seeming to sense his attention. "My army is yours to command. When you see my signal, you will take Dorinth in my name."

For a moment, Torj stared at her. *This woman...* My *woman...* For the first time in his long, battle-ravaged life, he felt *worthy.* Of the time he'd been given, and of her.

Gods, he wanted to go to her, to take her face in his hands, to put his mouth to hers and pour everything he felt into a kiss.

Instead, he bowed before her. "It would be my honor, Your Majesty."

Wren nodded, then scanned the rest of their company. "On my signal, then." With that, she motioned to Cal and Kipp, who rode out behind her.

Torj watched them go, fists still clenched at his sides.

You'll be the death of me, Embers, he called out through the bond. *I can't bear the thought of you out there alone.*

Dust gathered in their wake as she and the others rode away from him, but her voice came back, clear in his mind. *I told you, I won't be alone.*

No? I won't be there with you.

You're always with me, Bear Slayer.

In answer to her words, the bond hummed between them, a golden song in the dark. If they'd been together, Torj would have pressed his brow to hers and desperately tried to breathe her in, to let the power of her settle in his bones.

Soon this will be over. Her voice wavered through their connection. *And when it is, we need to talk about the future. We need to plan for all the good things...*

Such as? He didn't want to let her go, didn't want to watch as she rode off into danger. But no man commanded Elwren Embervale, and he wouldn't have her any other way.

Having a home of our own. With a garden. Where we can grow flowers and herbs...

When this is over, you'll be a queen, he reminded her gently.

So a home and a garden should be more than feasible, she told him. *And I want a cat.*

He suppressed a groan. *Not a cat... A dog.*

We can argue about it later. He heard the smile in her words, along with all the promise in the world.

I will come back to you, she whispered into his mind. *Always.*

Torj sent an image into her mind then, of him deepening

a kiss between them. He traced the line of her jaw and held her in place as his lips moved over hers, as his tongue explored her mouth, committing her taste and the hitch in her breath to memory.

You'd better, he told her as the image faded.

With a final glance toward the horizon, Torj swung himself up into his saddle and joined the others.

I love you, she told him through the bond.

The words eased something in his chest, ever so slightly. *I love you, too.*

CHAPTER 52
WREN

"The perfect strategy exists only in the mind; the necessary one exists only in the moment. Wisdom lies in building the bridge between the two."
—Kristopher Snowden, Drevenor Guest Lecturer

Kipp had chosen the location well. It was below a crest in the land that made it impossible to see from the guard posts of Dorinth, but still within short riding range from the capital. A vital strategic position that, once secured, would give them a direct path to the silvertide fields—and possibly Torj's salvation.

"The key is to eliminate as much of Silas' army as we can. That will create an opening for us," Kipp explained, pointing south. "The silvertide fields lie beyond that ridge. Once we've reduced his numbers from here, our forces can attack Dorinth while Silas scrambles to reorganize his defenses. Depending on where his other bases are, it will be a matter of days. When we're done here, we'll need to move quickly."

"It's not just about taking Dorinth," Wren added, meeting Cal's eyes. "It's about reaching those roses before Torj's condition worsens. And before Silas can harvest them for his shadow alchemy. He knows what they are to us now. He'll go to any length to stop us obtaining them. This is the first domino that needs to fall. If we succeed here, we gain access to both the capital and the fields. If we fail..."

She didn't need to finish. They all knew what rode on this mission—not just her crown, but Torj's life, and possibly the fate of all five kingdoms if Silas gained complete control of the silvertide roses.

Wren checked the sight lines as Kipp had shown her, determining how visible their position was from different approaches. "It looks good from here," she called.

"Good," Kipp replied, pointing down below. "You can see the path Silas' army will take—the terrain is easiest there."

"And the signal?" Cal asked, trudging across the rocky ground, spyglass in hand.

"One with dual purpose," Wren said with a smile, her lightning sparking at her fingertips. "Something that announces to the enemy I'm here, and that Torj can see from afar."

"Someone could have told me to bring my oilskin cloak," Cal muttered.

The trio made their way down the ridge. At Wren's instruction, their main force had visited the site and left their supply wagons and tents set up, and the ground was covered in the tracks of five hundred horses.

"We'll set up camp as though the entire host was here," she reminded Cal and Kipp. "I'm talking tents, bedrolls, campfires, the wagons unloaded, including the wine." Her voice didn't waver. She couldn't let it, not when so much depended on the next few hours.

The time passed in a blur of tasks.

"I think we need more horse tracks in and around the camp, and then some leading away," she called out to the others. "This is supposed to be a hive of activity, and we need every piece to feel authentic if we're going to pull this off."

Cal nodded and gathered their horses, riding all around the decoy settlement, adding to the old tracks there. He made it look like an entire unit had gathered at that very point before riding off.

As Wren finished up staging half-drunk goblets of wine and mead, Kipp watched her with a mournful expression. "Such a waste..."

"If we survive, I'll buy you a barrel of sour mead," she told him.

Kipp raised a brow. "Just one?"

"Two," she amended. "*If* we pull this off."

Cal cleared his throat. "As thirsty as I am, knowing the plan would be helpful."

"Right!" Kipp declared. "The plan is to let them capture you, Callahan."

"What?"

"Well, we have to make it look convincing—the rest of

us fled, and you bought us time, being the courageous Warsword that you are..."

"Sounds counterproductive at best," Cal muttered. "Suicidal at worst."

"And that's why you're not a strategist, my friend," Kipp replied cheerfully.

"I argued against it," Wren told him.

"Of course she did," Kipp interjected. "But only a Warsword would be daft enough to stay behind and think he could take on an entire army—am I right, Flaming Arrow?"

"Cheers." Cal huffed a laugh. "I suppose there's some truth in that..."

Kipp shot Wren a smug expression. "What did I tell you?"

"Doesn't mean I have to like it," she countered.

But Kipp simply shrugged. "Torj and the others should have eyes on the capital by now. It's time to give the signal."

Wren nodded and closed her eyes.

Bear Slayer... I'm lighting up the darkness just for you, she whispered through their bond.

And then she reached for her magic.

The first stirring of power felt like a breath of winter air in her lungs—sharp, clean, energizing. Slowly, it intensified, both within her and beyond, as though the sky itself were answering her call with something vast and ancient.

The hair on her arms rose as the power built within her, a pressure forming behind her eyes. She felt a surreal weightlessness as the wind picked up around her, bringing with it the first whispers of what was to come.

Magical energy hummed through her bones and a deep

resonance bloomed in her chest as the first clap of thunder sounded—the first strike of a war drum.

When Wren opened her eyes, the world had changed. Tendrils of dark cloud swept in, stark against the face of the moon beaming down upon them, the air heavy with the scent of imminent rain. She could feel Cal and Kipp watching her, but she focused on the silence around her, the way nature held its breath before the storm broke.

And break it did.

The first bolt came not from the clouds, but from her, as though her body were the channel between sky and earth. Violet-tinged lightning flashed across the dark expanse overhead in brilliant, jagged forks, and each lash sang in her blood.

The clouds opened up, and sheets of vicious rain pelted down, but Wren didn't register the sting across her skin. Instead, she felt the lightning in her veins as she brought it down upon the earth, strike after strike. She turned the violent tempest into a beacon for the enemy, and a signal of hope for Torj and her friends.

Through the downpour, she could see the approaching force.

Let them come, she thought. *Let them see whose kingdom they're trying to take.*

It was hard to hear the thunder of hooves over the thunder of her storm, but she felt the vibration of the approaching force beneath her boots.

"Here we go..." Kipp lowered his spyglass. "That's nearly five hundred men."

"So not a third of his army as we'd hoped?" Cal asked.

Storm magic was still pouring from Wren as she

answered through gritted teeth, "Not quite, but it's not insignificant, either. Silas took the bait. He's risking his men to make a grab for my power."

"Speaking of which..." Kipp's shout cut through the torrent of rain. "Time to go!"

Wren snapped out of her magical trance and reached for the reins Cal was holding out for her. Swinging herself up into her saddle, she urged her mare onward after her two friends, Cal falling back as planned.

The earth turned to mud beneath their horses' hooves as they galloped away from the site, from the enemy force that was fast approaching. Wren could barely see through the downpour.

There was a cry from just behind her—

Cal's face was tight with pain as he reached for an arrow that had found his shoulder with nearly enough force to unseat him. Blood immediately began soaking through his tunic.

"Cal!" she shrieked.

No, no, no.

"Keep riding!" he told her through gritted teeth. "I'll hold them off!"

In that moment, Wren saw everything with startling clarity. Cal was injured but could still ride. Kipp was their best strategist and needed to coordinate with Torj. And Wren—Wren was what Silas wanted most.

One of them needed to be captured to make the trap convincing, to give the enemy a false sense of victory. And the poison needed time to work. Most importantly, she could communicate with Torj through their bond, no matter where they took her.

Wren wouldn't stand for it. She didn't know why she had agreed to leave Cal behind in the first place, and now his blood was soaking the lands of her kingdom.

She yanked her horse around, placing herself between her friends and the approaching enemy.

"Wren, no!" Cal shouted.

In the distance, she heard Kipp shout something as well.

"Go!" she yelled, before she brought a bolt of lightning down. It hit the earth so hard that even in the rain it sparked, lighting the grass aflame. A wall of fire roared between them.

Cal brandished his sword beyond the flames. "We're not leaving you!"

"You have to," Wren insisted, feeding the fire with a gust of wind, ensuring her friends remained separated from her and the enemy as they closed in. "We need this. Remember, the roses come first—they're the key to everything. Don't worry about me! The pieces are in place. All they need to do is take the bait. And I'll make sure they do. Now go!" she shouted again. "Stick to the rest of the plan!"

The fire illuminated the panic-stricken expressions on Cal and Kipp's faces, but all Wren felt was relief. She heard the protest of their horses so close to the flames, and the hoofbeats as they were guided away, disappearing into the smoke beyond.

With her friends safe, she turned to face the enemy.

The front line of cavalry emerged from the rain and smoke, squinting at her—the lone rider waiting for them.

"It's her! It's the storm girl herself!" someone shouted. "She's trapped!"

At those words, their front line surged forward, and the

commander was upon her in seconds, his meaty hand grabbing her arm and hauling her roughly from her saddle, the rain still hammering them.

Irons were clamped over her wrists. Her magic snuffed out like a candle. The roar of the storm ceased, and the rain eased.

Wren expected a tonic to be forced down her throat, or a damp cloth to clap across her mouth. Instead, she gasped as sharp pain bloomed across the back of her skull, and her vision went black.

CHAPTER 53
TORJ

"A Warsword guards the midrealms with a vigilance that knows no bounds."
—A History of Thezmarr

Torj watched as Wren's lightning tore apart the sky on the horizon, and something within him both soared and sank. Pride at her power, terror for her safety. Through their bond, he could feel Wren's determination, her focus. But then, suddenly, a spike of fear that wasn't his own shot through his chest and he started.

"Something's wrong," he muttered, gripping the pommel of his saddle until his knuckles whitened.

Thea reached across and slapped his arm. "Wren can take care of herself. She's trusting us to do this part for her. Look there." She pointed to where riders were emerging from the perimeter of Dorinth. "It's working. They're sending out a force. And the guards are abandoning their posts—just as Kipp predicted."

Torj could see them now, like ants spilling from a nest. The enemy was emerging from its stronghold among the ruins, revealing not only their numbers, but their defense formations as well. A war camp had been built around the broken pillars and rubble. In the moonlight, the flag that Silas had hoisted above the remaining walls for all to see danced in the wind, taunting them.

"We need to attack now, while their numbers are lowered and the less experienced guards are likely on the watch posts," Thea said. "Wren created this opening for us, and we need to take it."

"But not all our allies have arrived," Zavier argued quietly. "Our numbers aren't at their strongest."

"Nor are Silas'," Torj countered. "If we sit here waiting for Leiko and Reyna to arrive, we'll lose the element of surprise. Silas' scouts will spot us and call for reinforcements. We need to ride while the capital is missing the bulk of its army." He addressed his fellow Warswords and commanders, ignoring the tug of worry in his heart. "Rally the forces from Harenth, the Devereux bannermen, and the Thezmarrians. We lay siege to Dorinth *now*."

Atop his stallion at the head of their army, Torj tipped back a double dose of Dessa and Zavier's strengthening potion. It coursed through him in a rush of ice, visible as it moved beneath his skin, his veins briefly filling with white light as his strength came back to him.

He strapped his gauntlets over his forearms, covering up the evidence. When Wren stood in the makings of the Delmirian throne room, he would tell her, but until then...

Dawn had not yet broken, but before them, the ruins of Dorinth were silhouettes against the gradually lightening sky. Morning mist curled low on the ground between the fragmented pillars and walls, while dew gleamed across broken stone.

When their forces were in position, Torj turned to address his fellow Warswords and the commanders of their joint army. "We need to split our efforts into four specialized groups," he told them. "One for the main assault on the capital, one to protect the field of silvertide, and another two to infiltrate from the flanks."

"This isn't my first battle," Vernich bit out, gripping his mace eagerly.

"Maybe not, Bloodletter, but it is for some," Torj countered with a glare before turning to the Master of Warfare. "What can we expect from the alchemists of Drevenor?"

Master Crawford looked as at home in the saddle as he did in the poisons dungeon of the academy, and there was a gleam in his eye that made him appear quite unhinged. But he spoke in the same calm, calculated way he always had, as though the army before him were merely a classroom full of students.

"My colleagues and I have come up with several concoctions to help incapacitate the enemy, including compounds that will amplify their fear responses, and powders that will cause them to hallucinate. We treated the water back at the camp with a subtle draft that neutralizes the harmful effects in our own forces. You will be immune, but if you see the enemy screaming for no reason, leave them to their nightmares. I assure you, they're far worse than whatever you could inflict with a blade. All paths lead to the underworld, my friends."

Torj suppressed a shudder, though he was glad to see the expressions across their forces suitably impressed and scared.

With that, he doled out his orders. "We need to move quickly now. Vernich and Graves, you take a unit either side of the stronghold and attack from the flanks at my signal. Hawthorne, Thea, you're with me. We'll take the main assault to the front of the city, leading the Harenth and Devereux forces. We'll leave a unit of Thezmarrians to guard the field perimeter."

With the help of his fellow Warswords, their numbers were split as instructed, and soon enough, he turned to address his own company of warriors—ready to fight, ready to die, if duty demanded it. Torj had given dozens of speeches like these over the years; he was well versed in the language of war, but somehow, this felt different... After all these years of running from the shadows, he now stood before the warriors not just as their leader, but as someone who had finally made peace with his own scars. The brave men and women before him were willing to face the enemy, and he owed them nothing less than to give them his all.

"A great wrong has been done here," he told them. "This wrong has not only been committed against one of our rulers, but against the midrealms as a people. Barely recovered from one war, we find ourselves thrust into the bloody maw of another, with yet another tyrant threatening us with darkness... I don't intend to let that threat come to pass. Do you?"

His soldiers shook their heads, rage shining in their eyes, knuckles white as they gripped their weapons.

"Then we take the bastards by surprise," Torj said. "We

take them like a knife between their ribs, and we show them what we learned during our time in the shadows."

"Ready when you are, Bear Slayer," Wilder said, jumping down from his horse and handing the reins to one of the soldiers.

"Be careful," Torj replied, giving him and Thea a nod.

"You worried about us, Elderbrock?" Wilder teased.

"Just concerned you can't keep up with Thea," Torj muttered.

Wilder snorted. "Piss off."

"If you two are done flirting, can we make a move?" Thea palmed two of her throwing stars.

"They're all yours," Torj told her.

Thea's answering grin was wicked. She flicked her braid over her shoulder and started toward the remaining outer walls of Dorinth, melting into the landscape with Wilder on her tail.

Torj watched as the Shadow of Death moved through the rubble of her ancestors' home, fluid as a dancer, swift as the wind. There was a blur of silver, and Thea's throwing stars went flying through the crisp morning air and into the throats of the enemy guards on patrol. In her wake, Wilder caught the men as they fell, clapping his large hands over their mouths to muffle their dying cries. He laid each body down soundlessly before moving on to repeat the motion with his wife's next victim. They worked seamlessly, as they always had, and when the last guard fell, Thea raised her hand in signal to Torj.

In turn, he motioned for the Thezmarrians to surround the perimeter of the rose field, while he followed the outskirts of the roses, advancing toward the would-be city gates on horseback with his unit. As they rode in silence toward their target, Torj scanned the broken walls for archers, but Thea and Wilder had left no man alive. Their approach remained unknown to anyone still within the stronghold.

As Torj closed the distance between him and the enemy compound among the ruins, the smell of stone and damp grew stronger, and the unit at his back became uneasy. When he reached the threshold, he signaled for them to stop, looking up to where Wilder and Thea were scouting from the ramparts. Silently, the couple descended the rubble and remounted their horses either side of Torj.

"As we suspected," Thea said quietly. "Their base is in the remains of the old throne room; it's a skeleton force, though there's no telling what alchemy supplies they have in their arsenal."

Torj turned to the unit behind him and pulled his mask up into place over his mouth and nose, motioning for them to do the same. They did as they were ordered.

When all their forces were in position, Torj took a deep breath and reached for his war hammer strapped to his back. He raised it above his head, and the air filled with the metallic song of a hundred swords being drawn in answer. With a roar that tore from his throat, he surged forward and bellowed, "Attack!"

CHAPTER 54
WREN

"A poisoner requires neither strength nor numbers—only
patience and an underestimated hand."
—Elixirs and Toxins: A Comprehensive Guide

Wren.

She woke to the sound of her name in the distance and the sharp, bitter aroma of her own smelling salts. The scent stung her nasal passage, and she jerked back, only to hit the hard bars of a steel cage. The metal was cold, even through her shirt, which she realized was still soaked through from the storm. *That's why I'm shivering.* Her teeth were rattling, which didn't help the throbbing of her head.

Gingerly, she reached up to touch her hair, the manacles around her wrists jangling as her fingertips met the matted mass at the back of her head. Her hands came away bloody.

"She's awake!" someone called loudly, making her wince as the sudden sound aggravated the pain.

Slowly, she blinked the world back into focus.

It wasn't her imagination. She *was* in a cage. A cage meant for livestock, if the smell was anything to go by... and beyond its bars, three members of the People's Vanguard stared at her.

"It's her, alright," one of them said. "Silas is going to be pleased. But what are you doing here, storm girl? Did your army abandon you after all your lies?"

"Something like that..." Wren muttered, trying not to grimace as the metal dug into her back. She figured the cage was probably the safest place for her, at least for the moment.

"She's not as pretty as the drawings," another man cut in. "Maybe if she smiled?"

The cage rattled as someone clapped their palm atop it. "Go on then, give us a smile," the third man jeered.

Wren blinked up at them. "You've taken me prisoner, chased off my only allies, and you're telling me to smile—"

"Donovan, get over here!" one of the commanders shouted from nearby. "Have you secured the perimeter yet?"

"Just about to!" Donovan called back before glancing again at Wren. "Guess you'll have to smile for me later."

Wren watched him go, her skin crawling. "I guess so."

From her crate, she watched as the People's Vanguard conformed to surprisingly regimented priorities. They secured the perimeter and gathered the maps Kipp had left behind, took inventory of the weapons and armor, and assigned guards to strategic points all around the site.

After a time, a new trio of guards was assigned to watch

her, and with them came a captain. He looked at her suspiciously.

"Why in the midrealms would they leave you behind?" he demanded.

"They didn't mean to," Wren croaked.

"It's true," one of the men chimed in. "They were fleeing as we approached."

The commander's eyes narrowed as he studied Wren. "Why should we believe you?"

Wren shrank back against the bars. "I don't care what you believe."

He crouched before her, gripping her cage. "How many in the force that left you behind?"

"In my immediate party? There was me and two others," she told him truthfully. "But before that? Three hundred? Four hundred? I don't know. They don't share the logistics with us women."

"And you expect me to believe that they left all this behind willingly?" he barked.

Wren drew a trembling breath. "I don't expect anything. But they were worried about the dark alchemy your forces use." She shook her manacles for emphasis. "They seemed to think that the Warswords in their company wouldn't be able to withstand it."

The commander huffed. "Well, that's true enough at least." He straightened and addressed his underlings. "I want you to search the tents for any form of correspondence. I want weapons, armor, and siege equipment loaded up. If there's any preserved goods, medicine—even livestock—I want it all. Take whatever personal items you want for yourselves. We'll be on their tail soon enough."

Wren drew her knees up to her chest. They'd taken her belt of potions and the dagger sheathed around her thigh, and she felt naked without them. She hadn't realized what a comfort the dagger had become to her, how her Warsword's iron will was with her always.

But she stopped herself from reaching for him through the bond. It was best the Bear Slayer didn't know how their plan had unfolded until *after.*

Through the bars of her cage, Wren watched the commander send scouts after Cal and Kipp as he redistributed useful supplies among his own troops and examined the food stores.

"Are we holding the position or pursuing, Commander?" one of the men asked, his gaze lingering on the barrels of wine nearby.

"I'm waiting on reports from the scouts," the commander said.

The soldier gestured to the empty wine goblets and tankards Wren had scattered throughout the camp. "They know how to have a good time at least."

The commander clicked his tongue in frustration. "Quit your griping," he snapped. "And if you're going to drink that, at least test it on the prisoner first. Who knows what they might have laced this stuff with?"

The man who approached her with a fresh goblet was the same bastard who'd told her to smile. Wine splashed over the sides as he shoved it between the bars. "Drink this," he commanded.

"I'm fine, thank you," she said lightly.

"I didn't ask if you were fine. I told you to fucking

drink it."

There was nowhere for Wren to go as he forced the cup to her lips and tipped it back, spilling most of it down her chin but managing to get a mouthful or two down her throat.

"Somebody needs to teach you some manners," he grunted as she wiped the wine from her face and grimaced. It tasted like warm vinegar, nothing like the wine Wilder bought from his friend Marise. But she didn't spit it out. She made sure to swallow it, made sure they saw her drink it.

She had never been gladder to have taken Cal's place. It was perfect that it was her in the cage.

"Well?" the commander prompted, glancing from his soldier to Wren's wine-stained clothes.

"Well, she hasn't dropped down dead," the man said, sniffing the goblet.

"Fine." The commander waved him off.

Stinking of wine and animal, Wren watched as the rest of the company discovered the liquor. They drank as they pilfered the camp, somewhere along the way forgetting to notice that their scouts had not returned from their pursuit of Cal and Kipp.

The campfires were relit, and soon, curious glances began to linger on her. Wren knew it was only a matter of time. She'd met plenty of men like them before.

It was the one called Donovan who approached her, leering. "Perhaps we should let her out to play for a while..."

"She's to remain untouched," the commander snapped. "Unspoiled."

"Bit late for that if she's been with that Bear Slayer

Warsword," someone called out from across the fires, a comment that was followed by raucous laughter.

Wren watched on as another hour passed. The nape of her neck prickled as the commander retired to one of the larger tents, and Donovan's eyes found her again. Predictable. It was all so predictable.

He approached, dragging a stick along the bars of her cage. "What's the matter, storm girl? You never seen a man before?"

"I have," Wren allowed. "I just don't see any here."

Donovan lashed out, striking the cage with his stick, hard. Wren flinched. The sudden noise and movement made her head hurt all over.

"I'd watch your mouth," Donovan hissed. "Might determine how you get treated in a place like this, if you get my meaning. I'd start putting in some effort if I were you."

Thanks for the advice, Wren wanted to say, but this time she kept her mouth shut, her gaze drifting to the soldiers across the camp. They were already rowdy from the drink, slurring their words and calling for refills.

"Are you pricks sloshed already?" Donovan called from beside Wren's cage. He was leaning on it rather heavily, Wren observed. She could have done without the close proximity. He stank worse than the cage.

The men around the campfires had indulged indeed. Some were stumbling, others drunkenly arguing over whose patrol was next... and some of their glassy-eyed gazes fell to her. They cleared their throats as they stood and started to stagger toward the cage.

They meant to make a game of her, that much was clear. A part of her felt untethered from the whole situation, as though she were watching it unfold from a distance, disappointed to find that men of the midrealms were as despicable as ever. Perhaps all that time with her Warsword had made her forget this foul side of mankind.

She could feel Donovan's eager eyes on her, lingering on her wet shirt and form-fitting pants.

"Donovan's got his eyes on the prize," someone leered.

She tensed at the attention, and the bastard Donovan noticed with a smug smirk. "Reckon you'll smile for me now, storm girl?"

She said nothing.

In the distance, someone let out a disgusting, wet belch, which was followed by a howl of laughter.

"Pigged out on the beef stew, did you, Higgins?"

"And the wine, and the mead," came the satisfied reply. "And now... for dessert."

Donovan's knee was bouncing by Wren's head, but when she turned to him, he cracked his stick against the cage once more. "Don't look to me for help."

"That wasn't what I was looking for," Wren muttered, low enough that her captor didn't hear.

Across the camp, one of the men stood, swaying dramatically on his feet. His comrades called out names and jests about his inebriated state.

Their calls were cut short as the man fell to his knees, and then face-first into one of the fires.

The men launched themselves into action, running for their friend, shouting wildly. And at last, Wren met Donovan's widening stare.

She let the corners of her mouth turn upward in an unhinged grin. Donovan's face drained of all color, and his hands shot to his head, rubbing his temples hard, a vein bulging in his forehead. He coughed. He cleared his throat. Coughed again, spitting on the ground.

And Wren smiled. She smiled as all around her, the enemy bled from their eyes and noses, as they screamed until they could scream no more.

When at last silence fell across the camp, Wren slid her hairpin from her messy bun and fitted it to the lock of the manacles *she'd* designed, with a failsafe for Thea. The irons fell away from her wrists after a few flicks of her pin.

Next, she unlocked the livestock cage—the cage she had left behind on purpose. The door swung open, and she climbed out, stretching out the aches and pains from being hunched over for the last few hours, her joints stiff.

There were corpses everywhere, and Wren surveyed the damage with laughter on her lips. Dark satisfaction washed over her as she stepped over Donovan's body.

She looked down at his swollen face, frozen in pain and fear, blood lining his eyes and nostrils.

"You were right," she said. "I did smile for you after all."

CHAPTER 55
TORJ

"If there is one truth a Warsword learns above all others, it is that blood flows the same from friend and foe alike. This knowledge becomes both their power and their burden."
—The Warsword's Way

The impact of hooves against ancient cobblestone reverberated through the city of broken white stone and rotting timber. Torj felt the uneven ground shift beneath his stallion's weight as they cantered beneath a massive archway, only half-intact, one side crumpled in a rough diagonal. They were greeted by the skeletal frames of what were once proud towers, now jagged against the brightening sky, while dark climbing vines and earthy-scented heather wove through the gaps between fallen blocks of masonry.

"Ride on!" he shouted back to his men, the wind

stinging his exposed skin as he charged through the outer circle of the city and into its heart. Broken pillars lay like fallen giants across what used to be the main thoroughfare, leading to the town square, where a giant bell tower still stood. Beyond were the ruins of a once great castle. The ancient white stonework was blackened in patches from old fires, cracked and weathered from seasons of neglect, and here, canvas tents were staked between ruins, surrounded by hastily established barricades.

A sentry's warning cry cut through the dawn stillness.

Torj kicked his stallion forward, the strengthening potion surging through his veins like liquid ice. "Take down the barricades!" he commanded, voice thundering as he raised his hammer and bore down on a guard who emerged, frantically attempting to raise the alarm.

Men spilled from tents and ruins, half-dressed and disorientated. Some reached for weapons while others stood frozen in shock. Torj's hammer met the shoulder of the first defender who stood in his path, the impact jarring up his arm as iron pierced through flesh and bone. Blood arced through the air like crimson rain.

"Form up!" came a desperate shout from within the enemy ranks. A commander in partial armor emerged from a large tent near the square, trying to organize the chaos. "To the bell tower! Rally to me!"

Torj signaled to Wilder, pointing toward the emerging threat. "Cut them off from the tower!"

His stallion reared as an arrow flew past, embedding itself in a wooden beam. The battle was condensing now, tightening around them as more defenders emerged from the encampment. The sharp clang of steel against steel echoed between stone walls, creating an all-too-familiar symphony. Torj dismounted, sending his horse back with a sharp slap to its flank—the narrowing paths between rubble would favor those on foot.

A guard rushed him, eyes wild with fear and desperation. Torj blocked the clumsy thrust, feeling the strength potion amplify his movements. He countered with brutal efficiency, his hammer finding the gap beneath the man's raised arm. Another defender appeared at his side, but Thea materialized like a shadow, her throwing star finding the man's throat before he could strike.

"They're trying to regroup at the gates," she called, blood spattered across her face as she moved to Torj's side. "Wilder says they have archers positioning on the western side."

"Take them down," Torj grunted as a glancing enemy blow hit his thigh. He swung his hammer straight into the soldier's chest, his sternum crunching beneath the iron.

Thea decapitated a man to her left, the head soaring through the air before it landed in the rubble with a sick thud. "There are more of them than we thought."

"We can take them," Torj replied, watching as the Master Alchemists made their way through the opening he and his company had created.

The screaming began as Crawford's alchemical compounds took effect. Defenders stumbled, clawing at invisible terrors, while others fought with desperate, unhinged strength. Torj pushed forward, each step measured, each strike calculated. The battle was spreading through the ruins like wildfire, men dying, people pleading for mercy, the wet shuck of a blade through flesh and bone cutting through all else—

"Wilder!"

The name tore from Thea's throat, and Torj whirled around to see the Hand of Death staggering forward, surrounded by a cloud of strange vapor.

Torj was instantly on Thea's heels as she cut her way through the bedlam toward her husband, Torj finishing what she started in her wake.

Wilder fell to his knees, and Torj's heart lodged in his throat as he reached his friend, skidding to a stop in the dirt and dropping to his side. A blur of silver shot through the air, and one of Thea's throwing stars pierced the throat of an enemy alchemist, his blood spraying the white stones red.

"Hawthorne," Torj urged, holding his friend up by the shoulder. "Look at me. Where are you hurt?"

"Not hurt," Wilder rasped, his eyes wide. "Can't feel..."

"Can't feel what?" Torj pressed, scanning his brother-in-arms for any sign of injury. He'd fallen, hadn't he? "Is it your legs? Talk to us, Hawthorne."

Thea cupped Wilder's face in her hands. "Tell me," she breathed. "Tell me what happened and who to kill."

But Wilder shook his head, dazed.

"Brother," Torj implored. "What can't you feel?"

Wilder's gaze met his, broken. "My Furies-given power."

CHAPTER 56
WREN

"Beware the woman who studies herbs with the same dedication warriors apply to maps. The path to destruction often winds through a garden of seemingly innocent blooms."
—An Encyclopedia of Deadly Plants

"Dear gods, woman," Kipp exclaimed as he regarded their dead enemies littered throughout the camp. "You're terrifying. *Actually terrifying.*"

Wren was securing her belt of potions around her waist, having found it and her dagger in the commander's tent, along with his body. "Why, thank you."

Cal made a noise of agreement. "Remind me never to piss you off."

Wren raised a brow. "Do you *need* more of a reminder, Cal?"

"Nope," he declared quickly, shaking his head at the

gruesome scene. "However, if I were a different Warsword, I might chastise you for changing the plan at the last minute. They were meant to take *me*."

Wren strapped her dagger to her thigh. "And if they had, you'd be dead. They tested the wine on me first. Luckily, I sorted my immunity to that particular poison years ago. You, on the other hand..."

Cal winced as he touched his shoulder gingerly. "Good thing I'm not a different Warsword then."

"My thoughts exactly," Wren replied, stepping over another corpse to stand before him and peel his armor back from his wound. Cal swore under his breath, but Wren ignored him as she examined the broken, bloody flesh. "The arrowhead went clean through. But I'm glad you didn't take it out without me."

"It was one of the first things you taught us," Kipp interjected while he rummaged through the pockets of the dead. "And we've seen what happens to people who don't do what you say..."

Wren huffed a laugh and reached for her medical supplies. "I'll have to saw the arrow off, so I can draw the shaft back through without making the wound worse."

"Sounds delightful," Cal muttered.

"I'd offer you some pain relief," Kipp said, wiggling a flask from one of the fallen soldiers, "but I'm afraid it might be a tad permanent."

Cal rolled his eyes. But as soon as Wren started to saw through the front of the arrow with a toothed-edge blade she'd found, the warrior stiffened. She worked as quickly as she could, trying to hold the shaft of the arrow stiff as she put the blade to the wood. Cal's face went blank, muscles feathering in his jaw as he ground his teeth against the pain.

When she was done with the tip of the arrow, Wren patted his good shoulder. "I'll patch you up as best I can, but then you'll need proper treatment when we rejoin the others."

"Will I be able to fight?" Cal asked.

"Depends..." Wren poured cleansing alcohol over the wound and he swore again. "How good are you with your other hand?"

"Callahan's had lots of practice being ambidextrous in his earlier, *lonelier* years," Kipp called with a wicked grin. "He'll manage."

Cal's cheeks flushed. "Fuck's sake, Kipp."

Wren fought back a laugh. "Well, you won't be using your bow and arrows. You'll only cause further damage to the injury and might cause permanent issues. If you were anyone else, I'd tell you not to fight at all, but..."

"But you know I will anyway," he finished for her.

"You Warswords are impossible."

Cal smiled. "So I've heard."

Wren finished wrapping linen strips around the wound and protruding arrow, not wanting to take it out without access to better supplies. "If you're already talking about fighting, you're fine to ride, I take it?"

"I can ride," he confirmed.

"Then we need to move. We can't waste the advantage this tactic gave us."

"Torj would kill us if we didn't ask," Kipp ventured. "Are you alright? They didn't hurt you?"

"I've got a lump on the back of my head the size of a

cauldron, but other than that, I'm fine," she replied with a wave of dismissal.

Kipp looked like he wanted to argue, but Wren was already striding toward her horse and fitting her boot to the stirrup. Gods, what she wouldn't do for a bath. She was covered in wine and blood, and she still stank of whatever animal had been in that cage before her. She could feel the matted hair on the back of her head as well, but there was nothing for it.

"You two coming or staying?" she asked, settling in the saddle.

"And miss you taking back your kingdom?" Kipp feigned shock. "Never."

There was blood on the pearly white of the silvertide roses. Wren saw it as she rode past the field into Dorinth, flanked by Cal and Kipp. The Thezmarrians had guarded the crop with their lives, and had now left a skeleton crew behind as the rest dragged enemy bodies away to be burned with their own dead.

Not yet daring to hope, Wren passed through the broken gates—and gasped at the sight within.

More bodies were strewn across the ancient cobblestones, and the lingering effects of Master Crawford's alchemy were evident in the surviving enemy soldiers still hallucinating, cowering from invisible terrors. Smoke rose from several small fires where tents and wooden structures had caught aflame during the fighting, tangling with the scent of blood and dust, and the sweet fragrance of the untouched rose field.

We won? she called down the bond to Torj, unable to see him amid the flurry of movement as their forces secured the perimeter and set up defensive positions on higher ground.

We won, came the reply, but his inner voice was flat, drained of the triumph she'd expected.

Wren scanned the ruins for him, an overwhelming sense of urgency flooding her chest. *Dorinth is ours?* she pressed, suddenly uncertain.

No, he told her. *Dorinth is* yours. *But we need you. Medical tent. Now.*

The words struck her like a physical blow. Wren urged her horse onward, abandoning Cal and Kipp to the chaotic aftermath of battle as she spotted Zavier and Dessa in the ruins ahead, tending to the wounded in the rubble.

When she reached them, she slid from her saddle, and before she could ask, her friends pointed.

Torj.

Her Bear Slayer looked up from where he was helping Wilder toward a tent, his face etched with exhaustion, minor wounds littering his exposed skin. The darkness of the strengthening potion still pulsed faintly beneath his forearms. Thea was on Wilder's other side, her face deathly pale, her eyes wild and panicked.

Wren rushed toward them. "What happened?"

"Shadow alchemy," Torj replied, his eyes roaming over her, scanning her for injuries as she had just done to him. His voice dropped to a whisper. "He can't feel his Warsword abilities."

"Wren..." Thea's voice broke. "You have to do something. He... he can't—"

Wren couldn't remember the last time she'd seen her sister so terrified, so desperate. The Shadow of Death reduced to pleading.

"It's going to be alright," Wren told them, squeezing Thea's hand in reassurance, willing confidence into her voice. "It's going to be alright."

"We know, Embers," Torj replied quietly, setting Wilder down on a fallen pillar. "You've got this."

Nodding to herself, Wren reached for her belt and took a small vial from one of its pouches, the contents catching the light like liquid silver. "Here, Wilder," she said. "Drink this."

With a trembling hand, Wilder did as she bid.

She held her breath, watching with the others as the potion took hold of the Warsword before them, his body shuddering. He closed his eyes, jaw clenched, bracing himself against whatever war raged within.

Thea fell to her knees before her husband, grasping his hands. "Wilder?"

"Give him a minute, Thee," Wren said gently, resting a hand on her sister's shoulder.

Wilder's chest heaved as he breathed through whatever sensations were coursing through him. The seconds stretched into eternity until finally, when he opened his eyes, they were clear.

"I'm alright," he rasped, looking to Wren with dawning relief. "It worked—"

"Wren!" Kipp's shout cut through the chaos around them, the edge in his voice making them all freeze. "Wren, come quickly!"

Cold dread washed over her. With her heart hammering wildly, Wren launched herself toward her friend, who was running ahead of her. Her boots slipped on blood-slicked stone as she sprinted after him, lungs burning—only to come to an abrupt stop at the entrance to the city.

A strangled noise escaped her as she looked out onto the field of roses.

The silvertide was aflame.

Silver petals blackened, curling in on themselves as hungry orange fire devoured their only hope against the darkness. The blaze spread in rippling waves across the field, consuming their salvation petal by petal, turning their cure to ash before her eyes.

CHAPTER 57
WREN

"A true warrior knows a hundred ways to draw blood and a thousand reasons to hesitate before doing so. It is in this tension that true mastery of war resides."
—The Warsword's Way

The heat of the flames singed Wren's skin. It was too late to stop it. Too late to flood the field with storm magic and save her one shot at curing Torj.

A sob broke from her lips as a chasm of grief opened up within. She could feel herself breaking, piece by piece, as the ashes of the silvertide drifted up into the wind around her.

Torj's voice filled her mind. *This is not the end. I promise you that, Embers. This is not the end.*

Wren's breath shuddered out of her as she fought back another sob, as she surveyed the scorched lands before her. They had won Dorinth, but at what cost? The victory was hollow without the means to a cure. Now, she would stand

and defend a shell of a city, while she couldn't save the man she loved.

Wren felt the eyes of a crowd on her, turning to find that her friends had gathered behind her, along with the commanders of their forces and the Devereuxs. She couldn't let herself fall apart any more than she already had. The terror, the panic, would come, but it would come in the privacy of her own tent.

She pushed her shoulders back and lifted her chin. "I want scouts positioned on every high point, watching for Silas. We may have taken the city, but he'll return in force," she told the Warswords. "We should search the castle ruins for any hidden intelligence or documents, anything that might help us understand his plans."

Kipp was already ducking away from the company, disappearing into the ruins.

"Cal," Wren called. "See to it that Dessa and Zavier remove that arrow and cleanse the wound. We'll need you in the battle to come."

The Master Alchemists came forward then, Farissa's brows knitting together in concern. But Wren spoke before her former mentor could voice her worry.

"The cure worked on Wilder. I need every available alchemist working on producing more with the few supplies we have left and devising a strategy for how to distribute it across our ranks."

"We can do that," Master Norlander replied.

"Of course," Master Crawford added. "And I'll ensure we have more offensive alchemy in our supplies as well."

"We're going to need it," Wren said, bowing her head in

thanks. She could feel Farissa trying to catch her eye, but she slipped away.

Don't fall apart, don't fall apart, she chanted to herself as she wove through the debris of discarded weapons and shattered shields. Her words must have followed the bond to wherever the Bear Slayer was amid the ruins.

This is not the end, Embers, his voice bloomed in her mind, strong and unyielding.

The broken pieces of her fallen kingdom blurred as she passed through the city, tears stinging her eyes, her heart lodged in her throat. Wren walked and walked, until she stood at the edge of Dorinth, until she was finally alone.

And when she stopped, she brought a tempest down upon the empty land before her.

Night had fallen by the time Wren returned to the heart of the stronghold. Her body was aching from being cramped in the metal cage, and she desperately wanted to wash the filth of the day from her skin, but the atmosphere of the camp brought a chill down her spine. People were watching her—people she didn't recognize, people dressed in far finer clothing than a war camp required. As she walked between the tents, she spotted Darian, whose face fell as she approached.

"I'm sorry," he said. "I'm so sorry. I couldn't stall him any longer. He's—"

Panic speared through her, her mind racing through all manner of horrific possibilities. "What is it? Is it Torj? Is he—"

Darian shook his head and pointed to a tent a few yards away. "It's not Torj."

"You're scaring me, Darian." Wren's heart raced, her clothes damp with sweat as she took a step toward the canvas structure.

"I'm sorry," was all Darian managed.

Fighting down the rising fear, dread sinking in her stomach like a stone, Wren reached the tent and, with a trembling breath, stepped inside.

Several lanterns illuminated the space within. It wasn't like the command tents she'd seen, strewn with maps and weapons. There was no council of generals awaiting her, ready to finalize orders and march into Delmira.

Instead, hanging against the center pole was a gown of pure white, its pristine silk a stark contrast to the muddy war camp around her.

"Your engagement has gone on long enough." Lord Lucian's voice cut like glass as the tent flap dropped closed behind him. "Before your coronation, you will marry my son. And when you walk into that throne room, it will be as *Darian Devereux's wife.*"

Spots swam in her vision, and her hands went numb. It felt as though someone was squeezing the life out of her, the air unable to reach her lungs. Wren braced herself against a table, which she now saw was covered in an array of jewelry.

The words that followed didn't sound like her, but she felt her mouth moving. "You can't be serious, Lord Lucian. Surely it's not befitting of a royal union to marry in the mud."

Lucian closed the small gap between them and grabbed

her arm, his grip hard enough to bruise not only her skin, but the bone beneath. "You can marry him in a damn pigsty for all I care," he hissed menacingly, "but you *will* marry him, and you'll marry him *now*."

For all her poisons and storm power, Wren froze. She had told herself that she'd never be at the mercy of a man, that she had all the strength within her to bring the bastard to his damn knees, but she froze.

His breath was hot on her face. "If you don't get into that gown this instant, I'll put it on you myself."

A tearing sound startled her, and she cried out as Lucian ripped her shirt away from her body, the cold air hitting her bare skin.

"Lucian," she croaked, hating the pleading note in her voice as she stumbled.

But he didn't stop.

More fabric gave way around her as he clawed at her, all the while muttering, "You'll need to wash this filth off. You can't marry my son in this disgusting state."

Wren couldn't breathe. She couldn't *breathe*.

A strangled noise escaped her as she tried to fight back, tried to clamber out of his reach, her magic suddenly failing her—

A pulse of power surged through the campsite.

A warning.

But it hadn't come from her.

Gasping for air, heart pounding, Wren looked up, still recoiling from Lucian's touch.

"I'll say this once, and only once." Torj Elderbrock stood before her, towering over Lord Lucian. "Take your fucking hands off *my wife*."

CHAPTER 58
TORJ

"A Warsword knows his weapon as an extension of himself. The wise Warsword recognizes when he has found something worth laying that weapon down for."
—The Warsword's Way

All Torj could see was red as he fisted the front of Lucian's doublet and tore him away from Wren. The nobleman's feet kicked out in a panic as Torj lifted him bodily from the ground and hurled him through the side of the tent.

Lucian screamed as his flailing body tore through the canvas and landed hard in the mud outside with a thud.

The sound echoed through the unnatural silence of the camp as Torj stalked through the torn tent after him. Blood roared in his ears, his vision tunneling in on Lord Lucian scrambling back.

"Elderbrock!" someone called, their voice sharp and commanding.

Warswords, bannermen, soldiers were all moving toward him, closing in. He could hear the pounding of their footsteps in the puddles, their shouts distant compared to the man at his mercy.

"You've just signed your death warrant, boy," Lucian spat, attempting to stand.

Boy?

He was a fucking Warsword of Thezmarr, and he was *done.*

Fury coursed like fire through his veins, and he clamped his hand around Lucian's throat, dragging him to his feet, squeezing his windpipe mercilessly, relishing the way his eyes grew bloodshot and bulged from his head.

"You put your hands on my wife." Torj's voice was low and deadly as he lifted Lucian once again before slamming him back down into the ground. "My fucking *wife.*"

"Torj." At the sound of the soft voice, the crowd that had gathered parted, revealing Wren, in her torn clothes, her body trembling.

A ragged gasp escaped him at the sight of her.

He released Lucian, who was unconscious in the mud, and rose to his feet. Torj went to her, drawing her to his side.

"I'm sorry," he murmured. "I'm so sorry. I was going to let you go through with it. I was going to stand by and watch the ceremony, like we agreed. But then..."

"Then he touched me," Wren said simply.

Torj nodded. "Then he touched you."

My wife. He could still taste the words on his tongue,

and around him, the wide eyes of bannermen and soldiers blinked in shock. But it was too late. There was no undoing it. No going back.

"You *bastard*," Darian shouted across the camp, charging for them. Torj gently pushed Wren out of the way as he allowed Darian's blow to hit his cheek. Knuckles collided with bone, and Torj grunted at the impact, momentarily blinded.

"First one's free, Devereux," he murmured so only his friend could hear. "But I won't be responsible for what happens next."

He saw the gleam of amusement in Darian's eyes before the nobleman masked it with a snarl of rage. "You think you can just steal my bride away?" he yelled, swinging his fist again. "Do you know what you've done?"

Torj caught the blow before it landed. "If you or your father lay so much as a finger on my wife again, I'll rip it from your hand and shove it down your throat."

He pushed Darian away roughly, and the nobleman rushed to his father's side. Lord Lucian was conscious now, bleeding, surveying Torj with a scathing look. He had seen that look before. He knew what came next: a verbal lashing, an onslaught of horrific consequences. But he couldn't bring himself to feel regret. Not after what the bastard had done.

Torj went to Wren and fastened his cloak around her shoulders, tugging it closed at the front to cover her tattered shirt and exposed skin.

"You're done for," Lucian spat. "A dead man walking. No more than a warrior brute born in the slums. And that's how you'll die, too." The nobleman withdrew something from his pocket, a piece of parchment, as his gaze went to Wren. "This is what you were willing to sell yourself for, whore."

Torj coiled tight, ready to launch himself at the bastard again, but Wren's gentle touch stopped him.

Lucian dangled it between them, taunting. "Everything you need to undo the Kingsbane's poison killing the Bear Slayer, right within your grasp." He snatched a torch from Lord Briar and held the parchment to the flame.

"No!" someone shouted behind them, but neither Torj nor Wren moved.

Beside him, Wren watched the information burn, the parchment curling and turning to ash before their eyes. "You were never going to give me that."

"Now you'll never know." Lord Lucian motioned to Darian, Lord Briar, and Lord Pendelton. "Gather our men. We're leaving. Let the Delmirian heir fight this war alone and see how she fares." He pinned Torj with a look of disgust. "You're nothing."

A current surged forth, and Torj felt Wren's hand thread through his, her power rising around them.

"He's my husband," she said quietly. She didn't need to raise her voice; the lightning flashing at her fingertips spoke volumes for her. "Get out, Lucian. Leave now before you're no longer able to."

Torj's chest swelled with pride as he watched his soul-bonded lift her chin in defiance. Clutching his cloak around her, Wren turned to the bewildered faces before them and addressed her allies.

"I cannot stand before you good people and ask you to risk your lives for a lie. Not when it would make me every bit the kind of ruler Silas the Kingsbane makes us out to be —putting my need for forces above your freedom, your right to choose with all the facts in hand."

"So what are the facts?" someone yelled.

Gods, it was all his fault. Torj had done this. He had turned her own allies against her with his big mouth and stupid soul-bonded heart.

As if in answer to the thought, a spark of magic flickered in his chest, and the glance from Wren told him she had felt it as well.

"The facts..." Wren scanned the people before her. "The facts are these," she said. "I am married to the Bear Slayer of Thezmarr. We were married by the captain of *The Furies' Will* on the way from Naarva. And together, we will fight Silas the Kingsbane. We will do everything within our power to ensure the survival of the five kingdoms."

The camp descended into chaos.

CHAPTER 59
WREN

"No crown rests upon a faultless head."
—The Midrealms Chronicles

Braziers and thick tallow candles illuminated the inside of the war camp armory, and the bare, muscular shoulders bunching with each strike of the hammer within. Wren stood at the entrance of the large canvas tent, watching her Warsword mend a shield, rivulets of perspiration running down the broad expanse of his back. Strength poured from him; she could feel it down the bond, thrumming alongside her storm magic.

"What are you doing here, Embers?" Torj's voice was a sultry promise, and yet he didn't turn around. She could sense the self-blame roiling in him.

"Looking for my husband." Wren took another step inside, dismissing the guards behind her with a nod as the flap dropped closed. It smelled of leather and steel, of smoke and oil. It smelled of *him*—of belonging.

"I'm sorry." He struck another dent from the shield. "I didn't mean... I'm sorry for what I've cost you."

"You cost me nothing I wasn't willing to give, nothing I hadn't already set in motion myself."

"What do you mean?"

"I was done with that lie the moment you became my husband aboard that ship."

He blinked at her. "What about Darian? The resources? The allies?"

"It was never about that, and you know it. It was always about saving your life, about buying time to find out more about the poison inside you. Lucian—" The name made her flinch, even after scrubbing the imprint of his hands from her skin. She sighed. "I don't want to talk about him right now."

For a moment, she said nothing, simply admiring how Torj worked—the confident swing of the blacksmith's hammer; the meticulous shifting of the shield, ensuring it yielded back into the correct shape. Locks of the Bear Slayer's silver hair had come loose and fell into his eyes as he moved. Wren drank in the sight of him as she circled the bench, her gaze dipping to the hard line of his mouth, the sculpted ridges of his tattooed chest.

Warsword. Bear Slayer. Lightning-kissed.

Husband.

At last, he looked up and caught her staring. "Keep looking at me like that, and the forge won't be the only fire in here..."

Wren felt the bond hum between them, a living connection that seemed to answer the yearning of her own body. She watched as Torj set down the hammer and moved the shield aside, and without thinking, she closed the gap between them.

The Bear Slayer tensed. "What are you doing?"

Wren reached for him, trailing a finger from the hollow of his throat down through the perspiration on his chest, and lower still. She traced a line down his chiseled abdomen, between the grooves that pointed below the laces of his leathers. Gods, he was everything.

"Wren..." Torj's chest rose and fell with each breath. "There are people right outside. What are you doing?"

Wren hopped up on the bench before him, opening her legs so he could stand between them as she whispered the words against his lips.

"Taking what's mine."

And then she kissed him.

Torj moaned as her lips closed over his, the sound deep and guttural. His mouth moved against hers, hot and heady and demanding, as though he were starved for her. Wren was all too willing to give him exactly what he needed. She gasped as his tongue swept inside and his hand found her throat, applying just the right amount of pressure there. Power and heat radiated from him, his touch searing her as he claimed her with deep, smoldering kisses that she could feel in her very bones.

"Gods, I've missed you," he murmured against her lips, and she felt the pain of his words echo in her chest.

"I've missed you, too." Her voice wavered as a rush of anguish caught her off guard. Ignoring the tears stinging her eyes, Wren dragged her nails down the hard planes of

Torj's chest, wanting to mark him, wanting the world to know he was hers.

The Bear Slayer hissed at the sting, his nipples hardening beneath her touch, but only kissed her more fiercely for it.

"I need you," Wren panted.

He squeezed her breasts through her shirt, and she arched into him. "You have me," he told her hoarsely. "All of me. For as long as I draw breath, Embers. And I have you, wife."

"Then show me, Bear Slayer. Show me who I belong to."

His hands were at the laces of her leathers then, tearing the knots apart and ripping the material down her legs. Torj dropped to his knees before her and spread her thighs wide.

"Perfect," he muttered, running his thumb down her center. "Fucking perfect."

Then, his mouth closed over her.

"Fuck," Wren cried out as Torj sucked on her clit. She grabbed his hair by the roots, and he made a noise of approval against her, the vibration making her toes curl. His tongue pushed inside her, only to be replaced by his fingers as he lapped at her, coaxing that addictive buildup of pressure, sending spirals of need rippling through her body.

She watched the tapered muscles of his back shift as he worked her, that powerful body kneeling at the altar of her pleasure. It was almost too much to bear. It *was* too much to bear.

"Now, Torj... I need your cock now," she managed as he teased her with his fingers.

He stood, his dark gaze hungry as he ripped open her shirt and bared her breasts. "Need to see all of you," he gritted out, his hands at the laces of his own leathers. "Need to see my *wife*."

Wren pushed his hands aside and undid the laces with deft fingers, freeing the hard length of him, her mouth going dry at the sight. The bench put her at the perfect height, and she positioned him at her entrance.

But the Warsword had other ideas. He rubbed the head of his cock through her wetness, teasing her clit again, coaxing desperate whimpers from her. She bucked her hips, trying to gain more friction, but he kept his touches featherlight, smiling wickedly as she felt herself coil tighter and tighter.

"You've driven me crazy these past few weeks," he rasped, sliding against her and grabbing her backside hard enough to bruise. "This ass has been tempting me to no end."

"Are you going to do something about it?" Wren bit the side of his neck before sucking the skin there, dragging a moan from the back of his throat. "Are you going to do what you showed me when we went through the mountain pass?" The thought of him touching her *there* made her breath catch.

"Not today, Embers. I want to take my time. Today is for fucking hard and fast."

"So fuck me hard and fast, then."

"Is that a queen's command?" he teased, still rubbing her clit with his length. "Perhaps I should just give you the tip..."

Wren bucked her hips in silent demand.

Smiling against her lips, Torj pressed the head of his cock inside her and stilled.

"Torj," she moaned.

And then he thrust, hard, filling her to the hilt.

A sob of relief broke from her as the sensation overwhelmed her, and she clung to Torj as he began to fuck her in earnest. With every drive of his hips, she clenched around him, the force of him all-consuming. The shield he'd been fixing clattered to the ground and the table rattled beneath her.

"Furies save me," she cried out as he hit that spot deep inside that set her alight.

Every stroke was a brutal claiming, a declaration. "No gods here, Embers," he growled, reaching between their sweat-slicked bodies. "And I'm not gonna save you. I'm going to ruin you."

As the rough words left his lips, his fingers found her clit.

Wren shattered.

For a moment, her vision went white, and she thought her heart might burst right out of her chest. Torj kept fucking her as the waves of her climax washed over her, causing her to shudder against him.

"Torj," she breathed into the crook of his neck.

"*Husband.*" He ground out the correction. "I'm." *Thrust.* "Your." *Thrust.* "Husband." *Thrust.* "Tell me, wife. I need to hear you say the words. Who do you belong to?"

"You. Always you." Tears stung her eyes. He tasted of home, of hope, of everything she had always wanted. "I—"

"I know, Embers," he murmured against her lips. "I know. I love you too."

His words washed over her, their pleasure entwining

down the bond, the force of that ancient magic fusing together, dancing in gold across their skin.

And then he followed her over the edge, spilling inside her with a shout and a rumbling moan.

Wren kept clinging to him, vowing that she'd never let him go.

CHAPTER 60
WREN

"The crucible teaches what words cannot: perfect timing. Too brief a heating leaves potential unrealized; too long burns away possibility."
—Alchemy Unbound

"I wish we had more time," Torj said, showing her the tremor in his hands as he dressed.

"That's what I thought as well. It shouldn't be happening like this," Wren told him, turning to face him. She brushed a lock of silver hair from his brow and smiled sadly, the golden bond materializing between them, shimmering in response to their roiling emotions. And then she paused, toying with the gilded ribbon between them, realization hitting her hard.

She had felt his pleasure as her own. At the end of the first battle at Drevenor, she had felt his pain... They could speak, mind-to-mind through the connection. They were linked. Always.

"The book said we could share physical sensations. That's the whole reason you tried to break the bond in the first place, isn't it?" she said slowly. "What if, by instinct, you're preventing the poison from spreading to me? What if you're using up your strength, your reserves, by stopping the poison traveling through the bond?"

"That's a bit of a leap, isn't it?" he said, staring at her hands as they covered his.

"Is it? You're a protector, Torj. You were long before you became my guard. And I'm your soul-bonded. It makes sense that a certain level of instinct would take hold..."

Torj stroked the back of her hand with his thumb. "If that's the case, then we need to be asking a different question."

"Which is?"

"Did Silas know? Did he somehow know about the soul bond, therefore targeting me in order to get to—"

Torj's breath shuddered out of him, his gaze becoming distant.

"Gods, *he actually told me*. I'm so sorry, Wren. I'm so stupid. There was a moment, during that first attack on Drevenor, when I had the dagger sticking out of my chest. Silas said, 'I can get to her through you.' Those were his actual words. He told me then and there. Fuck."

"This isn't your fault," Wren replied fiercely. "And now we know. We know you're not growing weaker because of the poison itself. You're expending your Furies-given strength stopping it from going down the bond."

"Is this where you tell me to stop? Because Embers... that's not going to happen."

But to her own surprise, Wren shook her head. "I won't tell you to stop. I'm not sure you could even if you wanted to. The bond has a mind of its own when it comes to instinct."

"Then what do we do?" he asked.

Wren's heart ached for him. She knew how much he was struggling with needing help. But she lifted his chin so that his eyes locked with hers as she said, "We defeat Silas. We save you *and* the rest of the world."

Torj gave a weak laugh. "Is that all?"

"That's all there is, Bear Slayer."

"Need a hand?" Torj offered as she reached for the breastplate that lay waiting for her back in her private tent.

Wren turned to give him access to the straps. "It's strange... you're usually taking my clothes off, not putting them on."

"That's definitely my preference," he replied, fastening the buckles over her shoulders.

As much as Wren wanted to haul his mouth back to hers and claim her husband again for the evening, she knew that they were out of time. "Take me to the command tent?"

"Only if you eat something on the way," he replied, rummaging through a bag and producing a squashed pastry.

Gratitude surged through Wren. When *was* the last time she'd eaten? "Thank you for thinking of me," she told him.

Torj huffed a laugh. "Always, Embers. Can't have that gorgeous ass of yours shrinking." He gave it a playful slap as she lifted the canvas flap and she jumped, batting his hand away.

"Not the time or place, Bear Slayer." But she couldn't keep the smile from her voice.

Wren knew she'd have some explaining to do as she and Torj emerged and found their friends waiting in the command tent.

"Is it true?" her sister demanded.

Kipp, Cal, Thea, Wilder, Dessa, and Zavier stared back at her, all of their faces astounded.

Wren returned her gaze to Thea, hiding a wince. "It's true."

Thea shook her head in disbelief. "*Why didn't you tell me?*"

"*That's* the issue here?" Wren asked, stunned.

"One of many," Wilder interjected, his tone stern as his eyes swept to Torj. "You could have given us a heads-up before you threw our main patron through a fucking tent wall."

"It was made of *canvas*, Hawthorne. He survived just fine."

But Thea elbowed Wren, snatching her attention back. "How did this happen? *When* did this happen? And again, *why didn't you tell me?*"

"I was going to—at Thezmarr. But then you told me that Wilder had proposed and that you were getting married. I didn't want to steal your thunder—so to speak."

Thea stared at her for a moment longer before she burst out laughing and threw her arms around Wren.

"Congratulations, sister. Don't think you're getting away without having a wedding party."

"Yes, congratulations Wren." Kipp surged forward, wrapping her in a hug as well. "I'm sure the men of the midrealms will be devastated."

As her friends hugged her and wished her well, Wren knew that behind closed doors, people were talking, spreading the word about her deceit and likely drawing into question her suitability as queen. But she also knew that the true test of her confession was not amidst her friends and family... It would be with those who had already rallied to the promise of a joint banner between the royal Embervale family and the noble house of Devereux.

Even so, the weight that had sat atop her chest like an anvil had lightened.

"Well, that was unexpected," Wilder said as he embraced her.

"It was necessary," she replied.

"Agreed. It's about time."

Wren smiled. "I know."

CHAPTER 61

TORJ

"A Warsword's sworn duty is first and foremost to the midrealms."
—The Midrealms Chronicles

"We've lost the support of House Blackthorn, House Merith, even the Rivertons," Kipp said as he sorted through his reports. "All of them are refusing to honor their pledges given the insult to the Devereux name. And of course, House Briar and House Pendelton are gone. They left with Lucian and Darian."

"It's to be expected," Wren replied slowly, though she looked pale.

Now he had the freedom to do so, Torj reached for her, covering her hand with his and eliciting a small smile from her before she continued. "But at least we have the masters of Drevenor with us. They're assisting Zavier and Dessa with the cure as we speak. In this war, having an alchemist is just as good as having a Warsword."

Torj nodded. "We're still hopeful that Audra will remind Leiko of his oaths to the other rulers of the midrealms—"

"But his forces are funded by the Devereuxs," Wren countered.

"Therein lies the problem. And we received word on Aveum's army," Wilder told them. "They were hit with a snowstorm at the base of the mountain ranges bordering Vios, and have been delayed."

"Is there any word on the rest of Silas' forces? What of the other strongholds close to here?" Thea asked. "Can we expect them to march on us as soon as they get word of our diminished numbers? Can we hold them off with so few in our ranks?"

"They're a few days' ride from us," Kipp offered. "So it's a matter of who gets here first—Aveum's forces, or the Kingsbane's..."

"Cal, how's the arrow wound?" Wren asked. "Are you fit to lead our archers?"

"I'm fine. Basically good as new. Ready to fight," Cal declared hurriedly.

"You'll live," Dessa corrected him. "But you won't be playing the part of the Flaming Arrow in this next fight if you know what's good for you."

"He doesn't," Torj said.

Wren huffed a laugh. "All you Warswords have that in common."

"If we're done here, there's another important matter on the agenda," Thea called, leading them outside, where she pointed to the Kingsbane flag flapping in the wind.

SILVER & SMOKE

Torj watched his soul-bonded climb the garrison wall, mud caking her armor, strands of wet hair stuck to her face in all her storm-worn glory. He'd never seen something so magnificent—not until she reached the enemy flag and tore it from its pole.

The sound of the fabric ripping echoed across the flooded encampment and was met with a near-deafening cheer from their forces. Tattered material danced in the breeze as the clouds retreated, revealing the golden light of dawn beyond.

Wilder clapped a hand on his shoulder. "We did it. We won the capital."

Torj nodded, bracing himself against a wave of dizziness. Between his friend's celebratory words was the truth: it wasn't over. They had the advantage, not a victory, and it had come at a steep price. The sacrifice of the silvertide roses was at the forefront of Torj's mind, the effects of the strengthening potion waning.

He had gone through his last two vials already, and as he and Wilder strode through the stronghold, he scanned the faces for Dessa and Zavier. He'd need more before the day was done. He just needed to get through the final battle, he told himself, then he would stop, would accept his lot in life—or death. But he had to see this final part to the end. He had to see Wren on her throne.

"You alright, Bear Slayer?" Wilder asked, brow furrowed.

Torj huffed. "I pummeled more traitors than you, didn't I?"

"Sure you did, old man," Wilder replied with a smirk.

"Fuck off, Hawthorne," Torj muttered, opting for silence

as they made their way to where Wren and Thea were inspecting the garrison.

Silas' forces had made use of the remaining structures in the city—stringing makeshift canvas coverings between the standing walls to create shelter. Fallen timber from collapsed buildings had been used to reinforce weak points in the existing walls, and to create basic barriers where the rubble allowed. The highest points in the city—the bell tower, the remains of a temple—had been tended to. They'd clearly housed some of the higher-ranking soldiers, where beds of straw had been made, and remains of rations were found nearby. There was decent visibility over the stronghold and the perimeter of the city, and Torj could see where, before the storm, temporary forges had been set up in the courtyards. One of the old market squares had been picketed off to hold their horses, who grazed on the wet grass that grew between the cobblestones.

When he reached Wren, she melted into his embrace without hesitation, brushing her lips against his. This was so new—the *not hiding*. It sparked something inside him as she claimed him for all to see. Her clothes were wet, her cheeks flushed with exertion and the rush of their brief reprieve.

"I've sent Vernich and Graves out to scour the lands for Silas. We put a real dent in their numbers, and thankfully, Thea and I were able to rid us of that vapor before we had too many casualties." Wren was breathless, energized by what had happened.

Torj spotted the tattered remains of the usurper's flag cast aside on a table behind her. "That's good," he said slowly.

"But?" she prompted.

"But we're not done. You know that, don't you?" He spoke the words carefully, not wanting to burst her bubble too soon.

"It's not my first war, Bear Slayer," she replied, her arms looping around his waist. "But I know to celebrate the wins when we have them, and while our warriors are gathering the prisoners and setting up our headquarters, I choose to celebrate... with you."

Over the top of Wren's head, Torj saw Dessa and Zavier talking with Kipp at the back of the makeshift shelter. "Is that so, Embers?" he said, pressing a gentle kiss to her temple. "I think you'll find that war camps offer little privacy."

"Who said anything about the camp?" she replied, peering up at him through her lashes.

He squeezed her, trying to share his warmth with her. "There are things to do..."

"I know. There always are." She sighed, her whole body sagging against him. "A girl can dream, can't she?"

"Who's going to stop you?" he murmured, giving her an extra squeeze as he echoed Thea's words from earlier.

As the sun rose higher, the sky a crisp shade of blue after the storm, he and Wren joined the others gathered around the table in the command tent, all of them weary and soaked through. The aches in his body were made worse by the cold, and he could feel the tender spots where bruises were blooming beneath his armor. He'd taken a few hits to the kidneys that were the main culprits, but he hid his grimace as he took a seat beside Wren.

"We need to decide what to do with the prisoners," Kipp said without preamble.

"How many are there?" Thea asked.

"Five dozen, or more. Some of the Guardians are still doing final checks," Cal replied, testing out his injured shoulder with a wince.

"There's a cellar down by the bell tower," Wren told Kipp. "You can put them in there for now. But make sure they have plenty of water and food if we have it. I don't want them being mistreated."

The strategist nodded. "That can be arranged. I'll set up a watch as well."

"Speaking of watches..." Torj shifted in his seat, sending a bolt of pain down his side that he barely concealed. He glanced at Zavier and Dessa to see if they'd noticed, but they were poring over the map of the capital. He forged on. "We need to reinforce all the perimeters as best we can. They'll know the weak points. We need patrols on constant rotation."

"Couldn't agree more," Kipp replied. "I get the sense there's something else you need, Bear Slayer?"

His gaze slid pointedly to the alchemists. But it wasn't Torj's need for a strengthening potion that saw him rise from his chair.

"There is," he told them. "Wren needs to be crowned queen. Tonight."

CHAPTER 62
WREN

"The histories of even the greatest rulers are marred by decisions they would unmake."
—Elwren Embervale's notes and observations

"Have you lost your mind?" Wren hissed, scowling at the Bear Slayer as he stood before their friends, their council, and told them that they needed to host a coronation during the chaos of war.

"Far from it, Embers. It's the most sense I've made in days," he replied evenly.

"What good in all the midrealms do you think that would do?" She was on her feet as well, her hands planted firmly on her hips.

"I think it would make you a legitimate ruler of the midrealms, one that any usurper would have more difficulty overthrowing, at least from a customary standpoint. You've

427

got nobles out there claiming that you're not queen until you wear a crown, nobles who won't honor their oaths until they see a queen on the throne. This is your chance to take what's yours."

The hum of the bond between them told Wren that there was something more to Torj's words, that there was another reason he was pushing this, but he tore his gaze away from her and addressed their friends.

"What is the point of risking lives and meeting Silas on the battlefield if the question of succession is raised afterward? With a crown on Wren's head, it's far harder to contest who should govern Delmira," he argued passionately.

"I agree," Kipp declared. "It's the most logical thing to do—"

"Do you think anyone will support me doing this while people are dying around us?" Wren countered.

"That's why they're here," Torj said.

"We don't have a crown, or a blacksmith to make one," she ventured. "Doesn't it need to be made with some sort of precious metal?"

"Leave the crown to me," Kipp told her. "But if you're concerned about the people dying around us, you're a healer, aren't you?"

Wren could have slapped him. "Yes," she ground out.

"Then I suggest you put your skills to use in the meantime, Your Queenliness."

Wren let out a growl of frustration. "One of these days, Kristopher..." she said threateningly.

"You'll knight me and set me up with a beautiful

maiden in my own estate? I wouldn't say no to that, Elwren —you know me well."

"Want me to hit him?" Torj muttered.

"At some point in the near future, I'll say yes."

"So it's decided," Torj said to the others. "Wren will be crowned at sunset. Hopefully that's enough time for everyone to retrieve what they need." He didn't pose it as a question, and no one speculated.

"What are you playing at?" Wren asked, shaking her head. "Becoming a crowned queen doesn't help us now. Crown or not, we fight with the numbers we have. No one is answering our call for aid now."

"Perhaps not," Torj said. "But when this war is over, when the dust has settled and you stand upon the ruins of this kingdom once more, I want there to be no question of your place in the midrealms. I want there to be no doubt as to who you are."

"And who exactly am I, Bear Slayer?" she demanded, planting her fists on the table and bracing herself against it.

"A fucking queen, Embers," he growled. "You always have been."

Around them, the group dispersed, no doubt sensing that it was best to leave her to deal with the Warsword alone. Only she didn't want to argue. She didn't want to plan the moment she'd been dreading since she'd declared herself heir of the kingdom.

"I'm going to tend to the wounded," she told Torj, brushing past him toward where they'd tethered the horses so she could retrieve her medical kit.

"Wren..." He started after her.

She threw up a hand to stop him. "When you're ready to

tell me why you're really pushing for this coronation, come find me. Until then, there's work to be done."

Wren left him there, staring after her as she made her way through the muddy streets to the medical tent that had been set up in her absence. Zavier and Dessa had beaten her there and were already making poultices and stitching injuries. When she spotted Cal lingering in the wings, Wren forced him into a seat.

"You did exactly what I told you not to, didn't you?" she said sharply, peeling away the blood-soaked bandage from his shoulder.

"Maybe," he said sheepishly.

"I did such beautiful work with those sutures last time, too," Zavier called wistfully from where he was cutting fresh linen into strips.

A smile tugged at Cal's mouth. "Sorry," he muttered.

"You're not in the slightest," Zavier quipped back.

Exchanging a glance with Dessa, Wren cleared her throat and stepped away from Cal. "Zavier, could you take over for me? I've just realized I've left a tonic brewing that will spoil if it's overdone."

When she passed the Prince of Naarva, he glared at her and muttered, "Subtle as a fucking war hammer, Elwren."

She simply smiled sweetly and moved over to Dessa, who was also grinning.

Wren lost herself in healer's work. For hours she administered pain relief to wounded warriors, sewed up gashes, and cauterized several deeper injuries. She tended to the prisoners as well. The members of the People's Vanguard seemed shocked to see her and her medical kit down in the cellar with them. No one spoke, no one tried to attack her, they simply showed her those who were injured and did what they could to help.

Wren reminded their guards that they needed plenty of fresh water and sanitary conditions. The enemy might be a monster, but she and her allies were not.

"I want to show you something," came Torj's voice from behind her as she washed her hands in a pail of water.

"Torj..."

"Just come with me."

Wren followed him wordlessly, the shadow of the bell tower darkening their path down one of the narrow, empty streets. She tried to picture Dorinth as a bustling city like Highguard or Hailford in Harenth, but her imagination failed her. She'd spent too many years thinking of Delmira as a burden, a place of curses and poison, something rotten to be cast aside and forgotten—like her.

"It's just here." Torj's voice cut through her preoccupation as he gestured to an old shopfront. The windows had been smashed in and boarded up a long time ago by the looks of the decaying timber facade. The metal frame above the door, where a sign might have once hung, was bare.

"What is this place?" she asked, taking a tentative step forward.

Torj pushed the door open for her, the wood groaning on its hinges.

Inside, Wren stopped short. Any aromas were long gone, only the lingering scent of damp remaining, but there was no doubt in her mind what this place had been. Light spilled from a lantern Torj lit and confirmed what she'd known in her bones. She was standing in an apothecary—

one larger than any she'd seen before. If she closed her eyes, she could smell it: the earthy scent of roots and mushrooms, the sharp vinegars and sweet honey, and the dried bundles of rosemary, thyme, sage, and lavender that might have hung overhead.

It had been ransacked, of course, broken vessels of clay and glass crunching beneath her boots and the shelves bare of the powders and potions they would have once stocked.

"There was a garden out back," Torj told her quietly. "The frames of the beds are still there."

"They would have grown fresh herbs out there, essentials to always have on hand," she murmured, her eyes skimming the dusty countertop and the set of brass scales that had been upturned and left behind. "Why have you brought me here?" she asked, her voice hoarse.

"I thought you'd like it," Torj said.

"And?"

"And I thought maybe when you're queen... you might want to restore it, back to its former glory."

Wren's heart was suddenly in her throat. "Why show me now? Why not when the battle is won and we're able to make such plans for the future?"

Torj met her gaze, and she *knew*. Wren knew why he wanted her crowned that night, why he was planting ideas in her head now rather than later.

"You don't think you'll survive the battle." The words rushed out of her, broken and hoarse.

"Wren..."

"Tell me the truth, Torj Elderbrock," she demanded, her voice suddenly sharp. "You have my heart and soul; you have *all* of me. And I deserve to know the truth."

432

His throat bobbed and he dipped his head in reluctant acceptance. "The poison..."

"Is spreading," she finished for him, reaching out to touch his chest where she knew it built up the most. "I can feel it through the bond. Every day it takes more of you."

His larger hand covered hers against his heart. "I'm needing more and more of the strengthening potion. One day it won't be enough, and though I'm not afraid of dying, I'm afraid of failing you in the moment you need me most."

"Torj..." Her voice broke. "What good is being queen, wielding so much power, when... when I don't have the power to save you?"

He kissed her then, desperate and deep, tasting of metal and smoke, of everything she couldn't bear to lose. She reveled in the taste of him, the feel of him pressed to her. She wanted to lose herself in him here and now. This couldn't be how it ended, not for them, not after everything they had been through.

He broke their kiss and rested his forehead against hers.

"Listen to me, Elwren Embervale," he growled. "If these are my final days, then they're yours. Every breath. Every heartbeat. They belong to you. They have since the moment I met you in the Bloodwoods."

"I refuse to accept it. These aren't your last days," she said fiercely. "I won't let you go. I don't care what it takes. I'll drain every drop of my storm magic, brew every potion and cure in existence..."

"My stubborn alchemist." He brushed his thumb gently over the scar on her cheek. "Always trying to solve everything."

"Don't." She dug her fingers into his muscular forearms.

"Don't you dare make light of this. Not when I can feel you slipping away. Not when you're giving up—"

"You think I want to?" he cut in. "You think I want to leave you behind? I'm trying to make this easier. I'm trying to make life *after me* easier."

"There is no life after you, Torj," she said, dragging his face down to hers, sealing her lips over his.

She kissed him hard, desperately, as though she could pour all the strength she had into him to keep him going. She memorized the taste of him, the hitch in his breath, the bruising press of his fingers as he clutched her body to his.

The kiss was brutal, each of them trying to devour the other, as though the more marks they left on their skin, the more tethered they were to the world, to each other. The bond was a taut, living thing between them, vibrating with their need, their anguish.

Wren untucked his shirt, slipping her hands beneath the fabric, aching to trace the heat of his bare skin. But she couldn't do this, not without him knowing that she wouldn't stand for a world without him.

She broke away, panting. "When this is over—"

"Don't make promises you can't keep." Torj pressed closer, cupping her face in his hand. "Just... be here. With me. Now."

Outside, she heard footsteps on the cobbles, and Wren pulled back, bracing herself against the pain that lanced through her chest.

A quiet knock sounded at the door, and Thea peered inside. "They're ready for you, Wren," she said softly, glancing between her and the Bear Slayer before ducking away.

Wren closed her eyes and inhaled deeply to steady herself. How had dusk come so quickly? Outside, a broken army waited. And her kingdom hung in the balance.

But she opened her eyes and turned to the warrior before her, letting him see the resilience, the determination she had forged throughout her years of grief and solitude.

"You are mine to protect," she told him. "And you always have been."

CHAPTER 63
WREN

*"Sovereigns of the midrealms must be crowned in the capital of
their kingdoms, with a crown of precious metal to mark the
occasion. So states the midrealms law."*
—The Midrealms Chronicles

A *queen of ruins*, Wren thought as she was brought to
what remained of her ancestors' throne room. The
debris that had lain dormant for decades had been cleared
away to the best of their forces' abilities, and the throne
itself had been... *mended* with odds and ends from the
deserted city. What had once been an ornate high-backed
chair was now a collage of warped metal and timber planks,
welded together to create what Wren could only describe as
a monstrosity. She supposed that, at least, was rather
fitting.

"Leaves a bit to be desired, I'll admit," Vernich said
gruffly from nearby.

Wren had never witnessed a coronation before, had

never given what she considered an unnecessary display of wealth and power much thought—until now. She was under no illusion that hers would be a far cry from those that had come before. But perhaps that was how it was meant to be. Maybe that was how she could make her peace with her fate. She wouldn't *be* like those who had come before.

"What happens now?" she asked Zavier, who was watching with a strange expression.

He shifted from foot to foot, shoving his hands in his pockets. "Mine was more, well... Just *more*," he said with a note of defeat. "There was a vigil of preparation where I was supposed to meditate. Then there was what they called *the robing*—where I was dressed in a bunch of ceremonial regalia. And when I say 'was dressed,' I mean by *other people*. They wouldn't let me put on my own damn tunic."

"I would have paid to see that," Cal muttered from the prince's side.

"I'm sure you would have," Zavier retorted, before returning to Wren. "I had to make the journey from the people's square in the outer city to the castle before I made the sacred vow and was crowned in the great hall. For what it's worth," he said, gesturing to the sparse setting, "I prefer this."

"As do I," Wren murmured, the back of her neck prickling as their forces gathered around the outskirts of the rubble.

"We at least got you a crown," Thea declared as she approached, one hand on the hilt of her sword, the other grasping something wrapped in a scrap of fabric. Kipp followed close behind, an unnerving grin on his face.

Wren gaped at her. "How? From where?"

Thea shrugged. "Kipp and I figured it out."

"Probably means it's stolen," Cal offered.

"Or melted down from a tankard or two," Zavier added.

Wren ignored them, looking to her sister again. "Who even has the authority to do this?"

"I do," came a sharp and familiar voice.

Audra, Guild Master of Thezmarr, swung down from her horse and crossed the remains of the throne room. Her hair was pulled back in its usual severe bun, but her spectacles were nowhere to be seen, and there was an impressive scythe strapped to her back. It reminded Wren of Anya, who'd wielded the same weapon in the shadow war.

Murmurs broke out across the gathered crowd as Audra strode forward. "I have the power to swear in a monarch, but we need to do it quickly. Silas' forces have regrouped. They ride for Dorinth as we speak. And they'll be here by midday tomorrow."

"What about Aveum's army? Harenth's? What about Tver?" Wren blustered. "Why in the name of the Furies are we wasting time on this—"

"Aveum and Harenth's armies have answered your call for aid, Elwren," Audra told her. "Tver... Tver refuses to honor its oath, citing the lack of a ruling queen as grounds for such treason."

Wren blinked, her knees buckling beneath her. "So without the aid of the Devereux bannermen and Tver's army, our force comes to what? Three thousand? Less?"

"Less. Right now, our odds are two to one. Worse, actually."

"Has King Leiko allied himself with Silas? With Lord

Lucian?" Wren pressed. "Will Tver's numbers reinforce those of the enemy?"

"We cannot know for sure," Audra said. "All we know is that you need a crown on your head before you rally the midrealms to your cause. Are you ready?"

No. The word resounded in Wren's mind.

You were born ready, came Torj's reply, strong, resilient, full of conviction.

Wren took a deep breath. "As I'll ever be, Audra."

The Guild Master dipped her head and motioned to the temporary throne. "After you."

Wren tried not to think about the slaughter ahead of them, or all the eyes on her as she made her way to what might have once been the dais. She tried not to think of the impending danger, of how, as she took her place in the wreckage, the enemy advanced upon them.

Audra addressed the gathered crowd first. "Today's coronation will be a condensed ceremony given the current circumstances, but it is no less legitimate than those that take place on a grand stage before the masses. The oath Princess Elwren of Delmira swears today will be recorded in the history books for the ages. It will solidify the Embervale line of succession for centuries to come." Audra turned to Wren. "Are you willing to take the vow?"

Wren swallowed the lump in her throat. "I am willing."

Graves passed a thick volume to Audra, who held it out to Wren.

The Constitution of the Founding Furies, the title read in gold lettering. Wren remembered it from her time at Thezmarr. It was the book Audra had wielded to her advantage when Thea sought to become the first woman warrior in decades. Now, it was the tome Wren would swear upon to take her kingdom back.

"Place your hand on the book," Audra instructed.

Distantly, Wren worried about the damage her sweaty palm might do to the ancient leather, but she did as she was told, finding the cover cool to her heated touch.

Audra cleared her throat. "Do you declare that you are the rightful heir to the Embervale throne?"

Wren fought to keep the quaver from her voice. "I declare that I am Elwren Embervale, true heir of Delmira, daughter of King Soren and Queen Brigh. With the passing of the firstborn daughter and the abdication of the second daughter, I am the rightful successor to the throne, and I shall take up the mantle as queen, as true ruler of this kingdom."

Audra turned to Thea. "Bring forward the crown."

Thea removed the fabric, and Wren stifled a gasp.

It was nothing like she expected.

The crown was *simple*. A continuous band of bright silver, slender and delicate in its construction, with a single central pointed motif. Simple and practical—the exact sort of design Wren would have chosen for herself.

There were no garish embellishments or spikes, no ornate arches, nor did it embody the same haphazard nature that her temporary throne did. It didn't look like it had been hammered together in the hours before. The steel shimmered in a familiar way... but there was no way they could have found Naarvian steel out here in the ruins to reforge anew, was there?

She glanced at Thea.

Wasn't me, her sister mouthed, stepping back as Audra handed the book off and took the crown.

"You may kneel," the Guild Master said.

Wren's joints cracked as she lowered herself to the ground, the broken stone biting into her flesh.

Audra held the crown over her head. "Repeat after me: I bond my life to this kingdom and its people."

"I bond my life to this kingdom and its people," she recited, her heart pounding.

"I shall serve as the protector of Delmira, and thus, a protector of the midrealms," Audra said.

Wren kept her head bowed as she echoed the sacred words. "I shall serve as the protector of Delmira, and thus, a protector of the midrealms."

"Elwren Embervale..." Audra paused, letting the significance of her final question linger. "Do you solemnly vow to lead the people of Delmira, to govern with justice and mercy, and to use the full might of your magic in its defense?"

"I do."

The weight of the crown settled atop Wren's head, the pointed motif resting against her brow.

Audra's boots disappeared from view as she stepped back. "Then rise, Elwren, Queen of Delmira."

Wren was shaking, shaking so hard that she was worried the crown would tumble from her head, but she rose from the rubble, from ashes long gone.

"Long live the queen!" Thea's voice boomed from the front of the crowd.

"*Long live the queen!*" came the thunderous response.

Wren didn't dare look to the crowd for fear of her knees giving out beneath her—but she need not have worried, for there was a rush of well-wishers, each taking her hands in theirs and kneeling. She fought the urge to pull them to their feet too quickly, her face flushing with embarrassment. All her life she had been an alchemist. For a time she had been a poisoner, striking names off a ledger. And now—

A firm squeeze of her fingers wrenched her from her daze, and she found herself looking at a pair of celadon eyes that matched her own.

"I don't know if *congratulations* is what I'm meant to say here," Thea said, brow furrowing. "But I think the most appropriate words from me are: *thank you.*"

"Thea, don't—" Wren started, but her sister cut her off.

"I mean it," she said fiercely. "Thank you. I know you did it for me. And it was selfish of me to let you."

"You are far from selfish, Thee."

Thea shook her head. "There won't be a day that goes by that I am not grateful to you for what you sacrificed. We once fought for the world we wanted, and we will do so again. But when we win, it will be *you* who has given me the life I yearned for."

Tears stung Wren's eyes as Thea bowed.

"Thank you, sister," the Shadow of Death murmured, kissing the back of her hand.

Choking back a sob, Wren pulled her sister to her. "It's my honor."

Thea smiled and stepped away, only for Wren's breath to catch in her throat as another Warsword took her place.

Torj Elderbrock came forward and knelt before her, his sea-blue eyes lined with silver. "I have made my vows to you before," he said quietly. "But I do so again with you as a crowned ruler of the midrealms."

"And what is it that you promise, Bear Slayer?" she asked, her voice trembling.

He held her gaze, offering his war hammer in reverence. "That I will protect you, that I will serve you, and that I will love you, as my soul-bonded, my storm wielder, my wife... and as my queen."

Wren let the tears fall as she pulled the warrior to his feet, the draw between them more powerful than ever. "Then my promise to you is the same, Torj. Always."

CHAPTER 64

TORJ

"A Warsword's armor is a prize bestowed upon him by the kingdom of Delmira upon completion of the Great Rite."
—The Warsword's Way

In the torchlight of his tent, the glass vials in Torj's palm gleamed, mocking him. *Two.* There were *only two* left.

"Fuck," he muttered. The hand that held the last doses of the strengthening potion shook, and he cursed himself for being so careless with the previous doses.

"I'm sorry," Dessa told him, her voice pained as she, too, looked at his tremors. "We ran out of a few things, and with the limited facilities here, we couldn't control the temperature—"

"Don't apologize," he said quietly. "You've given me more time than I thought possible. You did all that you could."

But Dessa was shaking her head. "It wasn't enough."

"It was *everything*," he said fiercely. "Every second more that I got to spend with her was *everything*, and it was because of you, Dess. And Zavier. I got to see her become a fucking *queen*."

"There's still the battle..." Dessa unrolled a pouch on the cot. "These won't be as powerful as the tonic, but they'll give you a burst of energy when you need it most. It's a potent mixture of dried iruseed. You're well acquainted with it by now."

"Yes."

"Good." Dessa held up a strange-looking capsule. "I made you three of these. It's a concentrated dose. I wouldn't recommend it to anyone unless—"

"They were dying?" Torj finished for her with a wry smile. "Had nothing left to lose?"

"Your words," Dessa replied. "Just don't take them all at once, and for Furies' sake, don't tell Wren I gave them to you."

"Duly noted."

Dessa sighed. "I already know I'm going to regret this."

"You won't," Torj assured her. "I'll always protect her. Even if it's the last thing I do."

"That's what I'm worried about," the red-headed alchemist scoffed, before rummaging through her pockets. "Here." Dessa handed him a thin silver chain. "The vials can be attached to that and tucked beneath your breastplate— easier to access that way."

"Thank you, Dessa," he said. "Truly."

"Thank her by staying alive," came Kipp's voice. His

head of auburn hair appeared through the canvas flap. "Zavier's asking for you, Dess."

Dessa gave Torj a businesslike nod. "Stay safe, Bear Slayer. Our queen needs you."

Torj simply saluted her with one of the vials as she left. He felt Kipp's eyes on him as he threaded the two doses of strengthening potion to the chain around his neck, tucking them beneath his undershirt.

"What is it, Snowden?" he asked, surveying the armor he'd laid out on his cot, wondering how the fuck he'd get it on with the way his fingers were trembling.

"I'm just here to confirm your position," Kipp replied evenly.

"Frontline," Torj said without hesitation. "I'll lead the charge."

Kipp sighed. "I suspected as much. Queen Reyna's forces are yours to command—"

Torj frowned. "Says who?"

"Says the winter queen herself." Kipp unfolded a map, smoothing it out in front of Torj. "You'll take the city gates. You can create a bottleneck there for a time, but those walls are old and in disrepair—they won't hold forever, so hit their vanguard hard from the first charge."

Torj nodded. "Archers?"

Kipp drew his finger along the map. "Across the walls, led by Cal, as long as the walls stand. Regent Liora's army will be waiting within, when they inevitably breach the gates."

"Anything else?" Torj asked with a note of dismissal.

Kipp studied him for a moment. "Don't do anything stupid."

"That's rich, coming from you," Torj said, trying to make light of the comment.

But Kipp, who was usually the most jovial person Torj knew—irritatingly so—was serious. "I mean it."

Torj bowed his head. "Same to you, then. Now, can I arm myself in peace?"

"Be my guest, Bear Slayer. It's the last moment of peace you'll have in a while." The strategist left.

Torj had the sense that Kipp had wanted to say more, that he'd held himself back. If they survived the upcoming battle, Torj made a mental note to ask him, but for now...

He took the ring Darian had given him from his pocket, rolling the fine band of silver between his fingers. His mother's ring. Not her wedding ring—gods, he would have tossed that in the depths of the sea the first chance he got. No, this was the ring she loved, the one that had been passed down through her family for as long as anyone could remember.

Torj hadn't been able to give it to Wren aboard *The Furies' Will*, for she'd still been wearing Darian's ring. But now, in a moment of weakness, he allowed himself to imagine sliding the circle of silver over her finger in front of all their friends. He wished he could have given her what Thea had. A real wedding. A celebration.

Torj threaded the ring onto the chain with his strengthening potions. It was a dream that would never come to pass now, like so many others, and he told himself he had made his peace with that. He had been able to call her *wife*, if only for a little while.

With the ring against his heart, his fingers brushed over the web of scars there. It hadn't been so long ago that he'd been convinced the old wounds were slowly killing him. And now here he was, dying from something else entirely. The irony wasn't lost on him.

He reached with trembling hands for his armor. It was too soon to take the strengthening tonic. Far too soon. He would have to get his armor on without steady hands.

Torj worked methodically, tightening buckles with his teeth, bracing himself against the tent's center pole as he strapped on his greaves. He was already sweating, which didn't bode well for leading Wren's frontlines and obliterating the enemy.

"Fuck's sake," he muttered as he fumbled with his sword belt.

Suddenly, the weight lifted from his tingling hands, and he glanced up to find Wilder Hawthorne securing it around his waist.

"The fuck are you doing?" he snapped, trying to bat his friend's hands away.

"Not sure you're in any state to pick a fight with me now, brother," Wilder replied, dodging his swipes and scooping up the breastplate from the end of the cot. "Besides, don't you remember when we were shieldbearers? You're the one who taught me how to fit armor."

"Well, I did a lousy job," Torj grunted. "Strap's too loose there."

Wilder laughed. "You won't say that when you're mid-swing of that giant hammer."

"I'll let you know."

"You do that, old man." Wilder clapped him on his armored shoulder. "I think you're needed elsewhere now."

With a wave of thanks, Torj was already striding for the exit and heading for the war tent.

There she is. His queen was at the head of the command table, a map of Dorinth spread out before her, her friends and council by her sides. Gone was her apron and dress; instead, Wren wore armor and her crown.

Elwren Embervale, his soul-bonded, his *everything*, was ready to fight.

He came to stand at her side, where he belonged. "What are your orders, my queen?"

CHAPTER 65
WREN

"The measure of a queen lies not in avoiding errors, but in learning from them before they become elegies."
—Elwren Embervale's notes and observations

"First, we need to focus on chokehold points," Wren heard herself say, her voice hard and unyielding. "We're outnumbered, so we need to identify two or three entry points to this stronghold that can be defended by smaller numbers." She turned to Torj, Thea, and Wilder. "You must have spotted these when Kipp, Cal, and I lured the initial enemy force from the city. Where are they?"

Thea stepped forward and used a series of pins to mark three positions on the map. "These spots here. It's where the remaining partial walls and parapets create natural funnels we can exploit."

Wren took a moment to consider. "I want a Warsword

and Thezmarrian unit stationed at each one. What about long-range weaponry?"

"I've got it covered," Cal interjected. There was no sign of the bandages that had been wrapped around his shoulder earlier. "The high ground gives us the advantage. I'll have archers positioned on any remaining parapets so we can provide ample cover from above."

"Good," Kipp said at Wren's side. "There's limited time, but I've got our shieldbearers creating some simple traps for when the enemy infiltrates the stronghold. Which they will. Without Lucian or King Leiko's manpower, we don't have the numbers to defend it indefinitely."

"Traps? Like what?" Vernich asked.

"Simple yet effective obstacles," Kipp offered. "Ditches and tripwires on the obvious paths up to the throne room, which is where they established themselves last time. They won't entirely stop the advancing forces, but they will slow them down and create confusion."

"What about pit traps?" Thea offered. "Wren could treat the spikes with poison, so even if they manage to climb out, they'll be weakened or dying soon enough?"

Wren nodded, ignoring the brutality of it all. "I can do that," she told her sister. "You and I can also cover our initial movements with storm magic. It may help wash away any traces of more basic alchemy that Silas intends to use. We only have enough of the counter-alchemy to give us an edge for a while, so we need to make it count."

"Do we have their positions?" Torj asked from her side, his towering presence steadying her as the plans unfolded before them.

"The enemy marches in one unified force from the

south," Kipp answered with a grimace. "Their ranks are a combination of the People's Vanguard fanatics, those who have been cursed with shadow magic and want violence for no rhyme or reason, and some of Silas' masked alchemist commanders."

"And Silas himself?" Wren pressed. "Do we know where he is among the army?"

Kipp shook his head. "There have been no sightings of him yet. But there's one last thing we need to decide on..."

Wren's heart was in her throat. She and Kipp had already discussed this, and it had left her reeling. "The final fallback position," she murmured.

"Yes." Kipp bowed his head in confirmation. "We need to establish a location within the ruins. Should the outer defenses fall, we need a place where remaining fighters can retreat before..."

Torj's warm fingers laced through hers and he squeezed her hand.

"Before the final stand," Wren finished for her friend.

Wren stole a moment of solitude atop a lone parapet, a moment to come to terms with the blood that would soon never wash from her hands. And so she stood looking over the edge of the decrepit wall, watching the sun rise over the ruins of what was once her homeland. The war camp of midrealms forces was sprawled beneath her position—hundreds of fires dotting the landscape like fallen stars, each representing soldiers who might not see another dawn.

She looked down to the black metal in her hand—a People's Vanguard mask.

Vernich had made good on his promise, finding her after her coronation and presenting her with a gore-splattered piece of obsidian. "Told you I'd rip one off another bastard's face for you," he'd said before stalking toward Kipp, who was talking animatedly to Graves.

It was a lesser version of the one Silas himself wore, but with a full mask at her disposal, it had taken Wren all of three minutes to realize she had been right in the Warren. The piece had been designed to prolong the effects of magic and alchemy by holding the essence within the depressed lines in the metal. It explained how Silas and his select commanders and alchemists could maintain their immunity to poisons and withstand certain attacks, but it didn't explain the enemy's ability to increase their strength so rapidly... She knew there was more to it, but she was out of time.

How could she have ever thought she wanted to specialize in warfare alchemy? She had forgotten the horror of it, the dread. In her thirst for vengeance after the shadow war, she'd forgotten that breaking things had never been her strength.

Healing had.

And then she felt him. The bond between them, an unspoken language.

She heard the reverence in his mind, in his heart. She saw the love in his eyes as he reached for her and crushed his mouth to hers.

I love you. I love you. Gods, I love you. Those words poured into her body with every kiss, every touch, with every thrum of the soul bond.

She dropped the mask and let her hands tangle in his silver hair, meeting every desperate brush of his tongue with a savage kiss of her own. They were prisoners in their armor, clawing at metal plates for just a skim of bare skin, but his teeth marked the side of her throat and licked over the hurt.

Fate waited for them on either side of the parapet, but her fate, her destiny was right there in front of her, under her skin and in her blood, in her soul.

The silvertide roses were gone. Her cure nearly completely used up by their own defenses.

And yet she refused to believe what was so plainly written across her Warsword's face.

Wren straightened, drawing her shoulders back. "This isn't the end, Bear Slayer."

"I—"

"You're needed on the frontlines," she said, her voice steel. "And when this war is done, I will show you exactly how wrong you have been. I did not wait nearly thirteen years only to say goodbye to you now."

"Wren—"

She silenced him with a single look. "On your way, soldier."

Wren waited until his footsteps retreated before she braced herself against the crumbling stone, choking back a sob as she at last took in the expanse of the enemy before her and the weight of the crown upon her head.

I love you, came the words from the gates below. She

imagined him mounting his horse, pictured him riding along the frontline with his war hammer raised.

Wren's fingers absently traced the vials at her belt—a habit from her days as a mere alchemist, when her biggest concern was whether a potion might bubble over. She hadn't been just an alchemist in a long time. Now she wielded vials that could end lives. She had carried that burden before, and would carry it again before her time was done.

She glanced down at her hands—the hands of a novice turned adept turned sage. Alchemist's hands, scarred from acids and burns, now holding the lives of thousands in her palm, her storm magic crackling there too.

A battle horn sounded in the distance, and Wren descended the uneven steps, to where her army awaited.

Thea was there, holding out her reins. "Torj designed the crown, you know," she ventured.

"I gathered," Wren replied with a soft smile, mounting her horse.

"But the steel... That came from me," Thea told her. "Remember Malik's dagger?"

Wren gasped. "You didn't."

But Thea smiled. "I did. And you know why?"

Wren shook her head in shock. Thea *loved* that dagger, had held onto it for well over a decade... She couldn't imagine her melting it down for anything, especially a crown.

Thea's expression softened. "Because when he gave it to me, he said the words: *Beware the fury of a patient Delmirian*... For a long time, I thought he meant me, and then for a while I thought he meant Anya. But it was you... I think he was talking about you all along." Misty-eyed, Thea cleared her throat and nodded to the battle ahead. "To war."

"To victory," Wren corrected her.

To her surprise, her sister pressed three fingers to her shoulder, the salute of respect for a Warsword, as she bowed low. "Your Majesty."

CHAPTER 66
TORJ

"History does not remember those who die quiet deaths."
—Bear Slayer, Warsword of Thezmarr

T orj led his unit of Thezmarrian warriors to the choke point he'd been assigned—a narrow path between two crumbling stone walls, with a makeshift barricade of debris and timber. From his position, he could see the second choke point, roughly a hundred yards away, with Vernich and Graves at the helm. Torj knew Wilder manned the third site, but he didn't have eyes on him, nor on either of the Embervale sisters, who had moved to the parapets above, to channel their storm magic into the attacking forces.

Torj signaled to his garrison to wait, even as the echo of the enemy's march drew closer and closer, their armor glinting in the morning light.

He kept his closed fist raised. They needed to hold their position. They needed to—

A thick silvery fog descended. Not shadow alchemy, but storm magic, billowing down around them, providing cover and distributing the cure Wren had worked so hard to create. She and Dessa had managed to turn it into a vapor that the Embervale sisters were now spreading across their ranks, protecting their forces from Silas' corrupted potions. Torj wished he could see Wren leading the midrealms army as she brought the mist into being, disguising where he and his company lay in wait, ready to strike.

This was it—the warrior's second, the intake of breath before the slice of a blade, the eerie calm before violence broke out, the unnatural silence of compounding fear. As the fog swirled around him, Torj rested a hand against the vials beneath his armor. *Not yet*, he told himself. Instead, he turned to the ranks behind him and combed his mind for something to say before the enemy was within earshot. He was tired of giving battle speeches, tired of rallying people to ride to their deaths. What words could he give them that would offer comfort from the slice of a blade or the hit of an arrow?

He thought back to his time training shieldbearers at Thezmarr. Two of those shieldbearers now stood as Warswords on the precipice of this very battle, another as a lead strategist at its helm. More had gone on to become great warriors of the midrealms. What had he told them?

Ignoring the tremor that had started in his leg, Torj straightened and cleared his throat. "Some of you have been here before," he started, projecting his voice to the farthest ranks. "For others, it's your first time facing what lies ahead.

None of us asked for this—of that, I am sure. And yet we cannot change what awaits us beyond the fog, nor can we change the fear that claws at us while we wait. But I always told the shieldbearers of Thezmarr that being a protector of the midrealms is not about hating the evil before you. No, it's about loving the land and its people behind you. But today it is about looking forward, to a future that promises freedom, not oppression. A cause I will gladly lay down my life for today."

Above, a flash of lightning split the sky. The signal. *Her* signal.

Torj drew a breath and raised his hammer for all to see, hiding the strain in his muscles as he called, "Remember that glory will not be found in failing to fall, but in rising when you do. So we rise! Again, and again! Until we vanquish this bastard and his bastard followers from our realm! Do you hear me?"

A thunderous cheer echoed behind him, drowning out his own heartbeat in his ears, and the distant sound of a drum.

Until the ground started to vibrate beneath Torj's boots, and dust rose from the path ahead... A sudden war cry pierced the air as a unit of the People's Vanguard charged up the narrow passage.

The enemy was upon them.

CHAPTER 67
TORJ

"An army is only as strong as its weakest man."
—The Midrealms Chronicles

The first clash of steel upon steel was deafening. The impact jarred Torj's entire body as he braced himself behind his shield. The soldier to his left fell almost instantly, blood spraying as a spear found his exposed neck.

"Hold the shield wall!" Torj bellowed from beneath the onslaught. "Hold it steady!" All around him, men and women of Thezmarr reinforced the barrier between them and the enemy's swords, shields slotting into place.

Torj glanced to the parapet above, his own voice sounding strange to him as he called, "Archers!"

Cal's voice carried across the chaos. "Loose!"

A volley of arrows blocked out the watery light as they rained down upon the enemy and the first wave of them fell. From the flashing glimpses Torj saw, the enemy was comprised of those corrupted by shadow magic—more animal than man, clawing for violence and blood—and those who were part of the fanatical People's Vanguard.

He fought all his natural instincts to break free from the defensive wall and send his hammer swinging into the second wave of attackers that launched themselves at his company. Instead, he braced himself again.

"Shield wall!" he commanded, feeling the ranks close in, taking the places of those who had fallen. The press of bodies was overwhelming, with the enemy assaulting their front and their own numbers enveloping the weakening flanks. The strike of blades and shields became distorted sounds echoing around the swell of the conflict, the scent of metal and blood thick in the air already.

Their formation held, and from above, Cal sent another volley of arrows down upon the attackers. Screams sounded, strangled and desperate as the second wave fell, giving Torj and his company mere seconds of breathing room.

"Now!" he yelled.

Torj dropped his shield. For those first few moments, he needed no strengthening potions or energy-boosting aids to lift his hammer; it went swinging. Bone crunched beneath it, and the slap of warm blood—not his—hit the side of his face and coated his neck.

"To the Bear Slayer!" someone shouted behind him, and he felt his forces surge.

Torj realized the enemy leader was using none of his deadly concoctions in the first wave of attack. The screams that surrounded him were born of flesh injuries and terror, the usual symphony of battle. Even in his weakened state, Torj was easily the strongest, most experienced warrior among those fighting, and he led the counter-assault, beating the enemy back. The wave of collision between the forces rippled from the point of impact outward, like the drop of a stone in a still lake, and the mass of armored bodies surged. But Torj followed his orders, utilizing the choke point between the walls for its intended purpose, cutting the People's Vanguard down as they charged through the narrow funnel.

The bodies of the fallen lay at his feet, piling up, creating another barrier. Silas' soldiers blanched as they realized they had to climb over their own dead to advance. But there was no sign of the Kingsbane himself that Torj could see.

Wren! he called. *Any sightings of Silas?*

He's certainly not leading his own army, came her strained reply. *He's got a handful of alchemists in his ranks—they're masked and protected by their own units—but no one from our forces has laid eyes on him yet.*

He won't be far, Torj warned as he knocked an attacker back with a punch to the throat. *He might be a coward when it comes to the fighting, but he'll want to be front and center if there is victory to be had.*

Stay safe, Bear Slayer, was Wren's response.

Torj's muscles strained as he swirled his hammer over his head and brought it down into the masked face of one of his attackers. Sweat and blood stinging his eyes, he looked around wildly, the claustrophobia of battle closing in around him. The narrow pass had become a killing field, the stench of it almost overwhelming. Beneath both enemy and ally boots, the ground was treacherous with blood-slicked rubble and discarded weapons, as many people slipping as being felled by blades.

Torj craned his neck to glimpse the state of the second choke point—Vernich and Graves were at the heart of the fray, their faces contorted in matching snarls as they fought back yet another wave of Silas' army while Wren and Thea's storms continued to rage around them. As with Torj's unit, the soldiers rotated to provide brief respite to those on the frontlines, but the Warswords stayed at the helm, where they belonged.

But the enemy was gaining ground. They were hitting the remaining wall with a battering ram, creating more space for their forces to surge through.

Wilder's choke point fell, Wren's voice sounded in his mind. *Get Cal to create cover for you and Vernich, then retreat to the secondary position.*

And you? Are you alright? Torj sent his panic through the bond, unable to glimpse Wren upon the parapet where she'd been before as he plowed his hammer through a line of enemy soldiers, their screams echoing off the piles of bodies.

I'm fine, came her distant reply. *Secondary position, now.*

Torj cupped a hand to his mouth and shouted, "Cal! We need a volley!"

"Nock!" Cal's voice cut through the bedlam. "Draw!"

Torj turned back to his unit. "Retreat to the secondary position," he barked, just as Cal's final order sounded above.

"Loose!"

"Pull back!" Torj shouted, the muscles in his arm

spasming violently as he raised his hammer to gain his unit's attention. *"Pull fucking back!"*

His commanders saw him and barked their own orders across the ranks. Arrows rained down, creating a much-needed pause in the fighting as the enemy pulled back to lift their shields. The dull percussion of arrows embedding in metal reverberated across the ranks, and shrieks of pain followed. Torj didn't look back. He clambered over the bodies alongside his company, hauling the injured to their feet and pushing them toward the rallying point.

As they retreated, the masters' alchemy rained down in clouds of powder that reacted with the enemy's armor, accelerating any existing rust—corroding the metal so drastically that it caved inward upon the wearer. All around him, people screamed.

The enemy swarmed the choke point, obliterating the stone walls that had created the narrow path. Someone shoved a set of reins into Torj's hand, and he swung himself up into the saddle, the motion second nature to him. His stallion was sturdy beneath him, and he urged Tucker toward the secondary position, where the remaining Thezmarrian forces were gathering, falling back into their ranks. He spotted Vernich and Graves taking their places in the frontlines atop their own stallions, and Audra rallying bands of shieldbearers at the rear, but there were notable absences.

"Vernich!" he called across the mayhem. "Where's Hawthorne? And Thea?"

The Bloodletter's gaze snapped up, wild with adrenaline. "Up top," he yelled back, pointing to one of the remaining walls. "An enemy unit attacked the archers. The happy couple are fighting them off while Whitlock covers our retreat. Get ready, the next assault is coming!"

Torj didn't look to the enemy; his eyes went straight to the rampart, the one where his soul-bonded had been stationed.

Wren? he shouted down their bond. *Wren!*

CHAPTER 68
WREN

"If you seek logic within the violence of war, you will find none."
—Elwren Embervale's notes and observations

"Thea!" Wren screamed, sending a bolt of lightning into an enemy soldier whose sword was poised at her sister's back.

Thea glanced at the man crumpling behind her. "Thanks!" she shouted over her shoulder.

Wren didn't even get the chance to sigh her relief. Heart hammering, she threw another spear of brilliant white light into an enemy unit ascending the parapet, sending them flying. She could hear Torj's voice distantly through the bond, panic edging his tone as he called her name repeatedly. Her heart clenched at the fear in his inner voice, but the madness surrounding her wrenched her attention away. *I'm here, I'm alive,* she tried to send back, but wasn't sure if he could hear her. It was taking all her strength to focus on channeling her storm magic while enemies closed in from every side.

"Where is he?" Thea shouted over the roar of battle, her swords a blur of silver as she cleaved through the necks of two attackers, spraying Wren with blood. "The bastard won't even show his face at his own fucking war?"

Wren wiped the mess from her brow with a grimace. "He's coming."

Wilder leapt in front of her just in time to deflect a spear. He threw the enemy soldier from the parapet into the ranks below, crushing several more.

"Our forces are in the secondary position," he said, barely out of breath as he pointed to the madness below. "The Kingsbane's army has breached all three choke points faster than we anticipated—they sacrificed their frontlines to overwhelm us with sheer numbers. They're advancing through the ruins, and we're running out of defensible ground."

He was right. Through the vortex of alchemy and storm magic, enemy figures broke from the mayhem with lethal purpose below, directing their ranks into a forked attack.

"Shit," Thea muttered. "They're using a pincer move to surround us."

Wren whipped around to the far end of the parapet. "Cal!" she shouted. "Redirect our archers!"

Cal already had them at the ready, arrows showering the rear of the advancing enemy below.

Wren caught sight of Kipp near the edge of the secondary position, his face turned up to her, waiting. She lifted her arm and slashed it down in a signal. Kipp nodded once and ducked away into the shadows of a half-collapsed building.

Moments later, the ground between the choke points and the secondary position rippled. As the enemy forces rushed forward, intent on overwhelming their defensive line, the earth gave way beneath their boots. Screams erupted as soldiers plummeted into the carefully concealed pit traps.

"Yes!" Thea breathed beside her, gripping Wren's arm in anticipation as they watched on. Those who weren't immediately impaled on the poisoned spikes were crushed by their comrades falling on top of them.

"It buys us time," Wren told her sister. "Not much else."

"We'll take it," Thea replied, pointing to Kipp emerging from the other side of their forces, already signaling to Torj and the others to ready the next line of defense.

But Wren's momentary triumph faded as her gaze returned to the larger battlefield. Her heart lodged in her throat as she saw how quickly the fallen were replaced, and how Silas' commanders were motioning to each other across the rallying numbers.

A hollow of dread opened low in her stomach as she realized the extent of her failure.

She had never won Dorinth.

Silas had delivered it to her, piece by poisoned piece.

Only to trap them within.

Wren watched in horror as the ground beyond her own army gave out, screams piercing the smoke-filled sky. But it didn't just cave in; it fell away to reveal a subterranean passage...

"Shit," Thea said at Wren's side. "The tunnels."

"What tunnels?" Wilder barked, slicing the hand clean off a soldier wielding an axe against him.

Realization hit Wren like a blow. "The underground network between the taverns. The one Kipp mentioned."

"How the fuck does Silas know about it?" Thea kicked another assailant from the rampart, his scream swallowed by the pandemonium below.

"How do you think?" Wren shouted, bracing herself as her power surged within. "Lucian was in that meeting. All his lackeys were."

She thrust her hands skyward, summoning a violent burst of storm magic that she directed toward the passage, hoping to collapse it before whatever awaited them surfaced from the dark. Lightning struck the ground at the tunnel's edge, sending rock and debris tumbling, but it was too late—the passage was too wide.

As the sparks of lightning faded, the extent of the enemy's plan became clear.

For from the depths of that tunnel, Silas the Kingsbane and his true army emerged.

Wren should have known it was coming. A man like Silas did not concede territory without a motive. She'd known that all along. He'd used the desperate common folk of the midrealms to bolster his numbers and then sacrificed them without a second of remorse.

There was no Devereux sigil stamped on the armor of his followers, but she could see the might of Lucian's coin in the weapons and numbers, in the formations that marched forth, fresh and eager to spill blood. Silas and his ranks rose from the hidden stairs below and lined the borders of the city, surrounding Torj, Vernich, Graves, and the rest of their forces.

There were those who were mad with bloodlust from the shadow alchemy, practically foaming at the mouth to unleash their violence upon her forces. There were soldiers wearing colors Wren didn't recognize...

And within the simmering alchemy and storm magic lingering in the air, Silas stood tall, gathering strength.

That was all it took for Wren to understand what she'd failed to see right from the start, ever since the Kingsbane had inflicted himself on the world.

Silas was a *summoner*.

The realization hit her with physical force, making her knees weaken and her storm magic crackle erratically around her fingertips. Cold sweat broke out across her skin as the pieces fell into place. Instead of summoning objects with his mind like Zavier, he had somehow learned how to summon strength *and* magic—first by muting it with the manacles and his alchemy concoctions, and then by drawing it to him with his own sovereign magic. The masks helped absorb and contain that power—

Silas gave a signal.

Those whose gazes were clouded with shadow alchemy surged forward in a mindless charge of brutality. They fought by no code, driven only by a thirst for pain and death. In a trance state, the enemy ranks seemed not to feel the blows to their own bodies, but simply raged on, screaming in victory whenever an opponent fell before them in a spray of crimson.

It was barbaric—sickening. Wren could smell the blood mingling with the smoke around them. The Warswords below carved through the chaos, cutting down as many incensed soldiers as they could, but more and more seemed to emerge from the passage—

A powerful gust of wind, not born of Wren or Thea's storm magic, swept through the battleground, sending debris flying. Ally and enemy alike braced themselves against the impact...

And membranous wings parted the fog as Talemir Starling landed amid the ruins.

CHAPTER 69
WREN

"With my body as a shield, my mind as a blade, I will not hesitate to sacrifice."
—Drevenor Academy Oath of Secrecy

Talemir set his wife Drue down, and she unsheathed a wicked-looking blade just as a second pair of wings snapped back, revealing another shadow-touched. Dratos Castemont landed beside the couple, along with Adrienne, another Naarvian ranger, who jumped down from his arms.

Shouts from all over the battleground told Wren that other shadow-touched warriors were taking up positions as Talemir, Drue, Dratos, and Adrienne launched themselves into the fighting. Wren recognized the golden explosions of sun orchid essence being used to combat the exposed shadow alchemy. Drue had brought Naarva's remaining supplies, it seemed.

Alight with her own fury, Wren threw bolts of lightning at the enemy from the parapet while Talemir dual wielded back-to-back with Drue, whose cutlass was a blur of silver amid the violence. Wren had forgotten how well they fought together, just like Thea and Wilder. Dratos matched the bloodlust of the enemy, splitting his opponents from navel to nose with his own blade, while Adrienne guarded his back with an axe and chain.

Wren looked to Silas, who had started to move through the bedlam, his mask still perfectly in place as he drank in the power around him. The momentum of the battle only seemed to escalate as he brought down warriors from both Aveum and Harenth as though they were nothing.

Heart pounding, Wren looked to Thea across the other side of the ruins. She fought with both lightning and sword as she and Wilder were swarmed by a unit of the People's Vanguard.

Further down the parapet, Cal was still leading the archers, having torn off his bandages again and taken up his own bow. Flaming arrows shot into the fray, but where one man fell, another emerged from the passage.

From Wren's vantage point, she could just make out Vernich and Graves advancing from the other side of the enemy entrance to the city, a force of Thezmarrians behind them, but their arrival had come too late. Thousands crowded the ruins, spilling savagery wherever they went.

The masters of Drevenor flung their fear potions into the throngs, causing enemy soldiers to drop their weapons and flee from invisible foes, but supplies were dwindling; Wren could see it in the lull between each attack.

Her gaze snapped back to the madman at the helm, as Silas' attention was drawn to the heart of the conflict—

"*Torj!*" His name tore from Wren's throat as, from a distance, she saw her soul-bonded tip a handful of pills into his mouth and charge for the Kingsbane.

And Silas fucking *smiled.*

Time slowed as Wren watched her hammer-wielding Bear Slayer carve through the ruins toward the enemy, his strength seemingly doubled since she'd last glimpsed him amid the mayhem. But Silas had potions raised, his mask strapped to his face, and she could feel the power in the air shift across the rubble, could see it shimmer as it was drawn to him.

Torj faltered, and Wren couldn't breathe.

The storm swirling around her wasn't enough. The potions at her belt were not enough. The dagger in her hand was not enough. *Nothing* was enough.

A scream sounded from somewhere—her, she realized distantly. Suddenly she was moving, running along the remains of the wall, following Torj as he hurled himself toward Silas, whose shields were drinking in his power, his life force at Silas' summoning, and blasting him back with corrupted alchemy.

Each blow to her Warsword made their enemy stronger while leaving Torj weaker. But he was still there, still her shield against the world.

Closer now, Wren threw concoctions from above, wracking her brain for what else they could do.

Torj's voice came to her.

Let's finish this bastard, Embers. Together.

But before she could respond, she saw it.

The gold thread between them flickering in and out of view, laced with... silver. Power surged through it, power that felt like coming home.

Lightning burst from her entire being, and as her Bear Slayer had once done for her... she leapt from the parapet.

CHAPTER 70
TORJ

"Soldiers are taught to accept their fate as they would accept the
weight of their armor."
—The Warsword's Way

W ren was airborne, hurtling through the maelstrom
of corrupted alchemy and storm magic, the wind
whipping around her. With her hair coming unbound in the
sudden leap, and her armor gleaming in the flashes of
lightning, she looked like one of the Furies incarnate.

Her own power guided her leap into the chaos, and
sparks flew as she landed in a crouch, forks of brilliant
white crackling all over her body. Elwren Embervale stood,
a vision of rage and retribution, a dark promise of justice to
come.

Alchemist. Storm wielder. Queen.

She took a step toward the usurper, a tempest gathering

at her silent call. She was growing stronger by the second; Torj could feel it through the bond, and in the charged air vibrating around him.

Silas had stolen his strength and power from his own people, but Wren... Her power was freely given by the land itself.

This is it, Torj realized. With a trembling hand, he reached for the two vials around his neck. He had already taken Dessa's iruseed capsules, but now, in this moment, it was time for his final strike.

The Bear Slayer removed the corks from the vials with his teeth and tipped the contents one after the other down his throat. The bitter taste burned twice as much, but the effect was immediate. All of his Furies-given strength rushed back to him in a colossal wave, and he raised his hammer, a war cry breaking from his lips as he charged across the wreckage. He knew he shouldn't relish the violence, that it was an ugly balm to the wounds within, but his hammer sang as it carved through air and man alike, a melody like no other, accented by the screams that sounded in its wake.

Torj, no!

Wren's panic was sharp down the bond, but he was resolute. He knew his purpose. It was the same as it had always been. Protect her. Love her. Help her rise to her own potential.

And so, when he reached Silas and swung his hammer, he knew it wouldn't find its mark. But it would buy her time. Time to take the power her kingdom offered her. Time to gather the strength she needed to bring the usurper bastard to his knees.

Enemy soldiers surrounded Torj before he could hit his mark, and he struck them down, over and over, while Silas watched. Blood sprayed by his hand, flesh and bone caving beneath his iron. For her, he would kill them all. For her he would raze the whole fucking force to the ground.

Dripping with gore, Torj looked up from the sea of bodies at his feet to see Silas holding a vial of shadow alchemy.

Silas looked from the onyx ribbons drifting within the confines of the bottle back to Torj. He flicked his hand in a signal.

A volley of enemy arrows blocked out the sun, and Torj couldn't stop them.

In the distance, someone screamed as each arrow punctured the flesh of his torso. One. Two. Three. Four.

Dazed, he looked down to see them protruding from his body, hot blood gushing from each wound.

Torj closed his eyes, and knew then what he had been saving himself for. He thought of nothing but Wren as he sent his power down the bond. As his strength left him, his knees weakened, and he fell to them in the mud, using his remaining energy for one last thing.

Silas' voice was laced with mock apprehension. "Do you truly think you're enough to stop me?"

"No," Torj answered, holding the grip of his hammer upright, as he smiled with bloody teeth. "But I'm just the calm before the storm."

A cry of fury sounded behind him, and a bolt of fiery lightning shot past him, kissing his shoulder as it hurtled toward Silas.

CHAPTER 71
WREN

"It is often written that sovereign magic is the most ancient in the history of the midrealms. It is not."
—The Midrealms Chronicles

Wren gasped as the lightning left her fingertips, not just with the force of her own power, but with the force of *Torj's*. She had never felt anything like it as it surged through her entire being. Her Warsword had poured his Furies-given strength into their bond, into *her*.

For all these years, he had protected her, had kept her safe, and now, he was showing her...

She was a reckoning all of her own.

She was the storm.

Alongside Torj's power, Wren drew magic from the very heart of herself, old sovereign magic that had run through the veins of her ancestors, magic that the kingdom of Delmira itself recognized in her. It was both within her and in the sky beyond, and she called it to her now in the ultimate warrior cry. Her lightning tore the sky apart in a blaze of blinding white. The dusk-kissed sky turned dark, heavy with thick clouds rolling in overhead, and they broke apart at her command.

Delmira. *Her* kingdom. The land that had bloomed with silvertide—roses that could have purified the shadow alchemy wreaking havoc across the midrealms. Roses that Silas had burned to ash just days ago, destroying the one cure that could have saved thousands, that could have saved *Torj*.

Storm magic heightened with Warsword strength blasted through the air, and Wren struck Silas with bolt after bolt, fast enough that he didn't have time to absorb it in the way he had before. Pressure built behind her eyes and in her lungs. Her whole body thrummed with power. Wren was stronger in her own kingdom, stronger than ever. The storm was in her blood, in her bones. She could feel Delmira calling her home, welcoming her with a tempest to rival all others.

The tether between her and Torj grew taut, and she distantly heard the gasps around them as the soul bond glimmered into being for all to see. A solid gold thread linking them, binding him to her.

Hold on, she called to him, the image of those arrows sticking out of his chest flashing in her mind. The pain of them lanced through her own upper body, but their entwined magic kept her upright as she fought her way toward Silas. His shadow alchemy gathered around him like a swarm, searching for power and strength to strip from hosts and feed back to him.

That was his endgame—not just to rule Delmira, but to

consume the magic of every wielder in the midrealms. To become a living god, feeding off the power of others like a parasite. It was why Queen Reyna and Regent Liora had allied with Wren despite any lingering misgivings between their kingdoms; perhaps it was why the Furies had soul-bonded her to Torj. If Silas won today, no realm would be safe.

There was a cry as one of Audra's Warswords faltered beneath his power, but Wren, barely aware of the ground beneath her feet or the shouts in the distance swallowed by thunder, wrenched the rain from the sky.

The downpour came in stinging sheets, a torrent she could hardly see through. As the drops hit the vapor, the alchemy hissed again, retreating into the rubble. But that wasn't enough. It wasn't nearly enough. Wren needed to cleanse her kingdom of this poison. She needed to flood its ruins and flush out the evil that had infiltrated her birthright.

Wren stood in the Delmirian soil, her rain flowing across the rubble, washing away the blood and debris. Everything else faded away, becoming a blur as her power surged around her. She could feel Thea's magic too, steady and solid beside her own, remnants of Anya's power echoing between them as well. It was as though the three Embervale sisters fought together once more.

Silas' scream of rage sounded, as did the cries of his men as they fell, but Wren didn't stop.

In the distance, she felt Thea's magic surging against the forces at the perimeter, heard the clash of steel once more as the battle raged on outside the would-be throne room. She flung out a hand, more lightning shooting from her palm this time, thunder clapping overhead—

Pain flared at her knees and she whirled around to see Torj keeled over in the ruins, broken stone and glass beneath him, his shoulders caving in. *His* pain. Wren forgot all else as she saw the labored rise and fall of his chest.

She ceased her lightning assault, ducking and dodging several flying vials as she lunged for the Bear Slayer, her heart in her throat.

"Torj," she panted, wrenching the arrows from him, trying to cauterise the wounds with her magic. "Don't you dare—"

"Embers," he murmured as the traces of lightning at her bloody fingertips kissed his skin.

"Together." Wren held out her hand. "Let's end him together."

They locked eyes, and Wren's breath caught in her throat as their fingers entwined and a bolt of energy burst through her. Through *him*.

"Wren..." Torj's voice was weak, but full of wonder.

The gold thread of their bond flared between them, but its usual warm glow shifted... transmuting, like metal changing in a crucible.

A scream echoed across the battlefield. Wren looked up as something hurtled toward them—alchemy, full of shadow and darkness. She clutched Torj to her. If this was to be the end, then she could make her peace with dying at Torj Elderbrock's side, with his hand in hers.

Glass exploded. Dark alchemy surged, and the scent of burnt hair filled her nostrils as she recognized the lashes of shadow from the previous war. The horrors of it began to flash before her, over and over again, the screams piercing enough to make ears bleed—

"Embers..." Torj's voice brought her back, no longer shaky, but husky and rich. Momentarily blinded, her eyes stung as she blinked, tears spilling down her cheeks as the gold of their soul bond bled away...

Giving way to a pure, brilliant silver.

The soul bond pulsed at their joined hands, a cord stronger than ever, wrapping around them both in intricate swirls. Wren could feel Torj's strength flowing into her, not just the borrowed power of the Furies, but his very *essence*—his unwavering loyalty, his fierce protection, his absolute devotion. She poured herself into the bond in return—not only her storm magic, but the love she had for him, the determination in her heart. All the while, the bond bloomed around them.

Shadow alchemy collided with silver.

And shattered.

A choked sound escaped Silas. But understanding flooded through Wren.

Gold will turn to silver in a blaze of iron and embers... giving rise to ancient power long forgotten.

The prophecy that had haunted her since the last war. Not just the joining of power, but its transformation into something new, something *good*. The silver light pulsed between queen and Warsword, like a map of stars in the night sky.

The silver bond between them wasn't just combining their powers—it was purifying them. Like the most complex distillation she'd ever attempted, it burned away everything corrupt. Wren could feel Torj's heart beating in sync with hers, could feel his breath in her lungs and his strength in her bones.

"How can this be?" she murmured. "The silvertide roses are gone. There is no more cure…"

But what the roses would have done through slow healing, their bond was doing in an instant—transforming that which was rotten into something pure, shadow into light.

Torj was pulling her to her feet, strong and steady, which was more than she could say for herself. With his wounds magically sealed, he pressed a hand to his chest in wonder, blinking slowly as he examined his other hand, which no longer shook.

"The poison's gone," he said, his gaze meeting hers once more, his sea-blue eyes bright. "The roses were never the cure. It was always you…"

The realization settled into her bones with the weight of ancient truth. All this time searching for something external, when the answer had lived within her all along. Not just her alchemy or her storm magic, but something deeper—the capacity to love fiercely enough to transform darkness itself. A power older than kingdoms or wars. Wren felt both humbled and strengthened by the knowledge, even as the world around them continued to burn.

Projectiles of dark alchemy came for them and broke against the silver light of their bond, which engulfed them both completely now. Wren could feel the wildness of her storms and Torj's Furies-given strength reinforcing their silver shield, the light shimmering as the enemy's attacks dissipated upon contact.

Around them, she saw the allies who'd rallied to her

cause—Queen Reyna's forces from Aveum, who'd braved a deadly snowstorm to cross the midrealms and fight; soldiers from Harenth, who had more reason than most to distrust a royal, whose towns and villages had been the targets of the People's Vanguard campaigns; as well as the warriors of Thezmarr and Talemir's shadow-touched, who had thought they'd seen their last war. Everyone she cared for still fought in the heart of the fray, caked with blood and gore, never once wavering.

Silas' voice drifted through the smoke.

"You pretend you're not like me. But you are—you're *exactly* like me. We both know that true power is taken, that it requires sacrifice."

As love filled Wren's heart for her friends, her family, and for Torj, the soul bond erupted outward—not just in their defense, but in attack, moving like liquid, cutting through the tainted alchemy and magic surrounding them.

Wren's hand remained firmly in Torj's as she spoke. "Sacrifice, perhaps," she said. "But true power isn't taken. It is *given*."

She could feel Silas' attempts to summon their magic and strength around him, but it wasn't working. Not how it had before. His strategy had always been to drain others, to take what wasn't his—first the strength of Warswords and other rulers, then Delmira, and eventually all of the midrealms. But the silver bond between Wren and Torj was something he couldn't corrupt or consume.

Wren threw herself into one last attack: a blaze of brilliant white light, of silver and smoke.

Alchemist fought alchemist. Storm wielder fought summoner. And Wren gave everything she had.

Silas could no longer summon magic from others, so he summoned anything and everything else, throwing boulders, discarded debris, and whatever else he could at them with all his might.

Gasps of horror sounded from the ranks around them, for the People's Vanguard hadn't been able to see the sovereign magic for themselves—until now.

A mass of stonework shot through the air by Silas' hand, crashing before Wren and Torj with a near-deafening crack, shaking the earth beneath them.

"At last, you're showing them who you truly are, Your Highness," Wren called, throwing another bolt of lightning in retaliation. "Silas isn't your true name, is it? For all your hatred and warmongering over royals, *you are one*, Andor Terling. Prince of Naarva."

The thud of weapons hitting the ground echoed across the battlefield as members of the People's Vanguard dropped them in shock. Their forces separated as they edged back, further and further, until they were almost in full retreat, their faces etched with horror.

Wren had many faults, she knew, but one thing she had in this gods-forsaken war was that she'd been herself, in the end. Alchemist. Poisoner. Storm wielder. Engaged to a nobleman. Married to a Warsword. *That* was what she had written to the people of the midrealms aboard *The Furies' Will*. She had told them her story, and Kipp had ensured that it reached every corner of the midrealms.

With everything she had, she had told the truth.

Silas had not.

And now, as her storm raged on, flooding the ruins of Dorinth and washing away whatever trance Silas had cast over the common folk with his shadow alchemy, the people of the midrealms saw the truth with horrifying clarity.

Some, Silas had manipulated in their moments of need and desperation. Others, he had drugged with dark alchemy, filling them with cravings for violence and blood.

Their loved ones had died for his cause. In his name.

And it was all a lie.

Fury flashed across Silas' face. "An entire kingdom fell because of your mother's selfishness," he spat. "You Embervales always win, don't you? Even now, when justice should prevail. Your mother had a choice! She swore an oath to protect us—an oath sealed in blood between friends. But when the darkness came, she chose only Delmira. My mother begged her... and Brigh turned away. Do you know what it's like to watch everything you love wither? Every Naarvian child who starved, every village razed—their blood stains your family's lands. Whatever happens to me, the people will remember: *your* family's legacy is built on betrayal."

"I had *no* legacy until now, Silas," Wren shouted. "Delmira suffered just as Naarva did—more so! It was a barren wasteland and fell *before* your kingdom did. Our mothers *were* friends. I read their letters, but I don't know what happened between them—nor does it matter now. Not when you're endangering the people of the midrealms." She projected her voice across the battlefield. "You claimed to fight for the common folk, but you've sacrificed them like pawns. You never wanted to free them—you wanted to rule them! To oppress them. You took their free will. You forced them into war with shadow magic."

Wren fought her way through the chaos toward him,

taking hit after hit of whatever he had left in his arsenal, but the blood roaring in her ears drowned out any pain. At last, he was within her grasp, and Wren reached for her hairpin in a flash of movement and pressed the poisoned tip to his throat.

After everything, Silas startled, blinking at her in surprise before a cruel laugh escaped him. "You think I'm not immune to whatever little potion you treated that with?" he jeered. "I'm a *Master Alchemist*, Elwren. I'm immune to everything you can imagine."

The pin fell from her fingers as Wren took a step back, and something heavy was pushed into her hands. With borrowed strength she lifted the object...

"You're not immune to this," she hissed, and swung Torj's war hammer with all his Furies-given power, caving in Silas' skull.

As he fell, the shadow alchemy that had threatened the midrealms began to dissipate, like ink dissolving in water. The silver light of Wren and Torj's bond spread outward in waves, washing over the battlefield, cleansing what the silvertide roses would have healed had they survived.

For a moment, the battlefield held its breath. Then, from across the ruins, Kristopher Snowden stepped forward, his armor splattered with blood, his face smudged with soot but radiating with pride as he looked at Wren, then slowly lowered himself to one knee.

"Hail Elwren Embervale," he called, his voice carrying across the ruins. "Queen of Delmira."

Thea was next, tears streaming down her dirt-streaked face as she knelt beside their friend. One by one, the people of the allied forces followed—Vernich the Bloodletter,

Ashlyn Graves, Wilder Hawthorne, Callahan Whitlock, Talemir and Drue, and even the rulers of her fellow kingdoms, the Queen of Aveum and the Regent of Harenth, who'd been guarded at the edge of the fighting.

The kneeling spread like a ripple through water, reaching the edges of the battlefield, where even former members of the People's Vanguard, now free from Silas' hold, bowed their heads to the woman who had told them the truth when their leader had fed them lies.

Torj remained standing at her side, his hand firmly in hers, their silver bond still pulsing between them like a life force. This was what the prophecy had always meant—not just a queen reclaiming her throne, but a new kind of power, born of love freely given rather than forcibly taken.

Wren knew that reclaiming her birthright was just the beginning. Rebuilding Delmira would take years. Healing the wounds between kingdoms, longer still. But as she stood in the ruins of what once was, hand-in-hand with Torj, she knew one thing with absolute certainty: there was so much hope for what could be. What Silas had tried to destroy with the remnants of shadow, she and her soul-bonded would rebuild.

CHAPTER 72
TORJ

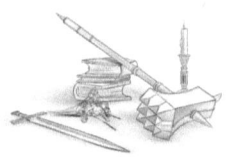

"Long may she reign."
—Bear Slayer, Warsword of Thezmarr

The battlefield went silent as Silas' body hit the mud, his head utterly pulverized by the war hammer in the Queen of Delmira's hands.

Those who hadn't already lowered their weapons in surrender did so now.

Amid the silver and the smoke, Torj went to Wren, his wife, and took her in his arms. "You saved me." He would forever be in awe of the woman before him. Of her ferocity, her determination, her spirit.

She smiled, and he'd never seen anything more beautiful. "I'll always save you."

Gently, he brushed her bloodied hair behind her ear, drinking in the sight of her. "I don't doubt it."

"Good," she replied, that warm smile still playing on her lips.

He kissed her, thoroughly, deeply, the battlefield around them fading away until it was only them.

"I want all my tomorrows to belong to you, Elwren Embervale."

CHAPTER 73
WREN

"Poison is often treated with poison. Venom is used to counter venom. There's a certain poetry in this symmetry."
—Elwren Embervale's notes and observations

In the days that followed, it became clear that what little had remained of Delmira's capital had been destroyed. The air was still thick with the scents of smoke and blood, and the faint trace of chemicals that lingered from exploding alchemy. The medical tents were full of those wounded in battle.

Knowing that her skill set was needed there, Wren delegated the handling of prisoners to Kipp and Torj, while she, Dessa, and Zavier joined Farissa and a handful of other healers who'd made themselves known to deal with the casualties of war.

Every dawn, a list was brought to her, naming those

who hadn't survived the night. Wren forced herself to read every name, to write to their families herself, to remember that the people of the midrealms who'd fallen were not just numbers on a piece of parchment. They had been people who believed in her claim enough to die for it, and that lit a fire beneath her, to see that right was done in the world.

"Your Majesty," a young messenger said with a bow as he handed her that day's list.

She still wasn't used to the title; it felt foreign, and she often caught herself suppressing the urge to look over her own shoulder, searching for someone more regal than she.

"Thank you," she replied as she took the scroll. As much as she had played the part of alchemist and healer over the past few days, she knew that time was coming to an end. She told herself that she was both queen and alchemist, and that perhaps that was exactly what her people needed—a leader who understood both the cost of war and the price of healing.

"Have you slept?" Torj's voice came from the tent flap.

Wren huffed a tired laugh and motioned to the purple smudges beneath her eyes, her blood-stained apron. "Not so much."

"I didn't think so." He pressed a hot canteen into her cold hands. "Drink that."

Removing the cap, she stifled a moan as she smelled the steam drifting from the liquid. "Peppermint and ginger?" she asked, taking a grateful sip.

Torj nodded. "Dessa told me it would help with the fatigue."

Wren smiled at the thought of her great Bear Slayer discussing herbs with her friend. "Thank you."

"I'm afraid you're going to need it." Torj guided her to a seat, gently pushing her down into it.

Wren's stomach bottomed out. "Oh?"

"We've had word from Darian."

"Is he alright?"

"He writes on behalf of his father..." Torj said slowly. "Lord Lucian wants an audience with you, to plead for a pardon."

Wren blinked, her tea forgotten. "What?"

"He insists that Silas had some kind of mind control over him and King Leiko, similar to what Artos used on Leiko during the shadow war. That they were forced to help him..."

Wren brought a hand to her face, pinching the bridge of her nose to alleviate some of the pain blooming behind her eyes. "What does Darian say?"

"Nothing," Torj replied. "He simply relayed his father's message, and Lucian's intent to speak with you in private."

Wren nodded. "When?"

"Tomorrow."

She laughed at that. "Doesn't sound like a request, does it?"

"We both know that's not in Lucian's nature," Torj said. "Kipp's had reports of forces gathering at the Devereux estate. Regardless of his claims, his influence is undeniable."

"And do you believe his story about mind control?" Wren asked with a raised brow.

"Not for a second. You?"

"I trust that bastard as far as I could throw him."

"I thought you might say that." There was a hint of a

smile on Torj's lips as he ducked out of the tent, only to return with a square box.

Wren set the canteen aside and stood. "What's that?"

Torj slid the box onto the nearby table. "Something you'll be needing before long."

Opening the box, Wren peered inside, moving the wrappings aside to spot something achingly familiar. She looked up at Torj, whose answering grin was wolfish, and then she laughed. She laughed until she cried.

Wren didn't know where to start when it came to ruling her kingdom. Dorinth had been all but razed to the ground, and the broader lands of Delmira had no people, no established regions. Aveum and Harenth's forces had begun the march back to their own kingdoms, and the ruins grew emptier by the day. It would take decades to rebuild. There was a chance the task might not even be completed in her lifetime. The mere thought was enough to make Wren want to crawl back into her cot. But the next afternoon, she spotted the Devereux banners on the horizon, and steeled herself for what was to come.

Darian rode at Lord Lucian's side, his face a mask of indifference, but for the slight dip of his chin when he saw Wren.

"Welcome to Dorinth," she greeted the noblemen as their horses reached the fallen gates of the city. "It's my understanding that you sought an audience with me, Lord Lucian?"

"It is, Your Highness," he said, dismounting with a bow.

"It's *Your Majesty* now," Torj growled from Wren's side. "Our queen was officially crowned several nights ago."

Lord Lucian gave another elaborate bow. "My apologies, Your Majesty. I am not as up to date with current events as I once was."

"Apology accepted," Wren replied with a wave of dismissal. "If you'll follow me, we've prepared some refreshments for our meeting, though you'll have to forgive the simplicity. We are still on rations here."

Wren and her guard led their guests to the makeshift council tent, where Kipp had set up a table and chairs for the occasion. She motioned for her guests to sit as she took her place at the head.

Lord Lucian took the seat at her left side, with Darian to his left. Torj stood just behind Wren, and she could feel the anger rolling off him in waves, vibrating down the bond they shared. She didn't risk a glance back at the warrior. She had to do this on her own.

"So, tell me, Lord Lucian," she said slowly. "Why have you sought this meeting?"

"Your Majesty, I wished to explain my actions in the recent conflict, to provide you with some much-needed background information as to why my forces were not here to defend you."

"By all means, continue..."

"As my son outlined in our correspondence to you, both King Leiko and I experienced a fog over our mental capabilities at the hand of the enemy, Silas. Without King Leiko's previous experience, we would not have recognized it at all, but he was able to identify it in the days after battle, once Silas' hold had loosened."

"I'm familiar with the mind control used over King Leiko in the past," Wren replied evenly. "You're sure it was the same? Back then it was a near-lethal combination of sovereign and shadow magic, utilizing the former King of Harenth's empath abilities... As far as I'm aware, the only person in the midrealms with an inkling of empath ability is Regent Liora, and as a distant relation, her magic is diluted. Not to mention, she's an ally of Delmira."

Lord Lucian sat back in his chair, seeming to relax as he forged on. "King Leiko swears it was of the same ilk—the same symptoms, the same level of control over our mental faculties. We were forced to hold our troops back. Forced to ally with the tyrant."

"And this mind control... Was it also responsible for your promise of a poison formula that didn't exist? And that particular taunt that was sent to me via our outposts?" she asked casually.

Lord Lucian nodded fervently. "Yes, the very same. I hope you know I would never wish harm on the midrealms. I have done so much to rebuild it after the shadow war."

Wren considered him. "I'm aware of how much you contributed to the restoration of Tver's castle."

"And I would be willing to do the same for Delmira," Lord Lucian added. "It would be an honor to see this mighty kingdom restored to its former glory."

"A generous offer," Wren replied. "In exchange for what?"

"A royal pardon," the nobleman said. "For all the former... indiscretions."

Wren rapped her fingers against the table. "I see."

"I hope you do," Lord Lucian continued. "With my

resources behind you, we could have the city of Dorinth rebuilt within five years. We could have it trading with the other kingdoms within a matter of months, particularly given the nature of the land. We could reach out to farmers and agriculturalists from other kingdoms, offering land in exchange—"

"We?" Wren interjected.

Lord Lucian placed a hand over his heart and bowed his head. "Yes, Your Majesty, *we*. You would have my full support in every avenue of development."

"Even though I have no intention of marrying your son?"

"I would advise against *two* husbands for the time being, Your Majesty."

Wren studied him before motioning to Kipp, who brought over the food and drink they'd prepared. "It's a fair proposition, my lord."

"Then *smile*, Queen Elwren. History is being made at this very moment!" Lord Lucian declared, his chest puffing out as he gestured to his own people, who brought bottles of wine from their supplies. "You will have a fully established kingdom at your feet in no time."

Wren declined the wine offered with a wave of her hand. "I'm avoiding such vices while I rebuild my kingdom," she told him. "Let us toast to our alliance in a simpler manner."

She watched as the refreshment tray was placed in front of them, and the Lord of Larkwood Valley was handed a small ceramic cup. He blanched at the sight of the teapot before them.

"I prefer to toast with wine, as is customary," he said stiffly.

"Given all that you've been through, I made something special for you," Wren said, her voice softening. "It's the same concoction that helped King Leiko all those years ago. It's a preventative against any empath mind control. You'll never have your free will taken from you again."

Relief washed over the nobleman's face. "You're too kind. I suppose you'll be drinking this as well, then?" He leaned forward, eyes narrowing slightly. "You can never be too careful."

"Of course, Lord Lucian." She lifted her own cup in a gesture of goodwill. "I'm always careful."

And then, Wren *did* smile.

She smiled as she poured his tea from the Ladies' Luncheon Teapot.

CHAPTER 74
WREN

"At the commencement of her reign, Elwren Embervale, Queen of Delmira, ordered hundreds of fields of silvertide roses to be planted across her kingdom."
—A New History of Delmira

Lord Lucian Devereux died two days later of natural causes. To Wren, his death felt both too easy and well earned—a quiet end for a loud man who had caused so much pain. His influence lingered in the confusion of his men, in the trust that had to be regained as Darian took his father's place as the lord and master of the Devereux fortune. The nobleman had played his part masterfully. During his absence, he'd convinced Lucian that he had orchestrated Wren's downfall from within, and at long last he'd gained access to the accounts, documents, and contracts in the Devereux name, transferring power piece by piece.

When it came, the poison was elegant, untraceable, its victim dying with the belief that he had won.

The depth of Lucian's treason emerged after his death: the evidence of his dealings with Silas, his plans to use Wren's power only to dispose of her at the opportune moment, the orders for the assassination of Torj Elderbrock, not to mention the proof of decades' worth of manipulation of the Tverrian kingdom.

Wren did take one central idea from the dead nobleman, though. She opened Delmira to the people of the midrealms, inviting those struggling to farm elsewhere to take a parcel of land for themselves in her kingdom and cultivate crops and livestock. It was Darian who impressed upon her just how vital agriculture would be to the economic development and sustainability of Delmira.

Before Talemir and Drue had left for Naarva, she had offered them the same—should any shadow-touched folk wish to make a fresh start, they would be given land in her kingdom and would be treated with the respect that they deserved. Talemir had been touched and vowed to pass on her offer to any who would hear it.

Unlike their mothers' fragile alliance, Wren and Zavier had forged something stronger in the crucible of scholarly pursuits and war. As newly crowned rulers of Delmira and Naarva, they were already drafting a new treaty—one built not just on mutual protection, but on genuine cooperation and trust.

Cal had surprised everyone by accepting Zavier's invitation to serve as Naarva's liaison to Thezmarr, overseeing military training and ensuring direct communication to the rest of the kingdoms.

"It's the end of an era," Kipp had sighed, slinging an arm over his friend's shoulders.

"And the beginning of a new one. Hopefully with less regrettable tattoos," Cal had quipped.

The inter-kingdom relations were just one of the countless responsibilities now weighing on Wren's shoulders, with the internal affairs of Delmira demanding even more of her attention and dedication. Whether Silas' claims about her mother's betrayal held truth or not, Wren suspected she might never know for certain. Regardless, she was determined to rule more fairly than her predecessors, forging her own path forward for the kingdom she had inherited.

"You need to appoint regional governors or lords, and from there, establish the best trade routes," Darian said over a meal one evening.

"Delmira was once the most prosperous kingdom in the midrealms," Wren answered, sipping from a full goblet of wine. "Can we assess the original routes and go from there?"

Darian nodded. "I was going to suggest the same. Do you have anyone in mind for regional governors?"

Wren pushed her plate back and rubbed her temples. "I don't want lords or noblemen from other kingdoms. I want the Delmirian people to elect them."

"That's a dangerous game," Darian started.

Wren shook her head. "It feels right. We're in this position because of the corruption of the nobility and the rulers. We need new leaders—leaders who have the people's best interests at heart, who understand the plight of the common folk. Delmira will adhere to the laws of the midrealms and the laws of Thezmarr."

"Well, then, I look forward to seeing this new world. May it be a rebalance of power and change for the better," Darian said. "I have the funding for the roads and bridges in place, with planners arriving by the end of the week to start work on infrastructure. Kipp assessed the previous layouts and made improvements, but for the most part, we are able to follow the design from the maps of the kingdom. We may even find foundations we can use."

"Good."

"What about defense forces? You're in a vulnerable position, with all this prosperous land but no military..."

"I don't even want to think about that right now," Wren muttered.

"You should. You, more than anyone, have seen how quickly power changes hands when there is wealth at stake. At least allow me to have some defensive structures built—watchtowers, walls and the like."

"The priority should be the people—"

"You barely have any people," Darian argued.

"They will come," Wren told him. "Vernich tells me that those who lived in the Warren plan to return to the lands above. Delmirians who fled decades ago wish to come home, and there are plenty of people throughout the midrealms who long for a new beginning. Delmira will give that to them. We will welcome everyone."

"A noble sentiment, but what if the kingdom is attacked—"

"Are we expecting an attack? Have you had word from Kipp's sources? Your own?" she pressed.

"No. But being prepared is the best defense."

Wren sighed and looked up from her clasped hands. She sought the four Warswords seated in their midst. Torj, Thea, Wilder, and Cal were all part of the negotiations and planning, and she valued their input more than anyone's.

"What do you think?" she asked.

Torj was the first to speak. "He's got a point. And years from now, when the kingdom has regained its footing and been built up again, you'll be glad for defensive structures."

Thea dipped her head in agreement. "You might not have the numbers to man the posts now. But one day you will, and when that day comes, everything will be in place."

Wren sighed again. "Alright, Darian. Build your watchtowers."

"They're *your* watchtowers, Majesty," the nobleman replied with a wry smile.

"Anything else?" she asked, eager to bring the discussion to a close.

"We're making good progress with the granaries and warehouses being built," Kipp answered, pushing her empty plate aside and smoothing a map flat before her. "Here and here," he pointed. "When the rubble has been completely cleared, we're prioritizing the rebuild of the forge and tanners. Land has been offered to skilled workers from neighboring kingdoms should they wish to offer their services."

"Clever," Wren replied. "And?"

"Well..." Kipp looked sheepish for a moment. "You might recall that we made a deal..."

"I do indeed, Kristopher," she said, raising a brow.

"Then, with your permission, I ask that I am able to collect that debt now."

Much to everyone else's surprise, Wren burst out laughing. And Kipp grinned.

"Are we finally going to find out what your deal was about?" Torj demanded.

"In part, I suppose," Wren replied. "Kipp assisted me with something, and in exchange, I promised to give him land to build a tavern in Delmira."

Thea's brows shot up. "You mean you won't be trying to take over the Flying Stag?"

"Please." Kipp waved her off. "One day I'll inherit the Fox, so I have no need for one of its sister taverns..."

"So what, then?" Cal asked.

"I'll be building my own from the ground up. It's always been a dream of mine."

Cal scoffed. "Since when?"

"Since Wren asked me for a favor, and I decided I wanted to build a tavern from the ground up," Kipp replied. "It's going to be called Professor's Corner."

For a moment, Cal blinked at him, before he burst out laughing. "Figures."

"If there's nothing else," Wren started, hiding her own smile. "There's one more item I want to add to today's agenda... The reopening of Drevenor Academy."

The tent went quiet, but Wren surveyed her companions with calm resolve. Fate had steered her away from her lifelong dream of becoming a Master Alchemist, the title she'd once coveted above all else. Yet while her own path had changed course, that didn't mean others couldn't continue where she'd left off— their success would be part of her legacy too, a different kind of mastery than the one she'd imagined.

"Wren..." Thea said gently. "Don't you think you've got enough on your plate without adding the rebuild of an alchemy institution in another kingdom?"

Wren laughed. "You'd think so. However, I've spoken with the High Chancellor and the other masters... I offered Delmira as a place to restart. More specifically, the cottage where I used to live. It would be small, nothing so grand as what it was, but... it's a chance to give back, and Delmira seems like the right place, in terms of its soil."

"You're sure about this?" Thea asked, frowning.

"It won't be what it was," Wren assured her. "No loyalty tests or deadly gauntlets. Dessa will make sure of that— she's going to continue her training with the masters so that she can become one of them. We want to create a place for alchemists, a home—in the same way that warriors have always had a place at Thezmarr."

"To the new Drevenor, then," Kipp declared, raising his flask.

"To the new Drevenor," Wren and the others echoed back.

Quiet moments were few and far between in the following days, but somehow Wren found herself wandering the outer streets of Delmira with her sister. Though the buildings were mere shells of what they had once been, without the chaos of battle, it was easy to imagine what they might become. Residences, shops, a city hall, perhaps even a school... Beside Wren, Thea was silently surveying the sights as well, a small smile on her lips, as though she, too, were picturing a future full of hope.

Thea wore a simple linen shirt and leathers, her sword strapped to her back. Wren still wasn't used to seeing her without the dagger that had graced her belt for so long. Its Naarvian steel had been repurposed for the crown now resting atop her own head.

She kicked a pebble from her path as they walked, trying to summon the courage to voice the question that had been plaguing her ever since the final battle. "What will you do now?" she asked.

Thea glanced at her, offering a wry smile. "I'm considering a trip to the Laughing Fox, just to get a meal that wasn't made by Warswords."

"That's not what I meant."

"I know." Thea looked out onto the rest of the capital, its ruins stark against the dewy morning light. "Wilder and I have been talking..."

"And?" Wren pressed with a note of frustration.

"We were thinking we might carry on the work you started as the Poisoner."

"What?" Wren snorted. "No offense, Thea, but you and the Hand of Death aren't exactly known for your subtlety— or for your expertise in alchemy."

Thea laughed. "True enough. What I meant was... we want to hunt down those responsible for the corruption in the midrealms. Anyone who is digging up old shadow magic artifacts, anyone who may have funded Silas, Lucian, or the People's Vanguard... We want to find them and end them. You took on that responsibility; you did that work alone. You're not alone anymore."

Wren's gaze followed her sister's to the entrance of the city, where she had torn Silas' flag from its pole. Beneath its shadow, Torj stood by the gates with Wilder.

"No, I'm not," Wren replied with a smile, drinking in the sight of her husband, his silver hair gleaming in the sun's rays, that part of her singing out to him, always.

After a moment, she could feel Thea's eyes on her.

Wren raised a brow. "What?"

"How did you do it? How did you save him in the end?" her sister asked. "He was dying."

"I saw it happen. I felt it happen... but I don't think we'll ever know for sure," Wren said slowly. "I suspect that Silas was trying to summon Torj's strength, but then the soul bond... It evolved somehow. It purified him of all the remaining poison inside him. It healed his wounds."

Thea was beaming. "Ancient power long forgotten, eh?"

"Apparently."

As though sensing their attention, Torj and Wilder glanced up as the Embervale sisters approached. Catching her eye, Torj smiled, and Wren had never seen him look more beautiful, more *hers*. He'd rolled his sleeves up to the elbow, the muscles of his forearms bunching as he pulled a rope rhythmically through his hands.

A lump formed in Wren's throat as she watched a square of fabric steadily climb the post, catching in the wind, growing taut.

A silvertide rose against a lightning-struck war hammer.

The new flag of Delmira, flying proudly overhead.

508

~

In the aftermath of the battle, it took far too long to get time alone with Torj. But at long last, they stood together on the blood-stained field where Silas had burned away the crop of silvertide roses, where so many had died.

"I keep waiting for a lull," Wren admitted as she surveyed the scorched earth. "A period where we're given the grace to process, to grieve... and it never comes."

Beside her, Torj made a noise of agreement, his warm fingers lacing through hers. "Such is life, Embers. It goes on. Always."

"I know." She sighed, squeezing his hand. "Ironic, wasn't it? That I spent so much time searching for a solution to the poison, to the alchemy, when it was within me all along."

"I've been thinking about that too," Torj replied as they walked across the ashes. "It makes perfect sense, really."

Wren glanced up at him, brow furrowed. "Does it?"

"You've always been a healer at heart... I don't think that part of you ever went away, even in your darkest moments. You couldn't find a cure, so you became one."

"If only you'd had that realization months ago," she said wryly.

Torj huffed a laugh. "If only."

"How do you feel now?" Wren had been monitoring him closely over the last few days and had seen no sign of tremors, no darkness surging through his veins.

"It was instant, Wren," he told her. "When the poison left my body, it was like a weight had lifted. Now I feel lighter, stronger than I ever did before."

HELEN SCHEUERER

A rush of relief washed through Wren. She had seen it with her own eyes, but the reassurance from his lips was the final confirmation she needed.

"And you?" Torj asked in return. "How do you feel now?"

Wren didn't hesitate with her honesty—not after all they'd been through, not after having had a lifetime of secrets between them once before. "Strange," she said. "No one can tell me how things truly ended between Silas and Zavier's mother and mine. And I find myself desperate to know, though it changes nothing."

"You're allowed to want closure, to want the truth about the past."

Wren looked up to the cloudless sky. "We need to look forward now—to the future. After the last war, I went about it all wrong..."

"How's that?"

"Those years nearly destroyed me, because I faced them alone. I won't make that mistake again."

"Nor I," Torj said, drawing her to a halt and resting his brow against hers. "Never again, Embers. From here on, we are united, always."

Wren's gaze fell to where their hands were joined. "The silver bond," she murmured. "Though it was no longer visible to the naked eye, she could still feel it thrumming between them. "Do you think it will always be there?"

Torj's eyes, sea-blue and clear of shadow for the first time in months, held hers. "I believe some things can't be unmade, Embers. Not by war or time, or even death."

A breeze stirred the ashes around their feet, and Wren spotted tiny green shoots peeking through the scorched earth—new growth already pushing through the devastation.

A smile touched her lips. "We're going to live well, Bear Slayer... I can feel it."

Torj pressed a kiss to her lips, lingering just a moment before breaking away. "Me too, Embers. We've earned our second chance and then some. Let's not waste a moment of it."

As they stood amid the ashes of what was lost, Torj Elderbrock kissed her soundly, and Wren's world lit up with color, with all the possibilities of what could be.

CHAPTER 75
TORJ

"What a storm breaks apart, it also clears away. The chaos is simply a prelude to what comes after."
—Bear Slayer, Warsword of Thezmarr

The first few weeks following the battle were hard. They camped among the ruins, living off rations and hunting game. Torj could see how tired Wren was, how much of herself she was giving to ensure that her kingdom was moving in the right direction.

Darian was instrumental in the initial planning; having been a part of the restoration of Tver all those years ago, he knew more than anyone that was required. King Leiko was nowhere to be found, leaving yet another kingdom in shambles, but Torj tried not to concern himself with that. They could only deal with one problem at a time, and it was his duty to look after Wren before all else.

Which was why he suggested they relocate to the cottage while the city was being rebuilt. It would mean a proper bed and some privacy, and Wren could also be closer to the plans that were unfolding for the new Drevenor Academy, which was where her passion lay. There, she could get her hands back into the soil; there, she could thrive in the wake of the war. Darian had argued against it, saying that a cottage in the middle of nowhere wasn't the place for a queen, but Wren had silenced him with a withering glare and the words, "That's *two* wars I've fought in now. Men lost the right long ago to have any say in my place in the world."

Torj chuckled at the memory as he scoured their campsite in Dorinth to make sure they hadn't left anything of value behind before the move. He was nudging rocks and debris with the toe of his boot when he heard it.

A faint mewing noise coming from a pile of rubble.

Crouching in the dirt, Torj peered between the rocks to find a pair of green eyes staring back at him.

"What in the midrealms..." he muttered, reaching into the small space.

A loud hiss sounded, and he snatched his hand back to see three scratches welling with blood.

"You little monster," he cursed, reaching in again. His fingers made contact with soft fur, and he ignored the swiping claws. With a grunt, he pulled the little creature from the rubble by the scruff of its neck.

The fluffball continued to hiss, and Torj held it at arm's length with a scowl, trying to get a good look at its wriggling form. It was a kitten. Black fur. Green eyes. With a bit of a vicious streak.

"You coming, Bear Slayer?" Wilder shouted from where he was hauling the last of the supplies onto the wagon.

"Just getting one last thing," Torj called back, staring at the kitten. The little beast glared back at him, and he laughed. "You're the one."

At long last, the cottage came into view. Around it, structures were being built for the new academy, but it was a damn sight better than the chaos of Dorinth. It was made infinitely better by the sight of Wren emerging from the nearby forest, a basket hanging from the crook of her elbow, full of silvertide roses.

Sensing him, she looked up, a broad smile breaking across her face.

You're home, she murmured into his mind as he jumped down from his saddle and strode toward her.

"I'm home," he said aloud, crushing his mouth to hers.

There was a loud meow of protest as she sagged against him, and Wren jumped back in surprise. "What was that?"

Torj shook his head, loosening the buttons of his jerkin, where a furry black head peeked out. "I brought you something."

The kitten leapt from his chest and landed gracefully on the grass, instantly winding itself around Wren's ankles.

She stared at it. "I thought you didn't like cats?" she breathed, crouching down and scratching it behind the ears. The damn thing purred.

"I like anything that makes you happy, Embers," Torj replied, drinking in the unbridled joy on her face.

"What's his name?" she asked.

Torj laughed. "Trouble. Monster. Menace. Mini Bloodletter... Take your pick. Though he seems to love you already."

Gods, she was so beautiful, so fierce. Standing, Wren cocked a brow at him. "Any more surprises?"

"Just one," Torj replied, dropping to a knee.

Wren's hand went to her chest, her eyes widening as he took the ring from the chain around his neck, where he'd kept it for all this time. His mother's ring.

"Elwren Embervale..." he said, his voice low. "I know we said our vows to each other aboard *The Furies' Will*, but I want to say them for all the world to hear. I don't want to spend another moment without the midrealms knowing that you are my wife. So I'm asking..." He drew a trembling breath. "Will you marry me again, Embers?"

EPILOGUE
WREN

Six weeks later

The alchemy conflict of the midrealms became known as the War of Silver and Smoke. Just like the shadow war that had come before, it had left an indelible mark on the midrealms and its people. Not a day went by that Wren didn't think of it, but it was different this time. Instead of mourning what she had lost, she was grateful for all that she had gained.

As she woke each morning, that was what she felt: gratitude. Gratitude for the opportunity to make Delmira something more, for the chances she'd been given, for the solid weight of the muscular arm tucked around her waist.

"It's too early to be thinking that hard, Embers," Torj's husky voice murmured against her neck.

"I was thinking how lucky I am to have you," she replied

with a roll of her hips, feeling the hard length of him against her backside.

"Is that so?" he said gruffly, tugging her tighter against him. "Do you need a physical demonstration?"

She laughed. "What I need is to get up and get ready. You're the one who insisted on this wedding party."

"I take it back." His words were still thick with sleep. "Don't need it. Just need you. In bed. Now."

"I don't think so, Bear Slayer," she said, batting his hands away and hauling herself from the warmth of their bed. "The next time you fuck me, I'll be wearing your ring."

A low rumble of need sounded behind her. "I do like the sound of that…"

Wren leaned down and pressed a kiss to his lips, careful not to linger too long and allow herself to be dragged back to bed. "Until the altar, then."

Wren found herself getting ready with Thea and Dessa in a small marquee they had set up for the occasion. Dessa lined her eyes with kohl and applied color to her lips while they drank sparkling wine from the bottle and teased Wren about her beginnings with the Warsword.

"Gods, when he was first assigned as your guard, you were *livid*," Thea recalled cheerfully. "Kipp and I had a bet going as to how long it would take you to poison him."

"I did no such thing," Wren said with a laugh.

"That's not entirely true," Dessa interjected with a grin. "Didn't you prick him with your poisoned hairpin when you snuck out one night?"

"That hardly counts," Wren argued as Dessa wove flowers through her hair.

Thea snorted. "Whatever you say, sister."

The tent rustled and Kipp's head appeared. "Are you ladies ready? There's a feast to be had!"

"There's a ceremony first," Dessa reminded him with a laugh.

"Yes, and *then* there's a feast, so let's hurry things along!"

"I hope you're not rushing the bride, Kristopher," came Farissa's voice from outside.

"I would never," Kipp replied with a wink.

But Wren was ready.

When she emerged from the marquee and saw Torj standing before the cottage with Wilder at his side, her breath caught. The Bear Slayer was as magnificent as ever, his silver hair pulled back into a neat knot, a few unruly strands framing his face. He wore simple warrior's garb, and his hammer was strapped across his shoulders as always.

They had promised to be themselves and nothing more at their ceremony, and looking at him now, all Wren wanted was the man waiting for her at the end of the rose-lined aisle.

She herself wore a simple gown, her belt of potions still fitted around her waist, though she'd allowed Dessa to braid a few sprigs of lavender through her hair. She looped her arm through Kipp's, her friend's chest puffing out as he escorted her down the aisle. As Wren walked, she saw the faces of everyone she cared for: Thea, Dessa, Zavier, Cal, Farissa, Audra, Talemir, Darian, along with the new friends she'd made over the past several weeks of building the academy.

When she reached Torj, she released Kipp and kissed him on both cheeks, the strategist looking suddenly misty-eyed as he took his place as celebrant.

Torj took her hands in his and she stood to face him before all their friends.

"Welcome, one and all," Kipp said, his voice ringing out across the small crowd. "We are here to celebrate one of the greatest triumphs I have ever had the pleasure of witnessing... The *official* union between the Queen of Delmira, Elwren Embervale, and the Bear Slayer Warsword of Thezmarr, Torj Elderbrock."

When Wren met Torj's gaze and he smiled, the silver bond shone between them for all to see.

The wedding feast was in full swing, and Wren's cheeks ached from grinning. She couldn't recall a time where she had been so happy. She stood barefoot on the grass, having kicked off her uncomfortable shoes the moment the ceremony ended. Torj was stealing glances at her from across the marquee, where he was speaking with Darian. Wren smiled at him from afar. The lightning-kissed, storm-blessed Bear Slayer was her *husband*. Husband and soul-bonded, and no words had ever felt more perfect.

The dancing had begun, with Kipp and Graves at the heart of the festivities. A towering presence emerged at Wren's side, and she looked up to find Vernich the

Bloodletter watching with narrowed eyes as the Son of the Fox danced with his daughter.

"I'm going to kill him," the Warsword growled.

But Wren put a hand on his arm. "I think Graves is more than capable of doing that herself if she wants to, don't you think?"

"If he does so much as lay a finger on her..." Vernich grunted, shaking his head. "Where's the fire extract?"

Wren pointed to the bar.

"Then that's where I'll be," the warrior muttered and stalked away.

Wren held in a laugh, but her attention was snatched away by Torj, who tensed in her periphery. She turned to face him and saw why.

An older woman had appeared at the entrance to the marquee.

She was not the frail, elderly figure Wren had expected. Grandmother Vara was straight-backed and tall, impressively so. She strode toward Torj with the confidence of a general in an army. Only when she reached him did her expression falter, her eyes lining with silver.

"Hello, my boy," she said. "I've missed you."

As Torj blinked at his grandmother and then took her in his arms in what looked like a crushing embrace, Wren found Kipp, who was on the outskirts of the dance floor now.

Thank you, she mouthed to him.

The strategist offered a salute.

It wasn't long before Torj introduced her to the woman who'd raised him, who'd set him on the path to being one of Thezmarr's legendary warriors.

"Vara, this is my wife, Elwren Embervale, Queen of Delmira," Torj said, pulling Wren to his side.

"Call me Wren," she added, hoping that there would be no unnecessary formalities between family.

"Well, Wren," Grandmother Vara said. "You're the most persistent individual I've ever come across."

Torj frowned. "What do you mean?"

"It was your wife here who tracked me down, with the help of a charming young fellow who kept offering me sour mead," Vara replied.

Torj turned to Wren, brows raised. "This is what you made a deal with Kipp for?"

Wren smiled. "Yes. We've been tracking Vara down since I started novice training at Drevenor."

Grandmother Vara reached for Wren and pulled her into a warm embrace. "Thank you for reuniting us," she said, before turning back to Torj. "And imagine that... After all this time, you marry a healer. Your mother would be so proud."

Wren's chest swelled. It meant more than she could say. Not only that Vara would think Torj's mother would be proud of who he'd chosen to marry, but that she had been called a healer, not a queen.

Grandmother Vara patted Torj's arm with a warm smile. "There will be plenty of time for us tomorrow, grandson. But tonight is for you and your wife."

As Vara peeled away, Wren felt Torj's gaze on her. She looked up to find him drinking her in, his eyes tracing over her face, her body, as his fingers laced through hers. "Gods, I love you," he said fiercely.

"And I love you," she replied, pushing up onto her tip-toes to brush a kiss to his lips.

Torj groaned, cupping the back of her head and deepening the kiss before breaking away. "Do you want to get out of here, wife?"

"More than anything," she murmured.

They didn't say farewell to their guests. Torj simply scooped her up in his arms and strode from the marquee, grinning at the cheers that echoed in their wake.

He didn't take her to the cottage, as she expected; instead, he carried her into the forest, to where the silvertide roses had blossomed tenfold. There, lanterns lit the way to a beautiful canvas dome that awaited.

"What is this?" Wren asked as her Bear Slayer set her down on the ground.

Torj huffed a laugh. "The bridal suite."

Wren answered with a wicked grin. "Is that so, husband? Are you going to ruin me?"

"It's you who's ruined me, Embers. And you did that long ago."

Inside, the tent had been adorned with cushions and throws and hanging lanterns. A small table to the side boasted a tray of fruit and cheese and a bottle of wine.

When they had settled inside, Wren reached for Torj, guiding his face to hers, claiming his mouth in a deep, passionate kiss. He moaned as she straddled his lap.

His husky voice skittered along her bones and lit her ablaze. "Tell me what you want, Embers..."

"You," the Queen of Delmira told the Bear Slayer. "It's always been you."

ACKNOWLEDGMENTS

In just a few short years, the Thezmarr world has taken on a life of its own... Perhaps that's why, as I end another story within it, these acknowledgments feel all the more momentous. *Legends* and *Ashes* changed my life completely, and as I sit here trying to find the right words of gratitude for all the support, I feel like I'm falling woefully short. It doesn't mean I won't try, though...

First, to my husband, Gary. Launching three books and getting married in the same year was ambitious to say the least, but your love and support got me through, like it always does. Thank you for ensuring my glass and plate are never empty, and for all the laughs in between.

To C.A. Wright, fellow author, editor, and most importantly, friend... Thank you for working your incredible magic on my books, and for keeping me sane with voice notes.

I'm deeply grateful to my P.A. and friend, Anne. Who knows what state I'd be in without you. Thank you for holding down the fort valiantly (and often).

Mum, thank you for proofing these pages, and for all your support as always. And all my love and gratitude to the rest of the Scheuerer fam back home in Sydney.

Thank you to my wonderful friends who always support

me in numerous ways: Eva, Lisy, Aleesha, Ben, Hannah, Natalia, Fay, Erin, Phoebe, Maria, and Joe.

Thank you to fellow authors Penn Cole, Kara Douglas, Nicole Platania, Emilia Jae, Tay Rose, V.B. Lacey, Sacha Black, Meg Cowley, Angelina J. Steffort, and Sheila Masterson, for being amazing friends and sounding boards.

As always, thank you to my agents, Ezra and Ethan, for all your hard work.

To Gillian Green and the rest of the team at Tor Bramble U.K., thank you for believing in this series and taking a chance.

A massive thank you to my street team, both past and present. I appreciate each and every one of you. Your efforts are inspired.

To the passionate Thezmarr community online who create art, theories, and discussions that continually move me... Thank you, thank you.

Last but never least, thank you, dear reader, for giving my books a chance. It's been a wild ride, and I can't wait to share what's next with you.

Much love,

Helen

ABOUT THE AUTHOR

Helen Scheuerer is the *Sunday Times* bestselling author known for her romantasy series, *The Legends of Thezmarr* and *The Ashes of Thezmarr*. Her work has been highly praised for its strong, flawed female characters and its action-packed plots.

Helen's love of writing and books led her to pursue a creative writing degree and a Masters of Publishing. She has been a full-time author since 2018 and now lives amidst the mountains in New Zealand where she is constantly dreaming up new stories.

Also by Helen Scheuerer